"When will I see you again?"

He adjusted his bulletproof vest and slipped his knife back into his boot.

"Let me think," I purred, enjoying how my change of tone stopped him in his tracks and piqued his interest. "Never. You will never see me again. I'm not interested and I'm tired of screwing someone I can't trust to tell me his real name."

"Turnabout is fair play." He grinned. He checked his gun and secured it at his hip. "And I think you were pretty interested twenty minutes ago when I made you see Jesus."

"Oh. My. God. You did not just liken sex with you to a biblical experience," I sputtered. His ego was bigger than his dick, and his dick was nothing to scoff at.

"If the shoe fits . . ."

"Listen, *David,*" I ground out between clenched teeth. "You're a decent lay and all, but you're not that good. I'm turning over a new leaf and I'm done having meaningless sex with ass-hats."

"Good luck with that, Ice," he replied, enjoying himself too much for my liking. He beat me to the door and flipped the lock. "I'll see you around . . ."

ALSO BY ROBYN PETERMAN

How Hard Can It Be?

Size Matters

Cop a Feel

ROBYN PETERMAN

KENSINGTON
Kensington Publishing Corp.
www.kensingtonbooks.com

KENSINGTON BOOKS are published by

Kensington Publishing Corp.
119 West 40th Street
New York, NY 10018

All Kensington titles, imprints, and distributed lines are available at special quantity discounts for bulk purchases for sales promotions, premiums, fund-raising, educational, or institutional use.

Special book excerpts or customized printings can also be created to fit specific needs. For details, write or phone the office of the Kensington special sales manager: Kensington Publishing Corp., 119 West 40th Street, New York, NY 10018, attn: Special Sales Department; phone: 1-800-221-2647.

KENSINGTON and the k logo are Reg. U.S. Pat. & TM Off.

First electronic edition: June 2014

ISBN-13: 978-1-60183-256-6
ISBN-10: 1-60183-256-7

First print edition: June 2014

ISBN-13: 978-1-60183-257-3
ISBN -10: 1-60183-257-5

Printed in the United States of America

This one is for
Candace.

You are strong and good and wonderful
and I'm so very lucky to have you in my life.
I think I will keep you!

ACKNOWLEDGMENTS

A book may be written by the author, but that is only the beginning. There are many people involved and without them I would simply have a story without the polish. I am grateful and blessed to have so many wonderful people in my life.
First and foremost my editor, Alicia Condon, who continues to delight me with her expertise as I continue to make her wet her pants! I am a better writer because of you.

My readers. All of this is for you. Without you, I don't exist!

My Pimpettes. You ladies are nuts and I adore you. Thank you for continuing to spread the word!

My beta readers. I love you more than you will ever know: Donna, Jennifer, Kris, Jim, Christi and Candace. You spur me to write faster and keep me afloat when I've jumped off the deep end. It wouldn't be half as much fun to write if you guys weren't reading!

My critique partners, JM Madden and Donna McDonald. You are brilliant writers and have a way with words that can make my biggest and most horrific mistakes seem like simple fixes. I am honored to call you my friends. When I grow up I want to write like you!

And last, but not least, my family. Hot Hubby, I wouldn't trade you for all the riches in the world. You and our kids are the best things that ever happened to me. Thanks for eating peanut butter and having no clean underpants when I'm on a deadline. You guys make it all worth it. Love you.

Prologue

"Is your name even David?" I asked as I yanked my panties back on.

"Is yours Melanie?" he inquired, buttoning his jeans.

"I asked first," I countered, wondering for the umpteenth time why being an idiot came so easily to me.

"Not David."

"Not Melanie."

We dressed in silence. I glanced around the hotel room and felt the need to do damage. Unsure whether I wanted to damage him or myself, I decided to get the hell out before I did something else I would regret.

"You know, I can't believe I've been sleeping with you on and off for a year and I don't know your real name," I said as I slipped my gun into its holster on my hip, promising myself I would never lay eyes on his ridiculously gorgeous nude body again.

"Back at ya, Ice."

"Ice?"

"Like your eyes, pretty girl. Icy blue and cold. I figure since you're not going to tell me your real name, I'll just give you one that fits."

"How about I call you, Ass?" I snapped. *What in the hell was wrong with me?* He hadn't forced me to do anything I wasn't more than willing to do. True, he hadn't given his real name, but neither had I.

"I've been called worse." He chuckled, revealing even white teeth and an orgasm-inducing smile. "When will I see you again?" He adjusted his bulletproof vest and slipped his knife back into his boot.

"Let me think," I purred, enjoying how my change of tone stopped him in his tracks and piqued his interest. "Never. You will never see me again. I'm not interested and I'm tired of screwing someone I can't trust to tell me his real name."

"Turnabout is fair play." He grinned. He checked his gun and secured it at his hip. "And I think you were pretty interested twenty minutes ago when I made you see Jesus."

"Oh. My. God. You did not just liken sex with you to a biblical experience," I sputtered. His ego was bigger than his dick, and his dick was nothing to scoff at.

"If the shoe fits . . ."

"Listen, *David*," I ground out between clenched teeth. "You're a decent lay and all, but you're not that good. I'm turning over a new leaf and I'm done having meaningless sex with ass-hats."

"Good luck with that, Ice," he replied, enjoying himself too much for my liking. He beat me to the door and flipped the lock. "I'll see you around," he shot back over his shoulder as he walked away.

"Don't bet on it," I muttered, and grabbed my purse.

"Oh, baby, I'm a gambling man," he laughed as he disappeared from my sight and hopefully my life.

I slumped down on the sex-destroyed bed and dropped my head into my hands. I had to get my damned life together. Was this all I had to look forward to? Mind-blowing sex with assholes not named David? The sex had been biblical, but the after-shame was getting debilitating. I was far better than this. What would my mother think? Or my brother, for that matter? I shuddered at the thought. I was an accomplished woman at the top of my game, and I deserved more than I allowed myself to have.

Done. I was done.

I grabbed my handcuffs, which had unfortunately been put to very obscene use about a half an hour ago, and left. I considered leaving my non-traceable Go-Phone in the room so there was no chance of another hook-up, but I needed it for work. With one last wistful glance at the sin-bed, I walked out of that room and into my new and improved life.

Chapter 1

Three months later

The office was small but tidy. My gut clenched in anticipation of the dressing down I was about to receive. I glanced at the organized stacks of paper waiting to be filed sitting neatly next to a pile of romance novels. I grinned and grabbed one—anything to take my mind off my latest major fuck-up. I'd been out of the hospital for nearly a month and I was ready to work again. I just needed to take my stern talking to and get on with it. I paged through the book and snorted. Why my boss kept this crap here was a mystery to me. I wondered if he read them.

Romance was for people who believed in fairy tales, and I didn't. Life was real and most people were bad. I skimmed the book and rolled my eyes. Nobody looked *that* good first thing in the morning, and making out without brushing your teeth at seven a.m. was not my idea of a good time. *Damn, the sex was pretty good, though.*

Of course, that made me think about *not David*, the egotistical wonder dick. I hadn't Go-Phoned him and he hadn't Go-Phoned me and since we hadn't made any other strangers-with-benefits rendezvous, I hadn't seen him in months. That smarted a little bit, but it was for the best. Great sex was great sex. I could get that anywhere. Although, he'd kind of ruined me. I hadn't slept with anyone but him in over a year. Whatever. At least he didn't know that.

I nervously tucked a strand of stiff blond hair behind my ear. Where in the hell was Steve? I knew I had it coming. I'd blown my cover twice in six months and that didn't bode well. I'd considered cutting my hair and coloring it before my meeting to show my boss, yet again, how easily I could disguise myself, but I figured a wig would do the trick.

Blonde wasn't really my color, but the last time I'd gotten an ass-chewing, I'd worn a red wig. Men preferred blondes according to Marilyn Monroe, and although Steve was gay, I figured being blonde couldn't hurt.

The ruckus in the hallway yanked me out of my pity party.

"This is ridiculous," a female voice shrieked. "You're not a fag. You fathered our two children and slept with me for . . ."

"Enough," my boss Steve ground out. "We're divorced and I am happily re-married. You're not allowed here, and if I have to get a restraining order, I will."

"You can't marry a man. It's against God's will. You'll burn in hell and you'll deserve it," his not so lovely ex-wife hissed.

"Jesus Christ, Helen. You need to leave now before I do something I will regret. Although there's not much I would regret at the moment."

"I'll leave," she said airily. "But you'll come back to me. Take this and read it. See the light, Steve. When you do, I'll be waiting."

"Don't hold your breath," he muttered.

I heard her heels clack down the hall. And that right there was why I would never get married. I'd rather chew glass and swallow it than deal with that kind of bullshit. Not that I'd get a divorce because I'd realized I was gay, but there were myriads of reasons not to be involved with anyone. Ever.

"Sorry about that," Steve sighed as he entered the office and tossed the Bible she'd obviously given him into the trash. "That was stressful to say the least."

"Um, are you okay?"

"I'm just dandy." He grimaced and took a seat behind his desk.

My boss Steve was a great-looking man in his late forties. Sandy blond hair and built like a brick shit-house. An ex–Navy Seal. From what I knew about him, he could kill a man with his bare hands, and I was fairly sure he'd been tempted to do just that to his ex-wife. He had two kids that he was devoted to and a husband that he adored. Clearly that didn't sit well with his ex-wife.

"Sorry you had to hear Helen mouthing off," he said.

"No problem," I said, feeling awful that I was adding to the weight of problems that had very obviously landed on his shoulders. "So, um . . . you wanted to see me?"

Steve tented his fingers, rested his chin on them, and stared at me. I fidgeted with my wig and put the novel back on the edge of his desk. *Fuck, why wouldn't he say something?* Never one to let a silence live out its life . . . I filled it.

"So I know you're a little unhappy with me at the moment, but I had no choice. Backup was stalled in traffic and the fucker was going to get away. I had to move. He sold to kids," I said at light speed in an effort to make him see there had been no other way. "Three sixteen-year-olds had already OD'd and he was scheduled to get a shipment that would hook and kill God knows how many others and I . . ."

"Do you have a death wish?" Steve asked quietly.

Shitballs. Yelling I could take. Yelling I could understand and process. Quiet was bad, really bad.

"No, I . . ."

"It seems to me that you do," he said, and tiredly ran his hands through his hair. "You broke procedure and could have been killed."

"But I wasn't and I . . ."

"This time," Steve interrupted me in a hard voice that shut me up quick. "This time you weren't killed, by sheer luck . . . not skill. You blew your cover with a cartel that wants your ass and will stop at nothing to get it."

"I stopped a thirty-million-dollar transaction and I won't apologize," I told him, adjusting my wig, which had slipped forward due to the fact I'd forgotten to pin the stupid ugly thing on.

"Show me your stomach."

Goddammit, I didn't have time for this. "My stomach is fine," I replied, straightening the neat piles on his desk.

"Show me your stomach."

I heaved a put-upon sigh and reluctantly lifted my shirt to reveal an angry jagged red scar. I'd taken a knife to the gut in my latest assignment gone awry. Of course the other guy had fared much worse . . . like six feet under worse. Luckily, his knife had missed all my major organs and arteries.

"Jesus Christ, Candace," he muttered. "That's it. I won't go to your funeral, young lady."

"You're not my dad," I shot back, worried about where the conversation was headed. He never called me Candace . . . always Candy or kid or idiot. Not Candace.

"Nope, I'm much worse. I'm your boss."

"So what are you saying? I'm fired? I'm reassigned? I'm what?" I asked in a voice I didn't recognize.

"You need a break. You're too involved—lost your objectivity," Steve said, watching me closely. "The drug dealers and the kids are hitting too close to home."

He was right and he was wrong—not that I'd admit the right part. I was an undercover DEA agent because my sister had died from a drug overdose when we were little more than kids. My brother Mitch had become an agent first. Needless to say, no one was overjoyed when I chose the same profession. My mother's fear of losing another child had almost debilitated her, but doing nothing had almost destroyed me. It was my way of paying tribute and it fit me. I was good at it. I needed it. I'd had to fight my parents and my brother on my decision. To this day, I felt their disapproval and doubt. It mattered to none of them that I'd been at the top of my recruit class, spoke three languages fluently, and had more weapons expertise than even my hotshot big brother.

My boss Steve had been the only one who had believed in me after I'd come out of training. He'd taught me the finer arts of jimmying car doors and disguise. He'd taught me the difference between revenge and justice. He'd been harder than hell on me and I loved and appreciated every moment of it. He'd believed in me and now he didn't . . .

"I know I screwed up and I promise you that I . . ."

"Save it," he said, slapping a folder down on his desk in front of me. "This is your medical report. To say that you're lucky is an understatement. This . . ." He pushed the folder toward me angrily. "This is proof of what being emotionally involved can do. It makes you sloppy and useless to me."

I said nothing. He was right. I was a constant blur of motion. Trying to fill up holes I couldn't define.

"There is strength in stillness and order. Protocol exists for a reason. Staying centered and uninvolved means you live to see another day," Steve said, pulling out another file.

"I know all that," I insisted. God, if I lost this job I had nothing. Less than nothing.

"Intellectually, maybe," he conceded. "But you're a liability to me at the moment and you're in no shape physically to go undercover."

"So you're firing me?"

"Hell no," Steve chuckled. "You're one of the best agents I have. Once you've healed and gotten your head back on straight, I'll kick your ass and send you back out."

I breathed a sigh of relief and my tense body went slack. Fuck, I'd thought my life was ending. In that moment I understood how much my work defined who I was. Whether that was good or bad, I had no clue . . . it simply was. Certain that sharing my revelation with Steve would be a bad thing, I kept my mouth shut. Difficult, as there was a silence I was tempted to fill.

"So what am I supposed to do?" I asked myself as well as my boss.

"Do you want to go to your parents?"

"God no," I shouted, and then slapped a hand over my mouth.

Steve's eyes narrowed and he waited. He knew my parents. He knew my brother. Hell, my brother Mitch had been one of his best agents until he fell in luuurrve and got out to become a plain old boring cop.

"If my mom knew about my stomach, she'd lock me in the house and go into a deep depression. I'm twenty-six and I will not go back," I snapped.

"A family that loves you is not the worst thing in the world," Steve said in his fatherly tone. I hated the fatherly tone.

"Yeah, well, a family that disapproves of what I do isn't going to be too excited about a knife wound in my belly. Just sayin'." I grabbed the silly romance novel and changed the subject. "You read this crap?"

"No, Kevin does," he said with a laugh.

Kevin, Steve's partner, was every bit as good looking as Steve. Many straight women had shed real tears upon learning the two men were gay and happily committed. Where Steve was intense and brooding, Kevin was light and joyful. They were wonderful parents to Steve's kids—far better than his religious zealot ex-wife, Helen.

"Well, these books are ridiculous. Happily-ever-afters don't exist," I snorted.

Steve shook his head sadly. "Ah, you have much to learn, Candy."

"Give me a break," I snorted.

"Exactly my plan. You're going on light duty until the doctors and I deem you ready for the field again." He opened the folder in his hand and skimmed the contents.

"Light duty? You're kidding me. Do you want me to file and answer phones?" I asked sarcastically.

"Nope," he said with a grin. "I'd like to keep my business. Your social skills leave much to be desired."

"Social skills are for civilians and fucktards," I snapped, unfortunately proving his point.

Steve cocked his head to the side and waited for me to bury myself deeper. I was a loose cannon, but I wasn't stupid. I stayed quiet. Difficult, but possible.

"God help the man who tries to tame you." He laughed and removed several sheets from the folder.

"No man will ever tame me," I told him confidently. "Romance is for sissies."

"How exactly should I take that? As a slur on my manhood or on my sexual preference?" he asked, eyebrows raised.

"No, I . . . shit. Um, I meant that it's, you know . . ." I mumbled and felt the heat crawl up my neck.

"Candy, you're missing out on a few things in life. Like a life mainly. I want you to take this light duty time to ease up and live a little. Have some fun, for God's sake."

I had no freakin' clue what he was talking about. A life? I had a life. I saved lives. And I had fun. I, um enjoyed tons of things, like . . . Whatever. This was ridiculous.

"Just give me my pansy-ass light duty assignment and let me get back to work."

Steve observed me critically for a moment, then went from father mode back to boss mode. "Fine. A dear friend of mine has received some threats on her life. I'm fairly sure they're innocuous, but Kevin is freaked out and wants protection for her."

"You want me find and eliminate the threats?" I asked, my expression hopeful. Maybe light duty wouldn't suck as much as I thought.

"Not exactly," he said, folding the papers in his hands and placing them inside the romance novel I'd just made fun of. "I want you on her and watching for trouble."

"You want me to be a bodyguard?" I gasped, unable to hide my shock and dismay. I was an undercover agent, for shit's sake. Not a rent-a-cop babysitter.

"Yep," Steve said, ignoring my stinky attitude. "Sue is a professor and an author. She's scheduled to headline an author's convention in a week and I want you on her. Innocuous or not, a threat is a threat." He handed me the book with a smile.

"Wait, I have to guard a woman named Sue who writes trashy romance novels, because someone may or may not want a piece of her?"

"That sounds about right," he said. "Oh, and she goes by Shoshanna. Shoshanna LeHump."

I waited for the punch line, but it didn't come. Who in the hell would go by the name Shoshanna LeHump? She sounded like a stripper.

"You're serious," I said, pinching my thighs to keep from laughing just in case he was.

"As a heart attack. Shoshanna married Kevin after her husband died so he could get his green card. They divorced when we met. Shoshanna actually officiated at our wedding ceremony. You remember, the one you were invited to but couldn't come because you were recovering from being shot in the ass."

That was a low blow. I hadn't been shot in the ass by anyone. It was actually quite big of Steve to state it that way. I had shot myself in the ass. I'd been testing a new firearm. The gun had been faulty. Hence, when I put it in my back pocket, it went off and I shot myself in the ass.

"I'm a little confused," I said, ignoring his comment about my ass debacle.

"In a round-about way, Kevin and I met because of Shoshanna. We owe her."

"She introduced you guys while she was married to Kevin?"

"No, no." Steve laughed. "But that does sound like something she would do. She's our angel because if she hadn't married Kevin, he would have been deported and we never would have met. She's the reason my life is full."

I was so tempted to roll my eyes, but I adored Kevin. And I loved Steve. And they loved each other. Hell, Steve sounded just like my pussy-whipped brother Mitch. He'd fallen in love with his fiancée Kristy when we were all on a bizarro drug bust that involved Bigfoot. Kristy had nothing to do with the crimes. She was with a crew of loonies searching for Bigfoot, a project that was unknowingly the cover for a nasty drug cartel. At first I didn't like her, but she proved herself in the end. Of course, it also helped that she didn't really believe in Bigfoot.

"So what's with the trashy novel?" I asked as he handed it over.

"Shoshanna wrote it. I would suggest you read it so you get a feel for her. Inside, I've put a list of potential suspects. You can question them this week before you leave for Wisconsin."

I looked the list over. Several professors at the U where this Shoshanna gal worked seemed to have rather large issues with either her success as an author or her subject matter. And there was some old woman named Evangeline O'Hara, who had been blackmailing Shoshanna for stories for what looked like twenty years.

"Holy shit," I muttered. "Here's your threat. This O'Hara woman has a motive like I've never seen."

"I'd tend to agree if she wasn't still in jail," Steve said. "Her calls and mail are monitored."

"I'll interview her."

"Absolutely and the professors at the U. Sue's one of the foremost profs of Women's Studies and these jack-offs are trying to get her tenure removed."

"Jealousy?"

"Possibly. More likely closed-minded bigotry toward her subject matter."

"Women's Studies?" I asked, surprised. "What are they? Dinosaurs?"

"Not what she teaches, what she writes," he corrected my misassumption.

"What in the hell does she write? Porno?" I laughed.

"Some might refer to it as porno, but it's technically classified as erotic romance," Steve said logically.

Again I waited for the punch line. Again it didn't come.

"So, um . . . is there anything in the university's by-laws that make her, um . . . sex books negate her tenure?" I asked. I'd almost said fuck books. Thank you, God, that that one hadn't slipped out.

"It's somewhat vague, but Shoshanna's lawyers are convinced she'd win and most of the board is backing her," he said. "But the controversy is unpleasant and drawing unwanted attention to the university. The longer it goes on, the more precarious her position is."

"I don't get it. She would win in court. What's the biggie?"

"The biggie"—Steve smiled at my choice of word—"is that Shoshanna loves the university and would leave before she caused too much trouble and bad press. It would be a sad day for her, the students, and academia if that were to happen."

"Why would someone hurt her then? Wouldn't it be smarter to just draw the situation out till she leaves of her own accord?"

"Yes and no," Steve said. "She's up for several prestigious awards, and two of the suspects in particular are up for the same award. I don't really get it, but apparently in the world of academia the more papers with stars on them, the more important you seem to be in that strange subculture."

"You think someone would kill or hurt her for that?" I asked, memorizing the names for later.

"Doubtful, but I've seen stranger."

Steve handed me a card.

"Here's Shoshanna's address. You're expected at dinner tomorrow night. Kevin and I will be there, as well as your brother, Kristy, Rena, and Jack."

That sounded like hell to me. To be stuck in a room with a porno writer and three sickeningly in-love couples would be enough to make me tear my own head off. My brother and his fiancée, Kristy, were bad enough, but their best friends Rena and Jack were downright nauseating.

"I don't think I can make that," I hedged, racking my brain for a good excuse.

"You have plans? Cancel them. This is work related, and you need to have a good time occasionally."

"I have a date," I blurted out, my mouth way ahead of my brain.

"Bring him," Steve said, waiting for me to cop to lying.

"Well, um . . . David is a little weird and I'd, you know . . . rather not subject him to my brother before I know if he really, um . . . you know."

"What does this David do?" he asked.

"I think he's a . . . banker."

"I see," Steve said, seeing entirely too much.

"Fine," I huffed, pissed at myself for lying and pissed at Steve for making me. "I'll come. Is Kevin cooking?"

"You bet." He smiled his first real smile of the meeting. "Shoshanna can't boil water and Kevin still cooks for her a couple of nights a week."

"Oh shit," I muttered. "What about the cartel that wants my ass?"

"Taken care of. Sent two agents to Mexico and ended it."

Fuck. I hated that. I hated that two people had to risk their lives to cover my fuck-up. Maybe Steve was right. I needed to get my head on straight.

"Are they okay?" I asked.

"Yep. Got back today. Hell of a ride. Been down there three months."

Three months? "Can I thank them?"

"Nope. These guys are deep cover. They don't exist in any database. Not going to screw with that. Just know it's taken care of."

"Right," I said, more furious than ever with myself. My vendetta against drug dealers had resulted in two of Steve's hard-core guys having to go to Mexico to clean up my mess. Not gonna happen again. Ever.

"It's done, Candy," Steve said, recognizing my frustration. "They're back and fine, but it could have gone either way. I wasn't planning on this, but shit happens. Remember that next time you want to go Rambo on a job."

"You have my word," I promised.

"Good. Now get out of my office. I have work to do. Oh, and by the way," he smirked, "blonde's not your color. Stick with your natural brunette. It's beautiful."

"Yes, sir." I gave him a mock salute and left. His chuckle followed me down the hall as I yanked the itchy blonde wig off my head and tossed it in the trash. I'd been living on luck and a prayer . . . and that stopped today.

Chapter 2

The private law enforcement gym was practically empty. It smelled a little musty and the equipment had seen better days, but I loved the place. I'd earned my black belt in karate in this very gym and felt a real sense of peace here that I sometimes had a hard time finding in my daily life. Steve's implication that I had no life rankled—possibly because it might be true. I just wasn't sure I was brave enough or cared enough to actually do anything about it.

Scanning the free weights, I settled on the lighter side. My healing knife wound kept me from a full workout, but I was getting stronger every day. My physical therapist was blown away by my progress. I was just pissed I wasn't back to full form yet. I dropped my gym bag on the floor and grabbed some five-pounders.

"What are you? A pussy?" an unfortunately familiar voice demanded.

Jesus Christ, who in the hell did I fuck over in a former life to keep running into these evil lesbian sisters?

"Nope, I had a little mishap at work and have to take it easy. What's your excuse?" I asked, eyeing her appalling choice of workout wear. Both Mrs. C and her sister, Edith, were somewhere in their late sixties and tended to favor sequins. Even at the gym.

Edith, clad in a shiny gold exercise top, cackled and punched her sister in the arm. "Yeah, what's your excuse, you old dyke?"

Mrs. C grunted and walloped her sister back. I idly wondered if they'd get into an all-out brawl. At least they weren't boring . . .

"Heard you got stabbed in the gut," Mrs. C said while she simultaneously smacked her sister in the back of the head. Edith came right back and knocked her sister's feet out from underneath her.

How in the fuck did they know that? "Well, that seems to be the rumor," I muttered, wondering how long I could take dealing with them before I did damage. Although, that would be an unwise choice on my part considering they had been in Vietnam, Special Forces . . . four tours. I was fairly sure only a few high-placed government officials knew of their existence.

"Yep," Edith crowed as she helped her sister back to her feet. "But rumor also has it that you put a dick-weed drug dealer six feet under."

"How in the hell do you guys hear all this stuff?" I asked. The info was classified and hadn't hit the media in any way, shape, or form. "You two run a knitting store, for God's sake."

The just stood there and grinned. A smile pulled at my lips because they looked so ridiculous, and they either had no clue or didn't care. I'd met them on the same drug bust where my brother Mitch had met his fiancée Kristy. They'd been part of the certifiably insane group of nut jobs searching for Bigfoot. Turned out they were far more than poorly dressed lesbian Sasquatch enthusiasts . . . they'd helped save the day by booby-trapping the trees with knitted snap traps.

"How is it that you lovely ladies are allowed to work out here?" I asked as I switched to twenty-pound weights. I was no pussy. I was a dumbass.

"Give me those goddamned things," Edith snapped, yanking the weights from my hands. "You wanna reopen that wound?"

"No," I huffed, annoyed that my pride had gotten the better of me.

"Anyhoo, we work out here because we're doing some government contract work and the generous city of Minneapolis has no choice but to let us hone our fine machines in their gym," Mrs. C said, sliding slowly into the splits. Edith, not one to be outdone . . . joined her.

Had I entered an alternate universe? I was going to be a bodyguard for a smut writer and these two sparkling, limber dingbats were picking off bad guys for the government when they weren't manning a knitting store?

As I stared at them on the floor, I idly wondered if I could do the splits. Holy hell, I really did need a life.

"So," Edith grunted, "heard you got quite the cushy assignment."

"I would truly love to know where you get your info."

"Not gonna happen." She gave me a wink.

"Figures," I muttered. I walked over to the treadmill and prayed our conversation was over.

"You are one lucky chickee," Mrs. C said, rolling out of the splits. "Edith here would give her left boob, it's the bigger one, to go to the SCREW-Con."

"I'm sorry, what the hell did you just say?" I asked, sure I'd heard her incorrectly.

"I said Edith's left boob is bigger than her . . ."

"Not that part," I snapped. "The other part."

"The SCREW-Con." She cackled at the look of horror on my face. "Society of Contemporary Romance Erotic Writers. Screw. You get it?"

"Yeah, I got it. Now quit fucking with me." I blew out an exasperated sigh and waited for the punch line . . . but it never came.

"Sweet baby Jesus in assless chaps, you really didn't know," Edith yelled, enjoying my discomfort. I certainly wasn't a prude, but I had no desire to go to a convention called SCREW.

"Clearly I didn't." I put my earbuds in, cranked up the volume on my iPod, and turned on the treadmill. This conversation was done. If there was anything else to know, I didn't want to know it. Despite the fact that Steve was my boss, I was going to rip him a new one for this. Being taken unaware by two sequin-wearing lesbians with uneven boobs was not on my schedule today . . . and apparently being ignored wasn't on theirs.

"You'll be bodyguarding one of the hottest pieces of ass alive," Mrs. C informed me while removing my earbuds.

"Sweet baby Moses in leather and a ball gag, I pray daily for Shoshanna LeHump to switch teams and come over to the dyke side," Edith shouted in full agreement as to the sexual magnetism of the infamous LeHump.

Stunned to silence and having no comeback for that one, I stared at them while debating my next move. Taking them down might set me back medically, and running meant I really was a pussy. So I tried the next best thing.

"You guys wanna go shoot some stuff? I'm about to implode and I need to find something inanimate to kill."

"Now you're talking, sister," Edith said, yanking me off the treadmill and out of the gym.

* * *

The gun range was empty. After signing in, the old gals announced that the targets were insulting, but they had just what we needed to spice it up. They set up targets that made Mel, the owner, cringe and threaten to ban us for life. Edith had a couple of words in private with Mel, and to my great surprise, he turned a blind eye. Those crazy women set up an old computer, two toasters, a vacuum, and a mini-fridge that they just so happened to have in the back of their car. They drew tiny bull's eyes on the appliances and started making wagers. Color me impressed. Maybe these gals weren't so bad.

"Youth before beauty," Mrs. C grunted, getting into her zone.

Laughing, I put on my ear protectors and goggles. Holding my Glock in my hand made me go to my calm happy place. I aimed and I fired—over and over and over.

"What the fuck?" Mrs. C gasped. "Guns down."

We holstered. She walked over to the appliances and whistled.

"What?" Edith shouted, still wearing her hearing protection.

"Clean bull's eye on every one."

"Clean a bull's what?" Edith yelled.

"Take your goddamned head gear off and get a look at this shit," Mrs. C said, squatting down to get a better view.

Both women eyed my handiwork silently, crossed back over to me and stared.

"Do it again," Mrs. C demanded. "Do it right now."

"No prob." I grinned and reloaded. And I did it again—and one more time for good measure.

"Jesus Christ in a corset, you should have sniped with us in Nam," Mrs. C whispered reverently.

"Wasn't born yet," I said, enjoying myself for the first time in a while.

"I've never seen anything like it. I think I came in my shorts," Edith added, saluting me.

"Gross," I groaned, backing away.

"Don't worry yourself," she cackled. "You're too young, too skinny, and too straight. It's your shooting that gave me a woody."

"Guys, enough. I'm a good shot. I'm supposed to be. I'm an undercover DEA agent, for God's sake." I rolled my eyes and debated whether they needed an anatomy lesson. Although who knew? Maybe they had dicks . . .

"She's the best I've ever seen," Mrs. C muttered.

"Not better than Mag the Hag," Edith insisted.

Both women dropped to their knees, genuflected, and quietly murmured Mag the Hag repeatedly.

Fuck, just when I was beginning to think they were kind of normal.

"Do you think it's possible?" Edith asked her sister, eyeing me suspiciously.

"Could be," Mrs. C said, rising to her feet.

"Um, guys, you're kind of freakin' me out here." Maybe it was time to go. Mrs. C's iron grip on my arm made escape impossible.

"She died in my arms. She was the best sharpshooter that ever lived." Edith's eyes welled with tears, making me notice her glittery yellow eye shadow. *How had I missed that?*

"I'm sorry, I know how it is to lose someone you love."

"I didn't love her." Edith laughed. "I hated her fucking guts, but I admired the hell out of her and would have done her if she was a dyke."

"Okay, then—gotta go," I told them, removing my goggles and peeling Mrs. C's claw off my arm.

"Mag the Hag, are you in there?" Mrs. C screeched into my ear, definitely damaging my hearing.

"What the fuck is wrong with you? You're insane and a menace to society. Not to mention, your fashion sense is vomitus," I shouted, and put my hand to my ear to check for blood.

"It's her," Edith said, dropping to her knees in front of me.

"Who's her?" I asked, glancing around in alarm.

"You. You're Mag the Hag reincarnated," Mrs. C rejoiced, trapping me in a bear hug. "God, I've missed you, you stinky bitch."

"I'm not Mag the Hag," I said, but because I was wedged in Mrs. C's armpit, it came out a little muffled.

"Of course you are." Edith tsked and bent to kiss my feet.

"This is the most glorious and fucked-up thing to happen in at least three weeks!" Mrs. C claimed, hugging me tighter.

"I really think you ladies need some help," I squeaked, trying to get some air into my squashed lungs.

"I'm gonna call Homer in DC. This will blow his mind," Edith said, and giggled after she'd finished adoring my feet. "He'll offer you a job so fast it will make your head spin."

"Thanks, but no thanks," I gasped, miraculously breaking away from Mrs. C. "I have a job already and I'm not Madge or whoever you whack-jobs think I am. I'm Candy and you're bat shit crazy."

"Exactly what Mag the Hag would have said," Edith shot back, secure in her debatable sanity that I was their reincarnated buddy.

"Okay then, I'll just be going." I grabbed my gun and quickly stowed it away. "I'll see you guys when hell freezes over and I hope you have an interesting rest of your lives." I made a run for the door.

"Hell froze over last Tuesday," Mrs. C shouted joyously as I hustled away. "We'll see you this weekend. We have a lot of catching up to do. You've been dead for years!"

"Not gonna happen," I muttered as I slammed the door behind me, only to be followed by their laughter as I hightailed it out of the building.

Chapter 3

What in the hell was I supposed to wear to a porno writer's dinner party? Glancing over at the unread romance novel, I rolled my eyes and started digging through my closet. I knew I should have read at least a chapter, but I was still pissed that I had to go to something called SCREW-Con. This was not what I was trained for and my apathy was definitely showing.

A dress. I'd wear a sexy little dress. Being the dateless mess that I was, I wanted to at least look good. I slipped on a fitted black halter dress, threw on some fun silver sling-backs, and twisted my hair into a messy up-do. A little blush, mascara and a swipe of lip gloss, and I was ready to go. Kind of. I needed an attitude adjustment. A stupid assignment was still an assignment and I was a pro. Even if it was glorified babysitting, I would take it seriously. I sat back down and went through the suspect list again.

Evangeline O'Hara; age eighty-four. Single. Incarcerated for blackmail of five authors for over twenty years and bribery of the Minneapolis police department. Sentence: ten years.

Jesus Christ, she looked like a melted wax figure. Her photo was so alarming, I quickly shoved it back in the folder. That interview should be a treat. She'd been convicted for stealing ideas from Shoshanna and the other authors and putting them out as her own. She'd made millions and had been brought down on live TV on the Anderson Cooper show. I made a note to get a copy of the broadcast.

Dr. Randall Steigmeister; age fifty-seven. Single. Tenured professor of Religious Studies at the University of Minnesota. Lost a sizable grant to the Women's Studies program a year ago. Grant went to proposal by Dr. Sue Lumpschlicterschmidt. *Holy hell, was*

*that her real name? Shoshanna LeHump was actually an improve-
ment.* Dr. Steigmeister had been actively campaigning to have Professor Sue's tenure removed due to the "sexist and degrading filth"
she produced.

I glanced over at the novel again and was sorely tempted to dive
in. I was curious to see what Dr. Randy meant by sexist and degrading filth, but I had almost run out of time. On to the last suspect.

Dr. Winnifred Junsen; age forty-eight. Divorced, no children.
Recently tenured Professor of Women's Studies at the U. Lost two
prestigious awards to Dr. Sue in the last six months. Unpopular
with students. On probation with the university due to bra-burning
incident in the football stadium. *WTF?*

So, Winnie and Randy were jealous and bitter and Evangeline
was unfortunate looking and insane. I rifled back through the folder
and pulled out photos of the professors. *Eww.* Pompous and well
fed. I was looking forward to either an interesting week or an an-
noying one . . .

Whatever. Maybe someone actually was gunning for Shoshanna.
The most obvious suspect was Evangeline, but she was in the slammer. I made notes to check on relatives and friends that could be
working with her. The other two looked harmless enough, but jealousy made people do outrageous things.

The novel stared at me from its perch on my bedside table. "I'll
read you tonight. I promise."

I grabbed my purse, gun, and keys and went to meet the infamous LeHump.

LeHump's house was typical for New Hope, Minnesota—nicely
manicured and quaint. Lots of hosta and hanging baskets along
with a huge Vikings football flag on a pole. I was the last to arrive.
Three huge SUVs were parked in the driveway. I giggled as I wondered if all the men inside were compensating for something.

"I can do this. It's just a couple of hours and Kevin cooked," I
muttered as I walked up to the front door. I didn't believe a word
of what I was saying, but if I kept repeating it, maybe it would
come true.

Damn it, why didn't I bring a date? Possibly because I didn't
have anyone to call . . . It would have been awesome to walk in
here with *not David.* The pure shock of seeing me with a potential

boyfriend would have taken all the pressure off of me and my knife wound, my lack of a social life, my inability to have fun or get laid, and the fact that I'd turned into a bodyguard . . .

Who in the fuck was I kidding? I couldn't do this. I quickly turned around and made a run for my car.

"Candy? Where you going?" my brother Mitch called from the doorway.

"Oh, hi. I just forgot my . . . you know, my um . . ."

"Guts?" He grinned and waited for me to make my way back up the front walk to hell.

"Yeah, my guts," I said as he trapped me in a gentle hug.

"How's the stomach?" he asked, tucking some fly-away hair behind my ear.

"Better."

"Really?"

"Really." I grinned and punched him in the arm. As much as he drove me nuts, my brother loved me and I loved him.

"This will not be bad," he said, reading my mind. "You'll get a kick out of Shoshanna, and you already know everyone else here."

"Define not bad," I said, following him into the house.

I entered the foyer and froze in my tracks. *WTF?* I knew plenty of Minnesota Vikings fans, but this was alarming. The entire décor was purple and white with some gold accents here and there. A large cardboard cutout of Brett Favre dominated one corner of the living room, and a pyramid of helmets hovered precariously as the centerpiece on the table. Purple shag carpet that would have made the Brady Bunch salivate covered the floor, and the walls were purple and white striped wallpaper with football decals all over it. I was speechless.

"You must be Candy!" a little bulldozer of a woman shouted with a mouthful of food. "Goddamn, you look like a fuckin' supermodel!"

"Um, thank you?" I whispered, unable to speak louder for fear I'd insult her home.

"You sure this Hot Mamma can protect me?" the little gal, clad in a Vikings sweat suit, bellowed as she grabbed some more cheese from the platter next to the helmets.

"She can shoot the teats off a cow from three hundred yards away," said my brother's best friend, Jack. "How's the stomach?"

"In general or right now?" I asked, watching the woman I assumed to be Shoshanna shove a hunk of cheddar into her mouth.

"Jesus Christ, Shoshanna," Rena groused, "where in the hell are your manners? Oh, wait . . . you don't have any."

"Shut your cakehole and try this cheese," Shoshanna said, and laughed with an orange mouthful. "It's fucking awesome."

Rena plopped down on her fiancé Jack's lap. "Candy, this is Shoshanna," she said, referring to the *fromage* eater. "Shoshanna, this is Candy."

"Damn glad to meet ya, Candy. I told the boys here I didn't need a bodyguard, but Kevin got his panties in such a wad, I had to go with it."

"I don't wear panties." Kevin chuckled and laid more appetizers out.

Although the food looked good, I was fairly sure I wouldn't be able to eat anything if Shoshanna kept shoving cheese in her mouth.

"What? Did you start going commando after our divorce?" Shoshanna cackled, and grabbed a few puffy-looking balls off the new platter.

"You know as well as I do that I wear boxer briefs," Kevin informed her, and handed her a napkin, which she promptly handed back. "Come to think of it, you probably don't know, considering the entire time we were married, I did the laundry."

This scenario was weird on several levels. Kevin had been married to the little gal with appalling manners, and now he was married to my boss, the ex–Navy Seal Steve. Steve had been married to the uber religious nut case Helen and had two kids. Now he was married to Kevin, and their wedding had been officiated by Shoshanna, ex-wife of Kevin, who wrote porno and liked cheese.

I glanced over at my brother who was copping a feel of his fiancée's ass, as their best friends, Rena and Jack, were doing their best not to grope each other.

I was in hell.

I considered making a lame excuse and running for it, but I knew it would be futile. I'd just have to suck it up and try not to watch Shoshanna eat.

"So," Steve said, pulling me aside, "you two will be leaving next Saturday."

"Right," I said. "Am I on Shoshanna this week?"

"No, Mitch and Jack are on her. You need to do the interviews and get ready."

"About that," I said, trying to burn my boss alive with a glare. "Are you familiar with the name of the convention?"

"I can't say that I am," he lied, trying to suppress his grin.

"It's SCREW-Con," I hissed. "You're demoting me to a body-guard and sending me to a convention called SCREW."

"From what Shoshanna says, it's supposed to be informative, and you could use some fun."

"It is," Shoshanna bellowed from across the room. "They have classes during the week at SCREW-U and a party on the final night called the SCREW-Ball!"

Damn, she had some good ears. I pulled Steve into the kitchen so I could rip him a new one out of everyone's earshot.

"Is this just a joke?" I demanded. "Is this to humiliate me or punish me?"

Steve watched me quietly as I unraveled.

"I mean, what the hell? Do you even think she's in danger?"

"What I think, what I believe, and what I know are in conflict with each other at the moment," he replied. "We have threatening letters and received another today. I'm unclear if we're on the right track with the suspects, but the potential for harm is there and the job is real."

"Is that what you think, know, or believe?" I asked, still trying to get a grasp on the situation.

"Irrelevant," Steve said.

"Fine." I rolled my eyes, glanced back into the living room, and caught the tail end of Shoshanna juggling the puffballs.

"No more business tonight," he said as he pushed me back to the circus. "This is about fun."

"Dinnertime," Kevin called out as he clapped his hands and pulled Shoshanna away from the cheese.

I found myself seated between Rena and Mitch and directly across from Shoshanna. Holy hell, how was I supposed to eat?

"So, Candy," Shoshanna yelled across the table, making me wince. "When you use handcuffs in a sexual situation, do you use your standard issue cuffs or fuzzies?"

I was speechless and grateful I had no food in my mouth or I would have choked.

"Oh, for shit's sake," Rena groaned. "Candy, you do not have to answer that."

Nodding mutely, I checked my watch.

"Fine." Shoshanna wasn't the least bit deterred. "It's just that my new book is about undercover agents who like a little spanky-spanky, and the two *male* cops at the table have not been very forthcoming with info for my research."

"Thank God for that," Kristy, my brother's fiancé, muttered, turning a shade of pink that led me to believe she and Mitch had done some research.

"It's just that metal cuffs could really do some damage, and blood would be gross. Not that I'm against two consenting adults going at it however they see fit. But the real problem here is that I'm not getting any, so I can't really experiment to learn the real outcome of metal versus fuzzies. Do you see my problem?"

Everyone went silent and pale. I briefly contemplated retirement as I realized I would be spending a week with Shoshanna and her mouth. Kevin was the first to recover his voice.

"Um, Shoshanna, I don't really think that's appropriate dinner table talk. You're scaring the hell out of Candy, not to mention my beautiful meal may go to waste because everyone has lost their appetite."

"What did I say?" she asked, truly confused. "Hey, pass the peas. I'm starving."

Slowly we all regained consciousness and began to pass the platters around the table. I lamented my loss of appetite. Kevin's dinner was truly beautiful—a perfectly medium rare beef tenderloin, a fluffy risotto with asparagus and mushrooms, French green beans with almonds, homemade dinner rolls, and the peas that the Porno Granny was after.

My brother and his best bud Jack still appeared to be in shock. Kevin and Steve were fine. I suppose they were used to the filter-free Shoshanna. Kristy was a bit subdued and Rena was A-okay. She dug into her meal as if we hadn't just heard the diatribe on bloody sex. If she could eat, then I could too. Who knew when I would get a gourmet dinner like this again?

"So you're writing a new one?" Rena asked as everyone blanched.

"Yep," Shoshanna said. "Starting a new series. I love the under-cover aspect. The hero and the heroine are in a big shoot-out with the bad guys—barely make it out alive. The adrenaline of blowing the heads off so many criminals is so intense they go at it like bun-nies in the warehouse next door to the pile of dead bodies. But, the kicker is they don't even know each other's names. They get sepa-rated when the local fuzz shows up and have to somehow find their way back to each other."

"Sounds a little complicated, Professor Sue," Kristy said.

"Not at all," Shoshanna replied. "It's totally hot."

"Who in the hell screws someone and doesn't know their name?" Rena laughed and punched me in the arm.

"Yeah," I stuttered weakly. "Who would do that?"

"What in the hell is wrong with you people?" Shoshanna shouted. "Back in the day, I screwed . . ."

"Oh my God," Rena shrieked, slapping her hands over her ears. "Stop. Now."

Shoshanna chuckled and shoved some peas into her mouth. Thank God, she used her spoon.

"Candy, are you all right?" Kevin asked.

"I'm fine. Why?"

"You're kind of green," he said with concern.

Mitch reached over and felt my head. "You're a little clammy."

"I hate that word," I said, removing my brother's hand.

"Well, you are," he said.

"I'm fine," I repeated, wanting the floor to open up and swallow me. I'd screwed somebody without knowing his name. Fourteen times. Not only had I become a bodyguard, I was a character in a porno book. Things were looking up . . .

Kristy, God love her, realizing my discomfort, *but hopefully not the reason,* steered the conversation away from my skin color. "So let me get this straight, they screw but they have no clue who they screwed."

"They know who they humped, they just don't know each other's names," Shoshanna corrected her.

"How in the hell do they find each other again?" Jack asked, drop-ping his head into his hands when he realized he had spoken aloud.

"Good question," the pea eater said with a large mouthful. "I can't figure that one out. I could make it random, but that's a little cheesy."

"Wait," Kevin interrupted. "How is it that they ended up at the shoot-out together in the first place?"

"Different branches of the government after the same bad guys."

"That actually makes sense," Steve chimed in. "The assholes at the FBI and CIA are always stepping on each other's toes because they're too assholish to communicate."

"Excellent," Shoshanna grunted. "All my research led me to believe those agencies don't even know who wipes their own butts."

"I wouldn't go that far," Steve said, laughing.

"I would," Mitch said. "I'm so happy to be out of that crap."

"I'm happy you are too," Kristy cooed, and blew my brother a sappy kiss.

I rolled my eyes and checked my watch again. Another half an hour. I would stay another half an hour.

"Back to my story. I need to do some more research and I need a research-ee," Shoshanna said, eyeballing me. "You got a boyfriend?"

"Me?" I asked, knowing I was the only other single gal in the room.

"Yep, you."

"No, and I don't want one."

"You gettin' laid?" she asked.

"Um . . ."

"I really don't want to know if my sister is getting laid," Mitch moaned, saving me from admitting I was clearly a slut.

"Fine," Shoshanna grumbled. "Do you wanna beta-read for me?"

"What's that?" I asked even though I knew I should have immediately said no.

"I give you chapters and you tell me if I got all the technical undercover agent stuff right. You get to read the book before it comes out and I'll pay you."

"God," Rena said with a laugh. "People would kill to get to read you before you came out."

"I don't think I'd be good at that." I had no desire to read my life in fiction. I was living it.

"You'd be great," Steve volunteered before I could say no. "Candy is one of my best, and her training is top notch."

"Done," Shoshanna shouted, jumping up from the table and retrieving a folder. "I'd e-mail it to you, but my goddamned computer doesn't like me."

She handed me a thick folder of pages. Why did I feel like that song? *Strumming my pain with his fingers, singing my life with his words . . .* What in the hell was the name of that song anyway?

"Your computer is fine." Kevin chuckled. "You're a menace to cyberspace."

"I've considered putting the fucker in the toilet, but getting electrocuted would hurt like a bitch."

"What's for dessert?" Jack asked, hoping to get Shoshanna's mind back on food. No such luck.

"My Pappi Joe, God rest his heathen soul, used to say if you didn't like something or someone, you should just pee on it."

"Now there's some solid advice," Rena muttered, and started clearing dishes.

Jumping up to help her, I idly wondered if there was a door to the outside in the kitchen. I wanted to ask for a doggie bag as I'd barely touched my meal, but that felt a bit awkward and rude. Kristy grabbed a few plates and hightailed it after us.

"Holy Christ Almighty." Kristy said, laughing. "That was some info I can't ever unlearn."

"You know, Candy," Rena said as she rinsed the flatware, "she is a little nutty, but she's one of the best people I know."

"Huh," I replied noncommittally and concentrated on putting leftovers in Tupperware. The kitchen matched the rest of the house. Deep purple linoleum covered the floor and the cabinets were a lovely complementary lavender with football helmet knobs.

"Really," Kristy chimed in. "She's brilliant. One of the most amazing and insightful professors I ever had. There are waiting lists for her classes."

It was difficult to reconcile the pea eater with brilliance . . .

"She's also a tremendous author," Rena added.

"I'm not sure I want to read the spanky-spanky secret agent novel." Shoving the food containers in the fridge, I started planning my escape.

"Trust me, you will." Rena grinned.

"Doubtful. Any gal who doesn't know the name of the guy she screws is a loser," I said, punishing myself and waiting to see their reaction.

"True," Kristy agreed, "but Professor Sue's heroines are strong and complicated. I'm sure there are good reasons for her being such a ho-bag in the beginning. Sue will weave it into her journey."

"Sometimes love starts out in hell." Rena hopped up on the counter and grabbed a cookie off a platter shaped like a beer can. "I fell in love with Jack when he arrested me, and Kristy fell in love with your brother because she'd just gotten out of a relationship with a married Dallas Cowboys fan who was too polite to tell her she'd been calling him by the wrong name."

"Bullshit." Kristy laughed. "I fell in love with your brother because of his ass."

I really needed to leave.

"But, the married Tony Romo lover part is true," Rena countered gleefully, and pilfered another cookie.

"Really?" I asked Kristy.

"Unfortunately, yes. On that note, I'm going back to the shit show in the dining room before any more of my dirty little secrets are revealed to my future sister-in-law."

She left and there was silence. Not uncomfortable silence, but a silence nonetheless. So, being me, I filled it.

"So, um, in the end . . . it might not be so bad to screw someone and not know his name?"

Rena put the majority of plates and silverware into the dishwasher while she considered my query. It took everything I had not to expound on my question and bury myself ass deep in humiliation. Not that I wasn't already there . . .

"Are we speaking hypothetically or literally?" she inquired as she handed me a very needed cookie.

"Hypothetically, of course."

"Oookay, was the *hypothetical* sex any good?"

"Very."

"Interesting. Was there more than one session of *hypothetical* sex?"

"Um . . . yes," I whispered.

"I see," she said. "More than ten?"

I nodded and snagged another cookie.

"Twenty?"

"No. Fourteen," I told her, dropped into a chair, and purposely banged my head on the table.

"Do you want to know his name?"

My head shot up from the table and I gave her a hard stare.

"Hypothetically," she quickly added, and unsuccessfully tried to hide her smirk. "If you had the opportunity to learn his name, would you want to know it? *Hypothetically?"*

"Until tonight, I didn't want to, but I feel like such a massive ho now, I think I'd better find out."

"Ease up on yourself, we've all been hos at one time or another. Although, fourteen times makes you kind of a top ho. Do you like the guy?"

"No," I blurted too quickly for even me to believe I meant it. "Fine. Clearly I like the sex part, but I don't really know him . . . He's cocky and . . ."

"No pun intended," Rena crowed. "Sorry it was too good to pass up."

Rena slid off the counter and scooped out two bowls of ice cream. Handing me one, she plopped down beside me and proceeded to dig in.

"Eat," she instructed. "Ice cream solves everything."

She was right. It did.

"Could we put an end to the hypothetical conversation for the moment?" I asked, praying she was a cool girl.

"Yep, on one condition."

"And that would be?"

"You take me with you when you interview that skank, Evangeline O'Hara." She grinned with such evil glee, I felt my own smile pull at my lips.

It wasn't exactly professional protocol to bring a non-officer to an interview, but having to rehash my ho-ish qualities was seriously unappealing. She did know Evangeline and could possibly be helpful . . . Ho talk or unprofessional behavior? The answer was surprisingly easy.

"You can come. I do all the talking unless I make it clear I want your input. If you step over any line, you're out. Deal?"

"Deal."

"Hey guys." Kristy popped her head back into the kitchen. "Shoshanna is giving a rundown of SCREW-Con. I think you'd better hear this, Candy. From what I understand, you're going as her assistant, not her bodyguard."

"Fuck," I groaned, and made a grab for the container of ice cream.

"What did you think you would be?" Rena asked, handing me a tub of whipped cream.

"I still haven't gotten over the fact that I'm going to a convention called SCREW. Really haven't thought much further than that."

"It's good you have us then," Kristy cackled and high fived Rena.

"What in the hell are you talking about?" The whipped cream settled like a lead ball in my esophagus.

"You're gonna need some outfits," Rena informed me getting her evil look back.

"Um, no."

"Um, yes," she shot back. "Hot sexy, porno-ee outfits."

"Absolutely not," I yelled, lamenting the fact I hadn't run when I'd had the chance.

"I don't see what the problem is," Kristy said. "When you were undercover on the Bigfoot drug bust, your nipples were practically hanging out of your tops."

"That was for a job," I snapped.

"And protecting Shoshanna's life is a game?" Rena's eyes narrowed dangerously. "I'd lay down my life for that profane little manner-less woman. If this is a silly little game that's beneath you, you need to speak up now and remove yourself from the case."

She had a point—a good one. What the hell was wrong with me? I was a pro and if I was being honest with myself, I kind of liked the outrageous Shoshanna. The thought of someone hurting her was wrong and wouldn't happen on my clock.

"You're right and I'm an ass. I promise you with my life, I will take care of her."

The ice cream no longer appealed. I couldn't swallow anything because my shame was lodged in my throat.

"Good." Rena hugged me tight. "We'll take you shopping on Wednesday."

"Sounds like hell." I grinned weakly.

"Oh trust me." Kristy joined the group hug. "It will be."

Chapter 4

The drive home was uneventful, but the partial manuscript of my life lying on the passenger seat called my name. Loudly. I parked the car in my driveway, grabbed the pages and read . . .

Holy hell, Rena and Kristy had been right. Shoshanna was one incredible writer. From her description, the story had sounded like a pornographic romp of idiots next to a pile of corpses, but the truth of the matter was far different. I felt better about being a slut because I was portrayed as a woman trying to find something real—something tangible that would last. I wasn't a ho; I was trying to make sense of a chaotic world and met my match in someone who was as screwed up as I was. A huge sense of loss settled over me when I finished the pages. I wanted to know what was going to happen to me next.

Wait the fuck a minute . . . Had I lost my mind? This wasn't me. This was a fictional character created in the mind of a pea-eating, cheese-loving Vikings fan. Disgusted with myself, I shoved the pages back in the folder and realized I'd missed a chapter.

To read or not to read . . .

I read.

Huge fucking mistake.

Upon finishing the spanky-spanky sex scene, I was so horny I thought I might explode in my car. I desperately tried to picture Shoshanna writing the sex so my libido would be doused, but I couldn't. *WTF?* All I knew for sure was that I needed to get laid. Now. By *not David*. My other half. The screwed-up version of myself who would make my life complete.

A single droplet of sweat trickled down my face and rolled

straight to my cleavage. This was ridiculous. I quickly started my car and rolled the windows down. Gulping fresh air and trying to clear my head, I did the only thing I could do in a clusterfuck situation like this. I picked up my Go-Phone and became one with my inner-ho.

He picked up on the first ring.

"Ice, how are you? Long time no speak," *not David's* panty-melting voice purred.

"I'm good," I mumbled. "And you?"

"Better now."

The zing of excitement that shot through my body tempted me to bang my head on the steering wheel, but I didn't want a black eye or a goose egg on my forehead if I was going to see the hotter than hell idiot. Sucking in a deep breath, I laid out my plan.

"I want to see you. I want your real name and I want to tell you mine," I sputtered on a single breath.

He was silent. Shit. This was the stupidest thing I'd ever done and I'd done some stupid in my time. He was probably married or engaged or gay. No, he wasn't gay unless he batted for both teams. I had fairly good gay-dar and really didn't think he was gay. But what did I know? Nothing. I knew nothing and now he was trying to figure out how to let me down nicely . . . or maybe he wasn't going to be nice. Maybe he thought I was a ho. Maybe I was a ho. If I hung up now, would he forget that I'd called?

"Luke."

"Look this was dumb and I'm drunk and I have the flu and I . . . wait. What did you say?"

"I said my name is Luke."

"For real?"

"For real." He chuckled and my nipples tightened. "Are you really drunk with the flu?" Amusement laced his voice. It made me want to slap him and ride him like a cowboy simultaneously.

"Um, no," I muttered, and wondered why my insanity wasn't scaring him off.

"I'd like to see you too."

"Are you sure?"

"Very. Why don't we have a drink at Mario's and see where it goes," he said.

"Like a date?" As sure as I was that I wanted to get in his pants, we were about to open a complicated can of worms and I was a sucky fisherman.

"Like a drink," he corrected me, sensing my panic.

"Okay," I whispered. "I can be there in fifteen."

"I can be there in ten," he shot back.

I giggled. He was as competitive as I was and it turned my crank like nobody's business. "I'll see you there." I hung up quickly so the ass-hat wouldn't have the last word. Of course I should have expected the text . . .

WEAR A DRESS

I rolled my eyes and to my great embarrassment, realized I was thrilled I'd dressed with care for the evening. I was sorely tempted to run in my house and put on some sweats, but he usually saw me in jeans and T-shirts. My plan was to blow his socks off and then his shirt and pants . . .

Oh God, was this living? If it was, it was scary and . . . well, it was scary.

It took me six minutes to drive to Mario's, two to park, thirty seconds to check myself in the mirror and swipe on some lip gloss, and twelve minutes to talk myself into going through with my drink-not-a-date. I was going to be late, but my inner monologue was demanding attention. My life was protocol and decisive action that oftentimes determined life or death. Things were black or white—good or bad. I could deal with that. I was very good at dealing with that. Love and happily-ever-afters were only fairy tales. I lived in reality.

Why in the hell did I think calling him and coming clean was a good idea? I'd been happy with my life and the occasional liaison with a guy named *not David*. Did I want to know if he left the toilet seat up or if he was a neat freak? No. No, I absolutely did not. Having a drink could only lead to ruining the very best sex I'd ever experienced. It was being around all the sickeningly happy couples at dinner that had made me weak. Damn it. And no thanks to Shoshanna, I was as horny as a teenage boy. Horny after reading fiction that could never happen in real life.

Order. Order was good. It made sense. It wasn't messy and people couldn't misinterpret each other or expect things from each other. Or break each other's hearts. Drinks with Luke would be a mistake, but I'd ruined it already. I'd set up new rules that I didn't want to follow. They'd lead to icky stuff. Shit.

I owed it to Luke and mostly my new big girl self to go in there and tell him I was insane. However, if he was interested in continuing the somewhat anonymous and uncommitted strangers-with-benefits thingie, I was good with that.

Grabbing my purse and making sure my gun was secured to my inner thigh, I was ready.

"Jesus Christ." I rolled my eyes at myself in the rearview mirror. Who in their right mind wants to date a girl who feels naked without a weapon strapped somewhere on her body? Nobody, that's who. I got out of my car, locked it, and took three calming breaths.

"Hey baby, you're exactly what I've been waiting for my whole fucking life," a male voice slurred.

Whipping around, I realized I was caught between my car and a big ugly drunk guy who thought he was going to get lucky. He thought wrong.

"I'm sorry, I'm sure I must have heard you incorrectly," I snapped, and realized he was a lot bigger than I'd originally thought.

"No, sugar, you heard me right." He licked his bulbous lips and advanced on me.

WTF? I was supposed to be on a date, not getting in a fight in the parking lot with an asshole who didn't know the meaning of no. Well, not actually a date . . . more of an offer to keep up the sham of a relationship that we'd had going for a year.

Damn, the fatass reeked. Had he drunk the bar dry?

"Why don't you just lift that sexy little dress up and I'll give it to ya good." He laughed and lunged in.

I quickly moved to my left and he fell clumsily into my car. If he dented my car, I was going to dent his head.

"Listen, bitch," he hissed, and grabbed my arm, pulling me up against his smelly, blubbery body. "You don't want to fuck with me."

"Excuse me," a very familiar voice called from about ten feet away. "Is there a problem here?"

"Get lost, buddy," my wannabe paramour slurred. "She's with me."

"Interesting," Luke said, holding his ground. "You good?" he asked me. His hands were clenched at his sides and I knew if I said no, my drunken attacker would most likely be lying dead on the ground in seconds flat. The fact that he didn't just step in and end my drama made me tingle inside and want to stick my tongue down his throat. God, a shrink would have a heyday with me . . .

"I'm good." I grinned and gave the sexiest and most considerate man alive the thumbs up. His returning grin made my knees week.

"You heard her," Drunkie snorted in victory, and wobbled unsteadily on his feet. "She's good with me. She's knows she's gonna get it real fucking good."

"Actually," I stated calmly, "I said I was good with the situation. Definitely not with you."

"Wait, what?" he asked, completely confused. Deciding I meant let's get it on, he began to unzip his pants.

Was he for fucking real? I was so glad it was me he was trying to rape instead of some poor unsuspecting girl who'd had a little too much to drink and couldn't defend herself. The more I thought about it, the more furious I got.

For a split second, I considered pulling my gun and making the inebriated asswipe pee his pants, but decided kneeing his balls into his chest cavity would be more fun. Plus, I had an audience. Leaning in as if I appreciated his disgusting attention, I pushed his head back. His hips jutted forward to balance his lumbering body and my knee went into action. I think I actually heard a crunch when I made contact. Having no real time to dissect the fact he may have had glass testicles, I quickly slammed my stiletto down on his instep and straight-armed my palm to his upper lip and nose. He screamed like a baby and went down like a huge rotting sack of potatoes. Out like a light. I hadn't even broken a sweat.

"Goddamn, that was hot," Luke yelled, pulling cuffs from his back pocket. "Let's get your friend over to that pole and leave him out here for the cops. Agree?"

"Agree." I laughed, more attracted to him than I'd thought possible.

"I'm pretty sure you broke his balls," he said with a grin.

"They did kind of crunch." I wrinkled my nose and wondered if we should check. Nope, that was even too gross for me.

"You wanna press charges?"

"You bet," I said, dragging the lump of shit to the pole. "He needs to pay."

"Allow me." Luke effortlessly pulled the loser to the pole. I stood and admired the way the muscles in his arms flexed as he worked. He cuffed the drunk and pulled out his phone. He made a quick call to the police, explaining the situation and that I would be calling in to press charges.

"You seem to know the cops pretty well," I told him, waiting to see if he would elaborate and tell me exactly what he did.

"The cops seem to know you pretty well," he countered, waiting for me to spill my secrets. I stayed silent, but something started to bother me. What the hell was it?

"I do believe we have a date to get to."

"A drink," I corrected, trying to remember my plan and figure out what was off. The simple fact that he was so beautiful was making my brain short out. "Should we leave him?" I asked, eyeing the unconscious jackass.

"Absolutely, it's all taken care of."

I snuck a glance a Luke. He looked a little thinner than the last time I'd seen him and he had a tan. Had he gone on vacation? Did he even live in Minnesota?

"You look gorgeous," Luke complimented me as his eyes roamed all over my body. "I mean, you're always hot, but this is *hot*."

"Um, thanks," I muttered, now out of my element. Destroying testicles and fighting injustice was easy. Making small talk with the sexiest man alive was torture.

Luke held out his hand and I took it. A zing of pure delight shot through me as I realized I was holding hands with a guy who still thought I was hot after I'd lodged another guy's nuts into his esophagus. Maybe I was being a little hasty. Maybe I would just see where this went . . .

Chapter 5

Mario's was a cute little Italian joint, dimly lit and full of romantic circular booths. This was my neighborhood. I wondered if Luke lived nearby too. We both slid into the booth and put our backs to the wall, ensuring that if anything went down we'd be certain to see it. Clearly, we were both in law enforcement. Or I was in law enforcement and he was a criminal . . . Our ingrained habit also ensured that our bodies were wedged together like we were conjoined twins.

"Hi," he said, looking down the front of my dress. "You wearing a bra under that?"

"No, and don't you think that question is a little forward?"

"Not really," he said with a grin, and ran his finger along my bottom lip. God, I was tempted to suck on it. Plus, he was right—he'd seen me naked more than anyone had in years.

"Luke what?" I asked, pulling back. I was slightly angled away from my perfect vantage point to scan the restaurant, but I was dangerously close to straddling him if he kept touching me.

"What do you mean Luke what?"

"I mean"—I rolled my eyes—"what's Luke's last name?"

"Oh, Luke's last name is Blakely," he announced grandly, clearly enjoying speaking of himself in the third person.

I giggled. Under the threat of death, I would never admit to him how much his cocky ego turned me on . . . or his hair or his teeth or his chest or his ass . . . He really was a ridiculous work of art. He had to be about six foot two. I was five foot ten and he had a good few inches on me. His eyes were a deep green and his sandy blond hair was just a little too long for him to be a regular cop. But his body? His body was to die for, and I'd seen it au natural.

"Hi there," a busty waitress purred to Luke, ignoring me as if I were invisible. "What can I get you, big boy?"

"I'll have a scotch, and my wife, who happens to be a rock star in the sack, will have a . . . ?"

I was speechless. *My wife? Rock star in the sack?* I mean, I appreciated his putting Boobs McGee in her place, but this was a little much.

I realized a very depressed Boobs McGee was now acknowledging my presence along with my *husband's,* but my voice was still MIA.

"Sugar lips will have a margarita," Luke volunteered. "Is that good?"

I nodded mutely and scoped the restaurant for alternate exits. He was a better player than me, and I was in over my head. Boobs McGee pouted, adjusted her namesakes, wrote down the order, and left.

"There are two exits. The door we came in and one in the kitchen. The kitchen is to your left through the swinging doors."

"How did you know what I was thinking?" I gasped. Was he a freakin' mind reader? I slid farther away and tried to think of nothing.

"I can read you like a book."

"No, you can't. I have a poker face," I insisted, desperately trying to regain my composure.

His intense stare made me feel naked and uncomfortable. "Maybe at work you do, but not in real life."

"My work is my life," I huffed. What a jerk. He was starting to sound like my boss, Steve.

"Now that's a sad state of affairs." He shook his head and moved closer.

I considered scooting farther away, but I didn't want to and I'd land on my ass on the floor if I moved another inch.

"You're making me nervous," I said, and then slapped my hand over my mouth. Where was my filter? Oh right, I didn't have one . . . Could I be less cool? This was a disaster. I wasn't cut out to flirt and date and be normal. I was cut out to shoot people. Standing up, I opened my mouth to make a lame excuse before I made my escape.

"Sit," Luke ordered.

I slowly eased my butt down on the edge of the seat as far away from him as possible.

"I have waited a year for you to make a move that didn't include a hotel room. You are going to sit here and get to know me and I'm going to get to know you in more than just a biblical sense. If I hadn't lost my cuffs to the fat bastard outside, I'd cuff you to me so you couldn't run."

"Um . . . okay." Shit, the thought of him cuffing me made my panties go damp.

There was a silence. A stupid, damn silence . . . so I filled it.

"You must get hit on all the time by humongous boobs, shit, I mean humongous women. Goddammit, I mean women. Women must hit on you a lot." My mortifying observation ended in a whisper.

Luke threw his head back and laughed. I wanted the floor to open and swallow me.

"How in the hell can someone who looks like you be insecure about anything?" he asked, still chuckling.

"I'm not," I snapped. *I am,* I wanted to scream. "And you didn't answer my question."

"Well, it wasn't really a question, more of a statement. And yes," he conceded, "I get hit on, but no more, I'd imagine, than you do."

"I don't get hit on much."

"That's good because I'd probably beat the hell out of anyone who looked at you."

"Possessive much?" I asked, wondering if he was serious.

"Occasionally," he said quietly.

Oh. My. God. He was serious. Uncertain whether to be pissed off or ecstatic, I decided pissed off was a safer emotion. "That's ridiculous. You don't even know me."

Luke blew out an exasperated breath. "That's what I'm trying to do here, but you're making it rather difficult."

He was right. I was so tangled up inside at having stepped so far out of my element, I was being bitchy. "I'm sorry."

"Apology accepted." He grinned and took my fidgety hands in his. "It's been a while. How have you been?"

"I've been . . . um." *In the hospital recovering from a knife wound after I fucked up a drug bust. I almost lost my job because I'm too tightly wound up in my work and I haven't been able to find anyone to have sex with because I'm too caught up in you* . . . "I've been fine. You?"

"Fine. I wanted to call you, but I've been away," he said.

Staring at the grooves in the worn oak table, I contemplated my next move. I could stay and talk or I could excuse myself to go to the bathroom and crawl out the window. That would be kind of a pussy move, and I'd destroyed a lot of clothes crawling out of windows. I really liked my dress, and heels were a bitch to climb in. Furthermore, I realized I did want to know him . . . or at least enough to feel less ho-like when I banged his brains out in about an hour. Fine, I could do this.

"Are you married?"

"Not even a little bit. You?" He was laughing at me, but that was a crucial question in my book.

"Nope and never gonna go there," I replied with confidence.

"It'd be a damn shame not to make some babies and pass on your genes." His lazy grin made my girlie parts jump to attention. Why did everything he said make me think of tackling him and making him see Jesus? Questions. Ask him questions. Guys loved to talk about themselves.

"Do you live in Minneapolis?" I retrieved my hands and sat on them. I didn't trust them. He was too pretty, and he smelled really good.

"I do, but I travel a lot."

"For work?" I asked.

He grimaced and looked up at the ceiling for a long moment. "Here's the deal, I can talk about every aspect of my life except work. Anything you want to know is fair game except that."

This was an interesting twist, but I couldn't talk about my work either. I didn't love that restriction, but I got it. There was just one potential problem . . .

"That's fine, but you have to tell me one thing." I leaned in close and he sucked in a quick breath.

"Baby, if you get any closer, we're going to get arrested for public indecency."

"That could be awkward if you answer my question incorrectly."

"If I answer it right, can we go back to my place? I'm in a little pain here." The evidence of his problem was obvious and delighted me to no end, but . . . Wait, how was I supposed to handle this?

Shit, it had been so much easier when I knew nothing about him. Although, I still didn't know all that much . . . It was clear he was funny, sexy, and he had put Boobs McGee in her place. He had an ass to die for and he wasn't married. He was honest about his work—kind of. He was amazing in the sack and he liked the fact that I could basically castrate someone with my knee . . . What in the hell was I worried about? He was perfect.

"Yep." I grinned and ran my tongue over my bottom lip.

"You're killing me here, Candy. Ask the goddamned question," he hissed.

"Fine. Are you on the right side of the law with your cryptic business or the wrong side?"

He blew a huge sigh of relief and grinned. "I'm on the right side. Can we go?"

"Do we know enough about each other?" I teased, getting hornier by the second.

He shoved me out of the booth and kept his hands on my hips as he quickly moved us through the restaurant. "We can talk the entire time," he said tersely. "Shit, the drinks."

"Just hand Boobs McGee some money and let's get the hell out of here." I was dangerously close to jumping him. His hands were burning themselves into my hips, and my knees were in danger of giving out.

"Hand who what?" He laughed, pulling his wallet out of his pocket and ransacking it for cash.

"The waitress with the knockers," I snapped. "The one who you falsely informed I was your wife."

"I thought that was a smooth move." Luke copped a feel of my ass and steered me toward the bar. He slapped fifty bucks down on the counter. "Hey, John."

"Luke, my man," the bartender shouted over the noise. "What can I get you and your lovely date?"

"She's my wife." John's eyes grew huge. "Just give this to the gal with the large chest and tell her we had to go."

"You got it, buddy. And congrats."

"Thanks," Luke said, rerouting us toward the door.

He was going to have to stop it with the wife stuff or I was out of here. Although a tiny part of me loved it. Could I really marry someone? Hell, could I really maintain a relationship more than a month? Before now I hadn't wanted to, but this crazy fool had me all confused.

Yes, I could do this.

I wanted to do this.

"Wait," I shouted, skidding to a stop in the parking lot, which was now empty of the fat bastard who'd attacked me. "What did you call me?"

"My wife?" he replied sheepishly.

"No. Before that." The feeling I'd had earlier that something was wrong returned with a vengeance. "Um . . . Sugar lips?"

"No, Luke. You called me Candy," I said, backing away.

"Of course I did. That's your name." He shook his head in confusion and ran his hands through his hair.

"You're right, that's my name, but I never told you my name." I waited for the explanation.

"You must have told me," he said with a lot less confidence.

"Nope." My eyes narrowed and my brain raced.

"Okay," he conceded. "I know your name. What's the big deal? You know mine."

"You told me your name. I did not tell you mine, which leads me to believe something is really fucked up here."

The suspicion bothered me and made me feel wary. My reaction would be considered extreme in normal situations, but my life was full of abnormal situations and trusting my gut, *as scarred as it was at the moment,* was how I survived.

"What else do you know besides my name?" I asked, hating everything at the moment.

"Confidential," he said quietly.

WTF? Confidential? All sorts of horrific scenarios blasted through my mind. Was he connected to someone I'd put in jail or, God forbid, killed? No, he would have taken me out long ago. Was I being monitored by the government? What the hell could I be monitored for? Was it because I'd fucked up a couple of times this year? "How long have you known about me?"

"A while," he admitted, and began to pace the parking lot. I tried to block out the way his jeans hugged his butt and how stupidly gorgeous he was. I needed to erase the fact that he made me laugh and that I'd just mentally prepared myself to try to have a real relationship with him. The joke was on me. Again.

"Is any of this real?" I demanded, willing myself not to cry. I'd thought he liked me. Was I a job? Was I an easy lay?

"It's real, Candy. Very real." He took two steps toward me and I took two steps back.

"You said you were on the right side of the law. I'm willing to believe that, but if you don't tell me what's going on, I'm so out of here."

"I can't." He sighed in frustration and shoved his hands in his back pockets.

"Clusterfuck doesn't even begin to describe this." I shook my head and pulled my keys out of my purse. "This was beyond a mistake and you have me completely freaked out. I'm going to walk to my car and you are not going to follow me. If I see you again, I will introduce your crotch to my knee." Son of a bitch, I was going to have to call Steve tonight and find out who Luke Blakely was and what he wanted from me. This absolutely sucked.

"Candy . . ."

"Nope. You can't call me that. You didn't earn it fair and square. Have a good life, and if I'm a job for you, good luck. I will make your life a living hell," I snapped.

"Jesus Christ." Luke threw his hands in the air. "Aside from the fact I can't tell you why or how I know your name, I don't really see a problem here. I'm crazy about you and I know you're crazy about me, or at least my oral skills."

"Oh my God," I shouted. "You are the most conceited ass-hat I've ever met. Turn the situation around. Would *you* be okay with this?"

He was silent. He couldn't answer the question because he wouldn't be fine with it either. I threw him one last withering glance and walked to my car. I turned my back on him, which could have been my last move ever, but for some reason I knew he wouldn't harm me—at least physically. Emotionally he'd just leveled me, and I didn't even know why.

I'd get to the bottom of this, and then I'd become a lesbian or a nun.

Chapter 6

It was obscenely early in the morning and the gun range was deserted. My Glock felt like a welcome extension of my hand. Ten rounds of target shooting had only minimally helped calm the tsunami in my stomach. After a sleepless night and no satisfactory answers from my boss, I needed to shoot stuff. I understood secrecy and covert necessities, but being told to drop it was grinding on my very last nerve. Not to mention my Go-Phone rang all night. Luke clearly wanted to flaunt his oral skills. I knew he wouldn't come clean, so I ignored his calls. I considered flushing the phone, but I knew my boss would not find that amusing.

Yes, my boss knew of Luke Blakely. Yes, he was an agent. No, I wasn't a high enough clearance level to know any more than that. Was he assigned to me? Not to Steve's knowledge. Was I in trouble? Again, not to Steve's knowledge. I was directly ordered to drop the matter, ask no more questions, and be satisfied that Steve would look into the matter. Would he share the results? Nope. I was on a need-to-know basis, and apparently I didn't need to know.

I needed to shoot some more shit. Where the hell were the lesbians when I needed them? The plain old body targets were unacceptable. I needed a refrigerator or at the very least a toaster. However, I'd shot the testicles clean off my target—twenty-three times.

My tummy growled with hunger, but the thought of food was nauseating. My hands began to tremble and I put my gun away. Confusion didn't begin to cover my feelings. I was driving blind, and that was a dangerous place to be.

Focus and precision. Deadly focus and precision. Forget Luke.

If I were in real danger or trouble, Steve would brief me. Luke was possibly watching me because I had fucked up. Maybe someone over Steve's head had assigned him to me. Maybe he was just an asshole. I scoured my brain to remember if I'd ever left evidence of my identity when we had met up. My real ID was hidden in a false casing on my gun. There was no way he could have found that. There was clearly another reason he knew my name and stats, and I wasn't going to find out. Fuck.

Thank God I had an assignment and I was leaving town. This was good. Forgetting Luke and his duplicity would be difficult, but doable. I suppose what sucked the worst was the pathetic fact that I'd thought he actually liked me . . . because I actually liked him, but no more. I might be gullible, but I wasn't desperate.

Interviewing Evangeline O'Hara would take my mind off trying to find unattainable answers about the sham my life had become. During my bout with insomnia, I'd reviewed all of her files. She was a piece of work. I actually looked forward to the interview, if only to get a look at her in person. There was simply no way she could look like her photos. Agreeing to let Rena tag along was a fortunate lapse in judgment, because she had been up close and personal with both Evangeline and Shoshanna and was privy to information I was sure the files lacked.

Shower. I needed to shower and eat and block the jerk from my brain. Never again would I be swayed by an ass, no matter how fine or muscled or perfect it was.

Time to step into my new life. Again.

"I think this is a waste of time—a dead end," Rena said, offering me a french fry. I declined.

We'd been driving for an hour and had stopped three times. Once for Rena to go to the bathroom, once for her to go through a drive-through for french fries, and once to go through another drive-through because she couldn't eat said fries without catsup. We were not stopping again.

"If you spill catsup in my car, you're walking home."

"Kristy said you were a hard ass, but I can see she was being kind." Rena burst out laughing. "Your phone is ringing."

"Your deductive skills amaze me."

"You gonna answer it?" she inquired, still chuckling.

"Does it look like it?" I ignored the phone. I knew who it was. Tomorrow I would get a new Go-Phone with a different number.

"Sounds like there's a story there." She giggled and continued to shove fries in her mouth.

I glanced over and gave her the evil eye, which only made her laugh harder. "I am a hard ass, I had no sleep, and you made me do something stupid," I snapped, and then regretted my words immediately.

"You think it's a mistake to take me with you?" she asked, and squeezed another packet of catsup on her fries.

"No," I answered. "You're probably an asset. What did you mean by this being a waste of time?"

"In a minute." She changed the subject. "What did I make you do?"

I drove in silence and refused to speak.

"Ahhhhh." She grinned and turned to face me. "What's his name?"

I heaved a huge sigh. Rena was like a gnat, she wasn't going to give up. She expected an answer and would keep bugging me till she got one. "His name is Ass-hat Son of a Bitch Douchehole."

"Damn, he must have had a hellish time in elementary school."

We drove in silence for approximately two and a half minutes before my dreaded need to fill it reared its ugly head.

"His name is Luke and he doesn't really like me. I think he was assigned to me, but I can't figure out why. The sex was just because I was there," I volunteered lamely.

"Did he say that?" she asked.

"Not exactly, but he didn't have to."

"Interesting. Do you read minds?" she inquired, dangling a catsup packet over my dash.

"Your point?" I asked. She was an idiot to bait me with tomato sauce.

"My point, little Miss Hardass, is that you are so terrified of getting close to people, any little slip up will send you running." She was quite satisfied with herself and I wanted to throw her out of the car. Why? Because she was hitting way too close to home . . .

"It wasn't a little thing," I huffed.

"Did he say he didn't like you? That you were a job? Or an easy lay?" she pressed.

"No, he didn't say that."

"Well, what the hell did he say?" Rena demanded, and pulled a candy bar out of her purse. "I'm getting ready to bleed like a stuck pig so I need chocolate," she muttered.

"Give me some of that," I said, hoping the chocolate would calm my nerves and divert her to another topic.

"Certainly." She chuckled and handed me half. "Answer my question."

"Fine," I shouted. My words bounced off the tight interior of the car, making Rena wince. "He said he was crazy about me. He invited me to a bar and introduced me as his wife to Boobs McGee, the overly amorous waitress, and he knew my name even though I never told him what it was."

"I'm a little confused," she said with a mouthful of candy bar. "Either I missed something important here or Ass-hat Son of a Bitch Douchehole has it bad for you."

"My name." I rolled my eyes. How could she not get the importance of his knowing my name? "He knew my name."

"Yeah. And?"

"In my world, that's fucked up. It means our meeting wasn't what it seemed."

"Do you want to know what I think?" she asked, foraging in her purse for what I assumed was more candy.

"No."

"Good." She laughed. "Then I'll tell you. I think if you were a job or an easy lay, he would have met you at a hotel and played hide the salami and left."

I hadn't considered that angle. Maybe she was . . . *WTF?* No. I wasn't going to let her or Kristy or anyone make me think I could be a normal girl ever again.

"He knew my name," I ground out through clenched teeth. "That's significant."

"Oh my God," she barked. "All you freakin' cops are so uptight—Jack, you, your brother. Quit looking for everyone to have an ulterior motive." She tore into another candy bar and kept on going. "So the fuck what if he was assigned to you, whatever the hell that could mean. Haven't you ever heard of falling in love on the job?"

"Only in fairy tales," I shot back, snapped off half of her candy bar, and shoved it in my mouth.

"If you weren't driving right now, I would take your hand off for stealing my premenstrual food," she hissed, and began digging through her purse again. "I have no clue if there's some kind of covert FBI CIA voodoo going on, but this sounds like a guy who likes you. Goddammit, these have been in here for a year," Rena muttered as she unwrapped some scary-looking peanut butter crackers. She sniffed them and stuck one under my nose. "Does that smell weird?"

"Kind of," I gasped, jerking away.

"Crap, I'm still hungry," she whined.

"Fine." I swerved off the highway and pulled into a convenience store. "What do you want?"

"Are you going in?" she asked.

"I am. I need to be away from you for three minutes. I need to adjust my attitude and I feel bad about stealing your period candy. I'm going to make up for my bad behavior by buying you some disgusting shit that's not rancid."

Rena's smile was contagious. I liked her. She was driving me nuts, but she was fun and smart and I didn't really have many girl friends. I didn't have many friends period.

"I want chips and some chocolate."

"Then you shall have it." I laughed and went in and bought it. God, I was entirely too uptight. Maybe Rena was right about my suspecting the worst of everyone, but she was wrong about Luke. It didn't add up and whether she understood it or not, I had to go on my gut with this one and stay away from Mr. Sexy Pants.

Walking back to my car, I felt lighter and happier. I had a friend. A friend who was in my car waiting for the disgusting gift I'd bought her. A friend who was talking on the phone. My phone. My Go-Phone. Fuck.

Yanking open the door, I lunged for the phone, but Rena was quick and evil. She blocked me with her foot and put Ass-hat Son of a Bitch Douchehole on speakerphone. I swallowed the scream lodged in my throat and flipped my ex–new friend off. She grinned and returned the favor.

"So who did you say this was?" Luke's voice came through loud and clear. This was beyond my worst nightmare. Rena was more of a loose cannon than I was.

"I'm Candy's mom. Who's this?"

"You sound a little young to be her mom." His voice was laced with amusement and I could picture his sexy lopsided grin. A thrash punk band started performing in my stomach. They were drunk and getting ready to dive off the stage and crowd surf. I was going to hurl. I angled myself so I would nail Rena when I let loose.

"Thank you," she said. "Now answer my question, young man. Who is this?"

"Luke."

"Well, Luke, how do you know my daughter?" She gave me the thumbs up and I almost slapped her. What in the hell did she think she was doing?

"If you're her *mom,* I'd have one answer. If you weren't her *mom,* I'd have another," he said with a chuckle, and my insides clenched. I went from nausea to arousal in a matter of seconds. Shit.

"Let's just say, for shits and giggles, that I'm not her mom for a moment," Rena said, getting down to business. "What are your intentions, Luke?"

"Assuming she's not sitting with you . . ."

"Never assume. That makes an ass out of you and me," Rena informed him with glee.

Oh my God, she was insane.

"Then I suppose I shouldn't assume I'm on speakerphone."

"That would make you an ass," she replied, and grabbed for the chips I was holding. No fucking way. She'd lost her chip privileges forever. Tearing open the bag, I shoved half the contents in my mouth and ate them. "Um, Luke?"

"Yes, Mom?"

"If you want her to hear your plea, you'd better start talking because I'm getting ready to be on the rag and she just ate my bag of chips. So this means I have to kill her and it would be a shame if she died thinking you were a total douchehole."

"Point taken." He laughed and I groaned. "Candy, I'm not following you. Well, I am following you, but not for work. I'm following you because I can't get you out of my head. Yes, I cheated and found out who you were. There was no way in hell I could let you totally disappear."

"That's hot," Rena chimed in, grinning from ear to ear. She glanced over and I gave her the double birdie. "She's still pissed. You're gonna have to do better than that."

I banged my head on the steering wheel and begged God for Armageddon.

"Candy, you are the hottest piece of ass I've ever had in my life. When you took that fat bastard's nuts out with your knee, I wanted to tackle you and make you see Jesus. You're funny and screwed up and sexier than anyone should be allowed to be. My plan, and I always complete my missions, is to get you into my life and back into my bed . . . Better, *Mom?*"

"Damn." Rena whistled. "This is making me horny." She tossed me the phone. "Talk to him. I'm going to call Jack and have phone sex."

With that little TMI nugget, she got out of the car and left me alone with the douchehole.

"Candy? Talk to me."

"No."

He waited and of course my ungodly urge to fill silences betrayed me. Again.

"It doesn't add up, Luke."

"Which part?"

"It wouldn't be that easy to find out who I am. There's more to the story, isn't there?"

I heard a frustrated sigh blast through the phone. "Yes, there's more, but . . ."

"No buts. You tell me or I hang up," I snapped. This yo-yoing was painful. He either really liked me or I was an assignment he couldn't fuck up. God, I so wanted him to like me.

"Candy, if I could, I would. I can't blow cover. If anyone ought to understand this, it should be you." He sounded defeated and I almost felt sorry for him. Almost.

Goddammit, I did understand, but rational thought wasn't part of my repertoire at the moment. This was personal and I wasn't very good at personal. "If you'll blow cover by telling me how you know about me, then I have to assume I'm a job. If I'm an assignment, you'll do anything to keep me in your sights. I'd do the same.

So again, good luck with tracking me. I'll make it very difficult for you. You might be good, but I'm better."

My heart painfully lurched as I snapped the Go-Phone shut, dropped it out of my car window, got out, and crunched it under my boot. What should have been a satisfying move made me feel like I'd just ruined my life. I barely knew this guy, except in a biblical sense; why in the hell was I so devastated?

"Ewwww," Rena said, examining the carnage that used to be my phone. "Guess that didn't go so well."

"No," I whispered, trying to hold back the avalanche of tears that threatened to fall.

"I'm really sorry. That was my fault. I thought I was helping." She leaned in and wrapped her arms around me.

My body relaxed against hers. "No, it's okay. It was actually good, I think. Part of me thought he was still a possibility . . . he's not." The tears finally flowed.

"I could have him killed," Rena volunteered. I grimaced at the irony. I was the type of person who was hired to do just that kind of thing.

"Thanks"—I grinned through my tears—"but no thanks."

"Do you want my opinion?" she asked as she rubbed my back.

"No, but I don't suppose that matters." I pulled back and waited for something obscene or profound.

"You're right." She giggled and then turned serious. "As much as you want to pretend he's not a possibility, you still think he is one. And so does he."

I contemplated what she'd said. I wanted to deny it, but what was the use? She was right and I was an idiot. If he had told me what I wanted to know, I would have lost respect for him. His dedication to his job was something I understood. I honored mine the same way. Fuck, I was living such a double standard. I wouldn't have told him anything either. My behavior was stupid and immature, but I was stuck. I didn't know what else to do. Did my self-preservation instinct outweigh my ability to be human?

"I bought more chips," she said, and handed me a huge bag. "Let's go interview an over botoxed skank. I promise it will make you feel better."

"You think?"

"I know."

Chapter 7

"**W**ait." I grabbed Rena's arm and yanked her to a stop as we approached the jail where the infamous Evangeline was incarcerated. "Tell me why you think this is a waste of time."

"Did you read the threatening notes Shoshanna got?" she asked. "I did."

"Do you know Evangeline's background in the literary world?" "I do."

"Then trust me when I tell you she couldn't have written those notes. The grammar was correct, there was punctuation included, and even though they had a fanatical religious undertone, they actually made sense," Rena replied.

"She's that stupid?" *How was that possible?*

"Yep. Although, I suppose someone else here could have written them for her."

"No, they weren't sent from the jail. They came from Saint Paul. It would have to be someone working with her on the outside." I removed the folder from my bag and glanced over the photocopies of the notes and the envelopes. The notes had been typed and were free of all fingerprint evidence. Whoever was doing this was well-versed in law enforcement tracking methods. Not a trace to lead to the perp.

"Holy hell," Rena hissed. "No one would work with her on the outside. She has no friends, and her only acquaintances are either serving time or were being blackmailed by her. Nope. No help from the outside," she stated with complete confidence.

"She has the most clear-cut motive," I muttered as I searched the file for any disciplinary actions on her jail record. None. She was a model prisoner.

"True," Rena agreed, "but I still don't think she's responsible for the threats."

I glanced over at my new friend and watched for any signs that she was hiding something—body language, red face, fidgety movement . . . Jesus, what was I doing? Was everyone a suspect?

"Do ya think I did it?" Rena crossed her arms over her chest and raised her eyebrow.

"Am I that transparent?" I groaned.

"No, I just get you. So answer."

I heaved a sigh and ran my hands through my hair. "No, I don't think you did it, but I looked at you. I did. I looked at you as a possibility," I spat, disgusted with myself. Did I trust no one? No, I didn't. It was becoming increasingly clear that no matter how good I was at my job, my job had taken over my life.

"What do you do for fun?" she asked, and pulled me over to a bench. "Sit."

I did.

"Fun?" I hoped I'd misunderstood.

"Yes, Candy. Fun."

"Um . . ." I racked my brain so I wouldn't sound as unsocial as I really was. "Work."

"Hobbies?"

"I shoot stuff," I mumbled.

"I think you need to branch out a little."

"Ya think?" I laughed. Even to my own ears I sounded pathetic.

"Look, I'm not attracted to boring people," Rena said. My stomach cramped. Was she breaking up with me? Dammit to hell, I felt the heat crawl up my neck. I wanted to change my answers, but I couldn't come up with a lie that sounded even remotely true. "You are not boring, but you're wedged so far up inside yourself, there's a chance you may never come out. It's kind of like sticking your foot up your ass and pulling it out of your mouth. You know what I mean?"

"Um, no."

"Actually that wasn't a really good example," she admitted. "You're in your own way. Clearly you're a good cop."

"Agent," I corrected her.

"Agent." She rolled her eyes and that heat I'd felt creeping up my neck landed squarely on my cheeks. "You can't go home to your job. You can't have sex with your job—well, you kind of did." She grinned and punched me in the arm. "Your brother is worried about you—so is Steve. And now because you showed up in my life, I am too. I don't take kindly to that, so you better be worth it."

"I want to be. For the first time in a long time I want to be." We sat in silence and shockingly I had no need to fill it. The truth would be so depressing and sad.

"What happened to you?" she asked quietly.

How did I answer that one? Nothing had happened to me. I never let anything happen to me. I had closed myself off a long time ago.

After my sister died of an overdose, I had a mission. Hell-bent on destroying people like the ones who had destroyed my sister and my family, I stopped feeling— It was too difficult. Mitch had been lucky. He'd left for college right after she died, and then everything fell apart—truly apart.

For the next several years till I went off to college, my family lived in silence. Hence my irrational need to fill it. We splintered, each handling our pain differently. Our once happy, loving family disappeared. My parents blamed themselves and became cold and distant with each other. I had no clue why they even stayed to-gether. It would have been better if they had screamed or cried or divorced.

My mother's need to control my younger sister and myself was debilitating. My baby sister handled it by withdrawing, and I han-dled it by excelling—in everything except being human. I was a straight A student, an award-winning athlete, and a cold bitch. Therapy might have helped, but we were proud, churchgoing Mid-westerners. We had God and each other. That worked out swim-mingly. During my time in training, I did a lot of therapy and had considered myself cured—till now.

Now my humanity and my desire to have friends and be loved were slipping through my formerly well-protected cracks. It was more frightening than hand-to-hand combat. Combat had a logical end. Life or death. Being vulnerable to other people was gray and messy and something I had very little experience with. I adored my brother and I loved my boss. Steve had become my de facto father and I knew without a doubt those two men would be there for me no matter how difficult I was. Friends and lovers were another thing altogether.

How to answer Rena . . . whether to answer Rena . . .

"It's too long to go into, but I think I might be finally getting past it."

"That's gonna suck," she said.

"What the hell does that mean?" I snapped. She had no fucking clue what she was talking about.

"Becoming human," she replied sympathetically. "Risking your heart, not just your life."

God, maybe she did know what she was talking about. And maybe she was right.

"Well, no worries, it will be fine." She smiled reassuringly and took my hand. "You have me and Kristy and Shoshanna now. You'll be human in no time."

I rolled my eyes and tried to suppress the grin that was coming straight from my lighter heart. "That certainly sounds frightening."

"Frightening doesn't even begin to cover it," she said, laughing, and yanked me to my feet. "Come on, it's about time you vomited in your mouth."

"I'm sorry. What?"

"Whoops, I meant it's time for you to meet Evangeline."

We signed in at the entrance of the jail and went through the first secure door, which promptly closed and bolted behind us. The second door would open once we'd complied with regulations. The walls were covered in lock boxes, and red security camera lights blinked rapidly in all four corners. I began to disarm.

"What the fuck? Are we in a cell?" Rena asked, glancing around nervously.

"Nope." I laughed. "I figured since you'd been arrested before, you'd know the drill."

"Well you *figured* wrong. I was never convicted of anything and never thrown in the pokey," she huffed. "Jesus Christ, you're a freakin' arsenal."

I removed my two guns, my cuffs, and a knife and placed them in a locker. "Give me your purse," I told her, and removed the folder and a pen from my bag. "We can't take anything in except my files, but our personal effects will be safe in here and we can get them on the way out."

Rena handed me her purse and I locked everything up.

"Can I have my cell phone? I was hoping to get a photo of the skank."

"Nope." I chuckled and shook my head. "No cell phones. No pictures."

"Dammit, I just lost thirty dollars," she groaned.

I rolled my eyes and tucked the key in my pocket. As soon as our belongings were stowed away, the second door automatically opened.

"How did you do that?" she asked, bewildered.

"I didn't. The little guy in the camera did."

"You're beginning to sound like my aunt Phyllis. She has Martians in her TV and cyborgs in her toilet."

"Awesome." I knew of her aunt Phyllis. I'd witnessed Phyllis's brand of crazy during the Bigfoot drug bust. Actually crazy wasn't remotely accurate, it was more like bat-shit loony, but I did like her. "We're being monitored and they watched us disarm."

"This feels kind of surreal," Rena whispered, moving closer to me.

"It is, but we're completely safe," I told her, and followed the guard on the other side of the door.

"You're here to see Evangeline?" the personality-free female guard grunted as she escorted us to a conference room.

"Yep."

"She's quite the hit here. Very popular," the guard gushed with admiration, all of a sudden full of life.

Rena choked on her own spit and I grabbed her arm before she volunteered something that would get us removed from the premises.

"You don't say, um . . . Sally," I replied, glancing at her name tag.

"Oh yes, she's the belle of the ball. Would you like me to stay in the room while you chat?" she queried hopefully.

This was bizarre. Did she have a crush on Evangeline? "No. That won't be necessary, but thank you." A deflated Sally left the room.

"What the fuck was that?" Rena demanded.

I quickly nodded my head to the corner of the room at the camera, letting her know we were being taped and she should shut her pie-hole.

"What the fuck was that?" she whispered.

I shrugged my shoulders and grinned. "Seems like Miss O'Hara has an admirer."

"Help me, Jesus," Rena muttered, plopping down in a chair. "Just try not to scream."

"Why would I . . . holy shit," I yelped, and slammed myself up against the wall as the most unnaturally large pair of boobs entered the room followed by a skeletal thin body and a face that could give a blind person a heart attack.

She was clad in prison orange, but the neckline of her jumpsuit had been altered to reveal her pickled cleavage. The bosoms actually started at her neck and the sheer weight of them was throwing her balance off, but her face . . . My God, I'd never seen anything like it. Her upper lip literally touched her nose and she had a permanently shocked look on her face due to her nonexistent eyelids. I was struck dumb.

I glanced over at Rena, who was enjoying my terror immensely. Although when she got her first gander of Evangeline, she gagged and latched on to the table.

"Shit," she gasped. "They're bigger."

"Ruby daaahhhling, it's so good to see you." Evangeline tripped her way toward the table. Years of ingrained training made me sprint over to catch her before she fell flat on her face.

"Arrrgrafabragah," she screeched, grabbing my hair for balance. Evangeline ignored the fact that she had a death grip on my head and continued her conversation with Rena. "Ruth, I need you to move. I have to sit there so the camera gets my best angle. Can't have my fans seeing me not at my best," she trilled, using me like a cane as she wobbled her way to the coveted chair. Rena bolted up and quickly moved as far away from the walking disaster as she could. It would have been nice of her to help me peel the freak show off my head, but I was clearly on my own.

"Excuse me, Miss O'Hara, I'm going to have to ask you to release my head. Now." I unglued her claws and helped her to her seat. I gave Rena the stink eye and cautiously moved back from Evangeline.

"My goodness," she cooed. *Sweet Jesus, her mouth didn't close when she talked due to her gargantuan lips.* "Aren't you a pretty little thing? Rutah, you have such lovely friends! What's your name?"

"I'm Candace Sanderson and I'm with the Drug Enforcement Agency. I'm here to ask you a few questions."

"Oh, Connie, how exciting," she shouted, making me cringe. She leaned in as much as her bloated chest would allow and lowered her voice to a whisper. "Is this about the Botox and Juvederm shipment? I had nothing to do with that, Corrine. It was that sneaky Tracey. She was trying to get into my pants. Of course, I led her on until I'd been plumped and frozen, and then I dropped her like a hot potato. If she ratted me out, Yvonne will kick her ass."

I was speechless. That was the most bizarre connection of words strung together I'd ever heard.

"Did they put Juvederm in your knockers?" Rena inquired casually from her safe corner.

"Of course not, Rula!" Evangeline laughed hysterically. "That was silicone! My lover Yvonne was able to procure a bit of the magic elixir. You see," she explained logically, "one can't let one's bosom go south. It's not good form. So clearly, Claudia, you're wasting your time if you're trying to pin the goods on me. However, if it would mean an extended stay at the prison resort, I might be willing to perjure myself and take the rap."

"Um . . . while that's all very enlightening," I stuttered, "that's not why we're here."

"Oh, thank God." She heaved a huge sigh, which made her lips flap. "Please disregard everything I just told you. I'd hate for my suppliers to be cut off. A woman must maintain her beauty, especially in the slammer, if you know what I mean." She tried to wink and it came out like a small seizure. My gag reflex kicked in and I decided to focus only on her forehead. Rena had gone mute. I assumed this was a little much even for her to process.

"Actually, Miss O'Hara," I started.

"Call me Evangeline, Cora," she insisted.

"My name is Candace," I corrected, and heard Rena snort in the corner.

"That's what I said, Crystal."

"Oookay then, let's get to the questions." I opened my folder and attempted to put my professional face back on.

"Wait," she shrieked. "Don't you need to pat me down? It's fine with me if you do. I won't fight you, Cassandra. I could be hiding something in my quivering cleavage," she purred suggestively, and ran her claws through her hair, which if I was not mistaken, and I was not, knocked her wig to the left.

"That won't be necessary today."

"Or ever," Rena muttered. I couldn't have agreed more. This needed to be over. Now.

"Evangeline, have you made any contact with Shoshanna LeHump since you've been incarcerated?"

"Shrilanka? How is she? We had such good times together!" Evangeline bounced joyfully in her chair at the mention of Shoshanna. The only parts of her body that bounced with her were her lips and wig.

"Please just answer the question."

She became truly confused, and for a moment I wasn't sure if she even knew where she was. "What was the question?" she asked.

"Have you attempted to contact Shoshanna LeHump in any way since you've been incarcerated?"

"No." She shook her head in embarrassment. "I know I should write her and thank her, but I've been so busy teaching poise and manners to the girls, I've neglected my social duties."

"Back the fuck up," Rena cut in, crossing the room and getting right up next to Evangeline. "You've been doing what?"

"Yes, Rainbow, I've found my calling and my sexual identity," she blabbered with complete sincerity and pride. "I'm a lesbian etiquette aficionado!"

"No."

"Yes, Reba, I spent my whole life with anger bottled up inside me because I was denying who I really was. My therapist, Dr. Calvert, has helped me see the light, and of course Yvonne has helped me reach my first orgasm. Her technique is so . . ."

"Stop!" Rena bellowed. "That's enough. I will need years of therapy to erase this visit and the visuals you just planted. I gotta get out of here."

I couldn't have agreed more, but I still had a job to do.

"In a minute," I told her, finally finding my professional face and manner. "Evangeline, you're saying at no time have you tried to contact Shoshanna LeHump in the last six months?"

"No." She shook her head sadly. "I know you must think I'm just awful." She started to cry. Her mascara ran down her face, making her look like a deranged clown. "Please give her my love. Tell Shodoodoo, I'm sorry for what I did and thank her for giving me a new life."

I looked around for a tissue but there was nothing. I honestly felt sorry for her and glad for her too. She was certifiable, but she did seem at peace and even happy. In my entire career thus far, I had never come upon anything like this.

"I think we're through here," I said quietly. "Are you all right?"

"Oh yes—" She beamed. I looked away in horror. She resembled a female ET with a terrifying makeup job. "You must let Suduko know I'm writing lesbian prison erotica now and I'm dedicating my first novel to her. And of course you, too, Rhonda."

"Please don't," Rena begged, and I almost laughed. She had gone as white as a sheet. "That is completely unnecessary."

"I beg to disagree. You have made my life better and now I want to repay the favor."

If Evangeline were sane, she would be brilliant. This subtle revenge was sheer genius, but she was insane and sincerely delighted to do something good for the women who had put her in the slammer. The slammer stay that had resulted in true happiness and, apparently, true love . . .

This had to go down as the weirdest day of my life.

"Thank you, Evangeline." I grabbed Rena, who was rooted to the floor, clearly trying to come up with a way to discourage Evangeline's generosity. "Time to go."

As I dragged Rena from the room, Evangeline had parting words. "Please visit soon. I'd love for you to meet Yvonne. We're getting married next month! I'll send invites."

We retrieved our belongings and sprinted to the car.

"I told you she didn't do it," Rena ground out between clenched teeth, still pissed she was going to be immortalized in prison porn.

"You're right, and that was the most alarming interview I've ever participated in."

"She's happy, isn't she?" Rena asked, digging back into our junk food supply.

"Gimme that." I grabbed the chips and threw a few back. "I believe she is. She's crazy and possibly in the first stages of dementia."

"Really?" she asked, shocked.

"Yeah, did you notice the moment she just went away?"

"I did. It threw me a little. I was so used to her being so damn evil, it was disconcerting to see her like that. Do you truly think she's happy?"

"I do."

Rena quietly contemplated for a few minutes. "I think Shoshanna will be glad."

"Glad that she's gone off the deep end?" I asked, surprised. I had a hard time believing Shoshanna would wish the worst on anyone—even someone as hateful as Evangeline had been.

"No. She'll be glad that she's finally happy . . . and I am too."

The rest of the drive was silent. We were both wrapped up in our own thoughts and they were heavy.

Chapter 8

After taking Rena home, I pulled into my driveway, slammed on my brakes, and froze. Thank God I was seated, because I felt dizzy and faint. An Olympic gymnastics meet in my stomach made breathing difficult. What the hell should I do? Back the car up and drive away? Act like I had the wrong house? Duck down and pretend I wasn't in the car? Now that would be pretty stupid, because I'd already been spotted.

He was on my front stoop—sitting there and watching my mini-freak with a huge grin on his face. God, he was pretty. I really should go. I did need some groceries and the store wasn't crowded at this time of night . . . If I got out and talked to him, there was a fine chance I'd strip him and tackle him. That could be embarrassing and illegal if I did it on my front lawn. Choice made—I had to leave.

Wait.

This was my house and I was a grown-up. He was trespassing and I'd simply get out of my car and tell him to take a hike. Although he always smelled really good and kissed like a rock star . . . Maybe I'd make out with him just a little bit and then tell him to get lost.

Stepping out of my car, I stopped. For the first time in what seemed like years, I took a moment to notice my surroundings. Dusk had settled in and there was a slight nip in the air. It smelled like fall, like a high school football game . . . like promise. That stomach tingling feeling that had eluded me in my own high school years rushed at me and made me breathless—the silly wonderful feeling that possibilities were endless. Stars were beginning to twinkle and I bit back the urge to giggle. There was a beautiful boy on the front porch of my quaint little Craftsman house and he wanted me. His motives might be suspect, but his desire was real and so was mine.

It was time to get gray and messy.

"Hi," I said in a voice that sounded far more carefree than mine.

"I'm sorry, I . . ." Luke started.

"No." I put my fingers to his lips and shook my head. "Don't ruin my buzz." He laughed and I continued. "I like you. I have no idea why since I hardly know you, but I do. I felt nauseous after I crunched my Go-Phone under my boot when I hung up on you and . . ."

"You crunched your phone?" he asked, delighted by my violent nature. *God that was a turn-on.*

"I did, but that's not really the point," I told him, trying to suppress my smile. "The point is, even though I don't trust you, I want you. So I've decided that I'm going to have you. Now." I expelled a huge breath and waited.

"Like now now?" he asked. "On your front steps?"

"Well, I considered it," I said, moving into his personal space, "but that could be a little uncomfortable and slightly illegal."

His breath hitched and everything south of my belly button clenched.

"Would you like to come in?" I breathed in his clean sexy scent and felt positively giddy.

"Is the pope Catholic?"

"As far as I know, but I'm Lutheran." I giggled and shoved my key into the lock.

We flew into the house all hands and lips and gasps. For a brief second I wondered if the place was clean and promptly forgot my worry when Luke found the spot on my neck that made me weak.

"Bedroom?" he asked in a rough voice.

"Um, I think it's . . ." Where in the hell did it go? I was lucky I still knew my name. "To the right," I hissed as his hands made their way under my shirt.

Without missing a beat, he tossed me over his shoulder and secured me with his hands up my skirt and planted firmly on my ass. I squealed and yanked his T-shirt out of his jeans.

"Five times," he groaned as he found my bedroom and slid me down his body. All of my soft molded to all of his hard.

"Five times what?" I asked as I tore at the buttons on his jeans.

"I'm gonna make you come five times and then fuck you so hard you won't be able to see straight."

He grabbed me as my knees buckled. No one had ever talked to me like that. Ever . . . and I loved it—so much so that I almost passed out in anticipation.

"We have to slow down," he muttered as he pulled his shirt over his head, revealing a six-pack that rivaled the hottest underwear model in the world. I ran my hands over his beautiful chest. It was covered in a light sprinkling of crisp blond hair that veed down to the opening of his jeans. I knew what was in those jeans and I wanted it bad.

"Strip," he demanded in a low voice that soaked my panties. "Slowly."

He backed away and watched me under hooded eyes. I slowly unzipped my skirt and shimmied it down my legs. My hands shook as I went to remove the Glock strapped to my inner thigh.

"Leave it."

"Really?" I asked, glancing down at my deadly weapon.

"God, yes. That's fucking hot." Oh. My. God. He was turned on by everything I thought was wrong with me. I was about to have orgasm number one without his even touching me.

"Oookay." I giggled and eased my nude thong over my bottom and my gun. "Wait," I gasped as a horrific flashback invaded my brain. "We can't do this."

"Have sex?" he asked, totally confused.

"We're totally having sex," I shouted. "Just not with my gun anywhere near my ass." I fumbled with the straps. *Shit, it was stuck.*

"What in the hell are you talking about?" Luke laughed as he watched my slow strip morph into a freaked out interpretive dance.

"I shot myself in the ass," I snapped, finally loosening the strap. Luke's stifled bark of laughter annoyed the hell out of me. "It was a new model and it was defective. I stuck it in my back pocket, resulting in my ass getting an extra hole," I huffed.

"Sweet."

I stopped and realized the story was actually kind of funny now that it was in my past . . . and I grinned. "I suppose you could describe it that way," I cooed and ran my hands over my bare bottom, transforming the laughter in his eyes to lust. "But quite honestly, I'm looking out for you."

"How's that?" he asked, crossing his arms over his chest and leaning back against the wall.

"It'd be a damned shame if that gun went off, missed my ass, and took your man jewels off."

"Point," said a suddenly pale Luke. "Remove the Glock."

"I'm on it, big boy."

Dammit, now I had a dilemma. How to finish my striptease without revealing the huge jagged red scar on my stomach . . . Turning out the lights would defeat the whole purpose and seem awfully suspicious. Maybe if I turned my back to him and pulled off my shirt and dove onto the bed I could hide it. No . . . but if I turned out the lights after I hit the bed—how in the hell would I do that? I'd have to get up to . . .

"Candy, face me and take off your shirt."

"I can't," I whispered. He was so into my tough girl persona and the way I looked, I was terrified for him to see me. My insides were so imperfect, I didn't want him to know the outside was too.

"You can and you will," he said gently. "Do it."

I turned and faced him. Why did it bother me so much? Had I not dealt with my wound yet? Was I worried he'd be turned off or was I more concerned that he'd know I wasn't as good as I pretended to be? Fuck it.

I removed my boots, shirt, and bra and stood completely naked in front of him. The burning lust in his eyes scared me a little, but it also gave me the confirmation I needed that my scarred body was still beautiful. He moved toward me and dropped to his knees. He reverently ran his fingers over my scar. I closed my eyes and my chest constricted. My breath came in short gasps.

"This is bad," he said softly, "but it could have been so much worse."

"You should have seen the other guy," I joked lamely, trying to catch my breath.

"I did," he replied. I tried to pull away. He held me fast and feathered his lips over my imperfection. It felt odd. The skin around my scar was still numb, but his lips caused a delightful little tickle sensation that made me shiver.

"Wait, what do you mean you saw him?" I pulled away when his statement registered in my lust-addled brain.

"After. All explanations after."

I took a deep breath in through my nose and blew it out of my mouth. He was playing by the rules I'd made. I looked down at his dark blond head lying gently on my stomach. His hands crept up and cupped my ass, pulling me closer to his worshipping lips. I wanted to demand he explain himself, but more than that, I wanted to be with him. Completely.

Explanations could wait.

"You're a little overdressed." I ran my hands through his hair and pushed all my worry and doubt to the far recesses of my mind. I wanted to be here right now in this moment with this man who was on his knees in front of me wanting me for exactly who I was.

"I do believe you have a good point." He stood and removed his boots and jeans. He looked like a freakin' Greek god clad only in gray boxer briefs. How in the hell was he not attached to someone? A man like him would have to beat the women off. He most likely had a different gal pal every night of the week. An ugly green burst of jealousy swept through me and I got mad at him.

"Stop thinking." His half smirk made me giggle and I wrinkled my nose at him. "What in the hell were you thinking?"

"Nothing."

"Men think about nothing. Women *do not* think about nothing." His large body loomed over mine as he backed me up to my unmade bed. "Spill it, pretty girl."

"Fine," I snapped, grabbing his shoulders so I didn't fall back on the bed. "I was thinking you probably have a ton of girlfriends or lovers or hookers and you have to beat women off of you and then I got mad at you for being a man whore."

"What the fuck?" He laughed and pulled my naked body flush against his almost naked body. "You are mad at me for the fictitious bullshit you created in your mind?"

"Yes," I muttered, and buried my face in his ridiculously perfect chest.

"Look at me."

"No," I replied, somewhat muffled due to the fact I had face-planted myself on his chest.

He reached under my chin and raised my eyes to his. "The talk takes place after the fun, but I want to be clear. I have no girlfriend, no wife, and no hookers. You?"

"Nope, no hookers." I giggled and rolled my eyes.

"Good to know," he whispered as his teeth found their way to the religious area on my neck. "Hell, baby, I don't even exist."

"You feel pretty corporeal to me," I moaned, and ran my hands over a butt so fine it almost brought tears to my eyes.

"For you, I'd pretty much be anything," he murmured in a husky voice that made my tummy flip.

The time for talking had ended. The time for action had begun. The first four orgasms made me scream and beg and call him all sorts of religious deities. He accepted the compliments with no humility whatsoever.

"I'm one away from fucking you till you can't walk," he said gruffly, grabbing his cuffs from the pocket of his jeans.

"I can't walk now," I gasped. I was a noodle. My legs and arms were worthless. "Have to stop. Your turn," I begged as I saw him coming for me with cuffs in his hands and the most evil sexy smirk on his face.

"No, baby, I said five for you and then I get mine. This time I'm gonna go slow."

Trying to get my bearings was difficult. My voice was hoarse from screaming after the almost violent out of body experiences he'd just provided for me. All lips, teeth, fingers, and orgasms . . . my orgasms. I'd never come so many times in such a short period in my life and it was very likely going to kill me dead.

"Look at me," Luke demanded as he cuffed me to my headboard. "See me. Watch me. Make me real," he whispered as his lips lowered to mine.

What did he mean? *Real?* My brain was cluttered and exploding with endorphins. He teased the seam of my lips with his tongue till I opened for him. In that moment, I realized I couldn't deny him anything. Ever. After a thorough and mind-altering exploration of my mouth, he dragged his lips from mine and visited my neck for a moment, then decided to hang out with my rock hard aching nipples for a while.

"God, your tits are fucking perfect." He licked, sucked, and nipped until I saw stars. I thought I was done after four, but clearly I was wrong. The strong pulls from his mouth on my breasts shot straight to my core and my body began to writhe in anticipation.

"Luke, I want to touch you," I cried out as he bit down on the soft underside of my breast, making me shudder uncontrollably.

"Nope," he said. "I want you helpless to anything and everything I want to do to you."

Holy hell, this man had my number so bad it scared me to death. The sex felt different this time. Was I more invested? Yes . . . No. If I were truthful with myself, I'd have to admit I'd been invested from the very first time we'd made love. I had no clue if that's what he considered it, but I had. It just took me a while to cop to it.

A buzzing knocked me out of my dream world. "I thought a little extra stimulation would destroy you," Luke said, brandishing my vibrator.

"You're trying to destroy me?" I tried to sit up, but his cuffs held me fast.

"Only for other men." He laughed. "Only for other men, baby."

With a grin that melted me, he pressed my vibrator to my over sensitive clit and I detonated. Behind my closed eyelids colors swirled. My hips jerked and my body felt like one big pulsing heartbeat. Despite the roaring in my ears, I heard him swear and heard the foil wrapper of a condom being torn.

"Spread your legs," Luke ground out through clenched teeth. "It's my turn now."

I opened my legs and eyes and saw a beautiful man almost out of control with lust lowering himself over my trembling body. I was still in the aftershocks of my orgasm as he lifted my ass in his big hands and pushed his body into mine. He was large but I was so primed for him, he buried himself to the hilt with one strong thrust. The sexy sounds he made as he owned my body prolonged my orgasm to the point of pain. My spasms gripped him like a vise, and I felt every gorgeous inch of the wild man inside me.

"So good, so fucking good, Candy," he moaned, and pumped harder and faster.

"Oh God," I gasped as a tightening started low in my abdomen. My exhausted body came to life and I met every violent thrust with an out of control abandon. I needed to fuck him as hard as he was fucking me.

"That's it, baby," he hissed in my ear, and bit down. "Fuck me. Make me come."

That was it. I was done. His dirty talk sent me straight to Jesus and all the angels and Saints and the Super Bowl with the Minnesota Vikings winning combined. I convulsed and flew into my sixth orgasm, taking him with me. He gripped my ass with such pressure, I knew I would have bruises, but I wanted even more. As the tingling ripped through my body, I screamed with what little voice I had left and felt his orgasm pulse into me with a strength that sucked all the breath I had left right out of me. I was fairly sure I was dead, or at the very least suffering a heart attack.

"Holy hell," Luke muttered, collapsing on top of me. His weight was a welcome blanket, but the cuffs were no longer my friend.

"Luke, my wrists hurt."

"On it." He jumped up and released my wrists and gently massaged them. "I think I almost passed out."

"I think I almost died," I countered, laughing.

"You are perfect," he murmured as he ran his magic fingers along my collarbone.

"Far from it." I paused and wondered if it was time to talk. "So what do we do now?"

"Well, I was thinking I'd like to hold you and fall asleep." He hopped up and disposed of the condom and flicked out the lights. Moonlight shone through the window and I was struck by how truly beautiful he was.

"You want to stay?" I asked. Did I want him to stay? I wasn't sure. This was majorly unchartered territory for me. What I did know was that I didn't want him to go.

"Does that work for you, pretty girl?"

"Um . . . yes. Yes, it does, but aren't we going to talk?"

"In the morning." He curled up next to me and held me. I felt the beating of his heart and the warmth of his body in the silence of my room—and I didn't need to fill it.

I didn't need to fill it because it was already full.

Chapter 9

I awoke as sore as I've ever been in my life, wrapped up in a warm human blanket that was very happy to see me. Unsure if he was awake or asleep, I stayed still and enjoyed being held. Dangerous, but I couldn't help myself. I dreaded the talk and selfishly wanted to be close to him until reality set in and made it impossible.

"Good morning, Sunshine," he murmured into my hair, pressing his very happy camper against my bottom.

"Morning." I couldn't hide the smile in my voice or the lightness in my heart.

"As hot and sexy as we both know that I am, morning breath is not working for me. Can I use your toothbrush?" Luke asked as his hands found their way to my breasts.

"Ewwww, that's gross," I said, removing his hands, which he promptly re-placed.

"You're kidding me. I had my tongue down your throat all night and you're telling me it's gross to use your toothbrush?"

"I suppose when you put it that way, I have no ground to stand on." I laughed and arched my back so my backside could say a proper hello to his front side.

"Jesus," he groaned. "Get on your hands and knees."

"Get a condom," I demanded. "And hurry." My exhausted, sore body had woken up with a vengeance, and I was beyond ready; no foreplay needed.

"Shit, I only had one."

"Are you kidding me?" I yelled. "You only brought one condom?"

"Oh my God," Luke barked with laughter. "I was sure you would knee my nuts and kick me off your property last night."

I flopped over to my back and glared at him in frustration. "I guess you were never a boy scout."

"What in the hell does that mean?"

"It means," I said as I rolled off my bed, "that you're not prepared. I, on the other hand, am."

Luke grabbed my arm and stopped me from going to my drawer for protection. "Are you on the pill?"

"Yes," I answered slowly, knowing where this was going and unsure if it was a good idea.

"I have a clean bill of health and haven't been with anyone else since we started sleeping together a year ago," he said, watching me closely for my reaction.

I knew he expected me to freak out. I actually wanted to freak out. He wasn't supposed to say anything like that, even though I wanted him to. Fuck. What was I supposed to do with this information? Truthfully, it delighted me and terrified me both.

"I haven't either," I whispered, looking away.

"I missed that," he said, and pulled me closer.

"I haven't either," I yelled, and tried to dislodge myself from his arms.

He had other plans. After he picked me up and deposited me in the bathroom, we brushed our teeth and he proceeded to pee.

"You have got to be kidding me." I rolled my eyes and looked at the ceiling.

"What? I had to pee. Don't you need to pee?"

"Yes, I do, but I am not going to pee in front of you." I wasn't sure if I wanted to laugh or scream. "If you leave the toilet seat up, I will hurt you."

"No worries." He grinned. "I didn't put it up in the first place."

"On my God," I muttered, leaving the bathroom. "This is never going to work."

"Yes, it is," he yelled after me.

I grabbed some yoga pants and a T-shirt and yanked them on before Mr. I Have No Inhibitions Whatsoever came back. He sauntered back into my bedroom in all of his naked glory and a pout settled on his pretty face.

"I thought I was going to get lucky."

"You were until you peed," I told him, and tossed him his jeans.

He laughed and pulled them on, neglecting to do up any of the buttons. If he thought that would turn me on, he was right. I trained my eyes on his face and waited.

"Don't you need to potty?" he asked, grinning like a naughty child.

Damn it, I did. I waltzed past him, slammed the bathroom door, and locked it. I wouldn't put it past him to barge in. The thought made me giggle and I bit it back. I ran a brush through my hair and swiped on some gloss. If we were going to talk, I needed just a little bit of pretty on my face. I avoided mascara just in case I cried, which I had no intention of doing, but I'd done a lot of things lately that were way out of my usual MO.

When I walked back into my room, he was gone. My stomach cramped and my breathing hitched. I slid down the wall to the floor and let my head fall to my hands. Had he left? Had he gone without saying good-bye? Was he pissed because I'd put the kibosh on his morning sex plans? What an asshole . . . and I almost let him do it without a condom. I was every kind of idiot all rolled into one. I got up and stomped out to my kitchen. I needed caffeine and then I needed to hunt him down and shoot his balls off.

I was so wrapped up in my ire, I didn't even notice the object of my wrath seated at the table with a cup of coffee in his hands and an icy glass of Coke sitting at an empty spot waiting.

"Men suck," I shouted at the cabinet as I yanked out a glass for my morning ritual.

"That's a little harsh."

"Shit," I screeched, whirling around and slamming myself up against the counter.

His chuckle made me want to slap him, but my relief that he was still here kept my hands glued to my sides. "I thought you left."

"So I can see. Sit down. I poured you a Coke."

"How did you know I drink Coke in the morning?"

He said nothing and just drank his coffee. It was time to talk.

"What's happening here?" I asked. "Who are you and what have you done with me?"

"I'm Luke and you're me before I found you."

"Come again?" I took a big swig of Coke and tried to decipher his riddle.

"I wanted to, but you wouldn't let me." He grinned and I blushed. "Damn, you're beautiful."

"Compliments will not get you back into my pants, but the truth might," I said quietly.

"Can you handle the truth?" His green eyes bored into mine and made me wonder if the truth was overrated.

"I suppose we won't know until you spill it."

His demeanor changed. I recognized the change. I lived by the same rules. He closed the human side and opened the cold agent side.

"The reason I'm telling you this is complicated. Normally, well hell, there is no normally." He laughed without humor and ran his hands through his hair. "I can tell you this because I'm getting out and you need to know."

That sounded ominous. Fuck.

"How did you find out my name?"

He raised an eyebrow. "That was the easiest part. You should never keep your ID in a false casing on your gun. I've known your name since the first time we were together."

Son of a bitch, I thought I was good . . . "Why didn't you tell me?"

"That goes back to you being me before I met you."

"Cryptic much?" I snapped.

"You'll get it eventually," he shot back lazily. "There were other reasons too. I needed to know who you were so I could find you again. There was no way in hell you were going to get away from me."

"Am I a job?" *Please say no. Please say no.*

"No, you're not a job, but one of my jobs had something to do with you."

What the hell did that mean? Wait. Fuck. He wanted me to make him real . . . He didn't exist. He was tan and had lost weight. I hadn't heard from him in three months . . . Mexico.

"Did you see the actual body or just photos?"

"Saw the body in the morgue, but saw photos of the crime scene," he said, and got up from the table. The tension in his body was palpable and he tried to mask it by making toast. The utter incongruity of his action made me laugh. He turned on me and his green eyes narrowed to slits. "You think it's funny that you almost died?"

"No." I swallowed the rest of my inappropriate laughter. "I think it's funny that you're making toast when you'd clearly like to spank me."

He said nothing and continued his toast making. He grabbed butter and peanut butter and jelly and honey from my fridge and cabinets. His movements were concise and angry.

"So you've been in Mexico."

He nodded once and buttered the toast.

"I'm sorry and thank you."

"I don't want you to be sorry and I don't want you to thank me. I want you out of this shit," he snapped.

"What in the hell are you talking about?" I stood up and attempted to keep my temper in check. Who did he think he was? My father?

"You're always going to be in danger," he shouted. "You have a fine chance of dying every single fucking day."

"So does everyone," I yelled back.

"Your percentages are slightly higher."

I couldn't really counter that one because he was correct. Up until now I'd never really thought about that very much, but Ass-hat Son of a Bitch Douchehole had me wanting things I'd never wanted before.

"You ended it in Mexico, didn't you?"

"Does anything ever end?" he asked tiredly. I stared at him and waited for more. "We nailed the kingpins, but there are always more behind them."

"If someone comes after me, I'll take them out."

"Goddammit, Candy, false bravado is going to land you six feet under." He slammed his fist down on the counter and his toast became toast.

I stared at the floor. He was right. I was losing my edge. When did that happen? How did it happen?

"In their headquarters there were pictures of you with explicit instructions to carve you up while you were still alive. The directive was to carve you, shoot you up with bad heroine, and let you bleed out."

I was mute. I had clearly taken out the wrong guy and was slated to pay heavily. It was Luke's reaction that mystified me.

"I have never enjoyed killing people as much as I did in Mexico." He violently shoved two more pieces of bread into the toaster to replace the ones he'd punched out. "Can I make you some eggs?" he asked politely.

"Um . . . no." My aborted death was too much to process, and I'd seen some real horror in my time as an undercover agent. However, the fact that Luke almost broke my toaster and then formally offered me breakfast was the thing that sent me over the edge, so I did what came naturally. I started talking. It was talk, cry, or shoot stuff. Crying was unacceptable. I liked my house and didn't want bullet holes decorating the walls . . . so talk it was. "You're right, that was stupid, what I said. It lacked foresight and planning. I know you don't want to hear me apologize, but it was my fuck-up you had to clean up and that makes me sick. You could have died and it would have been my fault and I never would have known. I would have thought you'd just found another stranger-with-benefits situation that was better than ours, when really I had killed you . . . not literally, but I might as well have pulled the trigger. Now that I know this . . . and why in the hell Steve didn't tell me this—wait. Why *didn't* Steve tell me this? Do you work for Steve?"

"Did. I did work for Steve. Not anymore. He was only recently briefed, and I informed him that I was going to tell you this."

"He agreed to that?"

Luke gave me a hard look and I backed off. Clearly Steve had agreed or Luke wouldn't have told me. Or Luke was really high up on the food chain.

"You shouldn't have taken a job that was personal," I told him, and waited for him to take my head off. He didn't disappoint.

"Are you kidding me?" he yelled. "I'm crazy about you. You are as damaged and insane as I am. I waited for you to make a move for a year, and then I look at pictures of you with your stomach ripped open and know that you took out one of the leaders of the nastiest most fucked-up drug cartels at the moment. I want you for myself and I want you alive. How in the hell do you think I wouldn't go down there and take care of that?" he demanded.

I was speechless . . . almost. "Luke, you don't even know me."

"Candy, I have been on you for a year. I have watched you and I know more about you than you could imagine."

"That's kind of creepy . . . and kind of hot," I muttered, trying to wrap my mind around the fact that he'd stalked me for a year and I hadn't noticed. "Why didn't you just say something when we were together?"

"And what exactly would you have done with that? Agreed to date and get married and live happily ever after with me? You would have run away. The same thing I would have done if someone tried to trap me."

"Why me?"

"Because you're you and you make me real. A civilian could never understand what I've done. Some of it I had to do and some of it I wanted to do. You are perfectly imperfect—so beautiful and so damaged. I am so fucking drawn to you, I can't see straight. That's why."

He stopped and stared me down, daring me to run. I wanted to. I really did, but I stayed. Little pieces of my heart began to shatter, but this was not going to work.

"What will you do?" I asked, unable to deal with all he had said.

"Do?"

"For a job. If you're getting out, what will you do?"

He shook his head and gave me a smile that didn't reach his eyes. Seeing him close himself off hurt in unexplainable ways. He'd asked for my life, put his heart out on the floor. But I couldn't go there. I simply couldn't.

"I'll figure it out."

"You're asking me to give up my reason for living," I whispered. Why did I ever ask him his real name? This was more than I could handle. Everything had been fine when I was a ho and he was *not David*. Wasn't it? Hell, I couldn't even remember now. That felt like another lifetime ago. I had nothing if I didn't have my job. He might think he knew me, but he had no idea who I really was if he thought it was okay for me to turn my back on my sister.

"Do you really think you're living?" he asked tightly. He was angry and I didn't blame him, but I was angry too.

"You know, Luke, you may have followed me for the better part of a year, but I wasn't following you. I don't know you and you don't know me if you think you can walk in here and tell me to quit my job because I might die. Up until recently, I didn't even care if . . . never mind." Fuck, why was I born without a filter for my mouth?

"Up until recently you didn't care if you died." He finished my statement correctly. "What happened recently that made you care, Candy?"

I glared at him while I considered what to say. Five points to me for not just blabbing out the first thing that came to my mind and five more points for realizing the first thing that embedded itself in my head was the right thing to say. At this point I had nothing to lose. "Fine," I snapped. "I won't play games. You happened, but this is ridiculous and too fast and happily-ever-afters only happen in fairy tales. Not in real life."

"Life is real and happily-ever-afters only happen if you make them. Fast is relative. We've been sleeping together for a year and neither one of us chose to sleep with anyone else. Does that mean nothing?"

"It means that we're compatible sexually." I narrowed my eyes and backed away as he advanced on me.

"It means a lot more than that and you know it."

He trapped me between the wall and my refrigerator. I could get away if I wanted to. He knew that as well as I did. Part of me wanted him to pull his cuffs back out and hold me down until I said yes to him. Yes about everything, but that would be a lie. I would hate him eventually for making me give up everything and I knew in my gut, he couldn't give this life up either. We were built differently from normal people. We were missing something inside. My only real fear at the moment was that maybe he was what I was missing.

"Your sister wouldn't want this for you."

"Stop," I ground out. "You are skating on thin ice. I'm doing this for her."

"She's gone, Candy. Do you really think she'd want you to exist in a living death for her? Haven't you done enough to avenge her?"

"Stop it. Now." He was tearing apart my walls and my reasons, and if too many came down, I'd be a shell. Hell, I was a shell, but I was a functioning shell. He didn't care for me if he wanted to destroy me. "Leave," I told him coldly. "Leave and don't come back."

"I'll leave, but I will come back. This is so far from over, you have no idea."

With that, he walked back to my room, grabbed his stuff, and slammed out the front door. As soon as I heard his car pull away, I slid down to the floor and I cried. Hard. He was wrong. He had to be, but if he was . . . why did my heart hurt so badly?

Chapter 10

The rest of the morning was a wash. Standing in the shower for forty minutes until the water ran cold didn't fix anything, so I moped around my house and cried. I tried to clean and do some needed housework, but focus was a problem. After washing the dishes with laundry detergent, I gave up. Grabbing my gun and my toaster, I went to the shooting range.

A handful of people watched me blow my toaster to smithereens. A large round of applause followed my performance coupled with an evil glare from Mel the owner. A group of people had rushed the desk demanding their own toaster target. I expected to be banned, along with the lesbians, very soon.

Snippets of my morning with Luke continually flashed through my brain, making me antsy and stressed. My need to pace and shoot appliances was wearing thin on me and most certainly on Mel, so I did what I'd been trained to do in difficult situations. I compartmentalized. I blocked it out. Pushing things away to deal with at another time was a talent of mine. The problem was, I rarely dealt with anything I pushed to the back . . . hence, I was a broken girl. Awesome.

Fuck him and everyone who wanted what I was unable to give. I had a job to do and some well-fed, pompous professors at the university to interview. Evangeline was off my list as a suspect. I was completely confident she had nothing to do with any threat to Shoshanna. As I replayed her interview in my mind, I couldn't help laughing. I sincerely hoped she did send me an invite to her and Yvonne's wedding. I would totally go.

* * *

Dressed in a conservative suit, low-heeled pumps, and pearls, I walked across the campus of the university toward the administration building. Fall was in the air and the leaves on the trees blazed red and gold in the mid-afternoon sun. I had informed Shoshanna of my schedule and asked her if she saw me to simply ignore my presence. It would do no one any good if she went into a diatribe on fuzzy handcuffs. I did have an answer for her on that subject, but I'd pushed that one to the back of my mind and had no intention of retrieving it.

Watching coeds in their bubble of academia made me wish for simpler times. I was happy at college. Well, not exactly happy, but I'd gotten away from my parents and was able to live freely without the hell that had been my home life. Observing the hand-holding couples and laughing sorority sisters, I shook my head. This wasn't what I remembered and it hadn't even been that long ago. I remembered loving my classes, but the people were a blur. I stopped in my tracks. Fuck, I hadn't lived in a long time. Aside from my brother and my boss Steve, no one knew me.

With a smile on my face that I was sure resembled a grimace, I picked up my pace and ignored the things around me I had no way of relating to. No time for wallowing in what couldn't be changed. Instead, I would focus on what I was good at. Although I was technically a temporary bodyguard, I was still doing the right thing. The good thing. The just thing. My brain could compute that—take care of those who are good and eliminate those who are bad. Black and white . . . no messy gray.

I checked in at the front desk and waited outside Randall Steigmeister's office. Single, fifty-seven, Professor of Religious Studies, lost sizable grant to Shoshanna's department last year and was hellbent on removing Shoshanna's tenure. His picture led me to believe he enjoyed his food immensely, and the writings I had read led me to believe he was more a right-wing Christian than an open-minded professor of Religious Studies. This should certainly be enlightening.

"Miss Sanderson," Randall Steigmeister bellowed grandly from his office doorway. "I am ready to see you."

"Thank you," I said, watching him try to take charge of the situation. I noticed his secretary discreetly glance down at her work in disgust as he snatched his mail from the basket on the edge of her desk. I was unsure if that look was aimed at me or him. "Hold my calls, Mrs. Sword."

"Yes, sir."

"This way, please. I'm a very busy man and I've a tight schedule today. I hope this meeting will be brief."

"That depends on you, Professor Steigmeister." I smiled brightly and followed a slightly put out idiot into his domain.

"So what can I do for you?"

"First of all, thank you for agreeing to see me on such short notice. The research I've done on you is very impressive and I feel quite sure this meeting is merely a formality." I smiled and squirmed nervously in my chair. His delight at my apparent inadequacy spurred me to drop and scatter all my papers on the floor. "Oh," I gasped. "I'm so sorry."

I quickly and awkwardly gathered my paperwork with no help from the now more confident pompous ass sitting across from me.

"There, there, young lady," he admonished, checking his watch. "Are you new to this, Miss Sanderson?"

"A bit," I stammered.

"Let's proceed. I am a very busy man."

"Of course. How long have you been a professor at the university?"

"Twenty-two years," he said. "Fourteen have been as a tenured scholar. I feel my mission in life is to open the minds of the population to the miracles of Jesus."

"Do you teach only Christian Religious Studies?" Had I read his dossier wrong?

"No." He laughed heartily and condescendingly at my question. "No, I cover world religions and the history thereof. I have a special relationship with Jesus, so that seems to permeate my rhetoric."

Taking in his office, I noticed the rather violent religious art he seemed to favor. All Christian.

"Congratulations, that's like, wow. And how long have you been acquainted with Professor Lumpschlicterschmidt?"

His nose wrinkled in disgust and his eyes narrowed slightly. "What is this interview about?" he demanded. "I thought you were here from the University Paper."

"No sir." Was he serious? "I'm from the DEA and you've been tapped as a possible suspect in some threats on the life of Professor Lumpschlicterschmidt."

"What?" he shrieked. "That's preposterous! What is she up to now?" He jumped up and paced the room. His bulbous middle strained against his several sizes too small faux suede elbow patched jacket.

"Please have a seat," I said. "This won't take long unless you refuse to cooperate."

"I've made no threats on her life," he hissed. "Yes, I have actively campaigned to have her removed from the university, but I would never lower myself to illegal or immoral means."

I partially believed him—he did have his own super special relationship with Jesus—but his nervous manner and beginnings of flop sweat meant he hadn't laid out the entire story. Sanctimonious asses like him bored me to tears. Give me a Porno Granny any day.

"What exactly do you have against Professor Sue's work?"

"Have you read it?" he yelled, turning an unflattering red. "It's filth. She is making millions off degrading filth and is dragging the reputation of this fine establishment into the gutter with her."

"Have you read it?" I asked.

"Of course not. I wouldn't dirty my hands with base pornography," he snapped, quite self-satisfied with his insult to Shoshanna's work.

"It seems to me you don't have much of an argument if you've not read the material you're so adamantly against," I stated calmly, and waited for him to bury himself a little deeper.

"I don't need to. It speaks for itself."

"I'm sure there are others who would agree with you."

"You have no idea. The integrity of an institution is only as solid as its faculty and board."

I nodded seriously and took a few notes. He relaxed, comfortable in my silent agreement with his philosophy, and played with his fountain pen. I wondered if all the parents paying big bucks for their children to be enlightened knew what kind of douchebags were doing the educating. He had no computer on his desk or any electronics other than a phone. Interesting.

"Do you teach any online courses?" I queried.

"Why? Are you interested?" He perked back up, assuming I was on board with his assessment of high moral standards.

"Possibly."

"Well, no. I don't. I don't believe in computers and such. They are instruments of Satan. Creativity and true thought come from the hand. The hand God blessed us with. I only accept handwritten work and I grade exclusively with a quill pen," he announced proudly.

Jesus Christ, this imbecile didn't know how to use a computer.

"I see that you're published, Professor Steigmeister. Certainly you didn't handwrite your thesis."

"Oh, but I did. Typing is what graduate assistants are for."

I was sure his grad assistants would be delighted to hear that. Much as I didn't like the jackoff sitting across from me, I didn't think he was truly a suspect anymore. He didn't have the technical skills to have produced the untraceable notes we'd received. His religious views were troubling considering the moral tone of the letters, but . . . time to fuck with him.

"What can you tell me about BDSM?"

"I'm sorry, what?" he blustered, and turned a much deeper shade of red. "I have no idea what you are speaking of."

Oh, but he who protests . . .

"Bondage, discipline, dominance, submission?"

"Really, Miss . . . Miss Sanderson! Your point?" he demanded imperiously.

"Abrasion, animal play, wax play, butt plugs?"

"Enough!" He was now a mottled purple, but strangely turned on by the terms. Evidenced by the erection that he tried to hide. God. Gross.

"You've read her books," I told him. "I think you take issue with her income. I think you know far more about BDSM than you'd ever let on. I believe your soapbox is rickety and jealousy can destroy people. I'd suggest you look up the word hypocrite."

"You need to leave immediately."

"I'm leaving." I smiled and handed him my card. "Don't leave town. Does your secretary type your correspondence?"

"Of course she does."

"Have a lovely day, Professor."

As I strolled casually out of his office, he shouted, "You can't possibly think I have anything to do with this."

I stopped and turned. "Actually, I don't, but I'd suggest you end your campaign against Professor Sue. It would be just awful if your peccadillos came to light. Jesus would be terribly disappointed."

Feeling nauseous yet strangely invigorated, I left his office and made my way down the hall to my next appointment. Mrs. Sword had happily handed over her hard drive. Normally I'd need a subpoena but a smile and a request did wonders when people didn't like their boss. No, I didn't think he'd written the notes, but I was fairly sure he'd back off his hate campaign against Shoshanna. I'd played a little out of the box, but who cared? Hopefully not Steve. My boss was very aware of my people skills, or lack thereof. I was getting the job done, and that was ultimately all that mattered. Right? Right. Plus, it was kind of fun. It was amazing to realize I was still useful when there wasn't someone with a bag of drugs and an Uzi pointed at my head. One down. One to go.

"Hi, I'm here to see Professor Junsen," I told the gender-ambiguous secretary. Was it a man or a woman? I couldn't tell.

"She'll be with you in a moment."

The voice gave no clue as to sexual identity. I covertly scanned for breasts, but the shirt was too baggy. Fuck, this was going to drive me nuts. "I'm sorry, I didn't get your name."

"Because I didn't give you one," it stated logically, and rolled its eyes at me.

"Hmm, you're correct." I didn't like the attitude and there was no way I could leave without figuring this out, so I flipped my badge and played my advantage. "Name?"

"Pat."

I almost barked with laughter, but I bit down on my lip. Hard.

"Is that a nickname?" I asked.

"Nope."

Fine, I was out of line. I despised not knowing things. My training was so ingrained, I had a hell of a time leaving stones unturned. But I was being rude. Pat's gender was none of my business and had nothing to do with my case. I shut my pie hole and waited. Damn, that was hard.

A buzzer went off on Pat's desk and Pat slapped it like a mosquito. "Professor Junsen will see you now."

"Thank you," I muttered still trying to unravel the Pat mystery. Oh well, some things were probably left better alone.

Professor Winnifred Junsen's office was just as offensive as Randal Steigmeister's, but in a vastly different manner. The walls were littered with feminist slogans and nude line drawings of what appeared to be very angry lesbians. *WTF?* There was clutter everywhere and an enormous pile of bras in the corner.

"I'd say nice to meet you, but from what I understand, you just terrorized a colleague of mine," Professor Junsen snapped from behind a massive desk. She was clad in some kind of muumuu and her short graying hair stood on end.

"Well, word certainly travels fast." *Fast was an understatement.* "I'm not one for feminine social graces. From my research, I'd assume you'd be quite comfortable with that."

Her laughter was grating and she came around her desk with an outstretched hand and tits flying in the wind. I almost suggested she grab a bra from the pile in the corner, but remembered she'd been disciplined for a bra-burning party on the football field. Wonderful. As I shook her hand, her unharnessed bosom actually hit my wrist. Our height difference and her inability to put her arms to her sides due to her rotundness made her braless state dangerous to others.

"So how can I help you?" she asked as she plopped down on a chair, legs spread and boobs swinging. She was a slob.

Holy hell, I was no Polly Priss, but disgusting was disgusting.

"Since you've been briefed by your colleague, I'll just get to it. How well do you know Professor Sue and what issues do you have with her being a best-selling author? Or is there more of an issue that she's aced you out in the awards department?" I sat back and focused on her face. I usually watched for body language, but I was in danger of making insulting observations if her badoinkees didn't stop bouncing. Evangeline would be horrified. Just the thought brought a smile to my lips.

"I'm glad to see your interruption of my day amuses you. You're barking up the wrong tree here. I take no issue with her porno smut anti-female-power fuck musings. I am a better professor and educator than she is and I believe she has paid off the board with her fornication-prose sin money to be awarded so many accolades."

Was she for real? "I'm sorry. Your choice of words is alarming on a few levels. You're not helping your case much, Professor."

"I don't have to," she grunted. "My brilliance and my dedication to the advancement of women will win in the end."

"How long have you been at the university?"

"Ten years. Tenured for one," she informed me proudly.

"And how many awards have you won?" I asked. She sat there and stared daggers at me. "I'm sorry, I didn't hear you."

"None," she groused.

"Interesting. When was the last time you corresponded with Professor Sue?"

"I don't. I have nothing to say to her. What do you want from me?"

"I want to know if you're jealous and deranged enough to write threatening letters to Professor Sue," I patiently explained. "I thought your buddy Randy might have filled you in on that little nugget?"

"What police department do you come from?" she demanded, grabbing a pen and paper.

"I don't. I come from the DEA and I usually deal with drug shipments and cartels and fucktards with machine guns. I'm taking a little breather because I thought it might be fun. Here's my card. You can call my boss or I can take you down to his office right now and you can meet him. We can have this meeting in a little room with two-way mirrors and armed guys who don't like feminists as much as I do. Your choice."

Winnie blanched and dropped her pen and paper and did a full three/sixty. "I wouldn't hurt her," she gasped desperately. "Ever. I plan to beat her fair and square. She rebuffed my sexual advances and I hate her, but I still love her and will make her pay academically."

I was struck dumb. Of all the things she could have said, that was not remotely what I expected.

"You're the last suspect on my list and you haven't made a promising case for your innocence," I said in a pinched voice, trying not to throw up in my mouth. "Spurned wannabe lover on probation for a bizarre bra-burning extravaganza. You probably need the awards you and Sue are up for to keep your job."

"Take me downtown," she pleaded.

"Wait. What?" I so did not want her in my car.

"I'll take a lie detector test." Holy hell, she was serious. "I thought if I burned the bras, Sue would be impressed and find me more attractive. I don't give a damn about the awards or my job,"

Winnie blubbered hysterically. "I just want her to go out on a date with me."

She was now in tears. Her body shook, which did unmentionable things to her bosom and forced me to look at the ceiling.

"Professor Junsen . . ."

"I love her," she shrieked. "Why doesn't she love me back?"

"Well, um . . . I'm fairly sure she's straight," I mumbled. What in the hell was I supposed to do here? My apparently profound observation about Shoshanna's sexual orientation sent Professor Winnie into an even louder round of snot-filled sobbing. Shit. "You just need to find a nice lesbian, who . . . um, you know doesn't like bras and stuff."

"Do you find me attractive?" she blubbered.

"I'm straight too," I said much louder than I intended. "Very straight, but if I wasn't, I might find you, um . . . or your, um . . . passion for women's rights somewhat interesting . . . kind of."

"Really?" she asked hopefully.

"Sure, but can I give you a piece of advice?"

"Yes. Please."

"You might want to consider wearing a bra."

"Do you think that would help?" she asked, glancing down at her swinging pendulums.

"Possibly," I whispered, sure I would burn in hell for lying.

"That's wonderful. Thank you. Could you do something for me?" she queried, wiping her nose on her muumuu.

"Is it legal?"

"Yes," she said solemnly. "Would you put in a good word for me with Sue?"

"Um, okay, but I don't know how much weight I pull."

Her face lit up and she bear-hugged me, squashing me with those boobs. As much as it grossed me out, I felt a little happy that I'd made her feel better.

"Professor Junsen . . ."

"Call me Winnie," she insisted.

"Okay . . . Winnie. Do you mind if I take your hard drive? I'll get it back to you tomorrow."

"God, no! Take it. You can take Pat's too. Pat only plays Scrabble on the damn thing."

Damn it to hell, why hadn't she used a gender-specific pronoun for Pat? I was never gonna find out what Pat was.

I'd come up empty. None of these suspects had panned out. All the same, I couldn't say I was disappointed. Well, maybe about Randy, he was an ass-hat, but Evangeline and Winnie . . . I kind of liked them from a distance. A great distance.

Who in the hell was threatening Shoshanna? I didn't know right now, but I sure as hell would find out soon. Of that, I had no doubt.

Chapter 11

After the interview weirdness of the day before, I was expecting a break today, but no such luck. I had almost forgotten about my little shopping expedition or I had just blocked it out. As I parked in front of Frisky Business, my butt welded itself to the driver's seat. I could not go in there. I knew what awaited me—Rena and Kristy. My new friends, armed with a list from Shoshanna detailing the appropriate clothing I would need as her assistant. Fuck . . . Why did this place seem familiar? I racked my brain trying to remember. I was certain I'd never shopped here before and I was certain I didn't want to shop here now.

If I drove away, I knew they'd come to my house and drag me back. That would be even worse than walking in of my own accord. The hot pink neon flashing light informing all to "Get Your Licks and Lashes Here" was alarming and disgusting. *Licks and Lashes?* I would confiscate Rena's and Kristy's phones the minute I walked in . . . if I walked in. The abrupt knock on my window scared the hell out of me.

"Get your ass out of the car." Rena stood there grinning like an idiot.

"I told you she'd be out here," Kristy chimed in. "You owe me forty."

"Fine," Rena groaned, "but you owe me thirty from the doughnut bet last week, so I only owe you ten."

"But you didn't get the picture of Evangeline at the pokey. That was thirty, so you still owe me forty."

They both stood there lost in confusion trying to figure out who owed who what. Did I really want to have friends? They seemed like a hell of a lot of work.

"Get out of the fucking car, Candy, or I'll drag your ass out," Rena informed me gleefully with her hands planted on her hips.

"And I'll take pictures," Kristy threatened, pulling her phone out.

I rolled down my window and stuck my hand out. "Give me your phones."

"Oh, come on," Kristy whined. "You're no fun."

"Phones," I snapped.

Reluctantly they handed them over. I put them under my front seat, got out, and locked the doors. "You'll get them back when we're done here."

"Nice move," Rena congratulated me and shoved me toward the entrance. "Very nice."

"Thank you."

We walked in and a huge sense of déjà vu swept over me. I *had* been here, but when and why?

"Oh shit," a male voice screeched. "We ain't got nothing here. We're clean. Motherfucker, Jesus, Mary, Joseph, and Moses, everybody duck and cover! The Feds are here."

About ten scantily clad male and female employees screamed and sprinted around the store looking for hiding places. It was like a Three Stooges episode, except there were ten of them and they were basically, for all intents and purposes, naked. Now I remembered. I'd busted this place four years ago for running a prostitution ring. Prostitution wasn't on my list of priorities, but when all payments were in grams of cocaine, hooking became my problem. Clearly, I'd made an impression. This was a clusterfuck.

"Freeze," I yelled. "Who's in charge here?"

"I am," came a muffled voice from underneath a pile of dildos.

"Get out here."

A tiny woman dressed in a corset, rubber miniskirt, fishnets, and combat boots crawled out from under the dildos and sheepishly approached.

"Are you still running a bordello here?" I inquired, trying to recall if she had been here four years ago.

"Absolutely not," she replied, completely insulted.

"Then why did everyone run around and lose their shit?" Rena and Kristy stood by me, stunned to silence.

"Because you're a Fed and last time you were here, you shot the hell out of the place."

"Oh, right. I did. Well, if you're not running drugs or hookers, we don't have a problem."

"Why are you here then?" the little rubber skirt gal asked skeptically.

"She's a customer. She's here to buy some hot, sexy garb to wear at SCREW-Con," Rena volunteered, stepping forward to shake hands with rubber skirt.

"No way," Little Rubber cackled.

"That's funny?" I snapped, wiping the smile off her face.

"Um . . . no," she stammered. "Just unexpected. What exactly do you need?"

"Here's a list." Rena handed over a sheet of paper with writing on both sides. "Are you an eight?"

I nodded. The size of the list made my stomach roil. Rubber gal took the list from Rena and hurried away to start collecting my own personal hell.

"You are such a fucking badass," Kristy whispered with delight.

"Dude, I am impressed," Rena added. "Your mere presence knocked over a tower of dildos and made the guy in the purple assless leather chaps pee himself."

"I can't do this," I muttered, and tried to turn and run.

"Nope," Rena said, and grabbed me in a hold she must have learned from Jack. I knew I was screwed.

"This is not about you. It's about keeping Shoshanna safe. Did you find anything out at the university?"

I hung my head and realized I was going to have to do this. It was a costume. I'd worn hundreds over the years and never balked. I wasn't going to start today. "It was a bust. None of them did it."

"Do you have any other leads?" Kristy worriedly asked.

"No, but I'll find him or her or them," I told the girls confidently.

"Then I don't want to hear any more bitching out of your cakehole about the outfits," Rena said as she pushed me toward the dressing rooms. "You'll need these to do the job right."

"Were edible panties on the list?" Kristy asked, holding up a box.

"No," Rena called over her shoulder, "but if they have strawberry in a medium, I'll take seven."

"How about raspberry panties?" Kristy yelled. "I don't see strawberry. Oh my God," she squealed. "They have chocolate. Mitch loves chocolate."

"Mitch is my brother," I groaned. "That is entirely too much information and the visual is vomitus."

"Whoops! Sorry." Kristy laughed.

This was going to be a long fucking day.

After an hour and a half of shoving myself in and peeling myself out of clothes made of rubber and other materials that should be used for tires, I was exhausted. I refused to come out of the dressing room so Kristy, Rena, and Rubber Skirt Gal, whose name turned out to be Joan, wedged themselves in every time I changed.

"Damn, you're hotter than Satan's underpants," Joan complimented me on the black leather pants and corset that were making it next to impossible to breathe.

"You really are," Rena said, eyeing me and my hooker clothes. "You're a knockout to start with, but this shit throws you over into the holyfuckingshitball category."

"Am I supposed to say thank you to that?" I asked, shifting in an attempt to get more air into my lungs.

"Yes, you are," Kristy announced grandly and began loosening the corset.

"Thank you," I gasped as oxygen rushed back into my body. I hoped one thank-you would cover both the questionable compliment and the saving of my life. "Everybody out. I'm changing back into my jeans, T-shirt, and shitkickers." I pulled a credit card out of my purse and handed it to Rubber Joan.

"Nope." Rena snatched my card from Joan and handed it back to me. "Shoshanna is buying—she insisted. Plus, this is going to cost a shit-ton. You're getting enough to have new slut-duds every day for at least two months."

"Oh my God. Put some of that back." I grabbed a pile and tried to hand it to Joan.

"Absolutely not. Shoshanna gave explicit instructions about what she wanted you to have and you'll have it. And," Rena gagged, "she threatened to eat every meal in my presence for a month if I didn't complete this mission. You're keeping the fucking clothes."

The three of us contemplated the reality of having to watch Shoshanna eat. I looked at the clothes and I looked at my friend. Her face was desperate, and I was fairly sure she would hurl in anticipation of her punishment if I put even one item back. Kristy, looking a little green, would probably vomit in solidarity, which in turn would cause me to throw up due to my overactive gag reflex.

"I'll keep the clothes." The ecstatic relief on Rena's and Kristy's faces made me giggle. "Now out. I need to be me again."

They filed out and I caught a glimpse of myself in the mirror. The pants molded to me like a second skin and held on to my ass almost as tightly as Luke had when we'd made love the other night. The loosened corset made my breasts spill out of the top. I didn't even recognize that girl. Luke would lose his mind if he ever saw me like this, but he would never see me like this. The thought made me weepy and I dropped onto the pink fur-covered chair in the corner. I would not cry for him. I would not cry for anyone. Why, why, why did I have to go and try to make things real with him? My heart hurt and a horrible unsettled feeling had moved into the pit of my stomach. No matter what I did, it wouldn't go away. Shit. Taking a deep breath, I attempted to push all my feelings to the back of my mind, but for the first time they wouldn't move.

Furious at myself for being weak, I yanked off the sex clothes and pulled on my jeans and T-shirt. There. I felt a little better. Just a little.

"Oh fuck, oh fuck, oh fuck," Rena whispered in terror outside of the dressing room door. "Get out here, Candy. We have to sneak out the back. Hurry," she hissed.

I pulled my gun from my purse and dove for the door. What the hell was happening? Knocking Rena to the ground, I aimed my gun out into the store and quickly scanned for trouble. At the sight of my weapon, the clusterfuck started all over again—sprinting, screaming, naked sex shop employees.

"Damn it," Rena exploded. "Put your gun away. You've completely screwed us now."

"What's happening here?" I ground out, unwilling to lower my Glock until I'd assessed the situation and had it under control.

"Well I'll be damned! Wasn't sure about you being Mag the Hag, but I was wrong. You are Mag beyond the shadow of a doubt," yelled an overjoyed Mrs. C.

"I'd say you just made at least three idiots pee and one may have crapped his pants," Edith crowed, sniffing the air. The shell-shocked employees all filed into a back room. This was clearly too much even for people who knew the ins and outs of butt plugs, passion fruit lube, and strap-ons.

"Do you see what the problem is now?" Rena grunted in disgust as she picked herself up off the ground. "Your trigger-happy fingers have just ruined my day."

"Sorry," I mumbled, and holstered my gun. "You could have been a bit clearer."

"How in the hell was I supposed to know you'd go all Rambo?" she demanded.

A bad day had just gotten worse. What were they doing here?

"You two are supposed to be working right now," Kristy admonished the sisters, and checked her watch. "Did you close up this early?" she demanded.

I'd forgotten Kristy owned the knitting shop the two old biddies ran. She was their boss and I was stupefied that they actually appeared contrite. They stared at each other, doing some kind of sibling lesbian telepathy, nodded, and Mrs. C stepped forward.

"Nobody was there and William Shatner didn't deliver the bolts of fabric, so there was nothing to do. We were bored and needed some new crotchless panties for SCREW-Con and so we left."

"Did you lock up?" Kristy was pissed and the gals were squirming.

"She did," they answered simultaneously.

"You were supposed to lock up, you old cow." Edith whacked her sister in the head.

"No I wasn't, you lazy dyke, you were," Mrs. C shouted, and trapped her sister in a chokehold.

"Do you mean to tell me you left the store wide open with no one there?" Kristy stepped in, separated the old gals, and got right up in their faces. Damn, she was brave. "If one of you mistakenly hits me, I will make you count buttons all night tonight and I will revoke the vacation time I gave you."

"Sorry," they muttered. "We'll go back and lock up."

"No." Kristy blew out an exasperated sigh. "I have to go over there and order new stock anyway, but just know this goes down on the list." They nodded and tried to pinch each other when they thought she wasn't looking. "Get your panties and then get your crotchless asses back to the shop. Or else."

I needed to get a few pointers from Kristy on handling the girls. It was like she was their freakin' mother. Amazing.

"Wait." Rena was puzzled. "When did William Shatner become a delivery guy?"

"He didn't." Kristy giggled, making her way to the door. "Our guy is the spitting image, so that's what we call him when he's not around."

"Oh fuck," Mrs. C muttered. "I thought it was really him. I've been calling him Captain Kirkhole for months."

Kristy froze for a moment and I watched her silently decide to let that one go. She was a smart girl. She knew when to pick her battles. My insides warmed when I remembered she was going to be my new sister. My brother had found a good one.

"Who's Mag the Hag?" Rena inquired as she warily stepped around the sisters and went to investigate the fuzzy handcuffs.

"She is," Edith said, pointing to me as she filled her basket with the dreaded crotchless undies.

"No, I'm not," I said, hoping I hadn't actually made anyone poop their pants.

"Yes, you are," Mrs. C shot back. "You are the reincarnation of the finest, most fucked-up sharpshooter ever born."

"You two are clearly smoking crack and I am not her. Never have been and never will be."

"Protest all you want, Mag," Mrs. C grunted as she tasted all the different lubes. "But you *are* her and we're finally all back together again. Good times ahead." Her face pinched, she spit out the lube and started licking the sleeve of her shirt. "Bubblegum tastes like monkeyass," she gagged.

Having no desire to ask her why she knew what monkeyass tasted like, I made my way over to the cash register, hoping someone had recovered enough to come out and ring me up. No one. It was not my day.

"Candy, I was hoping you could help us out." Edith ambled over, weighed down by her enormous quantity of edible clothing.

This was not good. I could feel it, but having them owe me might work to my advantage. "What do you need?"

"We don't exactly have tickets to SCREW-Con. They're sold out and we were hoping you could steal a few or sneak us in," Edith explained as she grabbed a ball gag and some rope.

I heard Rena's snort from across the store. I'd get her back later. "Um, not so sure about the stealing part, but I could ask Shoshanna if she has any extras."

I may as well have said The Second Coming of Christ. At the mention of Shoshanna's name, the old gals went positively giggly. WTF? Shoshanna was one hell of a lesbian magnet. First Professor Junsen and now the old sisters . . .

"Thanks, Mag," Edith gushed.

"I'm Candy."

"Yep, whatever you say." Edith grinned.

"Since nobody's working the counter, do you think we can just walk out with our stuff?" Mrs. C asked with two baskets full of sex-related things I'd never seen in my life.

"Absolutely not," Rena huffed before I had a chance to say the same. "What the hell is wrong with you lessies? That's stealing."

"Fine," Mrs. C pouted. "Someone get their ass out here and check me out or I'll tell the crazy bitch to start using dildos for target practice," she shouted at the top of her lungs.

Nine red-faced, puffy-eyed employees tentatively made their way out from the back room. Clearly, I'd made them cry. I felt bad.

"Where's the other one?" Edith demanded, looking around.

"Tommy shat himself," Rubber Joan whispered. "I sent him home."

Now I really felt bad. "I'm, um . . . sorry about all this."

"No problem." She smiled weakly. "Just please don't come in very often."

"I won't. I promise."

Rena, armed with Shoshanna's credit card, paid and we left. Edith and Mrs. C invited us to lunch, but Rena let them have it and told them to haul ass back to the store or she would call Kristy. They ran like the devil was on their heels.

"That was weird," I muttered as I handed Rena hers and Kristy's phones.

"Weird, but bizarrely fun," she said as leaned in to give me a hug. "You doing okay?"

It wasn't just a pleasantry. She really wanted to know . . .

"No, but I'll get there." I smiled and hugged her back.

"You will," she promised. "I know you will."

Chapter 12

"So none of them did it?" Steve asked as he rifled through a file on his desk.

"Nope. My report should be in your e-mail," I replied, sitting back in my chair and trying to relax. The utter lack of any suspect was making me antsy.

"I got it. You're positive?"

"Absolutely. Did the lab comb over the hard drives from the university?"

"Yeah, nothing. They were returned this morning." Steve sat down at his desk and ran his hands through his hair. I giggled because now it was sticking straight up on his head.

"What?" he asked, a small smile on his lips.

"You just created one hell of a hairdo." I laughed.

"Good. I needed a change."

"What's next?" I asked, glancing over at the file he'd pulled.

"Couple of changes. Honestly, I thought all the suspects were long shots and the notes were somewhat innocuous, but all that's different now."

"How?" I sat up and got the chilly feeling I always got when something bad had happened. He opened the file and handed me three sheets of paper. "Are these new?" I glanced over the copies of the typed pages.

"Yeah, these are copies. I sent the originals to forensics. I don't really expect them to find anything on them," Steve said with disgust. "Whoever this is, the perp's smart and has amped up the game."

"No shit, Sherlock," I muttered, reading the vitriolic content. "This is the first time a solid death threat has been made."

"I know and . . ."

"Daddy, Daddy," two little voices shrieked joyously, and two little bodies came barreling into the office.

"Hey, babies," Steve said, scooping up his kids and showering them with kisses. "What are you two little turds doing here? You should be in school."

"Mommy taked us here," his daughter Bella said with a giggle. "She go way on a trip and we get to play at you and Kevin's house for two years!"

"Weeks, Daddy," his son Devon said, correcting his little sister. "Mommy has to go away and we get to stay with you. Is that okay?"

"It's more than okay," Steve assured his seven-year-old son, trapping him in a bear hug. "Nothing would make me happier."

"Yay!" Bella shouted, crawling up Steve like he was a tree. "Kevin can be my horsey and I will ride him for five hours!"

"He's gonna love that." Steve laughed, putting her on his lap before she climbed up onto his head. "I think you guys missed somebody . . ."

"Candy," Bella screamed, flying off her father's lap and onto mine. Her sticky little hands held my face still for a sweet wet smooch.

"Hi, Candy," Devon said, ambling over for a hug.

"Hi guys," I laughed. "Long time no see."

"Daddy, can Candy stay at your house too?" Bella asked. "You can't do hair and I need her."

"We'll see." He grinned and grabbed Devon. Devon had a harder time with his dad being out of the house than Bella. I worried what that bitch Helen was trying to plant in his little seven-year-old brain. Speaking of . . .

"Hello, Steve," Helen, dressed to the nines, said formally from the doorway of his office. "Can you tell the girl to leave? We have some family business to discuss."

"The girl's name is Candy. You've known her as long as I have and she's the godmother of our children, Helen. She stays," Steve replied as pleasantly as he could for the sake of his children.

I sat still and held Bella firmly on my lap. She leaned in and laid her curly little head on my chest. She didn't seem too fond of her mother either. Devon tentatively crossed to his mother and stood unhappily beside her. She patted him on the head like a dog. I felt sick.

"A wonderful opportunity has just come up for me." She smiled and flicked invisible lint off her designer skirt. "I'm going on a two-week religious retreat to spread the word. You'll be taking the children, since you do so little in the first place, and I'll pick them up when I return."

"That's fine with me," Steve said tightly.

She was a piece of work. She didn't used to be like this when she and Steve were married. I'd never adored her, but I'd always liked her. Not anymore.

"Have you put any thought into our last conversation?" she cooed looking him up and down suggestively.

"No, I haven't and I won't."

"Suit yourself," she snapped. "Just remember I gave you the chance." She turned to leave, then as an afterthought, turned back to her kids. "Devon, what do you say?"

Devon looked lost; he had no clue what she wanted. "That, um . . . Daddy is going to burn in hell?" he whispered.

Helen laughed shrilly and hugged him tight. "That's right, baby. Mommy loves you." She left without a word to her daughter.

"Daddy?" Devon's lower lip trembled and he stared at the floor. "Are you really going to burn in hell?"

Steve got down on his knees in front of his son. "No, Devon, I'm not. My God is a loving God and since I'm a good person who lives a good life, I will go to God. Do you believe me?" he asked softly.

"I want to," Devon whispered. "Do you promise?"

"I promise." Steve took his son in his arms and rocked him while I held his daughter and rocked her.

"I think Mommy will burn in hell with the red devil," Bella announced. I silently agreed with her, but not being a parent, I wasn't quite sure if it was okay to voice my opinion.

"I think we shouldn't worry about any of that," Steve said. "We just need to make sure that we're good and kind and love each other, and God will take care of everything else. Okay?"

A relieved Devon relaxed in his father's arms. "Okay." He smiled. "I like that."

"Me too," Bella yelled. "Where is Hildy?"

"I'm right here, you rugrats!" Hildy grunted with delight from the doorway. Hildy was seventy if she was a day and had more energy than a twenty-year-old. She was short and round and had eyes that lit up with excitement at the smallest of things. She'd been Steve's secretary for as long as I could remember and everyone adored her. Her shock of gray hair stood straight up on her head no matter what she did to it and she wore sweat suits. Only sweats. Ever.

Bella shrieked and hurled herself at Hildy. Devon was only seconds behind.

"Hildy, I . . ." Steve began.

"I'm on it." She grinned. "Called my sister, Irma. She'll cover for me here at work for the next two weeks while I get to play grandma to my favorite little pooper scoopers."

"Hildy, I love you," Steve said gratefully as she gathered up the kids, promising a trip to the zoo and ice cream.

"I love you too," she said. "Just remember, Irma likes her rap music, so you gotta let her play her music or she'll get real crabby and pout."

"Got it." Steve laughed and kissed his kids good-bye.

We sat in silence for a few minutes.

"What? You're not going to fill up the quiet?" he asked me.

"No, I was waiting for you. That was intense."

"I'm going to try to get full custody. Devon's therapist has been worried for a while."

"Will the therapist testify?"

"Yes, I'm just worried about the kids losing their mother. I don't know if I'm doing the right thing."

"After the daddy burning in hell thing, I think you are." I wanted to hug him, but could tell he was about to blow. "I can come back in a little while if you want to call Kevin or just be alone." I stood up and moved to the door.

Steve looked at his watch and sighed. "I'd love to be alone for a few, but there's no time. Come sit back down. There's been a change of plans."

Seated again, I waited while Steve took a moment and texted Kevin. I really hoped he got custody of those kids. Helen was fucked up.

"Okay, the tone of this has changed. I considered keeping Shoshanna in town, but I think having her away from her home is a good idea at this point. This person knows where she lives and is probably aware of her regular schedule." I nodded in agreement.

"The convention isn't all that well publicized," Steve continued, "and there's been no mention of her writing erotica in any of the notes. I think she'll be safer with some of us on her in Wisconsin than she would be here."

"Some of us?"

"Yep," he said, leaning back in his chair. "I'm giving you a partner. It's smart and safe. I want a male. You can be with her in the ladies room, but I want someone who can troll the men's rooms and other places that would be unusual for a woman to be."

"Makes sense."

"I'll keep forensics on everything here. We've set up surveillance at her home and at the university. Her land line and her cell have been tapped and we've put cameras at as many of the mail drop boxes as we could manage around Saint Paul."

"What the hell is going on?"

"No fucking clue," Steve replied, tense with frustration. "It just makes no sense, which is why it bothers me so much."

"Have you briefed Shoshanna?" Was she going to take this seriously? Somehow I doubted it.

"I have and she laughed." Steve exhaled a loud sigh and shook his head. "She thinks it's exciting."

I grinned and dropped my head to my hands. This was going to be a hell of a week. "Are you sending Don?"

"No, Don's on a stakeout. I have someone more qualified. Actually he's overqualified."

"Who in the hell would that be?" I asked, running through the roster of male agents in my brain. *Overqualified?*

"That would be me," came a very familiar voice from behind me. Fuck.

I sat frozen and refused to turn around. If I pretended not to know him, would he go with that? Wait. Steve knew I knew him. What else did Steve know?

"This won't work," I said tersely, staring straight at Steve.

"Why not?" they asked in unison.

"Because," I ground out between clenched teeth.

"That's an extremely vague reason," Luke said, walking into my sight line and then taking a seat right next to me. His leg touched mine, and a snap of electricity shot through me. I moved my leg and kept my eyes trained on Steve—whom I wanted to kill.

"Candy, explain yourself," Steve said impatiently. "I have no time for petty bullshit. I need my best on this because I have no fucking clue what's going on here. State your issue."

"He doesn't work for you anymore. He got out."

"*He* decided he didn't want to retire after all," Luke informed me even though I refused to acknowledge him. "*He* thought it would be fun to work with a *girl*."

"Do you hear him?" I snapped to Steve. "He's an egotistical sexist asshole."

"Yes, he is." Steve gave Luke an admonishing glare. "But he knows what he's doing and I'd feel more confident about Shoshanna's safety if you two were working together. Is that going to be a problem?"

I stared down at my fidgety hands, tried to block out Luke's clean sexy scent, and considered what Steve had said. My feelings were not the priority here. They actually counted for nothing. Shoshanna's safety and well-being were the only objective. Period. Luke was good. I was sure of it. He was deep cover for God's sake. He didn't exist. He'd done things I probably couldn't even imagine. I snuck a glance at him and he was watching me intently with those green eyes, but I couldn't read him. I was unsure whether he was angry or amused. It didn't matter. As long as he did his job and I did mine, what I felt was secondary. Meaningless. I wasn't human and he didn't even exist.

"No problem," I muttered.

"No problem here either," Luke added. "When do we leave?"

"Saturday." Steve was all business now and pleased that he had gotten his way. "Luke's been briefed; he needs to be outfitted and to meet Shoshanna."

I gave Luke an evil grin at the realization that he was going to have to wear leather chaps and chains—then I blanched. *I was going to be wearing leather and corsets and fuck-me boots.*

"What do you mean outfitted?" Luke asked suspiciously.

"We're going as Shoshanna's assistants. The day and evening wear is specific," I innocently informed him.

"Will you be taking me shopping?" he queried, giving me a look that made my insides wiggle.

"Nope." I grinned evilly. "I'll be sending you with some experts."

"Really," he drawled, narrowing his eyes.

"Yep, you'll have a great time." I gave him a thumbs-up and dialed the lesbians.

"Luke," Steve called out as we were leaving.

"Yeah?"

"What the hell happened to you? Where's the brooding, angry, closed off fuck I've always known?"

Luke paused and stared at me so hard I felt the heat crawl up my neck. He took a deep breath and grinned. "He's finally found something that makes him happy."

Shit, shit, shit.

Chapter 13

It was Friday afternoon and I was already packed. It had taken two suitcases to fit all the rubber and leather in. I usually traveled with only an overnight bag—this was ridiculous. Rena had dropped off a kit of hooker makeup and listened to my dilemma about Luke.

"Wait, back up. You slept with him?" she asked, digging through my fridge. "You have really good stuff in here," she commented, pulling out the stash of chocolate I kept hidden in the back.

"I did and then I told him to get lost."

"Because he wanted you to quit your job?"

"Yeah."

"He's a total fucktard." She shook her head in disgust.

"Can you believe he wanted me to give up everything?" Thank God someone could empathize.

"He's a Neanderthal," she agreed. "I mean, your job is great. You kill people and you can have dinner with your job and then screw it. Your job occasionally stabs you in the stomach. It brings you joy and kinship and children. You can grow old with it as long as you don't get offed by a member of the Mafia or something silly like that. You are so right. I can totally see why your job is better than him. He's a douchehole."

"You're a dick," I snapped. "My job is all I have. It's why I get up, why I can function."

"First of all, I can't be a dick. I'm a girl, so bitch or vagina will suffice. Second of all, if you repeat the second half of your sentence three times really fast, you will realize that you're in trouble. Simply functioning is not living. If I thought you were living at the same time you were doing your job . . . that would be one thing, but you're not. Or am I missing something here?"

Was everyone against me? Ever since I decided to have friends, my life started falling apart. Or had it been falling apart for a while and it took having friends to realize it?

"Anyway," I said, ignoring all of Rena's profoundness, "even if I wanted to sleep with him anymore, I couldn't. We're on a job together. That's bad form and could fuck up the job."

"Now that I actually understand," she conceded. "But this shit is so far from over, and you know it."

Ignoring her point again, I changed the subject. "He had to buy sex clothes."

"Oh my God." She laughed. "Did you go?"

"Absolutely not. I set him up with some experts." I bit down on my bottom lip so I wouldn't laugh.

"Experts?"

"Yep. I sent Mrs. C and Edith."

Rena froze and her grin almost split her face in half. "Holy mother of God," she gasped. "You are so worthy of my friendship. They will eat him alive."

"That was my plan." I grinned back, totally delighted with myself.

"You're gonna pay for that, you know."

"No, I won't," I told her, my glee quickly fading. Was I? What would he do? What could he do? Shit.

"Oh baby," she cackled. "He is sooooo gonna make you pay."

After Rena left, I paced my house and tried to come up with all the ways Luke could get me back. Nothing concrete came to mind. Maybe he would think it was funny and enjoy his time with the insane sisters . . . Who was I kidding? He was going to hand me my ass.

He wouldn't do anything too awful. That wouldn't be professional . . . like what I'd done was professional. Damn, damn, shit, damn. I was in for it. A light knock at my door was actually a relief. It meant I could focus on something else. I checked my watch. There were still two hours before I had to meet Luke at Shoshanna's. I felt sure I'd be safe from revenge with Shoshanna around. Who was here? Had Rena left something?

I opened the door and tried to slam it shut immediately, but the angry guy on the other side stuck his foot in, making it impossible.

"Hi Candy," Luke said in a voice dripping with sarcastic sweetness as he pushed his way inside. "I just spent the most amazing three hours with some really good friends of yours."

"Um, if I say I'm sorry right now, will you leave?"

"Absolutely not, Mag," he said with a grin, and made himself comfortable on my couch. Great, he'd been made aware of my reincarnation.

"So you had fun?" I whispered, perched on a chair all the way across the room.

"A blast. I've never been more thoroughly castrated in my life. My ass is sore from being slapped and I might have sprained my dick getting away from your buddies when they tried to measure it."

"But they're gay," I stammered, appalled that they'd mauled him.

"Yes, they are. But when they correctly assumed that I was having sex with you, they felt it was their mission to make sure I measured up."

"And did you?" I giggled.

"I'm happy you're amused," he snapped, and narrowed his gaze. "Because payback is a bitch. And to answer your question, yes. I measured up quite impressively."

I sat silently on my chair and debated how to get out of this.

"There's no way out, beautiful girl. You now owe me and I always collect." He smiled menacingly. "Just so you know, I am the proud owner of some assless leather chaps and some leather pants that squeezed my nuts right back up into my body. There's a lovely vest that goes with that little number. You'll just love it. I have nipple clamps and chains and the girls insisted on a ball gag and a strap-on," he huffed indignantly. "They called me a fuck toy and challenged me to a contest down at the shooting range."

"Wow." I looked up at the ceiling and bit down on my lip so I wouldn't laugh. "How'd that go?"

"I kicked their Four-Tour-Vietnam-Special-Forces asses into the ground. By the end, they were on their knees begging my forgiveness and giving up every secret on you they had."

Shit.

"So Mag the Hag, what should your punishment be?"

"You could ground me or give me the silent treatment," I offered lamely.

"I was thinking more along the lines of a spanking." He pulled his T-shirt over his head and leaned back on the couch.

"I don't think so. Wait. What are you doing?" I demanded, trying to keep my eyes on his face.

"Getting comfortable." He grinned and unbuttoned his jeans.

God, from my vantage point it was clear he was going commando . . . help me, Jesus.

"I'm not sleeping with you. We're working together now and that's against regulation," I informed him haughtily, even though I couldn't rip my eyes from his crotch.

"Work starts tomorrow. I've never followed rules in my life. And who says I want to sleep with you?" he shot back, removing his jeans.

My tongue got stuck to the roof of my mouth, and no words would come. He was buck-ass naked on my couch, and it took everything I had not to fly across the room and jump him. My heart was beating so loud in my chest, I was sure he could hear it.

"So, tell me a little about Shoshanna."

"Well, I . . . um, she is . . ." I croaked.

"Cat got your tongue?" He smirked, got up off the couch, and moved toward me. "You don't look very comfortable, Candy. Why don't we remove that dress?"

"I thought you didn't want to sleep with me," I squeaked, running around to the back of the chair I was perched on. I was so turned on, my panties were soaked. It was like he read my fantasy diary. Shit.

"Sleep? No. Fuck? Yes."

"Is that my punishment?"

"Would that suit you?" His eyes bored into mine and I felt faint.

What in the hell was I supposed to do here? I wanted him so badly I was shaking. There was no denying that he wanted me as he stood there in all his glory with a raging erection. As far as punishments went . . . it was awesome.

"I guess that would work," I said to the floor.

"You have to beg."

"I'm sorry, what?" My eyes shot to his and I realized he was deadly serious.

"You heard me." He grinned lazily, primed to chase me if I ran. *God, he had my number.* "Take off your clothes, pretty girl."

I did have a choice. I knew with every fiber of my being he would stop the game and leave if I asked him, but I was enjoying playing as much as he was . . . maybe more. And he knew it. Could I beg? If he came any closer to me, the answer was yes. I would get down on my knees and beg.

"You have ten seconds to start removing your clothes or I will come around that chair and rip them off your body."

With trembling hands and a face flushed with desire, I pulled my dress over my head. A surge of heat rushed through me as the fabric brushed over my aching nipples. Unsure if my legs would hold me up, I leaned on the chair as I slid my panties down.

"Come over here and get down on your knees," he said gruffly, not moving an inch. He was dangerous and scary and sexier than any man had a right to be. He was turning my crank to a degree it had never been turned and I loved it.

I nodded and moved carefully around the chair. Getting down on my knees was a relief due to the fact that my legs had become noodles. I was now up close and personal with the biggest, most beautiful cock I'd ever seen.

"Is there something you'd like to do?" Luke casually asked.

"Yes."

"And what would that be, Candy?" His husky voice would be my undoing.

"I want you in my mouth," I whispered.

"You need to ask a little nicer and be a bit more specific."

"Please let me suck your cock," I begged as I felt heat creep up my neck and rush to my cheeks.

"Hmm, I don't think you want it badly enough," he tsked, and pulled me to my feet, pressing my body full into his. "Open your mouth," he demanded as his lips descended.

I whimpered in confusion as his mouth crashed against mine. All thought was lost and I gave back as furiously as I was getting. He kissed me senseless until I couldn't have told you my name or what day it was. All I knew was the taste and smell of the beautiful man who was devouring me.

As abruptly as it started, it stopped. He let go and my useless legs buckled. Thank God the chair was there to catch my fall. When he leaned in, his warm breath feathered against my cheek, sending shivers all over my body.

"Do you want to fuck?" he whispered in my ear.

"Yes," I hissed, arching up to him.

"How bad?" he asked, nipping my earlobe.

"More than I've ever wanted anything in my life," I moaned.

Standing up, he looked down at me. His eyes were dilated with lust and a thin sheen of sweat covered his gorgeous body. His lazy half smirk was firmly in place as he dropped his bomb.

"Good."

He turned away and pulled his clothes back on as I tried to process the fact that I wasn't going to get laid.

"Oh my God, you've got to be kidding me," I yelled as I grabbed for my dress and pulled it over my head. "I hope you get blue balls so bad they fall off."

"Payback is a bitch," he said, grinning.

"Yeah, well you just got your last chance with me in this lifetime," I huffed, searching for my panties. "Where the hell are my . . ."

"Got 'em," he purred as he tucked my panties into the pocket of his jeans.

"Give those back. They're my favorites," I snapped, holding out my hand.

"You'll have to earn them."

"I'll do no such thing. We're definitely even now. You won. Hope you're happy." I walked over to my front door and held it open. "Leave."

"You got it wrong," he said, backing me up against my door and invading my personal space. "I didn't win the battle—you've won every battle so far—but I will win the war."

"What in the hell is that supposed to mean?" I shoved him out of my face.

"It means you're mine." He laughed and walked out the door.

"When hell freezes over," I called after him.

He turned around and grinned. I wanted to slap him unconscious. "According to your dyke friends, and they instructed me to call them that, hell froze over last Tuesday, baby. See ya in an hour."

He got in his car and left.

Game was on and he was so going to lose.

Chapter 14

"Do you see my problem?" Shoshanna lamented as she plied Luke with cheese and crackers and a beer.

"Actually I do." Luke nodded his head seriously and sipped his beer. "I think it's a damn shame no one has been forthcoming with the information. I do believe I can help you out."

"Well, that's just fucking great!" she shouted, and slapped him on the back, causing him to choke on his beer. "Heimlich!" she shrieked, knocking Luke's beer from his hand and wrapping her tiny arms around him in an attempt to save his life.

"No, no, no," Luke gasped, removing the raving lunatic from his mid-section. "I'm good. It just went down the wrong pipe."

"Thank God," she said. "That would have been a disaster if I killed you."

"Not really," I muttered, tired of watching Luke charm the Minnesota Vikings sweatpants off of Shoshanna. In the last thirty minutes, I'd gotten about two words in.

"Now that's not nice, Candy." Shoshanna gave me the eyeball. "What do you have against Luke here? He's hotter than Satan's fucking underpants and he's been staring at your tits since you two arrived," she crowed with delight. "If I didn't know better, I'd say you two have played hide the salami."

"We haven't," I snapped at the same time Luke informed her we had. "Okay, fine," I admitted. "We used to, but that's over and you don't have anything to worry about. We are focused on your safety and getting to the bottom of this."

"Candy is correct," Luke agreed, "mostly. We are focused and professional. We will find who is threatening you and end it, but I will be having sex with her on a regular basis."

"No, you won't," I snapped, glaring.

"Yes, I will," he shot back lazily. "Shoshanna, do you have a problem with this?"

"Sweet baby Moses in a thong," she squealed with glee, "this is one of my books come to life! No problems here, but you seem to have a few," she told Luke.

"I'll work them out, trust me," he replied to Shoshanna while undressing me with his eyes.

I had never met or worked with someone so unprofessional in my life. What in the hell was he thinking telling Shoshanna all that crap? I knew he didn't play by the rules, but this was insane.

"A word?" I hissed to the loose cannon and nodded toward the purple kitchen.

"Shoshanna, will you excuse us for a moment?" Luke asked politely.

"Go for it, big boy! I'm just gonna grab some research material so you can help me out." She winked at us and ran back to what I assumed was a blindingly purple office. "Just yell when you two lovebirds are finished."

"Oh my God," I burst out. "We're just going to talk."

"Right," Shoshanna called over her shoulder, laughing like a loony.

"You are out of line," I snapped at Luke. "There are real threats on her life and if you expend one ounce of energy trying to get into my pants, which by the way is a lost cause, Shoshanna could die."

He watched my fit in silence and waited for more.

"Are you going to say something?" I demanded, crossing my arms over my chest, which he'd been ogling for the better part of an hour.

He walked right up to me and planted himself inches from me. Putting his hands on the purple stripes flanking my head, he loosely trapped me. "I have spent every day for the last several years expecting not to see tomorrow. I am so good at my job, the government decided to erase me from their rosters," he said in a tone that sent chills of unease through me. "I've done things that would give even people like you nightmares. God knows, they give me nightmares. I will guarantee you that I will find and arrest or destroy whoever is threatening Shoshanna and I will do it quickly. Life is short for people like you and me, so I will be pursuing you while I do what I'm paid to do. If you have a problem with that, take your-self off the case."

I was speechless. I would not take myself off the case. I might not have seen what he had seen in the line of duty, but I was no slouch. I was qualified and committed and I liked Shoshanna. He was high if he thought he could scare me away.

"You're fucking nuts," I said, ducking under his arm and putting some space between us. "I might not be as *well rounded* as you are, but I'm damn good at what I do. It's in me just as much as it's in you. So I will not be taking myself off the job . . . asshole."

"Tell me something, Candy," he said, breaking eye contact and examining the cardboard cutout of Brett Favre that had made its way to the kitchen since the dinner party last week. "Tell me that you're not attracted to me. Tell me that part of you doesn't wonder what it would be like to be mine, and for me to be yours. To have something real." He paused and ran his hands through his hair, and my stomach clenched in fear. This was too real for me—too messy . . . too gray. "Tell me all those things mean nothing to you and I will leave you alone, but think about your answer. Think hard."

He waited with his back to me. My brain was imploding in my head and my heart raced. He was serious. This was more frighten-ing than any violent, potentially deadly job I'd ever worked, and the stakes were higher. My hands trembled and the ringing in my ears made me grasp the counter for balance. My silence clearly un-nerved him and he took that as my answer. He turned to walk away and I panicked.

"Wait."

He froze with his hands clenched in fists.

"I have thought about all of that," I stammered, and his body vis-ibly relaxed. "I have, but it's too fast and I can't give up everything for something I have no idea would work . . . or last."

Luke turned and caught me as my knees gave way and I slid down to the floor. I wanted to curl up and hide from all the truth I'd just released. "That's all I need, beautiful girl," he said with a smile, and pulled me to his strong, warm body. "I will make you believe. I promise."

I laid my head on his chest and listened as his rapid heartbeat slowed. I had just done something scarier than facing the entire cartel that wanted to carve me up. I was fairly sure there was no way to shoot my way out of what I'd just admitted to . . . and as frightened as I was, I felt lighter than I had since before my sister had died.

I glanced up at my potentially terrifying future and exhaled a shaky breath. "We can't be screwing around during SCREW-Con. You know that, don't you?"

"I do"—he grinned and traced my lips with his finger—"but a tiny bit of nookie here and there should be okay. And once this fucker is done and put to bed, I'm taking you to an island, tying you up, and making you orgasm for three weeks straight."

I rolled my eyes as everything south of my belly button tightened in anticipation of a sex-a-thon with the insane man who planned to kidnap me. His smile was so happy and I knew mine matched. God, what had I done? Who cared? I had never felt this way before and I didn't want it to go away.

"That doesn't sound very fair," I purred, running my hands underneath his shirt.

"How's that?" he asked huskily.

God, I loved that I affected him as much as he affected me.

"I think I should be able to tie you up too," I reasoned logically, rubbing up against him.

"Fuuuuuck." He chuckled as his head dropped back onto his shoulders. "I do believe that could be arranged."

"Good." I pushed him away and put my agent face back on even though I couldn't hide my grin. "Enough of this. We have a job to do and we're going to do it right. Deal?"

"Deal."

As we made our way back to Shoshanna and the purple shag–carpeted living room, Luke copped a major feel of my ass. My instincts were to slap him, but my girlie parts disagreed. I could deal with a little grabby-grabby as long as we did our job. It might even make the job more fun . . . Wait. Who was I and what had I done with Candy? I glanced over at the very self-satisfied Luke and I realized I didn't care.

"As you two can see," Shoshanna said, holding up two sets of handcuffs, "I have metal and fuzzies. However, I think the fuzzies would be more comfortable. But it would make more sense for you guys to use the metal ones because that's what you carry and I want realism. Ya know? So what did you guys use?"

"The metal," I replied, and then screamed and slapped my hand over my mouth.

Luke, grinning like an imbecile, decided to expand on my faux pas. "We have used the metal. *Several times,*" he told a delighted Shoshanna. "But just the other day when I had Candy cuffed to her bed and I made her see Jesus a couple of times . . . six to be exact, the cuffs got uncomfortable and I wished I had something with some kind of soft fabric on it."

"You will shut your cakehole now, or there will be no island or Jesus or anything," I yelled at him. "Do. You. Understand?"

"Awwww, come on," Shoshanna pleaded. "I won't tell anyone. It's kind of like being a newspaper source. I'll protect your identity with my life."

"How about we just protect your life and you find some other sources? We're not available," I said firmly.

Shoshanna pouted until I saw Luke give her a covert thumbs-up, indicating he would be willing to spill the dirty details of our sex life. I would have words with him later.

"About the logistics," I said, and opened a file. "You're fairly well booked with appearances, panels, and parties. We might need to pull back a bit on some of this if there's even the slightest hint of trouble."

"No prob," Shoshanna said. "Anybody hungry? I've got some awesome Turkey Noodle DooDa Surprise from my buddy Nancy. I can throw some of that shit in the microwave and we can chow."

"Um, I'm good." Anything with cream of mushroom soup as one of the ingredients didn't sit well with my gag reflex.

"Just ate," Luke added quickly.

"It does look like puke," Shoshanna admitted, "but it tastes great! Come on, I'll make three plates."

"No," both Luke and I shouted at the same time. I glanced down at my hands and bit the inside of my cheek so I wouldn't giggle. We could take down a small army, but we couldn't face casseroles. Maybe we were a good match . . .

"Suit yourselves," Shoshanna muttered absently, lost in thought. "I'd rather eat cheese anyway."

She dug in and I glanced away, making a mental note to myself never to sit across from her at meals. "Okay then, Luke and I will go as your assistants. I'll be with you at all times except when

you're in your room. I have a room adjacent to yours with a connecting door and Luke will flank you on the other side. We also reserved the two rooms across the hall from you and eight more on
other floors. We'll move you daily so you'll be difficult to find."

"Jesus Harvey Simpson-Christ, that seems like a whole lot of
trouble for you guys. I really . . ."

"Shoshanna." I stopped her and my voice went serious. "I am very
aware that you think this is a game, but the tone of the notes has
changed and a solid death threat has been made. Steve likes that
we're getting you out of town to the writing convention, since no
reference has been made to your books. But we have no suspects
whatsoever and we're going to take all precautions we deem necessary."

"Damn, you're all hot and badass when you go tough-girl agent."
Shoshanna put her hand up to Luke for a high five. He slapped her
little paw and grinned in agreement.

"Enough." I shook my head and smiled. "None of the suspects
we had panned out."

"I didn't think they would," Shoshanna replied, cutting more
cheese.

"Why?"

"Well," she stated mushily with a huge mouthful of her favorite
treat, "Evangeline, God love her over-botoxed ass, is too stupid and
in the slammer. Junsen has a huge crush on me and wants a date
with me. If I were dead, that would be a little difficult. And Steigmeister lives in the dark ages. He can't use the computer and he's
too self-righteous to do anything illegal." She finished her explanation and shoved an ungodly amount of cheese into her already full
mouth.

"You could have saved me a bunch of time this week," I muttered, remembering all the fun I'd had.

"I told Steve all this, but nobody listens."

"Do you have any thoughts who it might be?" Luke asked the
question that was on the tip of my tongue.

"Nope, but the notes are weird. It's like whoever is writing them
doesn't know me. I wondered at first if the threats were even really
aimed at me."

"Do you have copies with you, Candy?" Luke asked, moving
over to sit with me.

"I have a new file for you. It matches mine, and we meet with Steve tomorrow morning before we leave to be briefed on any updates."

"Good." He was all business now. He took his file and scanned it.

"Oh, guys, there is one problem." Shoshanna slapped her little forehead as she remembered.

"What?" Our eyes shot up from our paperwork.

"I wouldn't have a male assistant," she informed us. "Highly unusual considering I'm a professor of Women's Studies and I write all women as Doms, so I've worked out another scenario. Candy, you'll be my assistant and, Luke, you'll be my cover model."

"Is that usual?" Luke asked, a little wary of the change in plans.

"Oh fuck yeah." She laughed. "Besides, you're hotter than hell on a stick and I'm sure you'll win the pageant."

"I'm sorry, what?" Luke swallowed hard and gave Shoshanna a look full of displeasure.

"Don't worry about it," she cackled. "Just bring your leathers and chains and prepare to have your mind blown."

I stared at my paperwork, enjoying myself way too much. I would definitely film the pageant on my phone. I'd have blackmail material for the rest of my natural life if I caught him strutting his stuff in chaps and chains . . .

"Fine," Luke said stiffly. "I'll just block that one out until I have to deal with it. However, I do have something that's bothering me. Who in the hell is watching you this week and where in the hell are they?"

A sharp rap on the door made me jump. Luke and I immediately pulled our guns and he quickly moved in front of Shoshanna.

"Who is it?" he yelled.

"Shoshanna's protection," shot back a very familiar voice from the other side of the door. It was Mitch. I holstered my gun and grinned with relief, but Luke's eyes narrowed to slits. WTF?

"Open the door, Candy," Luke instructed in a clipped tone. I moved to the door and let my brother in. I went to give him a quick hug, but he was focused on one thing only . . . Luke.

"Nice to see you, Mitch. Long time no see," Luke said mildly in a voice that made the hair stand up on the back of my neck.

"Right back at ya, Luke. I see that distance doesn't make the heart grow fonder," my brother replied with a smile that came nowhere close to reaching his eyes.

Fuck.

"Candy," Mitch snapped. "Kitchen."

"She stays here," Luke said as he holstered his gun.

Mitch and Luke did the macho stare down thing while Shoshanna and I watched. Shoshanna grabbed her notebook and started scribbling. I snatched it away and refocused on the testosterone contest. Were they serious? Yep. This was ridiculous.

"Luke, stay here with Shoshanna," I instructed firmly. "I'm going with my brother to the kitchen to have a little chat."

"Your brother?" Luke's eyebrows raised in surprise.

"That's right, motherfucker. Her brother." Mitch's smile reached his eyes this time, but it wasn't exactly pretty.

"Kitchen," I ground out through clenched teeth to Mitch.

"After you," he said, never taking his eyes off my pissed-off potential boyfriend.

Fucking awesome.

Chapter 15

Mitch paced the kitchen like a caged tiger that had lost its mind. I sat on the counter and watched him. It was clear he and Luke knew each other and even clearer that there was no love lost between them. Had they worked together? Had they dated the same woman? Ewwww, I pushed that one right out of my head. If that was the case, I didn't want to know. Why in the hell would they hate each other so much and how did Luke not know that Mitch was my brother? Hell, the family resemblance was almost impossible to miss.

"How often was Sanderson your last name when you were undercover?" I asked him.

"I've had over a hundred last names," he snapped, coming to an abrupt halt in front of me.

"And when Luke knew you, what was your last name?"

"Fuck if I know, but it wasn't Sanderson."

One question answered. Oh so many more to go . . .

"Why in the hell did you have to pick someone like him?" Mitch demanded.

"How do you even know that I picked him?" I shot back. Who the hell did he think he was? My father?

"The house is bugged, Candace."

"Shit," I muttered as the heat crawled quickly up my neck.

"Yeah and then some. Let's just reel off all the things I never needed to know about my sister. Call me crazy, but when I was sure it was you getting jiggy with one of the world's most dangerous assassins, I almost came in here and tore his head off."

"That would have gone over well." I laughed despite the fact my brother wasn't even remotely kidding. "How do you know each other?"

"Classified," Mitch said with disgust. "Maybe he'll tell you, but I won't."

"Yes, you will. You're out of the business now and you clearly know things you think I should know, so spill it, bro."

"Fine, little sis," he yelled. "We've worked together—many times. He's very good and fucking crazy. Without getting too specific, he's wanted by most of the criminal world. Dead. He's wanted dead by every cartel and organized gun-running, drug-smuggling crime group that exists. What he apparently just did down in Mexico is the stuff nightmares are made of. No one will ever forget that one," he hissed.

My stomach dropped and I thought I was going to be sick. I gripped the edge of the counter so I didn't fall off. "He did that for me," I whispered. "He was cleaning up my fuck-up. I'm the reason he was in Mexico."

"Jesus Christ, Candy. You killed the head of *that* cartel? Was that who almost took out your intestines?"

I didn't answer him. I couldn't. Had Luke put a death sentence on his already wanted head for me? This was not what I needed. My life was getting more complicated and screwed up than ever. The part about him being wanted meant nothing. Hell, I was wanted too. I simply hated the fact he'd led a raid with his emotions involved and that I was the cause.

"Was that who you took out?" Mitch repeated.

I looked up, startled. I'd forgotten Mitch was in the room. "Yes, that's who I took out."

If Mitch could have combusted, he would have. His strung-together run-on of swear words would have made me laugh in another situation, but I was fairly sure I would never laugh again.

"Why the hell couldn't you have hooked up with someone who wasn't a walking death trap?"

"I'm no prize myself," I snapped.

"Yes, you are. You're my sister. Any man would be luckier than hell to have you. It just can't be him."

"I don't see how the choice is yours, Mitch," I said quietly.

"How long have you been seeing him?" he demanded. I knew

how my brother's brain worked. He was looking for a hole or an advantage. I wasn't about to give him one. He was too good. No way would I tell him it had only been real for less than a week.

"A year."

"What?" he exploded. "A year and you're still alive?"

"Looks like it. And if I had died this year, it would have had nothing to do with Luke. I'm capable of that all by my lonesome."

"God, Candy." Mitch walked over and rested his forehead on mine. "I hate that you're still in this. Haven't you done enough? She wouldn't have wanted you to end up like this."

"Like what?" I pushed him away. Why did everyone feel the need to destroy me lately? Who had I fucked over in a former life that my karma had taken a nosedive into hell? "I'm good at this. It's right and I do it well."

"Do you love it?"

I paused. Did I? What a strange question . . . Did I love risking my life for people that would never know I'd saved them from anything? Was it enough anymore? Had I avenged my sister? Had I fixed my broken self? Would I ever take out enough of the bad guys? Did I really think somewhere deep inside that my family would be proud of what I was doing someday? Love wasn't the word I'd use. I wasn't even sure what it really meant.

"I . . ."

"Too long, Candy," Mitch said victoriously. "You took too long to answer, so that's your answer."

"That makes no sense."

"It makes perfect sense. If you loved it, you'd get up in my face and tell me to fuck off. You didn't, so it's time to get out and live. And you can't live with someone still ass-deep in this fucked-up world."

"That's an excellent point," Luke said from the doorway.

"I don't recall inviting you into this conversation," Mitch said tightly.

"You didn't." Luke grinned. "I invited myself. I agree with almost everything you just said to your sister. I want her out too and will do everything in my power to make sure that happens. However, I'm getting out also, so I'm no longer ass-deep in anything . . . Mitchy."

"Bullshit." Mitch crossed the room and stood toe to toe with Luke. Holy hell, were they going to fight?

"Enough," I barked, and hopped off the counter, getting between them. "Neither of you has the right to make any decisions for me. I am a grown woman with a mind, so screw both of you. If I get out, it will be my decision, not yours or yours. Mine."

"And him?" Mitch asked, referring to Luke.

I expelled a long breath and closed my eyes. Sink or swim . . . sink or swim. "He wants me, Mitch. He wants me just like I am—with my scars, the scars on the outside and even the uglier ones on the inside. He's good with my Glock strapped to my thigh and my total fucking fear of commitment. He's made me think about things and want things I've never considered a possibility for myself . . . I think I need that," I whispered, trying to make him understand.

Mitch stepped back and took three deep breaths to calm himself. He stuck his hands in the back of his jeans and turned his eyes on Luke. "Do you love her?"

"Oh my God," I shrieked. "Shut up! That is none of your business and I don't want to know the answer to that question." I heard Luke chuckle behind me and noticed my brother's shoulders relax as some kind of asshole telepathy passed between them. I wanted to deck him . . . both of them.

"If you hurt her, you don't have to worry about all the people who want you dead, because I will kill you . . . with my bare hands, and I'll enjoy it."

"Sounds fair." Luke cautiously crossed the kitchen to my brother and held out his hand. Mitch slowly took his hand from his back pocket and placed it in Luke's. With one last look of warning at both of us, Mitch left the kitchen.

"Hey, asshole," he called to Luke over his shoulder as he made his way to the front door, "the house is bugged. If I have to hear you talk about making my sister see Jesus ever again, I will make sure it's the last thing you ever say."

"Got it," Luke called back, winking at me.

The front door slammed and we stood in utter silence for a moment.

"That went pretty well," he said.

"Are you on crack?" I stammered. "That was hideous."

"No, hideous would have been if your brother or I was lying dead on the purple linoleum kitchen floor. *That . . .* was nothing."

"Sweet baby Moses in a thong," Shoshanna yelled, tearing into the kitchen. "That was tremendous. I got most of that down, but I missed a little bit of the . . ."

"Stop," I cut her off. "If you write even one word of what you just heard, I will personally go to Professor Junsen and tell her you're in love with her and I will give her the key to your house . . . and all of your bras."

"You are one tuff-ass broad," Shoshanna yelled gleefully. "We are gonna have one hell of a time at SCREW-Con."

"Screw what?" Luke asked alarmed.

"SCREW-Con," she repeated. "Society of Contemporary Romance Erotic Writers."

"Didn't you read your file?" I teased.

"I did and I'm very sure that was not in it. I do believe I would have remembered that one."

"That Steve is a sneaky fucker," Shoshanna cackled. "He left that tidbit out of Candy's too."

"We're done here," I said, exhausted from the drama. "We'll see you in the morning, Shoshanna." I grabbed my stuff, gave Shoshanna a quick hug, and waited for Luke.

As we walked down to our cars, Luke pulled me to a stop beneath the oversized Minnesota Vikings flag. "Do you want to make out by your car and send your brother into a fit? Or we could go back to your place." He grinned and waggled his eyebrows.

"No." I giggled. "We've done enough damage for the afternoon. And I think I need to be alone tonight."

"But it's our last nookie night before we have to be careful," he moaned.

He was right and I had considered that, but . . .

"If what you're offering is true, we have the potential of, um . . . many you know, nookie nights in the years ahead." *God, did I really just say that?*

The look of sheer joy on Luke's face made my breath catch in my throat. He picked me up, swung me around, and laid a huge one on my lips. "I will hold you to that, pretty girl. I will definitely hold you to that."

Luke walked to his car with a spring in his step and it was impossible to hide my smile. He honked his horn as he pulled away and I scanned the street for my brother. I spotted him in his car scowling at me. I grinned and waved. He shot me the bird and I returned the favor. This had been one of the best days of my life so far and I never wanted it to end. A tiny voice inside my head reminded me to beware of what I wished for, but I ignored it and shoved it to the back to deal with another day.

Chapter 16

Shoshanna's house was utter chaos Saturday morning—everyone was there and I already had a headache. I pinched the bridge of my nose and dove into the fray. Mitch and Luke gave each other a wide berth. It was clear Jack was siding with Mitch . . . However, Kristy and Rena were another story. They were on Luke like white on rice. He seemed to thoroughly enjoy the grilling they were giving him. He kept winking at me and I felt a little nauseous wondering what in the hell he was telling them.

Steve, Kevin, and the kids were helping Shoshanna bring her luggage out to the living room . . . all ten pieces. *WTF?*

"What do you have in there?" I tried to pick one up and doubled over. It had to weigh well over a hundred and fifty pounds.

"That one is full of vibrators for giveaways! They have the name of my latest book and a really nice picture of me on them."

Was she kidding? No one even stopped what they were doing. Thank God, the kids seemed to have no clue what she was talking about. Didn't anyone think it was appalling that Shoshanna had put her likeness on a vibrator? I was scared to ask what was in the other bags—so I didn't.

"He's hot," Rena announced as she crossed the room to me. "He's hot and he's so into you it makes me grind my teeth. I approve."

"Me too," Kristy agreed. "Now, your brother may take a little while, but I'll withhold panty privileges unless he eases up." She giggled and high-fived Rena.

"You would do that for me?" I asked, moved by her generosity and grossed out by the image of my brother having any kind of intimate relations.

"Of course," she said with a grin, and gave me a hug. "You're my friend and my future sister. I gather my ammo well and will expect a payback when I need it!"

"You got it." I stared at the two crazy girls who liked me. My friends. The feeling was new and precious. I was terrified if I expressed it, I might cry.

"Enough with the sappy bullshit." Rena rolled her eyes and slugged me in the arm. "You will be careful and you will solve the mystery. I'm sick and tired of this clusterfuck and I want it over."

"Deal." I hugged both of them and turned to find an adorable little rugrat demanding my attention.

"Candy, you was supposed to stay with us and do my hairs. Daddy and Kevin are terrible with my hairs. Just look at me!" She giggled and shook her head like a wet dog. I scooped her up and smooched her fat little cheeks. She snuggled into my chest and I buried my face in her sweet smelling "hairs."

"I think you look beautiful. Daddy and Kevin didn't do such a bad job."

"I know. Kevin said I be beautiful even if I have no hairs at all," she screeched with delight, and plastered wet kisses all over my face.

Glancing up, I felt eyes on me. Luke stood motionless on the other side of the room, watching me with Bella. The look on his face was one I'd never seen . . . a mix of longing and desire. I turned away. Way too much to handle at the moment. If he thought . . .

"Okay, everybody out. Give Shoshanna a hug and then haul ass out of here," Steve yelled over the din.

"Daddy said *ass*. That means butt," Bella squealed as Devon tried to control his fit of giggles at his father's use of potty words.

"Whoops," Steve said, turning pink. "Daddy owes the jar a quarter."

I stared at the man who was my boss—the ex–Navy Seal who had seen as many horrifying things as I had, probably more. He was blushing because he'd said ass in front of his children. He was going to put a quarter in a jar. He was married to a person he loved and he had a normal life. Was he proof that it could be done? That it could work?

I snuck a peek at Luke, who was watching the scene unfold as closely as I was. I wasn't sure if I could really ever get out . . . how could he be so sure? Or was he struggling too?

"Get your sorry hineys out of my house," Shoshanna grunted, pulling one of her thousand-pound suitcases toward the door. "Son of a biscuit, these weigh a ton. Mitch and Jack, take these out to the car for me, will ya?"

The guys took her cases and the gals followed them out. Kevin and Steve had a quick word and the house was almost quiet. I was quite impressed by Shoshanna's ability to curb her mouth in front of the kids. I wouldn't have called that one. Devon and Bella had tackled her and tickled her while she tickled them back. Devon seemed like such a happy, normal little seven-year-old when his mother wasn't present. Again, I hoped Steve and Kevin would somehow be able to get custody. As a gay couple, I knew they had an uphill battle. What was wrong with the world that a stable, loving, two-father family wasn't good enough, but an insane religious zealot with a vendetta, who didn't give a crap about her kids, was okay? I sighed and realized I couldn't fix that one. Kevin peeled the kids off a very happy Shoshanna and made his good-byes.

"I'll be home in an hour or so," Steve told him. "Just have to recap and brief Luke and Candy."

"Take your time. We're going to the mall to buy hair bows for the princess and a video game for the master of the house." The kids grinned, grabbed Kevin's hands, and dragged him out the door.

We were all business now, except for Shoshanna, who still thought the whole thing was a game. After leading us to the purple kitchen, Steve got right to it.

"We got another letter," he said, handing both Mitch and me copies.

"Shoshanna, have you seen this?" I asked.

"Oh yeah, they come here. I call Steve, he picks them up, and then you guys freak out."

"What's interesting is that they all say the same thing except for how they're addressed," Luke said, laying several out side by side.

"What the hell are you talking about?" Shoshanna asked, slapping a platter of cheese down on the table. I checked my watch, nine a.m.—entirely too early for cheese. "They all came to my house."

"No, not the envelope, the way they greet you," Luke said sarcastically in reference to the foul names that had been used.

"One hell of a greeting, huh?" Shoshanna laughed. "Cheese?"

We all quickly and politely declined. "Fucking awesome. More for me."

The gist of the notes was the same, except the last two, where death threats had been literally made instead of just implied. It was puzzling that the opening of each letter was different. I ran through the salutations . . . *Trollop, Vicious Whore, Insane Bitch*, and the list went on. Then the letters continued, *Your evil ways will destroy you. Atone before it's too late*. The last two arrived with the real threat . . . *You succeeded, now you die*.

"Have these been sent to the crypto guys at the FBI?" Luke inquired as he continued to stare at them. "We're missing something here."

"Sent them last week and faxed each new one as it came in," Steve replied. "Problem is they're backlogged and we're not priority."

"Jesus, I forgot to pack the Ben Wa balls," Shoshanna gasped, and hightailed it out of the kitchen. We were all silent for a moment. I wondered if anyone was going to touch that . . . Nope. We went on as if nothing unusual had just happened.

"Do we have anyone else that can decode?" I asked, mentally running through the specialties of all the agents I had worked with.

"There are two, but I was a little hesitant to bring them in." Steve dropped his head to his hands. "Because of the death threats, I had no choice. I called this morning. I should hear back from them within the hour."

"You'll have results?" Luke asked, impressed.

"No." Steve laughed without humor. "I'll have their answer as to whether or not they'll take the job."

"What the hell kind of agent has that kind of clout?" I was shocked. You can always debate with Steve, but what he says goes. Always. Luke seemed as surprised as I was.

"These agents are rather left of center. They don't exactly work for me," Steve continued. "They're known for their brilliance and shooting skills as well as their talent for destruction of hotel rooms and the massive expense tabs they incur."

WTF?

"Will they take this project?"

"If they don't, I'll sic Kristy on them. Apparently she scares the shit out of them."

"I'm confused," Luke said. "Kristy, the mild-mannered gal who was here? The one engaged to Mitch?"

"You got it."

"No fucking way." I started to laugh and I couldn't stop. "Those old hags can decipher code?" I gurgled.

"Yes they can." Steve shook his head and ran his hands through his hair.

"Um, still confused here," Luke cut in.

"Your girlfriends," I sputtered, completely freaked out that I was going to have to work with Mrs. C and Edith. "The ones who took you shopping."

Luke blanched. "The dykes?" he whispered, and without conscious thought moved his hand over his crotch for protection.

"Jesus," Steve groused, and gave Luke a glare that made many lose their shit. "What the hell is wrong with you? You don't call a lesbian a fucking dyke."

"Oh yes you do," Luke shot back defensively. "They specifically told me to call them dykes, lesbos, or queers. If I inadvertently used the term rug-muncher or muff-diver, they promised to remove my manbits with a dull butter knife . . . and then feed them to me."

Luke was sweating after that diatribe and Steve looked stricken.

"Sorry, man. I didn't know," Steve choked out.

"I've faced the unimaginable and they scare the shit out of me," Luke murmured as he kept his hand planted firmly on top of his privates.

"They'll take the job," I guaranteed a pale and shaken Steve. A man could go to war, but threaten his jewels and he became a little girl . . .

"How do you know?"

"I know because they worship the ground that Shoshanna walks on. They will take an obscene amount of pleasure in permanently eliminating anything or anyone that is a threat to Shoshanna."

"Okay great," Steve said, slowly regaining his authority and his color.

"Jesus," Luke groaned. "Will they be staying with us?"

Shit, I hadn't even thought about that.

"No, not initially. I'll need them here for a few days. I guess," Steve lowered his voice in terror. "I'll have them work out of my office until they find something."

"Will you be coming up?" I asked Steve.

"Possibly, but I want to stay on top of the forensics guys and monitor the house and the university."

I nodded and wondered what the coming week was going to hold. I'd be dressed like a rubber hooker and Luke would look like a male stripper from a gay biker bar. Shoshanna would be doling out vibrators with her likeness on them and the lesbians were going to get their wish to attend SCREW-Con. Unfortunately, they'd be locked and loaded and that was a scary picture. I didn't doubt their expertise. I'd have their back and I knew they'd have mine . . . I just didn't know if I could be around them for that long without trying to kill them myself.

"Candy—" Steve looked up from an incoming text. "You were right. They're in one hundred percent. And who's Mag the Hag?"

Luke laughed and I rolled my eyes. "Long, fucked-up story that only proves the old biddies are more insane that we thought."

"Do I need to hear it? Does it pertain?"

"Nope, but I can tell you."

"Or I can," Luke chimed in happily.

"I'm putting myself on a need-to-know basis. If I don't need to know, then I don't want to hear. You got it?"

"Yes, sir." I grinned and saluted him.

"I'm out of here. You have me on speed dial. I want you to check in periodically during the day and night till we get this solved."

"Roger that," Luke said, taking a piece of cheese and then deciding against it.

"I guess we should get going," I said, getting up from the table to give Steve a quick hug.

"Not looking like that you're not," Shoshanna informed us as she bounced back into the kitchen with an armload of what I assumed to be multicolored Ben Wa balls. "Steve, grab a shopping bag from under the sink before I drop all the vag-balls and make a mess. You two"—she nodded at me and Luke—"need to get changed into your work clothes."

"It's a six-hour drive," I griped. "There's no way I can sit in a rubber skirt for six hours."

"Then put on the leather shit," she reasoned, shoving Steve out the back door with the Ben Wa balls. "Steve, put them in the front and then lock it. I'll be damned if someone's gonna steal my balls."

She turned back to us and raised her eyebrows. "Move it. We got a Con to get to!"

"Fine," I groaned.

"I don't know if I can do this," Luke said as he followed me out of the room.

"What? The job?" I asked, shocked.

"No. The fucking clothes." He laughed.

"At least we'll look like idiots together," I told him, taking his hand in mine and going to our suitcases.

"Fucking awesome," he muttered.

I couldn't have agreed more.

Chapter 17

"Absolutely not," Luke choked out. "You are not fucking wearing that."

"You think I want to look like this?" I snapped as quietly as I could, just in case Eagle Ears Shoshanna was in hearing range. I felt like an ass in tight black leather pants and a matching corset. "I'd rather chew glass and swallow it. And if you think I'm overjoyed that you're wearing *that,* you're on crack," I hissed, referring to his leather pants and shirtless ensemble.

"Are you kidding me?" He rolled his eyes and yanked at the chains around his neck. "I look like one of the fucking Village People."

I bit back a laugh and had to agree.

"Put a jacket over that. I will beat the hell out of anybody who looks at your tits. Those are mine."

"Um, no . . . actually they're mine," I informed him sternly and tried to tuck my overflowing bosom back into the corset. I secretly loved his he-man possessiveness, but I wasn't about to let him know that. "You're gonna have to let that 'tude go. This is tame compared to some of my other outfits."

Luke leaned back and banged his head on the wall. "These clothes do not bode well for me not being able to screw you blind," he said, closing his eyes to get away from my boobs.

I giggled and realized he had a fine point. This was going to be difficult. His shirtless state made my fingers itch to touch him . . . shove him down . . . and stick my tongue down his throat. Tearing my eyes from his pretty parts was hellish, but necessary. We had a job to do—a serious job and my overactive, underused sex drive had no place in the equation.

"We can do this," I told him, trying to convince myself as well. "We will do this. Come on, let's go."

"You have to swear to God and the Minnesota Vikings you will come to that island with me, or I'll drag you into one of the purple rooms in this house and do what I want."

"Oh my God," I gasped. "This isn't our house. It's Shoshanna's. That is just wrong."

"Are you kidding me?" He laughed. "She would have no problem whatsoever with that. She'd probably stand outside the door and take notes. Island. Promise. Now."

"Fine." I rolled my eyes and my insides danced with anticipation. "Island. Yes. Now move." I walked away and he groaned. He'd clearly gotten a good look at my bottom, which was molded into my leather pants within an inch of its life. I gave my hips an extra swing and heard some lovely swearing. God help us all . . .

The SUV was big and black with tinted windows.

"Is this fucker bulletproof?" Shoshanna asked with delight.

"Yep," Luke answered, getting into the driver's seat.

"Hey, I wanna drive," Shoshanna whined. I'd heard about Shoshanna's driving skills from Rena and there was no way in hell she was going anywhere close to the driver's seat.

"We're not insured for you to drive," I explained, giving Luke a look so he wouldn't contradict me. "It's a company car, so we have to comply with regulations." I thought that sounded pretty good, and Shoshanna, while not happy, seemed satisfied.

"Actually, it's mine," Luke said, and I pinched his leg. Finally getting my drift, he quickly added, "But I'm the only one insured to drive it. Plus I'm a guy with a dick, so I have control issues and have to do all the driving. Always."

My mouth hung open as I attempted to figure out if he was serious and decided he was. We would have problems in life . . . of that I was sure.

"Got to love a guy with a dick," Shoshanna cackled behind us.

This was going to be a long ride.

"So Luke," Shoshanna yelled from the back, making me wince, "what the hell is your deal?"

"And by that you would mean what?" he replied.

Holy hell, it occurred to me that I didn't know his deal—at all.

Did he have a family? Where did he grow up? Did he really even live in Minnesota? What was his favorite color? Favorite food? Favorite position? Well, I did kind of know that one . . .

"Ya know, ex-wives, criminal records, love children. The usual," she said, and I choked on my spit.

"None of that." He chuckled and my grip on the dashboard loosened. *When had I grabbed the dash?*

"Family?" she prodded. He clearly didn't want to talk about himself. This was the first time I truly appreciated Shoshanna's pushy behavior. "Mother, father, brothers, sisters?"

"None of the above," he answered in a clipped tone.

"What the hell, were you hatched by aliens?"

"You're not going to shut up, are you?" Luke asked the little gnat in the backseat.

"Nope." She grinned, leaning forward.

"Fine." Luke blew out a frustrated sigh. "Put your goddamned seat belt back on and I'll talk."

"I don't wear them. I find them to be constipating."

"I find them to save lives, so put it on. Now." He spoke to her like a child and she obeyed like a child and then stuck her tongue out at him . . . like a child.

"If I have poop-shoot problems, it's going to be your fault," she warned him. "I'll make your life a living hell."

"I'll take my chances."

I hadn't uttered a word. I was as curious as Shoshanna, probably more—but I refused to chime in. Just as I didn't want to know if he was under the crazy assumption that he might be in love with me, I wasn't sure I wanted all the dirty details of his life. Was that why I hadn't asked? Was it fear?

"I'm in my family's business," he stated flatly, without emotion. "My parents had me and weren't quite sure what to do with a baby, so for the first part of my life I lived in Minnesota with my grandparents."

"Is that where you live now?" Shoshanna queried.

"I live in their house, but they passed back when I was in high school."

"I'm sorry," she said, patting him on the back and laying her little head on his shoulder.

"Shoshanna. Seat belt," he snapped.

"Goddammit," she muttered. "Didn't think you would notice."

"Unless you have a neck as long as a giraffe, there's no way not to notice."

"Point!" she yelled. "So then did you go to your mom and dad?"

He was quiet and I realized this was a touchy subject. He glanced over at me and I gave him a little smile. He took a deep breath and kept talking.

"I've lived everywhere and I don't remember most of it. My parents were far better assassi . . . agents than they were parents. I was a prop and somewhat of a nuisance to them. They got blown away on a mission when I was sixteen, so I came back here. I inherited my grandparents' estate and also my parents' estate along with their island and their myriad of homes around the world. The end."

Wait, what? Was that the island he wanted to take me to?

"Holy fucking shit." Shoshanna whistled and threw herself at the back of Luke's head in what I guessed was a show of sympathy, but his surprise on her impact almost caused us to crash.

"Seat belt," Luke and I shouted. Shoshanna slunk back to her seat and fastened her belt.

"Sweet Mother Mary in a miniskirt," Shoshanna exploded, never one to let being chastised get her down. "You're fucking Batman."

"Nope. I'm fucking Candy."

"Oh my God," I hissed, and punched his arm. "Shut. Up."

"Seriously," Shoshanna said with a laugh and leaned forward, yet again. "You're an orphan who's richer than shit and you fight crime! You're fucking Batman."

It was hard to argue her logic . . . but he was loaded? He owned an island? I mean I did well for myself since I seldom ever did anything that required money. I'd been able to buy and pay off my cute little house and pay my bills, but I certainly wasn't rich. Never really wanted to be.

"Do you have an Alfred?" she demanded, totally into her superhero theory.

"No. No Alfred." Luke heaved a put-upon sigh and shook his head. I suppose he was thinking this was going to be a long ride too.

"Do you have anyone?" she asked quietly.

Luke stole a quick glance at me and then looked away before I had the chance to look away first. "Maybe," he answered Sho-shanna. "I hope so."

Fuuuuck, this was a ton of pressure I hadn't expected or wanted. My stomach churned and my hands clenched to fists. How in the hell was I supposed to be all things to someone when I couldn't even be that to myself? He was asking too much. I rolled down the window to get some fresh air to clear the tsunami inside my head. My face felt hot and my body felt cold . . . A large warm hand crept over and took mine. My balled-up fists relaxed and a sense of calm immediately washed over me. I turned to him, startled by my reaction, and he just smiled that beautiful smile and winked. He knew.

"Goddamn, you two were made for each other. You remind me of me and my Herm, God rest his soul. He was the whole package and he had quite a package if you know what I mean. I used to call him Mr. Wonderpecker."

I did not want to hear anything about Herm's pecker and I certainly wasn't up for answering questions about Luke's, *as impressive as it was,* so I quickly changed the subject. "Shoshanna, I read in your files that you have a daughter."

"I do. Her name is Sue Junior and she's a rocket scientist."

I waited for the punch line . . . it didn't come.

"Really?"

"Yep," she said proudly. "She's smarter than a whip, but as socially awkward as I'm profane. I keep hoping for some grandkids, but she told me she thought passing down our DNA was a bad idea."

"Oookay." I was still stuck on the fact that her daughter was a rocket scientist.

"Anyhoo, I've got Steve's kids to dote on when they're not with his nasty bitch of an ex-wife, but I am lonely."

"You have tons of friends and people who adore you," I said, feeling the need to fix her.

"Oh God yeah, and I love them too, just like family, but it's different when you lose your other half. Herm's been gone almost nine years and I miss him every day."

"I'm sorry," Luke said.

"Nope. Don't be sorry. I had love—the real kind—and I had it for a long time. Herm loved everything about me. He loved that I could use the word fuck as a noun, a verb, and an adjective in a single sentence." She chuckled. "All my qualities that Sue Junior finds appalling are the things Herm adored."

I stared straight ahead. If I spoke, I was afraid I would either cry or profess my undying love to Luke. Neither would be appropriate at the moment. Shoshanna was explaining what I was feeling, not the use of the word fuck part, but the fact that Luke found all the things about me that I thought were relationship deal-breakers to be assets. How was it that a tiny, foul-mouthed, Porno Granny was making my life make sense? How was it that she was *strumming my pain with her fingers and singing my life with her words*? And what in the hell was the name of that stupid song?

"You're daughter's wrong," Luke told her. "Your DNA is outstanding and I would be honored if you were my mother, creative use of the F-word and all."

"Goddammit," she groused. "Now I'm gonna cry, you son-of-a-bitch. I'll tell you what, when we get back to Minneapolis, I'll adopt you. I'll have my lawyer draw up the paperwork this week and you can meet your sister Sue Junior at Christmas. Maybe you can talk some sense into your sister's head, because I sure as hell can't."

Luke was speechless and I coughed to cover my burst of laughter. She was serious—as a heart attack. I had a feeling no matter what Luke said, he was getting a new mama.

"Um, Shoshanna, I . . ." Luke began.

"It's Mama," she corrected him. "Now since you're working, I'll let you call me Shoshanna, but in private it's Mama and I won't hear any back talk. You understand?"

"Um . . ."

"Good," she shouted, cutting him off again. "I have always wanted a goddamned son. Getting death threats has turned out to be fucking awesome."

Flabbergasted best described Luke, and I could no longer hold back my giggles. He glanced over at me with a look that screamed "what am I supposed to do?" and I lost it.

"I don't know what the hell you're laughing at, little missy," Shoshanna sang from the backseat. "I'm gonna be your mother-in-law."

That shut me up fast, and now it was Luke's turn to enjoy himself. I racked my brain for a comeback, but Shoshanna was a last word kind of gal. I decided saying nothing would be my safest bet.

"So kids," she continued as if she hadn't just dropped several nuclear bombs, "I have a goody bag for you." She hoisted a large hot pink bag over the seat. "I need some shut-eye and if I keep this shittin' seat belt on, I'm gonna fart in my sleep. And trust me, that would be bad for everyone." She took off her seat belt, lay down, and started snoring within seconds.

We drove in silence and listened to Shoshanna snore. Several times I tried to find my balls and start a conversation, but the words got stuck in my throat.

"You don't have any questions for me?" Luke inquired, noticing my latest aborted attempt to speak.

"Um, yes, but I don't know where to start."

"Anywhere. Start anywhere."

"You're loaded."

"Yep. I'm loaded. I could care less about that since most of it's blood money, but it doesn't suck not having to worry about paying bills. I've given a shit-ton of it away, but it just never seems to run out."

"You have an island?" It was difficult to absorb. I had never met anyone who had a freakin' island.

"Yep and that's where you've agreed to go with me."

"Does anyone live on it?" What in the hell was this conversation? It felt like a cheesy Lifetime movie where the poor girl finds out the dude she's been doing the nasty with is a sheik.

"Caretakers. I haven't been there in about two years. I assume it's still there." He grinned and waited for me to scream.

"I can't date a bagillionaire," I stammered. "I live in a tiny house and I like it. I love outlet malls and Target. I don't own a ball gown and I don't ever use more than one fork even when they put out two at a restaurant. I shoot people and I don't fit in to polite society. I have shitty people skills and you should probably find an heiress or someone who has some designer shoes."

"Do I look like someone who grew up with a silver spoon in his mouth?" he asked.

I stared at the floorboard, still finding reasons this could never work.

"I grew up in hell. My grandparents were good people, but they were old when I was a child. My parents didn't want me, but eventually had no choice. I didn't spend my youth in boarding schools playing cricket and eating caviar. I was witness to things a kid should never see. They fucking used me as bait for drug lords and a child sex slave ring. I saw more blood and death by the time I was eighteen than most people see in ten lifetimes. I don't own a tux. I don't use six forks. I drink beer out of the bottle and I want you in my life. Permanently."

"I . . ."

"I'm not finished. You are the only woman who has made me stop and want things that I thought were unreasonable and impossible. I started to care if I died and I didn't hate the fact that I had a chalet in France because I've imagined bringing you there a hundred times. You're as fucked up as I am and I mean that as a compliment. You're everything I never thought I could find and I've decided to keep you."

"Do I have a choice?" I whispered, trying to suppress my delight. He passed all the tests I didn't even know I needed him to take. He was broken, but strong and beautiful and good . . . and I wanted him.

"No, you don't." He grinned, relief at my tone softened his features. "Besides you already made your choice back at Shoshanna's purple abode."

"You mean your mama's house?" I teased.

"Was she serious?" he asked, still totally thrown by Shoshanna's edict.

"I'm pretty sure she was." I glanced back at the sleeping Shoshanna and smiled. She was beautiful and I think Luke was secretly moved by her offer. Not that he'd actually take her up on it . . . but in the end, he might not have a choice. She was a force of nature.

"I need a lighter subject," he said, popping on some sunglasses that made him look hotter than he already was. "What's in the bag?"

"I'm not sure we want to know." I reached in and extracted the first thing my hand touched—a supersized vibrator with a smiling Shoshanna on it. "Oh shit," I gasped, and dropped it on Luke's lap. He glanced down and blanched.

"Tell me I'm not seeing what I think I'm seeing," he begged.

"What do you think you're seeing?" I asked on the verge of hysterics.

"I think I see my mama on a vibrator," he snorted.

"That's exactly what you see. Welcome to your new family," I squealed, unable to hold it back any longer. I didn't know if I'd ever be able to use a vibrator again. Shoshanna's smiling face on the vibrating part was seared into my brain. Years of therapy couldn't erase that image.

"Help me Jesus," Luke laughed.

I'm not sure how long we laughed, but it was cathartic. All the tension and fear of what might come was gone for the moment. I was happy and my stomach muscles ached from laughing. I put the bag on the floor; we could check out the other items later. Reaching over, I took Luke's hand in mine and we rode the rest of the way in silence, listening to the loud, but lovely snores of his mama.

Chapter 18

I didn't know what to expect of SCREW-Con, but it certainly wasn't this. Hundreds of bizarrely clad people roamed the atrium lobby of the Marriott. Conversations were loud and animated and everyone appeared happy and excited. Some wore leather and chains, some had on sweatpants and T-shirts, and some looked like regular Joes off the street. The main problem, from a protection standpoint, was the sheer number of people. This was a clusterfuck. Keeping Shoshanna safe was going to be difficult at best. I glanced over at Luke, who assessed the crowd and kept Shoshanna slightly behind him. I moved in and flanked her back.

"I love this," Shoshanna shouted, trying to hug a few fans.

The moment she spoke, she was rushed. She was a rock star and a goddess in this group. My hand went to the weapon in my purse, but I wisely didn't pull it. Luke stepped up and raised his voice.

"Back off, everyone. Shoshanna is delighted to see you all, but she has, um . . . strep throat and is contagious," he informed the excited crowd.

"Oh my goodness," a gal in head-to-toe black leather cried out. "You feel better, Shoshanna! We love you!"

"In a show of love and support for Shoshanna LeHump, I'd like to ask everyone to raise their hands in the air and keep them there until Shoshanna leaves the room."

I shot Luke a glance. What was he doing? The crowd looked ridiculous, but we could see their hands . . . and the fact that no one held a weapon. He was brilliant.

"Fucking awesome," Shoshanna shouted, raising her own little arms high. "This will be our new move."

The crowd roared with approval and began waving their arms

back and forth to a melody only they could hear. Keeping my eyes
wide open, I carefully monitored the mass of groupies. They all
complied with Luke's rule and seemed to enjoy it immensely. It
was a hell of a lot easier to keep Shoshanna from getting shot this
way.

"Shoshanna, when does the new book come out?" a hefty gal in
green rubber yelled from the back.

"In two weeks, but I brought a whole bunch of early release
copies for you guys," Shoshanna bellowed back, causing a deafening roar from the crowd.

"Who's the shirtless hottie with you?" another rubber- and
feather-covered woman asked, leering at Luke.

"He's my new cover model. His name is Duke LeHump and he's
hotter than Satan's fucking underpants." She slapped her soon to be
son on his ass and the crowd went nuts. Luke was still processing
that his new name was Duke LeHump and clearly didn't register
that his mom had just smacked his butt. If I wasn't so busy scanning for killers, I would have dropped to the floor in hysterics.

"Is he a relation?" Someone with a squeaky high voice wanted
to know.

"He's my son," Shoshanna crowed. "But don't tell anyone," she
begged the crowd of at least one hundred and fifty. "The adoption
isn't final yet."

Again, the hordes roared with laughter, thinking it was a joke . . .
little did they know.

"What about the girl? She's a hottie too," a huge man sporting
man-boobs and a fuschia brassiere demanded. "I want her outfit.
It's so me!"

Luke's head shot to the man. His possessiveness was going to
have to stop. His focus should be Shoshanna and Shoshanna only.
He visibly relaxed when he saw the size and outfit choice of my admirer.

"She's my assistant," Shoshanna crowed with pride. I held my
breath and waited to hear what my name was going to be. Why
hadn't we had the foresight to figure this out before it became
Shoshanna's lone decision . . . "Her name is Mandy Dandermanschmidt and she is the bomb!"

WTF?

"Okay everyone," Luke called out to the crowd. "We have to get

Shoshanna settled in. Just keep your hands in the air until you can't see her anymore."

"Anything for you, Duke LeHump," purred a gal who was seventy if she was a day, flirting openly with Luke.

"Wait!" Shoshanna grabbed a bag and started hurling Ben Wa balls at the crowd. "Grow some balls!"

The crowd shrieked with delight and dove for the shower of balls bouncing around the lobby. Luke grabbed Shoshanna, picked her up, and made for the elevators. I followed close behind, keeping my hand securely attached to my gun.

I noticed a group of ridiculously handsome scantily clad men being pawed by a group of overzealous gals about thirty feet from the elevator as we waited. The men huddled together like a heard of frightened cows in a thunderstorm. They tried to hold on to their clothing as the randy ladies tore bits free for souvenirs.

"What in the hell is happening over there?" I asked, feeling sorry for the guys.

Shoshanna glanced over. "Oh, those are the cover models. They'll be your competition in the pageant," she told Luke. "Sweet baby Moses in a basket, that does seem a little out of control," she muttered.

Luke glanced over and blanched. "Shit." He looked up to the heavens for intervention but none came. I grinned, but I actually did feel his pain. "Where in the hell is the elevator?"

"Hang on." Shoshanna slipped out of Luke's arms and hustled over to the involuntary strip show. She stuck her fingers in her mouth and let loose with the shrillest and loudest whistle I'd ever heard rip. I was sure the people standing closest to her would sustain significant hearing damage. "Ladies," she shouted at the stunned and temporarily deaf group. "I realize these men are panty-melting hot, but they are human beings and we will not objectify them the way men have objectified us for hundreds of years. We will admire their beauty, their greased pecs, and their tight asses, but we will also honor their brains and talents. We will not rip their clothes off. That is rude and I'm fairly sure illegal. Now step back and let me meet these lovely and well-built hunks."

She made her way through the now contrite crowd to the seriously grateful pretty boys.

"Thank you," the one who resembled a Greek god gasped. His

blond hair, tanned skin, and blue eyes were silly gorgeous. He was joined by what appeared to be the most muscle-bound and sexy Hispanic twins I'd ever laid eyes on. Of course there was no missing the man with hair flowing to his waist and a body to die for . . . and the African American hottie with the rockin' bod and eyes that could make you melt and the . . .

"Put your tongue back in your mouth," Luke hissed in my ear while eyeing the crowd for trouble. This new pack of women weren't aware of the *Shoshanna hands in the air move* and Luke was taking no chances. "You're mine and if you flirt with even one of them, I'll shoot him."

I choked on my laughter and elbowed him as I scanned the perimeter of the crowd for newcomers. "You will not shoot anyone other than a bad guy," I told him. "And I will hazard a guess that most of those insanely beautiful men bat for the other team. Soooooooo, maybe I should be warning you."

"Funny," he grumbled.

"What are your names?" Shoshanna asked the boys.

"Jim," the Greek god replied, shaking Shoshanna's hand.

"Cesar and Cheech," the steamy Latin twins answered, kissing Shoshanna's hands.

"Teddy," Mr. Sexy Hair chimed in.

"Rocky," the mocha-skinned beauty added, bowing to his savior Shoshanna.

"Well goddamn if you're not a pretty bunch! I brought my own model too. Wave to Duke LeHump," she instructed her new buddies. "He's my son and has a wonder ass."

The men nodded in agreement and dutifully waved at Luke, who shook his head and closed his eyes.

"He's a little shy, but he twerks like a motherfucker!"

There was an audible moan of agony from Luke and the ladies shrieked with glee.

"I challenge you to a twerk-off," Teddy, the hair dude, shouted at Luke. Teddy's eyes narrowed, and he gyrated his hips to punctuate his point or show off his package . . . I wasn't sure which. Good God, he was serious.

"This is fucked," Luke muttered under his breath. "If he challenges me again, I'll have to shoot him. Actually if he looks at me again, I'll shoot him."

Was his solution to everything to shoot it? Wait . . . that was my solution. Shit. "Um, no. That won't really help anything. Look, if you play along, I'll give you a blow job later." I said the first thing that came to my mind and boy, was it a doozy. I knew he was serious about shooting Hair Teddy, so I had to distract him . . . who was I kidding? I was dying to go down on him and had found an excellent excuse to be a hooker.

Luke was speechless, but the huge grin that practically split his face made me giggle. "Deal?" I asked innocently.

"Oh my hell, yes," he hissed. "Grab Shoshanna, we're out of here."

I moved in to pick up Shoshanna if necessary while Luke covered me. I hustled her back to the elevator just as the doors opened. Miraculously we were the only ones who got on.

"This is gonna be great!" Shoshanna bounced up and down like a Ben Wa ball as Luke and I relaxed for the first time since entering the hotel.

"You have the keys to all the rooms?" he asked.

"Yup." I held up the bunch and handed him his. "Shoshanna, you have a panel in an hour. Let's go relax for a bit and make some plans. I want to check in with Steve."

"Sounds good. I'm gonna register Duke for the pageant online. I'm a VIP so we can bypass all the bullshit lines."

"About that . . ." Luke snapped.

"Look, I should have checked with you guys about the names, but they were the first things that came to mind and I figured you didn't want to use your real ones, being that this is a covert operation and all." She still hadn't stopped bouncing and I had to smile despite the fact that my new last name was Dandermanschmidt . . . I did have it better than Duke LeHump.

Luke simply gave up and ignored the new name and twerk-off altogether. "Check on the dykes' progress," he told me.

"What dykes?" Shoshanna asked, confused.

"Mrs. C and Edith are decoding the notes," I said, assuming she knew of the gals. Everybody else did.

"Holy shitfire on a hemorrhoid." She laughed. "Those nut jobs make my mouth look clean! Love those girls."

Girls was pushing it, considering Mrs. C and Edith had to be in their seventies, but she did have a point. I cringed at the thought they would be here in a couple of days. Luke's color had paled considerably and I guessed he was thinking the same thing I was.

"I have the hotel plans," he stated, all business—this was the part he could handle. "We'll take Shoshanna through the employee corridors. We'll use the service elevators and avoid crowds as much as possible."

"Good thinking." Shoshanna nodded her head and kept bouncing. "Oh, Candy, have you ever had a Brazilian wax?"

"Um . . ." How was it that half the stuff that flew out of her mouth rendered me speechless?

"Yes." Luke grinned. "She has."

The heat raced up my neck and landed on my cheeks, which I knew were now a flaming red. I was going to kill him and he'd just lost his blow job privileges.

"Are you in the market for one?" Shoshanna inquired, oblivious to my embarrassed fury. "Because they're doing them on level C. They'll even do little hearts or airplanes."

Mute. I was mute. Nothing would come out. I shot Luke a look that implied if he said anything, I would pull my gun out of my purse and shoot him. He grinned and wisely stayed quiet.

"No, I'm good," I croaked, forcing words to come out.

"I was thinking about getting one, but having the hair ripped off my vag when no one but me is gonna see it just seems like a waste," she reasoned. "What about you, Luke?"

"He probably should," I said before he could decline. "I mean what if his pants fall down during the twerk-off? It would be nice if he was all spiffy and tidy." I grinned evilly at him.

"She's got a point," Shoshanna agreed.

"There will be no twerking," Luke ground out. "I don't even know what the hell that means. I'm not doing any fucking pageant and I'm not getting my balls waxed. Period. End of story."

"Oh come on," Shoshanna said, giving him a hug. "You have to do the pageant. It will reflect badly on me if my son doesn't support his mother. You can keep your hairy balls, but you have to do the pageant. Please?"

"Fine," he huffed, "but I will not twerk, whatever the hell that is. And since I am going to do something that I will never be able to live down in this century, you will do everything I tell you to do this week. No questions asked. Deal?"

"Deal. But you know, twerking isn't hard. I'll pull up a video in the room."

It was going to be an interesting week.

Chapter 19

"So they did what?" I asked Steve, holding my cell phone away from my ear due to the fact he was screaming.

"They made twenty copies of all the notes, pinned them up all over my office, and shot at them," he bellowed.

"They opened fire in your office?" I was shocked and actually surprised. "What did they hope to accomplish by that?"

"I have no fucking idea, but the local cops showed up and cleared the building. Those insane dykes hid in the air vents and are still in the goddamned building," he grumbled.

"Do you think they just wanted some privacy?" I asked.

"They could have just asked," he shouted. "This was the stupidest fucking idea I've ever had. They are complete menaces."

Luke sat across the room and listened to our conversation. He could have been in the other room and heard it, Steve was so loud.

"If they don't figure this out, I will have them wiped off of every known roster that exists and then I'll kill them."

"Can you do that?" I asked.

"What, kill them?"

"No. Wipe their identity off the face of the earth."

"Of course I can," he huffed. "And if they keep this shit up, I will."

Damn, I didn't know Steve had that much power, but Luke apparently did. He sat quietly and didn't move. Was that what had happened to him? That was awful.

"Before the firestorm, had they found anything?"

"Yeah," Steve said, calming down. "Something about the order of the notes is important. They were onto something and then they opened fire and shut the fucking building down."

"What are you going to do?" I asked. My eyes were drawn across the room to Luke, who had eased his leather pants down and was sitting with his dick in the wind. I gasped and laughed. What the hell was he doing and where was Shoshanna? I vaguely heard the shower running as Steve described in great detail what he'd like to do to the sisters, but I couldn't focus on anything except the happy camper that Luke had released from his pants.

"I think you owe me something," he said softly.

"What's that?" Steve yelled over the phone.

"Nothing. I just have to get ready to go. Call you later."

I hung up on my boss and raised an eyebrow at Duke LeHump.

"Come here, Candy," he said in a voice that brooked no bullshit, and I almost fainted. My nipples hardened and a dance started in my lower abdomen. How did the man do this to me?

"We might get caught," I said as I crossed the room and got down on my knees.

"Isn't that half the fun?"

"You think having your mother catch me going down on you would be fun?" I teased.

"Look, I never went to normal high school or had a normal date or made out in the backseat of a car when I was a teenager . . . the least you could do is suck my dick while my mom is in the shower."

"Oh my God." I burst out laughing. I knew part of what he'd said was serious and it made my heart hurt, but the fact he was now referring to Shoshanna as his mom was hilarious. "I suppose I could help you out."

I leaned in and took him in my hand. He was hard and smooth and perfect. I ran my tongue around the head of his cock and licked the small drop of pre-cum. He was salty and delicious. His head dropped back on the chair and he moaned his approval. His hands death-gripped the arms of the chair as I slid him into my mouth. His hips began an involuntary pumping motion as I took him deeper in my throat. God, I adored this man and I loved what I could do to him. His strong hands wrapped themselves into my hair, guiding me to his needs. Picking up my pace and realizing I would need to change my panties, I went to town using my hands, my tongue, and my lips.

"Jesus, Candace," he hissed. "You are killing me. Faster, baby. God yeah, just like that."

"So guys, you ready? I just need to pee and then we can sneak down to my panel," Shoshanna bellowed from the bathroom. I almost choked on Luke's dick . . .

I quickly disengaged as he yanked up his pants. I ran across the room and sat nonchalantly on the bed.

"Lipstick," he told me frantically.

"What?" I whispered loudly.

"Fix your lipstick. It's all over your chin."

"Shit." I grabbed a tissue from the box by the bed and scrubbed. "Better?"

"Yes, but my hairy balls are killing me. I'm not sure I can walk."

"Well Mr. I Want to Get Caught by My Mom, you're going to have to."

"If I pulled down my pants right now, they'd be blue," he groaned.

"What's blue?" Shoshanna asked as she made her entrance. Holy shit, and what an entrance it was. She was decked from head to toe in purple leather with Minnesota Vikings decals placed strategically over her body. Her leather was nowhere as skintight as mine—*thank God*, but it was fitted and alarming.

"Nothing is blue," I told her.

"Right," Luke muttered under his breath.

"That's an outfit," I said, hoping I sounded complimentary.

"Thanks," she preened. "It's new. I normally just wear my sweats, but I figured since I was making you two lovebirds dress up, I should too."

"What do you mean by lovebirds?" I demanded, wondering if I hadn't got all the stray lipstick off.

"Nothing." She grinned and waggled her eyebrows. "Come on, kids. I have a nipple clamp demonstration to do."

We'd apparently been busted after all . . .

We made it to the conference room without incident. Luke was walking slightly bent over, but that was his own damn fault. The minute we hit the room, the entire audience of at least two hundred raised their hands in the air. Word had clearly traveled fast.

"Hello, my Street Walkers," Shoshanna greeted her fans. Her legions of fans had named themselves *Shoshanna's Street Walkers* and they were an obsessed and rabid group. They had online chat rooms and LeHump clubs all over the country. Shoshanna often visited and lunched with her fans. She adored them as much as they adored her.

The crowd chanted her name as she took her place at the front of the room. Grinning, she sat on the table, kicking her little legs back and forth and waiting for the din to die down.

"I am delighted to be here and I can't believe how many of you came."

"We love you!" someone shouted from the back of the room.

"I love you too," she yelled back . . . and the room went nuts. I glanced over at Luke and he shrugged. She had rock star status here. It was amazing.

"Okay, calm down." She laughed. "The panel today was supposed to be about fetish wear, but I thought a demonstration of how to correctly use nipple clamps might be fun." The Street Walkers chattered excitedly.

"Now, I want you to remember that trust and a partner you can communicate with is imperative. What else are you supposed to have?" she asked her minions.

"A safe word," a gal in the front said.

"That's right, and what else?"

"After care?" a timid man on the side said.

"Absolutely," Shoshanna said, giving him a thumbs-up. "But you also need education, and I can't stress enough that you need to communicate. Everything that you do must be safe and consensual. Always."

"Do you live the lifestyle, Shoshanna?"

"Nope, but I've studied it and taken classes with some outstanding Doms. Of course, when my Herm was alive, we did like a little spanky-spanky and a little tie me up action, but it was mild compared to what some others enjoy."

"Are Haven and Michael going to have their baby?" someone called out.

Haven and Michael? Who in the hell were they?

"I don't want to spoil anything, but . . . YES," she shouted excitedly. "And Donna and Bruce are going to have a huge misunderstanding and JoJo will play a large part in that little issue."

"Oh my God," exclaimed a woman with a multicolored Mohawk. "I don't think JoJo is a good influence. How can you do that to Donna and Bruce? Haven't they been through enough already?" she demanded, pissed off. Luke stepped toward Shoshanna and she shooed him away.

Good Lord, they were talking about fictional characters. I thought they were discussing real people . . . wait, they were real people to them. Shoshanna was such a gifted writer that she gave her characters life and all these people were emotionally invested in her creations.

"It's okay, Duke. Rose, here, is right," she said, referring to the Mohawked fan. "Rose, you have to understand that Bruce and Donna are damaged, and to give them an easy happily-ever-after isn't realistic and isn't fair to them or you. They'll have to work for it and their journey will be fraught with misunderstanding and heartache. Nothing worth it is easy. Hell, Herm was dating my sister when we met, and let me tell you, that was a clusterfuck."

"What happened?" I asked, unable to stop myself.

"Well—" Shoshanna smiled ruefully. "I knew my sister wasn't crazy about him, so I challenged her to a game of poker for him. I kicked her ass, she handed him over, and the rest is history. Okay, who wants their nipples clamped?"

We had no clue who was raising their hands, because all their hands were already raised. Shit. And then it got ugly . . .

The chant started in the back and got louder as more of the Street Walkers caught on . . .

"Duke LeHump. Duke LeHump. Duke LeHump."

"Absolutely not." Luke shook his head and stared out at the audience angrily. That did shut a few up in the front. Luke's mean look was scary.

"Pleeeeeeeaaaaaassssssseeeeeeee?" Shoshanna begged him with a sweet little grin on her face—and Luke caved. I think she actually had power over him. The fact that she was insisting on becoming his mother must mean a hell of a lot more than he was letting on.

The next thirty minutes were horrific. It was clearly demonstrated to me that never in my life would I let anyone put pinchers decorated with pink feathers on my nipples. Luke was a good sport, but he left the room with not only blue balls . . . he also had red nipples.

"Come on, guys," Shoshanna said to Luke when it was over. "You have a pageant rehearsal in ten minutes."

Luke froze and I swear he was going to cry. I stepped up behind him and palmed his asstastic butt.

"I'll finish what we started earlier to make up for all this," I promised.

"Blow job and you ride me like a cowboy while you wear the corset and those fuck-me shoes," he bargained.

I paused and considered even though I knew my answer was a resounding yes . . . "I think that works for me," I purred. "But we wait for Shoshanna to go to sleep and we do it across the hall in your room."

"Did you set up monitors in her room?" he asked.

"As soon as we got here. You saw me do it." *Holy shit,* that's how Shoshanna knew we were fooling around . . . all she had to do was glance over at my TV, which I had left on, and she could watch the *Luke and Candy Porno Hour.*

Luke was struck by the look of horror on my face. "Oh hell, she did see us."

"Beware of what you wish for, my friend. Beware." I copped another quick feel of his butt and shoved him out the door, and the three of us went to the first pageant rehearsal . . . from hell.

Chapter 20

Moving quickly through the bowels of the hotel, we made it to the rehearsal without incident. The conference room was enormous, and a stage with a runway that extended out into the audience had been built. A giant glittering silver disco ball hung from the ceiling and wildly colored balloons littered the floor and the stage.

"Don't you love the condoms?" Shoshanna squealed with joy. "I just adore the promotion of safe sex."

"What condoms?" I asked searching the room. Thankfully, it was a small group. It should be easier to keep her safe in here.

"What do you mean what condoms? They're fucking everywhere." She picked up what I'd thought was a balloon and handed it to me. "Lick it. It's flavored."

"No. I'm good," I said, quickly dropping the inflated birth control to the floor.

"You have got to be kidding me," Luke groaned as he took in the room. "I'm a cold-blooded killer not a twerk-happy romance cover model."

"I thought you didn't know what twerking was," I said, stepping over the condoms as we made our way to the front of the room.

"I don't, but it seems to be the *in thing* and I certainly want to fit in," he snapped sarcastically.

"It will be fine, son," Shoshanna consoled him as she hustled on ahead of us.

"Why does she do that?" He shook his head, disgusted with himself. "It's like Catholic guilt. She says something mamma-like and I do whatever she wants."

"Well, I'm Lutheran so the guilt thingie is a little foreign to me, but she is a brilliant professor and clearly has manipulation down pat." I glanced at him. He was lost in thought, halfway pissed off and halfway amused. Some part of him wanted Shoshanna to be his mother and the thought of disappointing her was bugging the shit out of him. He was as unused as I was to needing other people.

A large gal somewhere in her forties cleared her throat. She had pink hair and was covered in tats and wearing a business suit and high tops. "All right, boys. My name is Medusa Schmadden and I'm the pageant coordinator. Everyone strip down to your underpants and let's begin."

Luke turned white and I thought he was going to faint. "I'm not wearing underpants," he practically whimpered. Medusa's eyes narrowed and she stomped over to Luke.

"What's your name?" she demanded.

"Um . . . Duke LeHump."

"The contest contract you signed specifically stated that you would wear underpants to all rehearsals. I don't know how much clearer I have to be. Leave your pants on for today, but I expect to see you in your underpants tomorrow or you can do the rehearsal in the buff. Do you understand?"

"Yes," Luke said with murder shining from his eyes.

Medusa took a shocked step back, turned on her high top, and marched away.

"Hey, Duke-man, she's a total cow-bitch. Don't listen to her. She hasn't been laid in twenty years," the gorgeous hunk named Jim told a furious Luke. "Just ignore her. I do. It pisses her off and she starts to pull her hair out. Last year we were so successful she was partially bald on the right side of her head by the end of the week."

"Do you do these a lot?" I asked Jim. Luke moved quickly and placed his arm around my shoulders, staking his territory. I shot him an annoyed glance. He may as well have peed on me.

"A couple of times a year," he admitted sheepishly. "It's good money on the side. I also do about thirty or forty covers a year."

"What's your regular job?" I liked this guy. He was sweet and funny. My gay-dar was a little confused. I couldn't peg him.

"Can you keep a secret?" He grinned and leaned in. Luke pulled me closer and I had to stifle a laugh.

"Yes. I'm very good at that." I elbowed Luke. He grunted and backed off.

"I'm a writer. I write espionage and adventure mysteries. I'm a wannabe Clive Cussler." He shrugged his massive shoulders and winked.

"That's awesome. Are you published?" I asked as Luke huffed and puffed beside me.

"No, not yet," he admitted, "but I have a great agent and my manuscript is at several of the big publishers as we speak."

"Congratulations," I said. "How is it that you end up doing this?"

"Well, I was going to conventions as a writer to learn, and an agent suggested I try out the cover dude thing while I wrote so I didn't have to have a day job. I did and it worked and here I am."

"Jesus Christ in a bikini," Shoshanna yelled, scaring the hell out of poor pretty Jim. "I love that fucking story. Who's looking at your manuscript right now? Maybe I can give them a call and help that motherfucker along."

"Oh my God," Jim whispered, looking pale beneath his tan. "You would do that? Without reading it?"

"Hell yeah," she grunted, and slapped his ass. "Anyone who would march around in his underpants to have the time to write is a serious writer."

"I think I love you," he said, trapping her in a bear hug. I almost pulled my gun, but realized Jim was practically naked and couldn't be hiding a weapon anywhere. "I have it on my laptop. I'd feel better if you read a couple of chapters before you endorsed me."

"Outstanding!" Shoshanna shouted. "Pull it out, baby, and let me see it."

"There will be none of that," Medusa shrieked, misunderstanding Shoshanna's directive. "I don't care if you are Shoshanna LeHump. I'm the only one who tells these boys what to do."

"Relax your crack, Medusa. I'm talking about his book, not his dick. You should get your pea-fucking brain out of the gutter and do your job. And by the way, if you get in my son's face one more time, I will make sure you never work in this industry again. Are we clear?" Shoshanna put her little hands on her little purple hips and waited.

"I'm sorry," Medusa grumbled somewhat contritely. "I'll keep that in mind."

"You do that." Shoshanna was a momma bear when it came to her boy. I snuck a peek at Luke, whose expression was somewhere between shock and pride. He was so totally going to be adopted.

While Shoshanna and Jim huddled together and read his chapters, we got barraged by the rest of the competition.

"So Duke LeHump," Hair Teddy cooed. My gay-dar was pinging with Teddy. "Are you ready to twerk?"

"Teddy, is it?" Luke inquired tightly.

"Yes, darling. It is."

"I will not be twerking—today, tomorrow, or ever. So you can take your twerk and shove it up your . . ."

"What Duke means to say," I cut Luke off before he pulled his gun and shot Hair Teddy dead, "is that we've heard you're the master twerker and we know Duke doesn't stand a chance against your skill and twerk-finesse."

Teddy was appeased and gave us a lewd hip shake to seal the deal. "God," he gushed. "It is so wonderful to be appreciated and feared for my talent. Those Hispanic steroid twins think they can take me. They are foolish," he hissed, and gave us another ungodly sample of his specialty.

"Are they not regulars on the circuit?" I asked, hoping I got the lingo right. Luke stood mutely beside me. I knew he was watching Shoshanna, but I could use a little help with old Teddy . . .

"No," he said, throwing an evil eye and a hip grind their way. "From what I heard, they're huge in Mexico and trying to horn in on my territory."

"But you guys look totally different." I was confused. What was the problem?

"True," he agreed. "No one has a mane like mine." He shook his hair and struck a pose.

"Wow," I stuttered. "You are . . . really, you know, something."

"Thank you." He held his pose and continued talking. "Rocky the Chocolate God is my only true friend and occasionally my lover. We've done a series of male-male covers together and he would never even think of trying to out-twerk me. His specialty is juggling. He's wonderful."

"I, um . . . wow." Was he for real? He was and it was all I could do to not burst into laughter.

"Mandy. May I call you Mandy?" Teddy asked, and twisted his body slightly to a new and alarming pose.

"Yes, of course."

"Mandy, you are an exquisitely gorgeous woman and your breasts are fabu. Are they real?" he inquired.

Luke tensed beside me and I knew he was going to blow. "He's gay," I muttered under my breath as Teddy began doing something that reminded me of Lamaze breathing.

"I don't care," Luke whispered. "I'm going to shoot him anyway."

"Why thank you, Teddy," I said, stepping in front of him just in case Luke lost his mind and pulled his gun. "They're real and Duke can vouch for them. His talent is staring people down and he's my lover most of the time when he's not being a dick."

"Oh." Teddy sighed forlornly. "I was hoping he was gay. Duke, if she ever bores you, Rocky and I could show you a very arousing and energetic time."

"That won't be necessary," Luke managed to say. "Mandy is quite acrobatic and has a mouth like a vacuum."

I was dumbfounded. My first instinct was to reach for my gun and shoot off his pride and joy and my second instinct was to laugh. Thank God the second prevailed.

"Congratulations, Mandy. It's rare I hear such a compliment given to a woman. Please excuse me, I must inform Rocky that we won't be having a three-way tonight." He bumped and ground his way across the room, stopping in front of the twins, Cesar and Cheech, to do a nightmare-inducing hip maneuver that threw the twins into their own pelvic-thrusting frenzy.

"Enough," Medusa grunted from the runway. "Save it for the stage. Get your gyrating asses up here and show me what you've got."

"Give me your phone," Luke demanded, holding out his hand.

"Why?" I asked.

"Because there will be no record of this. Ever."

I grinned and handed it over. He was as smart as I was and that was a huge turn-on. I was going to make him beg later and he was going to love it.

The rehearsal wasn't going well. Luke refused to do anything Medusa told him to do and since she was clearly terrified of Shoshanna, she just left him alone. Teddy and the twins kept up a jerky pelvic thing going that looked like they had bees in their pants. Rocky juggled condom balloons and Jim just watched and grinned. This was awesome. Shoshanna and I sat in the audience and watched the shit show.

"Jim is a fantastic writer," she said quietly.

"Really?" I was happy for him. When Shoshanna found a project, she went full steam ahead. He'd be published in a month.

"Absofuckinglutely," she said. "Fresh voice, incredible characters, and a plot I wish I had thought of. Can't wait to read the damn whole thing."

"Will you make a call?"

"Already did." She grinned and held up her phone. "He's gonna be huge. I can feel it in my bones and he's just the cutest thing ever."

"Is he straight or gay?" I asked, watching the action on stage.

"Honestly, I'm not sure," Shoshanna answered. "Highly unusual that I can't tell, but I can't."

"Yeah, me either."

"Did you hear about the protesting outside?" She pulled some Corn Nuts out of her bag and offered me some.

"No." I sat up and scanned the room for newcomers. I quickly walked to the back and locked the doors to the room. I'd gotten too comfortable and so had Luke. The flirty crap had to stop. Sitting back down, I accepted a handful of the teeth-breaking snack. "Are they protesting the convention?"

"Yeah, it happens every year, but apparently these guys mean business."

"What do you mean and how did you hear this?" How in the hell did she have more information than we did?

"Jim told me. He said they've literally set up a camp across the street from the hotel and they have signs and bullhorns and the kind of Christian attitude that makes God puke."

Great, we would need to check that out. I was starting to wonder if we didn't need more bodies on the ground. Having Mrs. C and Edith here would be a relief. Holy shit, I never thought that would cross my mind . . . ever. I made a mental note to check with Steve on their progress. If it wasn't quick enough, then I wanted more manpower here. The vastness of the convention and the size of the hotel were working against us, and until we had someone in custody, I wouldn't be happy.

"You will not leave the hotel for any reason whatsoever," I told her. "After the rehearsal we'll go to the room and Luke or I will case the protesters."

"Goddammit, I want to come. This is so perfect for my book, and I want to watch you guys in action. Please?" she said sweetly.

"Nope." I grinned. "That might work on your son, but I'm a hard-ass bitch and you will stay in the fucking room or I will kick your butt."

"Jesus, you're cold." Shoshanna laughed.

"Just call me Ice."

"Look at that!" Shoshanna giggled and pointed at Luke, who was grooving ever so slightly to the pounding beat of the European Techno Pop. "Isn't he cute?"

Cute wasn't the word I'd use. How in the hell did he do it? Even dressed in nothing but Village People tight leather pants and barely moving, he was sex on a stick. I couldn't even see anyone else up there and there were some damn pretty boys on that stage. He caught my eye and gave me his sexy lopsided grin and I melted. He did the smallest pump of his hips and it shot straight to my girlie parts. Lord help me. I was lost and pretty sure I didn't want to be found.

Chapter 21

"There are around forty to fifty protesters. They have campers and have set up what they're calling Jesus Town," Luke said with disgust. "Men, women, and children. They're using the kids for their own ends. Makes me sick."

There was so much more to that statement than he was openly revealing. I knew his parents had used him in unforgivable ways and it broke my heart. My parents might have been cold and screwed up after my sister died, but they loved me and would never knowingly hurt or harm me.

Luke had taken Jim with him to check out the protesters, since Jim was the one who had briefed Shoshanna. I knew Luke would grill him to see if he had any involvement in the death threats. I liked Jim, but I would do the same. No one was innocent until we found the guilty party. No one.

"Did you see anyone you recognized?" I asked.

"No, but I've only seen pictures of the professors you questioned. I might not be able to identify them. I want you to take a walk down there in about an hour. They have a sing along against pornography planned."

"Awesome, just what I've always wanted to see." I rolled my eyes and noticed how tired Shoshanna seemed. "Shoshanna, you don't have anything for three hours until your signing. Why don't you lie down?" Sometimes I forgot she was in her late sixties and this was a lot on her.

"You know, I think I might do that." She yawned and gave me a loopy grin. "Not as young as I used to be." She walked through the connecting door and went to her room. I turned on the monitors.

"I'll make sure her doors are locked," Luke said, following her. I watched her crawl sleepily into bed as Luke fastened the chains on her door. He walked over to the bed and carefully draped a blanket over the already snoring Shoshanna. He bent down and softly kissed her forehead. My heart lurched and I felt an overwhelming need to cry for the little boy that Luke never got to be. I quickly turned off the monitor. I would turn it back on when he was in the room. This moment was private and should be his alone.

"So, did you talk to Steve?" he asked a moment later, plopping down on the couch and turning the monitor back on.

"I did." Lord have mercy, he was beautiful. He'd changed into some worn-out jeans and a T-shirt to walk the crowd of protesters. Leathers and chains would have been a poor choice since he wanted to blend in. I looked away. Work, I was here to work, not ogle the hot guy on the couch. "The gals think they might have broken the code, but they need a little more time. They should be here sometime tomorrow."

"Great." He shuddered and laughed. "I didn't think this trip could get any more fucked, but I was wrong."

I smiled and agreed. The combination of characters was becoming overwhelming, but it was what it was. No amount of complaining would change it. At least we'd been given twenty-four-hour advance notice . . . Although the anticipation might be worse than if the sisters just showed up unannounced. Whatever.

"There's another note." I handed him the copy I'd printed from Steve's e-mail. "Same shit, different endearment."

"The death threat is still there," he observed.

"Yep."

"Read me all the salutations. That has to be the key." He was terse and frustrated. Hell, so was I.

"Let me see." I quickly pulled the notes from the file and dropped everything to the floor. "Shit, hang on," I said as I gathered them back up. I went through them one by one. "*Stupid Woman, Evil Bitch, Emasculating Slut, Sinful Shoshanna, Irritating Monster, Trollop, Vicious Whore, Insane Bitch, Meddling Idiot,* and *Nosy Harlot.*" I shook my head in disgust. I'd seen much stronger language and more descriptive threats in my time, but these notes set me on edge. Such blatant hatred was unnerving.

"Fucking lovely," Luke muttered, closing his eyes. "Sounds like a whack job and those are the worst."

"I just don't get it. She has no clear enemies and the point she made the other day about being unsure the threats were even aimed at her won't leave my head."

"Agreed. While they're offensive, they don't scream Shoshanna."

We sat in silence for a few moments. My need to fill it was replaced by the storm inside my brain. Who in the hell was doing this and why? With so little to go on, could we really even keep Shoshanna safe? I loved danger, but not when it threatened those I was becoming attached to.

"I just want to lock her in the room until this is all over." I put the notes back in the file and pinched the bridge of my nose.

"Aren't you forgetting something?"

"What?" I picked up the folder and reopened it. "Did I leave something out?"

"No, you left something undone."

"Undone?" What the hell was he talking about? The monitors were on. Shoshanna was snoring happily in her bed. I'd checked in with Steve and I'd briefed Luke on the new note. The crazy-ass sisters were coming tomorrow. I would walk the crowd in an hour . . . What else was there?

He crooked his finger at me and gave me a lazy smile. Every nerve in my body jumped to attention. And I went from business to pleasure so fast I had to grab the chair for support.

"Ohhhhh, that." I rolled my eyes.

"Yep, I believe you made me a promise. I negotiated for extra terms and you agreed, although I might switch it up a bit. We have a snoring client and a monitor to spot any movement. I'm pretty sure you need to pay up, beautiful girl."

"Well, as interesting as that sounds, your mom *is* in the next room and if I recall correctly, you're very loud."

"You're the screamer," he shot back, sitting up and removing his shirt. "God, your tits are a weapon in that corset. Loosen it."

"Seriously? Here?"

"Very serious. Now."

I shrugged and started to cross the room to him as I loosened my leather torture wear.

"No. Stay there in that chair. I want you to strip and then you'll do what I tell you to do."

I nodded, afraid if I spoke I'd say something I'd be embarrassed about later. Outrageous terms for sex and male body parts were the only things floating in my brain.

"Take everything off slowly," he instructed in a voice that made me weak. "Keep your eyes on me. Watch how much my body wants you." He slid his jeans and boxer briefs over his hips and huge erection as I tried to remember how to remove my clothes. I'd put them on, so I should be able to take them off . . . Right? My hands trembled as I peeled the leather pants and thong from my body. The corset took a little more effort, but I finally succeeded. "Put those heels back on." His voice was husky and his lids were hooded.

I carefully stepped back into my shoes and waited for his instruction.

"Sit down on the chair and spread your legs."

I did. He was pushing every button I had and he knew it . . .

"Show me how you touch yourself," he said gruffly. "And watch me while I show you what I like to do to myself when I think about you."

Oh. My. God. I had never done anything like this. It excited me and scared the hell out of me. I felt vulnerable and a little slutty . . . and I loved it. I watched, rapt, as he took himself in his hand and stroked. It was so hot, I forgot my orders.

"Touch. Now," he said, increasing the speed of his hand. "I'm going to make you come without touching you."

I slowly reached between my legs and was shocked to find how wet I already was. With small tight circular motions on my clit, I closed my eyes as the tingling pressure began.

"Look at me," he hissed.

My eyes shot open and locked with his as we brought ourselves higher and closer to orgasm. The sexy sounds that came from the back of his throat as he watched my now flushed body join my hand in movement almost undid me. I pressed down on my clit with the heel of my hand as I pushed my fingers inside of me. My hips undulated with a fierce desire of their own as he watched me intensely.

"So fucking sexy," he said as he sped up and got rougher with himself. His almost violent strokes were going to send me over the edge, and the look on his face caused my breath to come in short uneven spurts. "I'm gonna come and you're gonna come with me. Do it," he demanded in a voice that made the blood rush to my ears and my heart pound like a hammer in my chest. "Now."

I pressed down on my clit with two fingers and slammed my legs shut, trapping my hand and letting my body take over. My head fell back on my shoulders and the buzzing in my ears increased to a roar. I heard him swear as I came so hard I thought I would pass out. His moans of ecstasy as he came prolonged the orgasm ripping through my body. I gasped for air and bit down on my lips so I wouldn't scream. The aftershocks rocked my limp body and I slowly opened my eyes. He was standing over me with an expression of pure male satisfaction on his face. I hid my face in my arm and giggled.

"That was so fucking sexy." He dropped to his knees in front of me and took my chin in his hand. His searching stare took my breath and I leaned in. His lips gently brushed mine. He ran his tongue along the seam and I opened to him. The kiss was different. It was tender and sweet. It held a promise of so much, I had to close my eyes or I would cry.

"It's okay," he whispered. "I've got you."

He took my hand and led me to the shower. He washed my body in silence and I did the same for him. The orgasm had been amazing, but it was the emotion afterward that rendered me silent. This was what I wanted, wasn't it? He was beginning to own me, body and soul. He hadn't said anything more about me giving up my work, but unfortunately he didn't have to. I was coming to the decision he wanted all by myself. I had no intention of telling him that or that I was in grave danger of losing my heart to him. It was simply too scary—and still too soon.

"Am I hot or am I hot?" Shoshanna trilled as she modeled her purple rubber jumpsuit.

"You look like a freakin' alien," I said as I checked myself out in her mirror with trepidation. "Fuck," I muttered. "I look like an alien too."

Wearing a hot pink rubber miniskirt and a black rubber boob

tube with black thigh-high fuck-me boots and hot pink feather ear-rings, I looked like a fashion disaster with a rubber fetish. I feared what Luke would be wearing when he arrived in our room. I prayed to God it wasn't rubber.

I'd walked the picket line after our shower and didn't recognize anyone. The protesters were unsure of my allegiance as I was dressed normally. I smiled and made polite small talk with several. They were convinced that it was Gomorrah inside the hotel with public sex displays and sacrifices going on. One misguided imbe-cile informed me that the sinners were fornicating with goats and sheep. I feigned shock and moved on. They appeared to be stupid and harmless, but I planned to take another walk first thing in the morning. There were three more busloads of God-fearing anti-porno Christians scheduled to arrive.

"I think I might make the *New York Times* bestsellers list," Shoshanna told me. "My agent said I'm a shoo-in, but I won't be-lieve it till I see it." Her eyes were huge and her excitement made my eyes water.

"My God," I gasped. "That would be amazing."

"I know," she shrieked, and jumped into my arms. I hugged her little body tightly to mine, but when I tried to put her down, we re-alized our rubber had basically fused together.

"Oh hell," I groused as I literally peeled her off of me. "Rubber is for fucking tires—not clothes."

Shoshanna, who found the humor in everything, grunted with joy and went to find a notebook. I supposed this, too, would make its way into one of her books.

"You guys ready?" Luke asked from the other room.

"Holy Mary Mother of God in a jockstrap," Shoshanna shouted. "My son is one hot motherfucker."

Fear paralyzed me. If Shoshanna thought he looked good, there was a fine chance he was wearing a matching rubber jumpsuit. I slowly left the bathroom and sighed in relief when I saw him. He had on his leather pants and a strategically ripped shirt. Kind of Flash-dancey. He looked silly, but Shoshanna was right. He was hotter than hell. What the hell couldn't he carry off?

His eyes narrowed to slits when he saw me. "What are you wear-ing?" he inquired with immense displeasure.

"Rubber," I hissed, and flipped him off. "Don't you crawl up my ass about it either. I feel like an alien and I look like a hooker. I warned you that it would be bad."

"You're *my* alien hooker and I forbid you to wear that."

"There is so much wrong with that statement, I don't know where to begin. Shoshanna, put the fucking notebook down."

She sheepishly dropped her notebook and pen and slunk to the other room. "Let me know when you're ready," she said, trying to swallow her glee.

"You." I poked him in the chest. "Are not the boss of me. If I want to look like a rubber hooker from hell, I damn well will and you have nothing to say about it."

"You are going to cause me to shoot someone," he informed me.

"Are you serious?" I was flabbergasted. It was just an outfit, for God's sake.

"Deadly," he replied, crossing his arms over his chest.

I realized I could turn this into a win-win situation if I wanted to . . . I hated the outfit. It was rubber and smelled weird and my ass cheeks hung out of my skirt. If I caved, he would be happy and so would I. Rolling the consequences of letting him win around in my brain was interesting. If he got his way with my hideous clothing choices, I would be more comfortable, but he would have gained far too much ground. I paced the room and tried to figure out whether letting him win would outweigh my loss of power.

"Nope."

"Nope?" His eyebrows raised in displeasure.

"That's right. Nope. I'm wearing this, and if you don't lay off, I'll remove my panties."

"You wouldn't dare."

"Try me," I snapped, getting up in his face.

He grabbed me by the arms and put his lips to my ear. "I want to fuck you so bad right now it's not funny. Every man that looks at you tonight will want the same thing and that makes me insane. You are a walking wet dream and you belong to me. You got a problem with that?"

"I should, you arrogant pig, but I just can't think of it right now."

He chuckled and then dropped the real bomb. "Oh and Candy, just so you know . . . I'm in love with you."

"Don't you dare say that," I yelled at him. WTF? What right did he have to say something like that? "You cannot say stuff like that. Do you hear me?"

He smiled his wicked sexy smile and watched me unravel. "You can yell all you want, but it won't change a thing. Oh . . . and don't worry, baby. You don't have to say it, but I know you love me too." He winked, slapped my rubber-covered ass, and walked over to the door.

I thought my head was going to explode. "You are such a conceited fucktard. I should shoot your ass," I stammered. "You have no idea what's inside my head. You are so full of yourself and . . . and assholish." *Jesus Christ, I did not just say assholish. It wasn't even a word.*

"What the hell is happening in here?" Shoshanna asked with concern.

"I told her I loved her; she cussed me out and threatened to shoot me." He grinned.

I flipped him the bird and shoved my Glock into my purse.

"Sounds like love to me," Shoshanna said, giving her son a high five.

"That's what I thought too."

"Holy hell, you people are nuts," I shouted. "We're gonna be late. Move it. Now."

I gave them the silent treatment all the way to the signing while Luke grinned and stared at my tits. Shoshanna, clearly taking her son's side, bounced like a ball and hummed the wedding march. This fucking day couldn't be over soon enough. The thought of the lesbian sisters coming sounded like a vacation compared to being ganged up on by my kinda boyfriend and his insane almost-mom.

Wait . . . did he really mean what he said? Fuuuuck, I think he did.

Chapter 22

Shoshanna sat at a long table covered with her books and swag. Jim sat to her left. He was wide-eyed and positively giddy. He really was something to look at. I noticed Luke's disapproving stare as I discreetly checked Jim out. He moved his hand to where his gun was hidden and raised his eyebrows. I rolled my eyes and laughed. He was crazy. One hundred percent certifiable . . . and I loved it. Dammit.

Shoshanna stuck her fingers in her mouth and let loose with one of her deafening whistles. I'd seen the move coming and quickly covered my ears. Jim wasn't so lucky. He blanched and covertly checked his ears for blood. The chatter in the room ceased and the large group waited with excitement.

"Everybody, my hotter than Satan's underpants son, Duke LeHump, has created my new signature move." She raised her little arms in the air. "I would be fucking honored if all of you would do my move until you leave. It makes me feel proud and I hope to hell all of you are wearing deodorant."

I'd never seen so many hands shoot up at the same time. It was like a unison bust of two hundred and fifty people. Amazing. This was going to make a potential nightmare doable. I had to hand it to the fucktard. He was brilliant.

"Now form a nice line and I'll start signing! Oh, and I want you all to meet my new protégé. He's mind-bogglingly talented and I'd read the goddamned phone book if he wrote it. He'll be published next year and will be happy to sign anything you got!"

"Will he sign my boob?" a busty gal in a leather ball gown asked.

"I don't know." She turned to a red-faced Jim. "Will ya?"

"Um, sure," he said nervously. Shoshanna was like the Fairy

Godmother from Cinderella. She was full of magic, and I was sure this was only the beginning for Jim.

"What's that sexy writer's name?" another fan yelled.

"His name is Jim . . . Jim, um . . . What the hell is your last name?" Shoshanna shouted, clearly forgetting Jim was seated right next to her.

He winced in pain. I was sure his ears hadn't healed from the whistle. "It's Jim Kallenminski."

"What the fuck kind of name is that?" she bellowed. *That was rich coming from someone who called herself Shoshanna LeHump.* "That's just not gonna work for an author. I have a great idea," she gushed, and stood up on her chair. "We're gonna give Jim a new last name! Are you Street Walkers in?"

The crowd went nuts and names came flying faster than the employees running around in Frisky Business when I walked in to buy my rubber hooker outfits.

"LeHump," someone shrieked.

"Already taken." Shoshanna laughed.

"Williams."

"Peterman."

"Fauntleroy."

"SexyAss."

"Jameson."

"That's it!" Shoshanna bellowed. "Jim Jameson. Are you Irish?" she asked a laughing Jim.

"No, but I like the whiskey." He grinned and a few of the gals in the front melted.

"Sold!" Shoshanna hugged Jim, sat down, and got to business.

I kept my eyes on the crowd while Luke watched the ones closest to Shoshanna. We worked together like a well-oiled team. No words were necessary. It was perfect. I felt the tingle and was secure in the knowledge he was on the same wavelength. I couldn't believe he could really give this up. Granted, it wasn't our usual job, but there was still risk involved. Hell, had I become an adrenaline junky? Stop. No time for thinking about anything other than finding and eliminating the threat.

The mass of fans came in all shapes and sizes. They were mostly women, with a few men thrown in here and there. The excitement was palpable and the questions were many.

"Shoshanna, is the next book Bruce and Donna's story?"

"Yep, I love those two bastards and I can't wait to see what happens to them," she answered, and signed the woman's book.

"What's going to happen? Will they be able to work it out?" The woman was a mess, truly on pins and needles about two people who weren't real.

"That's to be determined," Shoshanna told her. "But I'm watching them carefully." She glanced over and winked at me. No fucking way. Were Luke and I actually Donna and Bruce? I was going to kick her little purple rubber butt when we got back to the room. Of course that wouldn't be for a while since Luke had a pageant rehearsal after the signing. Lord, I hoped he'd worn his underpants tonight . . .

The crowd was fairly calm and respectful. It was evident that Shoshanna was adored and revered. It was actually fun to watch. I noticed Luke looking on with pride and I almost got choked up. Refocusing on the crowd, I froze. Luke's head snapped to me and his eyes zoned in on my subject. What the hell was Pat of the unidentifiable sexual orientation doing here? My stomach felt light and my hand went to my gun. As if this person knew they'd been caught, Pat's gaze met mine. Pat's eyes grew huge. Pat turned and quickly ran out of the room. Was it fucking Pat? Was Junsen here too? Had I missed something major during that interview? I turned to Luke and mouthed, "I'm on it." He nodded and tensed. I knew he would stay with Shoshanna and keep her safe. I had an ambiguously sexed suspect to chase.

I was seconds behind Pat and saw her speed-walk down the hall and turn to the left. Girl. I'd just think of her as a freakin' girl . . . Hauling ass, I avoided the meandering crowds as much as possible. The damned thigh-high stiletto boots I wore were making the chase somewhat difficult, but I'd dealt with worse. Like the time I'd taken a knife to the thigh and had to run a mile to the pick-up point. Now that sucked.

Pat slipped into a door marked cleaning closet. I had her. Her ass was mine. Opening the door, I found her standing there with a mop in one hand and a squeegee in the other. She was trembling and her eyes were wild.

"Hi Pat." I smiled and leaned back on the door, making her escape impossible.

"What do you want?" she snapped, shaking like a leaf and brandishing her mop like it was a sword.

"I think that's my question, among a few others."

"You will not get me fired, copper," Pat shrieked, and made a mad dash for the door.

I put my left foot out and tripped her . . . him . . . it. As she went down, I gave her a swift undercut in the stomach, knocking the wind from her lungs. When she hit the floor, I dropped down and slammed my knee into her lower back, yanked her arms behind her, and bound her hands with the strap of my purse.

"That was really fucking stupid, Pat," I said, giving the leather purse strap a little extra yank for good measure. "First of all, I'm not a fucking copper. I'm a cold-blooded DEA agent who enjoys shooting shit. You made me run in stilettos. I don't appreciate that. I could have twisted my ankle and then I would have been really mad as opposed to just mad."

"What's your fucking problem?" Pat grunted, gasping for air.

"Apparently you are. Why'd you run?"

"Because."

I waited for more but it didn't come. "Wrong answer." I pressed my knee into her spine and she screamed. I hoped no one was directly outside the closet. This would be kind of hard to explain.

"I'm not supposed to be here," she choked out. "I called in sick and I don't have any more sick days."

"Right."

"I swear," she whined. "I could lose my job if you say anything. I need my job. I'm saving for transitional surgery."

Still no clarity on her sex, dammit . . . Irrelevant. "Why were you at Shoshanna's signing?"

"I wanted to get Junsen a signed book and plead Junsen's case. She loves Shoshanna and I love Junsen. I thought maybe we could have a three-way relationship."

Jesus, this was getting icky. "Let me get this straight. Junsen loves Shoshanna and burned bras on a football field to prove her dedication to her. You love Junsen so you're going to get a signed book from Shoshanna, the woman Junsen loves, to prove your adoration to her and possibly begin a three-way."

"Yes," she hissed.

"And you called in sick and could lose your job . . . ." It was so fucking stupid, it had to be true. "What do you know about the notes?"

"What notes?" Pat asked, bewildered.

"The threats on Shoshanna's life."

"What?" Pat grunted. "I know nothing. I'm a pacifist."

"Could have fooled me with the mop and the squeegee thing you had going."

"Look I have a rap sheet and I freaked," Pat whimpered. "I'm just starting to get my life together and you could screw it up."

"What did you do?"

"I ran a fake Viagra ring and sold to major pharmaceutical companies."

"Holy shit, you're Limp Dick Smith?" We'd been making jokes about that case for three years. Everything in my gut said Pat was not our man . . . or woman, but proof was necessary. "Do you have ID on you?"

"Yes, back pocket."

I pulled out the wallet—a man's wallet—and checked the ID. Pat Smith, age thirty-one, sex . . . scratched out with a pin or nail. WTF? I grabbed my phone and called it into Steve. After about a ten-minute wait, I had my answers. Pat was most definitely Jesse Limp Dick Smith. Her foray into a life of crime had made national news and been fodder for every late-night talk show for months. Pat, aka Jesse, had gotten off on a bizarre technicality that I couldn't recall and had gone into the witness protection program because there were thousands of furious men that wanted her dead. But the real proof was Steve's latest information. While I had my knee embedded in Pat's spine a message had been left on Shoshanna's bugged cell phone. A muffled woman's voice had left a cryptic message—"Time is up." The call had been too short to trace.

"Alrighty-roo," I said. "I'm going to let you up. You're leaving the convention and going back to Minneapolis tonight with some local law enforcement guys who will make sure you don't come back."

"Are you going to turn me in to the university?"

"No, I'm not, but you and Junsen need to get it through your heads that Shoshanna is straight."

I loosened the purse straps and helped Pat up. On unstable feet, she extended her hand to me.

"What's that for?" I asked, taking her hand and shaking it.

"For keeping my secret. You're a tuff-ass mo-fo."

"Thank you. You really are going to have to leave," I said, feeling a little bad about her limp.

"I know. It was stupid for me to come in the first place. I just thought . . ."

"Look, go home and tell Junsen how you feel. You never know what might happen if you just lay it out there."

"Yeah," Pat said, rubbing the raw skin where the straps had been. "Maybe I will. Oh and Candy?"

"What?"

Pat inhaled deeply and blew it out slowly. "I was born a hermaphrodite. I'm saving up to become a woman. According to my therapist, the Viagra thing was payback because of my deep-rooted hatred toward men."

"Okay . . . wow," I muttered, unable to come up with anything more profound. "Can you get back to your room alone? Your escorts will be here in a half an hour."

"Sure," she said. "Will you call me when you get back to Minneapolis? I haven't told many people my deal, and I think we could be friends."

I didn't know what to say. Part of me felt great and the other part was completely skeeved out. She waited, expecting rejection. Was she really that different from me? I lived a half-life too, telling no one what I really did or who I really was. I'd only recently found friends and I'd spent a good portion of my life with a vendetta. I was able to fulfill my anger on the right side of the law . . . Pat had fulfilled hers on the wrong side.

"Yes, I'll call you. I'm new to the friend thing, so I don't want anything too overwhelming or time consuming, but we could give it a shot." I heaved a huge relieved sigh. I knew I had done the right thing when I saw her shy and grateful smile.

"Okay, I'll catch you back in the Twin Cities." She limped out of the cleaning closet and left. I took a brief moment to gather myself and headed back to Luke and Shoshanna. I eyed every woman I passed. Who in the hell was it? The lesbians needed to get here now.

Chapter 23

Rehearsal was a treat after the bizarre takedown in the cleaning closet. Luke was up to speed. He'd spoken briefly with Steve and I'd filled him in on the rest.

"Did you have fun?" he asked, grinning.

"Yeah, at first I did," I said thoughtfully. "But then I felt bad and Pat asked me if I wanted to be friends and I realized I wasn't that different from her and I told her as long as she didn't take up too much time, I would try it out."

"Wait. What?" He was totally confused. It did sound strange . . .

I shrugged my shoulders. "Too hard to explain."

"All right, everyone strip and get on the stage. We have two days till the pageant and it's a fucking mess," Medusa Schmadden yelled.

Luke heaved a hellacious put-upon sigh and walked to the stage.

"Goddamn," Shoshanna whispered, and shuddered. "This death threat stuff isn't as fun as it was last week."

"You're going to stay in the room tomorrow. I have reservations about you being here right now, but the doors are locked and Luke and I are both here."

"Well, hell," she muttered. "I have a panel on fuzzy handcuffs versus metal tomorrow. I hate to disappoint my Street Walkers. Could I Skype in?"

I thought for a moment, then shrugged. "I'm okay with that." It was a good compromise. She'd be safe and her fans would be happy. "We'll just tell everyone you're sick and need to stay in your room. I'll speak with the coordinators and get monitors set up. Luke and I can set up the feed in the room."

"Can Jim come up tomorrow? I want to work on his book with him."

"I say yes, but I want to run it by Luke. His background check came up clean."

"You guys checked him out?"

"Yep. I turned in a list of everyone we've been in contact with. Haven't gotten all the information back yet, but Jim is good."

"Teddy, if you don't can the hip thrusts, I'm going to castrate you," Medusa screamed.

Teddy threw his hair back and stomped off the stage. He stood in a corner and pouted.

"Son of a bitch," she groused, and pulled on her hair, which was looking a bit thinner. "Everyone take five." She made her way over to the devastated Teddy with Rocky close on her heels.

"*Mom,* you do realize I will make you pay for this for the rest of your natural life," Luke said as he flipped the chair next to me around and straddled it. Shoshanna grinned and blew him a kiss. He was in his freakin' underpants and still managed to have the upper hand. Jim and the twins, Cheech and Cesar, joined us. I was in the middle of a men's underwear ad come to life.

"Cheech and Cesar," Shoshanna said, pinching their cheeks. "How are you enjoying your first American Romance convention?"

"Isss okay," Cheech muttered sullenly. "That faggot Teddy is pussy. I will beat him and then I will beat him."

We all sat in shocked silence for a moment and wondered if he was joking.

"I am making the kidding!" he shouted, laughing and offering his hand up for a high five to Jim. Jim gave him a half-assed slap, and we all chuckled uncomfortably.

"My brother's understanding of the English language needs some work along with his sense of humor," Cesar said sheepishly in perfect English. "We are used to being the stars. We always win everything we do. We are . . . how do you say it? Um, unused to being challenged."

"This be no challenge," Cheech boasted. "No offense to you"— he nodded to Luke and Jim—"but we are the best and we will have the win of what we came here to do and make our families and country proud."

"You're gonna do just great." Shoshanna patted him on the head. "This is all good fun and the exposure you'll get will help you launch a career right here in the good ole U.S. of A."

"Actually," Cheech said, leaning in and coming dangerously close to my boobs, " my dream is to be the next Pat Sajack. I love the Wheel of the Fortune and I will have relations with the Vanna White."

Again with the shocked silence . . . However, there was no uproarious laughter this time. He was serious. Cesar kept talking as if what his twin had just said made complete sense.

"Yes, Cheech will be a TV star and I will be on *Top Chef*. I will win and open up a chain of restaurants and be very rich and famous."

"Oh my, what do you cook?" Shoshanna asked. Was she trying to be polite or was she really interested? I was beginning to doubt the sanity of the twins, and my estimation of their intelligence was taking a steep nosedive. Not to mention their time was limited if they didn't stop ogling my rubber-encased boobs. Luke's displeasure was quite obvious to everyone except the brothers.

"I am taking lessons now. It is not hard and I have confidence I will succeed."

Jesus, they were idiots. Conceited dumbasses. Lovely.

"Hey you," Cheech said to me, clearly oblivious to the steaming Luke. "Why don't you and me go at the bar and get the drinks together?" He waggled his eyebrows and pointed at his crotch. They had gone from being hot and sexy to being stupid and pervy.

"Thanks, but no."

"Why not?" he demanded. "I will show you the good time better than the boring American mans."

"She's married." Luke cut him off in a clipped tone. "Back off or her husband will kick your ass."

"I don't see no husband," Cheech said, confused and surprised.

"I'm her fucking husband," Luke snapped. "So stop looking at her and talking to her. And if you so much as lay a hand on her, I will remove it."

"Okay, gringo." Cheech laughed and backed away. "No problemo."

"Come on," Cesar said, slapping his brother in the back of the head. "Sorry about that. You might find it hard to believe, but he has a hard time making friends . . ." He grinned and walked away with his utterly confused brother.

"I have the friends," Cheech hissed at his brother as they crossed back to the stage.

"Right, my brother. Sure you do."

"What the fuck?" I whispered to my little group. "That Cheech is as dumb as a box of hair. Cesar seems kind of okay, but oh my God."

"I'm gonna have to shoot him," Luke said.

"Is that your solution to everything?" I asked, shaking my head in disbelief.

"Do you have a better one?"

"Well yeah, I . . . um . . . No. I don't, but you can't go around shooting people for looking at me. It's immature and just doesn't bode well for the future."

"So . . ." Luke grinned and crossed his gorgeous arms over his stupidly perfect chest. "You're admitting we have a future."

"I'm admitting nothing," I huffed. I hated being backed into a corner. "I'm just saying you can't shoot anyone unless they're breaking the law or trying to kill you."

"Wait. I'm confused. Are you guys married or not?" Jim asked.

"Not," we said in unison and then Luke added, "yet."

"Okay," Jim said, and laughed. "And your hobby is shooting people?"

I realized that Jim had no clue who we really were or what we really did. I was halfway tempted to tell him, but Luke shot me a quick look. Luke was right. Shoshanna was safer if we kept our cover. There would be time to tell Jim who and what we were later. I hoped.

"Duke's just screwing around," Shoshanna chimed in, saving us from having to make up a joint lie that matched. Luke rolled his eyes and mouthed, *No, I'm not,* when Jim was turned away.

"All right, people," Medusa shouted. "Teddy is feeling better and we need to get something done before the girls show up."

"What girls?" I asked Shoshanna. "Nobody said anything about girls."

"Oh yeah, I forgot that part. They bring in some female cover models and they dance with the guys during the show." She leaned in and chuckled. "Last year that got a little out of hand. I thought the convention organizers banned it. Those gals were fucking wild."

I did not like the way I was feeling. I hated it. Some super sexy slut bag was going to come in here and rub all over my guy while he was in his underpants? Wait. He wasn't my guy . . . well, he could be, but was I really ready to commit to him after a week? I suppose if I counted all the times we'd had sex, I could add two more weeks to it, but that was technically cheating. I didn't even know his freakin' name until last week. Although, he knew my name all along and had stalked me for the better part of a year . . . I could count the two weeks of sex as one since it was somewhat anonymous . . . Fine. We'd been together two weeks. That did not merit losing my mind and shooting unsuspecting women no matter how slutty they were. I definitely wouldn't shoot them. I felt better.

A loud banging on the door ended my ridiculous inner monologue. Medusa sprinted across the room and opened it. Palming my gun, I got in front of Shoshanna.

"Sweet baby Jesus on a unicycle, here they come," Shoshanna groaned.

Through the door came a bevy of large-breasted, overly made up, scantily clad gorgeous women. I had a decision to make . . . to shoot or not to shoot. Not. I would not shoot innocent hooker women even though they made a beeline to Luke and began pawing him.

"Ladies," Medusa shrieked, pulling another clump of hair from her head. "There were supposed to be six of you. I only count five."

"Elle ate dinner so she couldn't come," squeaked a brunette with a voice that could attract dogs from five miles away.

"What in the hell does that mean?" I muttered.

Shoshanna mimed sticking a finger down her throat and raised her eyebrows.

"Gross."

"And sad," she commented. "I hate that women buy into the whole media circus of how they should look. It's a sorry place to be if you adhere to that bullshit."

I nodded my head and watched as the nightmare unfolded. Luke, to his benefit, was removing the women from his person. This did not seem to stop them. I found myself reaching for my gun and quickly pulled my hand back.

"What am I supposed to do?" Medusa moaned. "Whatever. Ladies, pick a guy and let's get started. Maybe Elle will show up."

"Not gonna happen," quipped a blonde in a gold lamé string bikini. "She ate a burger, fries, and an extra-large chocolate milk shake. That will take at least two days."

The girls tittered and all headed for Luke and Jim. I felt itchy and pissed. This was not working for me—at all.

"You okay?" Shoshanna asked with a knowing smile on her face.

"No, but I'm about to do something really fucking stupid to make it better."

"You gonna shoot somebody?"

"Nope, something even dumber than that." I sucked in an enormous breath, pinched my cheeks, and adjusted my boobs. They might not be as big as the ones on the stage, but at least they were real. "I'll do it," I yelled, and immediately regretted my impulsiveness.

Luke's head jerked up and his grin made me want to slap him and then strip him. My insides were in hell. A full halftime marching band doing a heavy metal medley had taken up residence in my stomach and I thought I was going to hurl.

"Great," Medusa said, taking her hand from her hair for the first time since the rehearsal had started. "Get up here and pick a guy."

"I will be your partner of the guy," Cheech said, proving his worth with a gyration that made me choke on my tongue.

"Absolutely not," Teddy cut in, and produced his own gag-inducing hip thrust. "She has a lovely bosom and a mouth like a vacuum. I shall partner her."

"What are we? Chopped liver?" the one with the squeaky voice whined as her hand moved dangerously close to Luke's ass.

"I'm flattered that you all would like me to partner with you, but I'll stick with my husband." I walked over to Luke and knocked Squeaky's hand away. "If you put any part of your body on him again, I'll shoot it off," I told her under my breath. She blanched and moved quickly to the other side of the stage.

"Nice move," Luke said, and palmed my butt.

"I am so mad at you right now," I hissed.

"What the hell did I do?" He laughed and tried to put his arms around me.

"You," I ground out, and slipped from under his arm, "were standing up here in your underpants with women pawing all over you. Because of you, I almost shot five women dead. That is unacceptable. You are such a dick."

"Oh my God, you're blaming me because I was standing here doing nothing—actually I was trying to peel them off—and somehow it's my fault that you wanted to shoot them?"

I thought about it for a moment. "Yep. That's right."

He grinned and pulled me close. "Goddamn that's hot. And I don't know if you're aware of it, but you called me your husband. That means we're engaged."

"How in the hell did you come to that conclusion? I was just going along with the lie you already told. It means nothing, so don't read into it, big guy."

Luke's grin practically split his face. I could deny and deny until I was blue in the face. As far as he was concerned, we were now engaged . . . my brother was going to be thrilled. I tried to tamp down the smile that was pulling at my lips, but failed. He grabbed me in a bear hug and pressed his lips to my ear.

"You are so into me," he whispered.

I rolled my eyes and let my body relax into his. Honestly, what was the point of even fighting him anymore? We both knew that eventually he would win . . . and that I wanted him to.

"Let's begin. Ladies, bend over and touch your toes. Men do a little sexy bump and grind," Medusa bellowed, and turned the techno pop up to an ear-shattering decibel. From there on out it was a clusterfuck of epic proportions . . .

Luke got an erection from bumping and grinding me, so he plastered his front to my back and refused to move. Teddy and Rocky decided to ignore the girls and twerked with each other. I tried to keep my eyes averted, but it was like a train wreck—I had to watch. Cheech and Cesar circled their partners, doing what appeared to be a tribal sex dance complete with grunting sound effects. They humped the air with such intensity they were dripping with sweat and sprayed the appalled women with their effort. I was sure they'd collapse from sheer exhaustion. Jim was in hell. His gal pal was trying to strip him and he was hanging on to his underpants for dear life. I realized I could never un-see any of this. It would be burned into my brain for eternity . . . Again, I wondered who I'd fucked over in a past life to deserve this torture.

"Enough!" Medusa shrieked, practically in tears. She turned off the music and pulled on her hair. "That was hideous. If I had eaten dinner, I would have thrown it up from watching that horrifying display."

I actually had to agree with her.

"What is the matter of the problem?" Cheech demanded, truly confused. "I was in the zone and the womens were digging the sex-iness of my crotch moves."

"Is he for fucking real?" Squeaky asked. "That was disgusting," she hissed, grabbing her friends and making a beeline for the exit. I quickly followed and locked the door after them. Luke dropped to a squat on the stage to mask Mr. Happy in his pants.

"Let's just call it a night," Medusa said wearily.

"I have an idea," Shoshanna, never one to let well enough alone, volunteered. She ran up on stage, dragging me with her. "Mandy, you stand in the middle and freeze like you're a mannequin. Boys, pretend you got locked in a department store overnight and you find the most beautiful woman in the world, but she's frozen— a block of perfect ice. The only thing that will unfreeze her is a dis-play of love for her. One at a time, you will fucking go for it . . . But, you can't touch her." She winked at her son, who gave her a thumbs-up. "Duke will go last and he will wake her from her slumber and they will live happily ever after."

"What?" Teddy gasped. "I will be the one to wake her. I have the longest hair."

"No," Cheech insisted. "I will do the wake of her. I have the package that is huge."

All the other men laughed derisively.

"I do," he shouted. "I will show to you the package of the win-ner."

"No," Shoshanna yelled, startling him enough to halt the display of his weenie. *Thank God.* "You know the rules. You can't expose your penis. Ever. You will be disqualified and shame your country. You don't want to embarrass Mexico, do you?"

"No." Cheech hung his head and let go of the waistband of his underpants.

"I get to wake her because I'm her husband," Luke informed the models. "And if anyone has a problem with that, we can go out back and take care of it."

"I actually love that idea," Medusa said, getting excited. "It's brilliant and we've never done such high concept before. This could be award winning," she muttered, pulling me to the middle of the stage.

This was going to be frightening, but infinitely better than twerking with my fake husband. I simply had to stand there and do nothing—I could do that. The guys all seemed to be fine with the change, especially Jim, who would not have to fight to stay clothed. As long as no one touched me, Luke wouldn't have to shoot anyone and now that the gals were gone, my trigger finger was less itchy. Win-win.

"Great," Shoshanna said. "Let's work!"

"All right, everyone," Medusa sang, giving Shoshanna a quick and heartfelt hug. "You heard the lady. Let's work!"

Chapter 24

I woke up the next morning sore. Not from anything fun like sex. Nope, I was sore from having held my mannequin pose for two hours while Medusa and Shoshanna created a masterpiece. I had to admit it was far more interesting than the twerk-fest that had been emerging as the show's centerpiece. In the new and improved version, the guys got to strut their stuff and Luke just had to walk up at the end and kiss me silly. Worked for me.

I'd slept alone. Luke slept, or rather kept guard, across the hall. Secretly I'd hoped he would push the issue and screw me blind, but he didn't. He was right—we were working. It did occur to me that he might be waiting for me to make the next move. He'd have to wait. We had a potential killer to catch, and completing our mission sooner rather than later was imperative.

Mrs. C and Edith were expected around lunchtime. Shoshanna would Skype from the room and Luke approved Jim working with Shoshanna later in the day. She was safe for the moment.

"Are you going to case the new protesters?" Luke asked, delivering coffee and doughnuts to the suite. I glanced at the offering, sad that he had forgotten my Coke. "Why the long face?" he asked, grinning as he pulled an icy bottle of Coke from the bag I'd missed. "Did you think I forgot?"

"Um, yes . . . actually," I answered, embarrassed on several levels. There was no reason he should remember every little thing about me. I didn't want him to, but at the same time I did. I was starting to notice and remember all sorts of wonderful and frightening things about him. The lack of lifting the toilet seat was alarming, but he did have excellent aim. He smiled easily and when he was really happy, he hummed quietly. He carried his past in his eyes and from time to time, I saw raw pain and anger there. Shoshanna seemed to calm him—almost as if she knew. Hell, maybe she knew more than I did. If I was being totally honest and completely conceited . . . I knew I made him happy. The further I relaxed into the inevitable direction of our future, the more relaxed he became. Surprisingly, I did too.

"Do you guys want to demonstrate the fuzzies versus metal for me and the Street Walkers?" Shoshanna asked as she stuffed almost an entire doughnut into her little mouth.

"No," I said, relieved I had a real excuse. "I have to go do a meet-and-greet with the new Jesus-lovin' porno protesters. I'm sure Luke would be delighted to help you out."

He flipped me off and sipped his coffee. God, he looked gorgeous in his ripped jeans and T-shirt. "Actually," he said, changing his mind and smirking evilly. "That's not out of the realm of possibility. I could do imitations of all the amazing sounds you make when you're cuffed to the bed."

"Great," Shoshanna tried to say. However, her mouth was full and it sounded more like, Gwaurt . . .

"I'm out of here," I informed my posse. "I'll call if I need you."

"Do you have the pen and Bible?" he asked.

I held up the items in question and tucked them back into my purse next to my gun. "Got them. And thank you. I've never used one of these babies yet."

"Youb neber used a Blobble?" Shoshanna choked out through the mass of dough in her mouth.

"Not the Bible," Luke corrected a relieved Shoshanna. "A camera pen. State of the art and hot off the assembly line. It also has laser ability. You can take a photo while you zap your perp."

Clapping my hands with delight, I tackled Luke in a hug. No one ever got me cool stuff like he did. No one. "I am so excited to have one of these. It's almost as good as a new gun," I gushed, showing Shoshanna my new beloved toy.

"You two are something else." She swallowed and then laughed. "You're more thrilled that he got you a fucking pen than if he got you a diamond ring."

That silenced both of us. I was frozen in uncomfortable shock and Luke was contemplative. He wouldn't dare. That would screw up everything. Shoshanna, as much as I had grown to love her, was opening a can of shit-storm.

"I wouldn't want a ring unless it shot bullets out of it," I said flippantly, avoiding any in-depth conversation on things that scared the hell out of me.

"Yeah, yeah, that's what they all say." Shoshanna chuckled and then shoved another doughnut into her mouth.

I decided to get the hell out while her ability to speak was hindered by her healthy breakfast. No telling where she would go next. "I'm outta here. I'll see you guys in an hour or so."

The protesters had doubled their numbers, but not their intelligence level. I was evangelized by numerous offensive do-gooders. It was helpful to learn that fornication sent unmarried women straight to hell. I was curious if it did the same thing to men, but didn't really want to engage. Masturbation caused blindness and hairy palms in males and hair loss, stunted growth, and webbed feet in women. The information apparently came straight from scripture. My knowledge of the Bible was somewhat limited, but even I knew they were on crack.

I asked a few of the most hardcore female protesters to sign my Bible. Since we had nowhere to start, I figured taking pictures of the biggest haters couldn't hurt. Each time I had my fancy new pen out, I randomly swung it around and took pictures from behind me and to my sides. I'd download my findings into the computer later and see if anything caught my eye.

Pass after pass and I saw no one familiar. Even though I knew Pat had gone home and I was secure that she had told me the truth, I still looked for her and Junsen. Would I ever get past my distrust issues? Did I want to? Wasn't that what made me a good agent? Shit, I was thinking far too much. I shut down that part of my brain and continued to watch for suspicious women. I took copious numbers of pictures with my toy. Playing with new gadgets was delightful and I took full advantage, taking more pictures of *God's Chosen Ones* than was necessary. Some I took in movement and some still. I turned the pen at all different angles and held it upside down too. I'd read the quality was outstanding and could capture clear images even while an operative was running or driving. Running would make me stand out too much, but I was dying to try.

"Would you like to join in our crusade?" a mousey woman with a JESUS FOR PRESIDENT T-shirt inquired.

"No, thank you. I'm just getting some exercise."

"Well, if you change your mind, we will be here for you. You look like too nice a girl to be involved with the hell-smut inside that hotel." She smiled and raised her hands in prayer.

Why did I want to deck her? Was it her closed and judgmental mind or was it her sub-par intelligence? The people inside that hotel were there because they enjoyed reading sexy romance. So what? Yes, some of them participated in the BDSM lifestyle, but from everything I'd gathered and witnessed, it was consensual and safe and hurt no one. They weren't burning Bibles and judging the idiots outside. The attendees hadn't spoken about the protesters except to say they felt sorry for them.

I knew for a fact that Shoshanna and several of the other big authors funded charities and did more good for less fortunate people than probably all of these God-fearing Christians had ever done. Shoshanna spoke openly for women's rights and I knew she was a large contributor to Kristy's women's shelter.

The people inside the hotel were not corrupting children, having group orgies, or compromising animals. They were having a great time . . . making new friends, greeting old ones, and standing in lines for hours to get autographs from their favorite authors. Most appeared happily married and they'd chosen a safe and nonjudgmental place to gather and celebrate their kink. It was a free country, but I would think Christians could find something a little more constructive to do with their precious time.

These people reminded me of Helen, Steve's zealot of an ex-wife. All holier than thou to the world, but as mean as a snake in private. Only truly concerned with themselves and their own needs. Who in their right mind would poison their children against a loving and wonderful father? Helen's facade was impressive, but her insides were rotten.

I knew my anger at Helen was behind my need to put the mousey gal in her place, but I didn't care. At all. "Does your group do anything for the poor?" I asked the gal in the JESUS FOR PRESIDENT T-shirt who was clearly unaware that there was supposed to be a separation of church and state in our country.

"Of course," she answered indignantly. "We show them the way of the Lord."

"Do you feed them or educate them or help them get out of abusive situations?" I asked. "Do you build homes or teach them about bullying or nutrition for their children or do drug intervention? Do you actually do any of the things Jesus would do if he were here?"

"Well, I um . . . we offer baptism," she added triumphantly. "Jesus baptized hundreds of millions of evil Jews."

"Um, actually Jesus was a Jew," I informed her. "He was. I promise you. And get this, he didn't pass judgment on Mary Magdalene, and she was a hooker. I really think you might find something more Christian-like to do with your time. Don't you?"

Mousey gal turned and ran. I was sure she was going to get a big-time Jesus lover to come back and put my heathen ass in place. As much as I was jonesing for a good fight, verbal or physical, I knew it wouldn't help the job I was supposed to do. Shit. I never got to have fun. I quickly and quietly made my way back to the hotel before I did something I'd love in the moment and regret terribly later.

Chapter 25

"It was awesome," Shoshanna squealed. "Luke let me cuff him on camera and then he told stories—detailed stories about using cuffs safely while in sexual situations. He did the most amazing impressions of you. You have quite the vocabulary, young lady. I would hope when you give birth to my grandkids, you'll clean up that filthy mouth."

My stomach dropped to my feet and I felt my skin heat up. He did not do that . . . did he?

"I'm joking," she said hurriedly before I could pull my gun out and shoot Luke. I wouldn't shoot to kill, I'd just injure him real good.

"You were going to shoot me." He laughed, grabbed me by the waist, and swung me around. "God, that's hot," he shouted.

"You think it's hot that I was going to put a bullet in you?" I demanded, trying unsuccessfully to get away from him.

"I think it's hot I get you so riled up that you feel the need to kill me occasionally."

"I wouldn't have killed you," I muttered. "I just would have hurt you a little."

"Well, Jesus Christ in assless leather chaps, that's good to know," Shoshanna grunted. "I just got a son; I'd hate to lose him so soon."

Luke put me down and I adjusted my T-shirt, which had ridden up and exposed the matching bra to the panties he had stolen when he had left me high, dry, and frustrated a few days ago.

"I didn't realize my prize had a matching partner," he said, trying to lift my shirt again.

"Stop it." I slapped his hand and ran behind the chair. "Shoshanna, tell your son to lay off or I'll shoot him." Of course, the grin on my face weakened my threat.

"You heard her, boy," she said, enjoying the game. "You've been warned."

"Fine." He mockingly threw his hands in the air. "I know when I've been beat. So, back to business. Did you find anything interesting out there?"

"Interesting? Yes. Helpful? I don't think so. I did take a ton of pictures. Do you know how to upload them from the pen?"

"Yep. Give me your laptop."

I handed it over and he dismantled the top of the pen and inserted it into my computer. "It should come up in a few," he said, watching the screen.

I glanced over his shoulder, still amazed by the technology. "Everything has been slow. I think everyone in the whole hotel has been on their computers at the same time."

"It might take a while," he agreed. "What time are the dykes coming?"

I checked my watch and shuddered. As much as we needed them, I still dreaded their arrival. "Any time now. They have our room number, so I assume they'll come directly here with whatever information they have."

"I just hope to God it's something we can use," Luke said, still watching the laptop screen.

"Me too," Shoshanna said. "I mean, this is a nice room and all, but I want to be with my people."

"Hopefully you will be, but until we get this solved, you're staying in the room," I told her, hoping she realized the gravity of the situation.

"Yeah, yeah," she said. "I'm just glad Jim is coming soon. Gotta do something or I'll go nuts."

My cell buzzed and I saw it was Steve. "Hey, what's up?"

"You guys in the room?" Steve asked, sounding exasperated.

"Yes. What's wrong?"

"Hell if I know. Apparently Edith and Mrs. C are there, but there's a problem."

"Okay." I shrugged my confusion to Luke and put Steve on speakerphone. "What's the problem?"

"Fuck if I know," he shouted. "Those pains in my ass won't tell me. Their location is on the back south side of the hotel by some sort of gate. They want you to come down."

"I'll go," Luke said, holstering his gun and pulling on a light jacket to cover it.

"They want both of you," Steve groused. "I told them that was a no go. One of you had to stay with Shoshanna and they told me to . . . well, suffice it to say it was highly unpleasant what they told me to do, how to do it, and what to do it with."

"I'll be fine in the room alone," Shoshanna said. "I'll lock it up and I won't let anyone in, not even these guys. They have a key and if they insist on having me open the door, I'll know the bad guy is with them."

"Holy shit, Mom. That was brilliant," Luke said, hugging her.

"Did you just call Shoshanna, Mom?" a confused Steve asked.

"He did," Shoshanna crowed. "It's a long story, but a goddamned good one. I'll tell you when we get back."

"Fine. Tell the old ladies that another note came to Shoshanna's house. We picked it up about thirty minutes ago. I've scanned it and e-mailed it to Candy's computer."

"The Internet is slow," Luke told Steve. "Tell me what the salutation was."

"Let me see," Steve mumbled, rustling through papers. "Here it is. It says *Extreme Fool*. The rest of the letter is identical to the others."

"I think the different greetings are the key."

"Agreed," Steve said. "The old bitches think the same thing. Now lock Shoshanna in, give her a weapon, and go find the troublemakers. I want this shit over. Today."

"On it," I said, and Steve hung up. I handed Shoshanna the pen. Even though the camera had been dismantled, the laser should still work. It was safer than leaving her with a gun that could be turned on her by someone who knew how to use it.

"You want me to draw on someone?" she asked.

"No." I took a deep breath so I wouldn't sound as stressed out as I truly was. "There's a laser in the pen. If you depress the top, you can shoot someone. Make sure the writing end is pointed away from you, or you'll shoot yourself."

"Motherfucker, that would suck," she said, examining the pen.

"It wouldn't kill you, but it would knock you out cold and that is not anywhere in our plans," Luke said, watching her figure out the pen.

"Can I try it?"

"No," we both yelled in unison.

"It only carries enough charge for a few shots, so you will save them until you need them," I explained, doubting my sanity at having given it to her.

"Which you won't," Luke added.

"I sure as hell hope not," she muttered, still staring at the pen.

"This is such a bad idea." I shook my head and began to pace.

"If I thought they'd come up with just one of us, I'd tell you to stay, but they're fucking crazy," Luke said, and handed me my purse.

He was right. There was a reason they wanted both of us, but it had better be good or I was going to kick their asses.

The fastest way to the meeting point was out the front door and through the throngs of protesters. I wanted to avoid the mousey gal at all costs. I was in the kind of mood that if she looked at me wrong, I'd take her out, and I simply didn't have time for that at the moment.

"They better have a good reason for this," I muttered as we zig-zagged our way through the riled-up crowd.

"The atmosphere out here is turning hostile," Luke observed as we made our way past the last of them.

"I noticed that. It wasn't like that an hour ago. I wonder what's going on."

"We'll figure that out after we get the nut jobs."

As we rounded the corner, I gagged and Luke stopped short.

"What the fuck?" he said, and lifted his arm to protect his nose with his sleeve. "What is that smell?"

"God," I gasped. "It smells like skunk."

"It smells like a herd of skunk," he choked out.

"You mean a surfeit," I corrected him.

"A sure fit?"

"No, dumbass." I giggled. "A group of skunks is called a surfeit."

"And you know this because . . ."

"Jeopardy," I said, trying to breathe through my mouth. The

odor was so heavy I could taste it. Breathing was losing its appeal. "Holy hell, they can't possibly be out here in this."

"We have to go to the checkpoint. If they're not there and this is some kind of fucked-up joke, I'll shoot them," he informed me.

"I will too."

He grinned happily and I grinned right back. "Plug your nose and let's go."

He took my hand and we walked into what smelled like the bowels of hell . . . and it was about to get worse.

Mrs. C and Edith stood about twenty feet away by the gate where we were supposed to meet them. They were pissed and they were soaking wet.

"If you hadn't forgotten the goddamned SCREW-Con tickets, none of this would have happened, heifer," Mrs. C hissed at Edith.

"You say one more word about that and I will choke you to death and enjoy it," Edith shot back. "I wasn't the one who stepped on a goddamned gaggle of skunks."

"It wasn't a gaggle," Mrs. C said, walloping her sister. "It was one fucking skunk. And a group of skunks isn't called a gaggle, it's called a herd, jackass."

"I call bullshit," Edith yelled, diving at her sister and trying to choke her. Mrs. C sidestepped her and popped her in the back of the head as she went down.

"Bullshit that," Mrs. C grunted, and kicked her sister in the butt for good measure.

"It's called a surfeit," I yelled with my nose plugged.

"What the hell?" Edith gasped, and rolled to a defensive crouch. Mrs. C pulled an Uzi and aimed it at us. Clearly, they hadn't heard our approach. "Put the gun down, idiot," she snapped at her sister. "You could have killed Mag the Hag and her concubine. That would have been quite the clusterfuck, considering you also forgot the fucking tickets," she shrieked.

I stood patiently and waited for them to get it all out of their systems.

"Did she just call me your concubine?" Luke asked me.

"Um . . . yes." I giggled. "I believe she did."

The gals had about fifteen minutes of sister bitch fight left in them before they were able to pull themselves together sufficiently to hold a somewhat normal, albeit horrifically smelling, conversation. I'd never seen so many creative takedowns in my life. The old coots were extremely limber and if they'd been younger, I might have suggested they go out for Cirque du Soleil, but they were pushing seventy and they liked to kill people. Probably not a good fit.

"So Mag," Edith wheezed, trying to catch her breath after being socked in the stomach with the butt of Mrs. C's Uzi. "We have a little problem here."

"That's right," Mrs. C added, breathing heavily. "Fuck-for-Brains forgot the tickets and we couldn't get in. The hotel dick-wads thought we were with the religious ass-munchers protesting outside. We tried to explain nicely that they were mistaken, but . . ."

"But," Edith cut her sister off, "my sister got impatient and called the little hotel turd-knocker a fucktard and they kicked us out."

"Interesting," Luke said with his fingers plugging his nose. "And the rest of the story . . . ?"

"Right." Edith gave her sister the stink eye and kept going. Mrs. C flipped her off and began to make a show of sharpening her rather intimidating bowie knife. Lovely. "So, the fat cow here decided we should scale the building and crawl through your window."

"You agreed to it, you stinky hooker," Mrs. C snapped.

I truly thought Edith was going to self-combust. I'd never seen her so mad. "Yes," she said steaming, "But I didn't agree that we needed a quarter mile running start from the skunk-infested field behind the hotel."

"You agreed if we got a good jump we'd stand a better chance of getting to the second-story ledge, smelly ass."

"If you make one more odiferous comment, I will knock your head into your shoulders. Permanently."

I glanced over at the building. There was no way they could have jumped to the second story. They were insane, they smelled like hell—and we had to work with them.

"Why are you wet?" Luke asked the question I was afraid to hear the answer to.

"Shit for brains"—Mrs. C pointed at her sister—"thought it

would be a fine idea to wash the scent off in the hotel pool. I'm fairly sure the sirens you hear in the distance are a direct response to that assmonkey move."

"Did you have a better idea?" Edith ground out through clenched teeth.

"Douche," Luke said.

"What?" I laughed at his new name for the gals.

"Did you call me a douche?" Mrs. C demanded, brandishing her knife.

"No," Luke said. "I didn't call you a douche. I implied that you need to douche."

"Well of all the . . ." Edith sputtered, picking up her Uzi and aiming at Luke's head.

"He's right," I said, stepping in front of Luke out of habit. Luke chuckled and moved me to his side.

"Thank you for protecting me, light of my life, but I can handle it." He walked over to Edith and put his hand out for her machine gun. She reluctantly handed it over. "Douche will remove the skunk smell. I'll run to the drugstore and get some. You and your stench will remain outside with Candy until I get back."

"Wait one goddamned minute, you're telling me if we had dunked ourselves in douche instead of pool water, we wouldn't smell like skunk ass?" Mrs. C asked.

"Close," Luke told her. "You wouldn't smell like wet skunk ass, which, by the way, is far worse than plain old skunk ass."

I had to agree. My gag reflex was on overdrive.

"Well Jesus Christ, that's the best news I've heard since we found out Candy here was Mag the Hag reincarnated," Edith crowed, and went to hug Luke.

"No," he yelled, backing away. "While I appreciate the sentiment, I'd probably hurl all over you and we certainly don't need to add that to the mix."

"Roger that," Edith said, saluting him.

"I'll just run to the store and . . ."

"No need. We have four cases of douche in the back of our van," Mrs. C informed us.

I was speechless and Luke went pale. The burning question was why they had four cases of douche in their van, but neither one of us was willing or able to touch that one.

"I'll be right back." Edith sprinted in the direction of the field.

"Watch out for the fucking skunk," Mrs. C called after her. "We parked under a tree just in case we had to make a quick getaway. Parking lots suck for that."

I nodded mutely and Luke just stood there. I knew he was sill stuck in the mystery of the massive amounts of douche.

"It will never make sense," I whispered to him. "Drop it or you might go insane."

"Roger that," he mumbled, still trying to let it go.

"So thank God all the paperwork was in a waterproof folder," Mrs. C said, handing over a thin lime green plastic case. "We've deciphered it, but I think we need Shoshanna to figure it out."

"Did you run it by Steve?" I asked, praying Edith would return quickly. My eyes were watering and my nose felt singed.

"Nah, he's kind of pissed about a little mishap in his office and we figured it out on the drive up. No time. Although we should probably give him a call. He is involved."

"Probably," I muttered, thinking that it was stupid not to have informed him first, but the sisters worked with their own set of rules. I just hoped they really had something . . . because we didn't.

"Got it," Edith bellowed as she arrived, carrying four huge boxes. "Do we just shove it in our . . ."

"No." I cut her off before Luke and I had to hear whatever term they favored for female genitalia. "Pour it all over your bodies and rub it in."

"Strip," Mrs. C told her sister.

Luke and I couldn't turn away fast enough. "Let us . . . um, know when you're done." I'd seen too much in my short life that I couldn't erase. Mrs. C and Edith naked and douching their skunky bodies off would make my brain implode and I would most likely die.

After twenty minutes of staring at the back of the hotel and imagining them scaling it, they were done.

"You can turn your pansy asses around now," Edith told us.

We turned to find them decked out in sequined halter tops, leather pants, and combat boots. They looked like drowned circus clowns, but the smell had abated somewhat or else I'd just gotten used to it.

"I smell like spring rain," Edith boasted.

"And I smell like extra cleansing vinegar and water in a field of wildflowers," Mrs. C added.

"That's fantastic," Luke said. "Now lets get our asses back up to the room and figure this out."

We trudged back around the building. Although the smell was better, it definitely still lingered, as proved by the parting of the Red Sea of protesters as we made our way to the hotel entrance. The wrinkled noses and gasping of the Jesus lovers would have been humorous if I hadn't been a participant. This day was only getting worse and I worried what else it held in store . . .

Chapter 26

"What in the hell is that smell?" Shoshanna screeched when we entered my room en masse. The sisters were positively sheepish in the presence of their idol.

"Sorry," Edith muttered, getting down on one knee and genuflecting to Shoshanna. "We had a little run-in with a skunk's ass. We douched thoroughly and we are deeply mortified to offend you in any way." Mrs. C dropped to her knees beside her sister.

"Get your asses up." Shoshanna laughed. "You kill me. I hope no harm came to the skunk."

The old dykes paled considerably and mumbled something incoherent about the skunk being happy, healthy, and fine—prancing off into the field of wilderness behind the hotel to play with his skunk friends. I realized we'd completely forgotten to inquire about the skunk, but from their ridiculous story, I was certain the skunk would no longer use his ass again. Ever.

"Okay, time to get to work." I sat down at my laptop and started poring through the massive number of pictures I'd taken. The quality was outstanding.

"Talk to me," Luke told the old gals. "And by the way, another note arrived when you were in transit and it . . ."

"Don't tell me," Mrs. C cut him off. "Let me guess. The greeting has to start with an E."

Luke paused and checked the copy he held in his hand. "Yep. You were expecting that?"

"Yeah," Edith chimed in. "The E makes it *mine*. Of course, it could have been a T or a D, but it wouldn't have made as much sense. *Mind* or *mint* wouldn't have worked."

"Explain," he said.

"I'm dying to hear this," Shoshanna added.

"You're not dying anytime soon," Luke told her, and put his arm around her.

"Are you Shoshanna's concubine too?" Edith asked, impressed.

"Fuck no!" Shoshanna cackled. "Luke's my son."

"How in the fuck did we not know this?" Mrs. C demanded of her sister. "Have our sources been slacking?" She was utterly shocked and pissed.

"I'll take their balls off when we get back," Edith promised her.

"Wait." Shoshanna jumped in quickly, fearing for the testicles of people she didn't know. "It's a new thing. I'm adopting him. The paperwork is ready—we just have to go to the courthouse and file when we get back."

Luke seemed surprised and flustered. As much as he secretly wanted this to happen, I don't think he'd really thought it would. God, I couldn't love Shoshanna more.

"Are you open to some new daughters?" Edith asked, wondering if she and her sister had a shot. It was clear they'd never get to date Shoshanna, so I supposed being her daughters was the next best thing.

"Nah," she told a disappointed Edith. "Already got a daughter, but I am looking to add to my friendship tree."

The old gals perked up immediately and slapped each other a high five. I tried to suppress my giggles and failed. I buried my head back in my computer before I said something to the gals that might start a fistfight. The pictures were fascinating. I'd gotten an alarming number of photos of the mousey gal. Boy, Mousey had some bad teeth . . .

"Enough of the chitchat." Luke was all business and sexier than hell.

"Right," Mrs. C said, pulling out her copies of the notes. "If you put the threats in order and take the first letter of each greeting, there's a message. Pretty unsophisticated, but then again I don't think we're looking for someone with a shit-monster load of brains."

I half listened as I scanned the pictures. The shots I'd taken from behind me were starting to get interesting. There was a man and a cloaked women talking with people intently. Riling them up. I noticed fist bumping and angry faces. WTF?

"Yep," Edith said. "Fairly amateur, but they do have some knowledge of police procedure because there's not a print to be found on these notes."

"So it's a cop?" Shoshanna was appalled. She held the law in high esteem. Her son was a DEA agent, for God's sake.

"No." Edith shook her head. "Someone in the field wouldn't have used such a simplistic code and I don't think they would have left the cryptic message we found."

"Look at this shit," I told Luke. "Here's the reason the crowd was getting hostile." He moved in and leaned over my shoulder. "Look at that man and the woman. They're doing something to the crowd."

"Can you go in closer?"

"Let me see." I moved in and blew the picture up. It got blurry and I still couldn't make out the woman's face.

"Keep scrolling," he said. "See if you captured a better shot of her."

"On it."

"Do you think the God-heads are involved?" Mrs. C asked, checking out the pictures.

"Don't know," I muttered, scrolling quickly, "but my gut says yes."

"I know you think we're full of shitfire and hot air, but you are Mag the Hag."

The visual of shitfire and hot air was not a good one. The girls had such a riveting way with words. Hell, I was halfway beginning to believe I might be Mag, not that I would ever admit it. The pure agony of the time I'd have to spend with them catching up would keep my lips zipped for eternity.

"Candy, keep looking," Luke instructed. "Ladies, back to the notes."

"Right. The message is about Steve."

"Wait. What?" I stopped mid-scroll and turned to the gals. "It's about Steve and you didn't call him?" Were they insane *and* stupid? "What if he's in danger?"

"I don't think he is. It's Shoshanna this person is after," Edith said, but pulled out her phone and texted Steve the information. "He's gonna scream like a girl and I'm just not in the mood," she said, indicating her text.

"What the hell does it say?" I asked, exasperated. They needed to just get to it.

"It says, *Steve is mine,*" Edith said. *"Steve is mine."*

"Well, what the fuck does that mean?" Shoshanna was bewildered.

"I don't know," Mrs. C said. "We were hoping this would make sense to you."

"Well, it doesn't," Shoshanna replied.

Something in my gut clenched hard and I started scrolling like a mad woman. The cloaked woman and the note were connected and I had a feeling I knew exactly who she was. I just needed the proof. Why couldn't I find a shot with her face? Dammit, there had to be at least one.

Edith's phone started ringing. Shoshanna started freaking and Luke started swearing. It was all I could do to concentrate, but I knew I was right.

"Goddammit," Edith groaned. "It's Steve. Do I have to answer this?"

"Yes," we all shouted in unison. The chatter continued and it was driving me nuts. I simply had to block everyone out and focus on the task in front of me. We were so fucking close I was starting to tingle.

Edith was listening to a tirade from Steve. Though I couldn't make out what he was saying, I could tell he was pissed. Luke stood next to her and listened in. Shoshanna was pacing the room and Mrs. C was doing something akin to yoga. Scroll. I had to scroll.

"What?" Edith bellowed. "You're fucking kidding me!"

"Give me the phone," Luke snapped. "Get your laptop open and pull up the e-mail he just sent. Now."

Edith hustled over to her bag and went to work. Mrs. C, having finished her meditation, was arming herself to the teeth.

"I love the smell of napalm in the morning. Smells like victory," Mrs. C grunted as she tucked a wicked-looking knife into her boot. Holy God Almighty, she was quoting *Apocalypse Now*. This did not bode well.

"Right," Luke said in a tight voice to Steve. "You're sure? Do you have the e-mail pulled up?" he asked Edith.

"Almost," she said.

I scrolled and froze. I was absolutely sure the picture I'd just found would match the one in the e-mail Edith had received from Steve. I couldn't believe it, but then again it made perfect sense.

"Got her," I yelled.

"Me too," Edith added.

"What the fuck?" Shoshanna exploded when she saw the picture. "It's Helen?"

"Who's Helen?" Mrs. C asked. "Actually I don't care who she is. I'm going to shoot her. Somebody show me a goddamned photo," she huffed, and checked her Uzi.

"Helen is Steve's ex-wife," I told her.

"He's gay," she informed me as if I didn't know.

"Yes," I agreed. "And therein lies the problem, I think."

"Why does Helen want me dead?" Shoshanna dropped into a chair and ran her little hands through her hair. "What the hell have I done to her?"

"It makes no sense to you or me, but I'm going to go with the guess that you were married to Kevin and now he's married to Steve," I said, taking a screen shot of the picture and forwarding it to Steve. We had our girl, now we just had to find her. I grabbed my purse and headed toward the door.

"No," Luke said. "You'll stay with Shoshanna. You're the only one of us she knows, and if she sees you she might run or God knows what else."

He was right, but I was pissed. I wanted to take her down for so many reasons I couldn't begin to count them. I was ready to fight him on it, but I stopped myself. I would never go Rambo on a case again. Ever. If I went down there and she recognized me, I could jeopardize everything. My needs were secondary. Shoshanna's life and safety were paramount. Not to mention Luke's and the old gals'.

"I'm good with that."

Luke watched my internal struggle and gave me a quick nod of approval. "Edith and Mrs. C, we're going down. We will not kill her unless it's absolutely necessary. I want to take her as quickly and quietly as possible. Alive."

"Can I use chloroform?" Edith asked, holding up a rag and a bottle.

"Yep." Luke nodded, impressed at how well equipped the gals

were. "Chloroform, good. Uzi, bad. Just make sure you don't breathe it in."

"Aww fuck, commander boy." She laughed. "I'm totally immune to that shit."

Luke's eyes grew large, and Mrs. C gave him a thumbs-up to confirm Edith's story. "You two are something else." He shook his head and grinned.

"You don't even know the half of it," I muttered, and double-checked that my Glock was loaded.

"Is she working alone?" Edith doused her rag in chloroform and shoved it in her pocket as she continued her questions.

"There's a man with her in the pictures, but my gut says she's going solo on this."

"I agree," Luke added, "but I want him too."

They were locked and loaded and still managed to look like tourists—not a weapon in sight. Although there was still one major problem . . .

"Lose the sequined halters," I told the sisters. "You stand out like a sore thumb."

"On it," Mrs. C said, dropping her halter to the ground. I shrieked and slapped my hand over my eyes. I didn't mean for that to happen, but I should have known better. "Does anyone have a T-shirt?" she asked, completely uncaring that her torpedo tits were swinging in the wind.

"I do," I choked out, and ran to my suitcase with my eyes on the floor. I yanked out the first two that my fingers touched and handed them over with my eyes closed.

"Didn't take you for such a prude," Mrs. C guffawed, and pulled my T-shirt over her head, effectively covering her boobs.

"I'm not," I mumbled. "You just took me by surprise."

"Mag, you haven't changed one goddamned bit," Edith said, and slapped me joyfully on the back, sending me barreling into Luke.

"You know, Candy, with a body like yours, you could be a stripper," Edith teased, and flashed me her boob.

"Candy only strips for me. Period," Luke informed them, and winked at me. "We've got work to do. Quick, quiet and out of there."

"God," Mrs. C yelled, hopping from one foot to the other. "This is gonna be fun."

The door clicked behind them and they were gone. I took a deep breath and noticed a very quiet Shoshanna. She was pale and shaken and looked so small in the chair.

"It will be all right. I promise." I wrapped my arms around her and hugged her tight. "Luke and the girls are the very best and this will be over in the matter of an hour or less."

"I just don't get it," she muttered, holding on to me. "Is it because Steve is gay?"

"I guess so, but it's more because Helen appears to be severely mentally imbalanced. She can't fathom his homosexuality, so she has to lay the blame somewhere."

"God, I feel so sorry for her."

I was stunned to silence. How could Shoshanna have compassion for someone who wanted her dead? I was overjoyed at the thought of nailing Helen. It would mean Steve and Kevin would have a good shot of getting those kids and there would be one less hate-filled fanatic running around. But maybe Shoshanna had it right and I had it wrong. Could I still want her put away and find it in me to feel sorry for her? Too heavy. I'd think about that some other time. I needed to stay focused and present for Shoshanna.

"I'm really tired," she said. "Would it be okay if I lie down for a bit?"

"Of course." I was worried about the toll this was taking on her. She was tough, but this was a world of shit she didn't belong in. This was not helping my attempt to feel sorry for Helen. "Come on, let me tuck you in."

Once she was safely snoring in her bed, I went back to my connecting suite. I had pulled her blinds down and cracked the door between our rooms. Glancing over at the monitor, I saw she was sleeping soundly and that eased my mind a bit. However, I had so much freaking pent-up energy inside of me, I had to do something. I paced the room and got a whiff of myself. Hell, I smelled like skunk ass. I'd sponge off and then I'd do a hundred crunches and sit-ups. Having a plan made me feel better. I checked the monitor one more time and then hustled to the bathroom.

Chapter 27

It felt great to be clean. Leaving the door open, I scrubbed quickly, trying to remove all the skunky scent and idly wondered if the gals had any more douche. I sniffed my skin. Nah, I was good—didn't need to douche. My phone and my gun were on the counter. Clean in three minutes . . . a new record. I yanked on some black yoga pants, tennis shoes, and a jogging bra, strapped on my holster, and slid my gun in. As I tucked my phone into my bra, a shiver crawled up my spine and I froze. Something was wrong—I could feel it. My brother Mitch called it my Spidey Sense. I called it my stay-alive radar.

Rushing back into the room, I ran to check Shoshanna. The door was closed and locked. I went to bang on it and stopped short when I noticed the monitor. Fuck. Helen was in the room and she was wielding a large sharp knife at a terrified Shoshanna. So much for compassion. Helen was going to die today.

Going to my calm place, I grabbed a file from my bag, cranked up the volume, on the monitor, and went to work. Lock picking was an illegal specialty of mine, and I was good. With my eyes on the lock and my ears glued to the sounds from the monitor, I went to work. Time and silence were of the essence.

"So, whore," Helen hissed, and sat down in a chair. "What do you have to say for yourself?"

"I'm confused, Helen," Shoshanna said calmly. "What have I done to you?"

Good, Shoshanna . . . stay calm. Keep talking . . .

"What have you done? What have you done?" Helen shrieked. "You ruined my life. That's what you've done."

I glanced over at the monitor. Shoshanna was cornered by her bed and Helen was in a chair she'd moved between the door to the hallway and the door to my room, making escape impossible for Shoshanna. Son of a bitch, the lock was more complicated than I thought. I considered texting Luke, but my fingers were occupied, time was short, and Helen was insane.

"Tell me how," Shoshanna said in a quiet voice. "Tell me how so I can help you."

"You can't help me," she snapped, and gave Shoshanna a grin that sent chills through my body. I pulled the monitor closer to the door so I could keep my eye on the situation. Last resort was to shoot the lock out and take her down, but I wasn't sure if the knife was her only weapon. "You've already caused enough damage, so now you have to pay."

"If you're going to kill me, I think I have a right to know why."

"Actually you don't, but I'm feeling generous at the moment so I'll tell you." She laughed and played with the knife. "You broke up my marriage," she spat.

"But you were already divorced," Shoshanna said shakily. "I didn't even know you."

"Shut up, bitch," she snapped. "It's my turn right now. I'm making the rules and what I say goes. Do you understand, slut?"

"Yes," Shoshanna answered meekly. "Sorry."

"Not yet, but you will be. So as I was saying, you're clearly a faggot-loving piece of shit. Which by the way, you'll burn in hell for."

Shoshanna sat silently and waited.

Smart. That was smart. Stay quiet. Helen might blow at any moment . . .

"Because you married a filthy homo, he was available to my husband. When Steve lost his way from the path of God, he strayed to the sinners. It's your fault that Kevin"—she hissed viciously—"tempted my husband to the devil. Your fault," she screamed, getting up out of her chair and advancing on Shoshanna.

Goddamned fucking lock . . .

"You're going to get caught, Helen," Shoshanna told her. "How do you think you're going to get away with this?"

"Ohhhh, I already have gotten away with it," she said sweetly, running the blade under Shoshanna's chin. "You have a little work to do before I kill you. Are you ready?"

Jesus Christ, don't tell her we already know it's her . . .

I had pulled my gun and was ready to shoot the lock out, but paused. Shoshanna had more time. Helen wanted something. Wedging the file into the lock, I heard a small click. The lock was layered—I needed to hear at least three more clicks.

"What do you need, Helen?"

"Don't call me by my name," she yelled, and paced the floor in small circles. "You don't deserve to utter the name of a child of God."

"Sorry, you're right."

"Too late to repent," she said breezily. "I gave you many chances and you failed."

She pulled a piece of paper and a pen from her pocket—that's when I noticed she wore thin rubber gloves. No prints . . .

"You're going to write a suicide note, my dear. You're going to denounce the disgusting practice of homosexuality. You're going to say you witnessed Kevin molesting my children and that Steve was aware of it and did nothing. You're going to apologize to God and let the world know that faggots are evil and should be jailed for sodomy and child molestation. You're going to ruin his life like you ruined mine and then you'll die. It's fairly cut and dry. Did you get all that?"

Shoshanna was shaking and tears were running down her cheeks. She just needed to hold on a little longer. I was two clicks in. Helen was going down. Hard and fast.

"I don't think I can remember all that," Shoshanna whispered. I saw her glance toward my door and I prayed she knew I was trying to get to her.

"That's fine," Helen said amiably, handing her the paper and pen. "I wouldn't expect a fag-hag like you to be that smart anyway. Here's a copy. You can work from that and then sign it."

Shoshanna sat down and began writing. Her hand shook and she kept wiping tears from her eyes.

Three clicks. One more fucking click . . .

I was sweating and pissed. I decided that texting Luke was a necessary pause. What if I couldn't get the fourth click? It was not Shoshanna's day to die.

Helen in Shoshanna's room.
Has knife.

Locked out. Picking lock.
Proceed with caution.

Send. He would understand. He wouldn't bust in. He'd come here and check the monitor and we'd figure it out, but my plan was to be in and done by the time backup arrived.

"I don't have all day," Helen said in a bored voice. "Hurry up. I have a new man friend waiting for me and I want this done."

"I'm writing," Shoshanna said softly, trying to steady her voice. "There's a lot here."

"It's rather brilliant, don't you think? I mean really. I can't believe I thought the entire thing up myself. God has watched over me and guided me," she gushed proudly.

She was fucking crazy.

Shoshanna didn't utter a word. She kept her head down and continued writing.

"I'm not sure if we should do it in this room. Blood is so very difficult to remove from carpeting. How about the bathroom?"

Not a word from Shoshanna.

"I asked you a question," she shrieked. "You will answer me or I'll make it hurt real bad."

"The bathroom would be fine," Shoshanna muttered. "This pen doesn't work. Do you mind if I use mine?"

"Whatever," Helen snapped.

Motherfucker, why couldn't I get the lock popped? Oh. My. God. Shoshanna had the laser pen in her hand. Brilliant.

"All right," she sang. "Time's up."

Helen was crazed and excited. This was bad. She paced the room like a caged animal and kept glancing at herself in the mirror.

"He was a fool to have thrown me over for a man," she hissed. "He will be so fucking sorry."

She ran over to the bathroom door and opened it . . . only she fucked up. She opened the door to the hallway, not the bathroom. Should I stay on the lock where I could watch the monitor and see what she was doing or go to the hallway? Would Shoshanna actually use the pen on Helen? I gave myself thirty more seconds on the lock; if it didn't pop, I was out of here.

"Come on," she grunted, pulling Shoshanna to her feet and slicing her cheek. And that was when all hell broke loose.

Shoshanna screamed in pain and dropped to the floor. Helen

tried to drag a wailing Shoshanna to the bathroom. Shoshanna lifted the pen and shot Helen somewhere in the vicinity of her legs as the door from the hallway to Shoshanna's room flew open violently. The fourth and final click popped on the lock and I burst into the nightmare of confusion.

My eyes had to adjust to the low light and I heard a grunt and another scream. A body knocked me to the ground and I pulled my gun.

"What the fuck?" a man shouted.

The laser had slowed Helen and the impact of the hallway door flying open had slammed into the back of Helen's head and sent her flying. Shoshanna was huddled on the floor in a ball holding the pen and, sobbing, and Jim stood there freaked out and confused.

Jim. Jim was coming to work with Shoshanna, heard her scream, and plowed through the door. The body on top of mine was Helen's. I rolled her off and connected the butt of my gun with the back of her head. Twice.

"What the fuck is happening in here?" Jim bellowed, now on the floor beside Shoshanna. "I mean what the fucking fuck?"

Shoshanna was sobbing incoherently. I kicked the knocked-out Helen and moved to them. "You and Shoshanna just saved Shoshanna's life," I panted from exertion and adrenaline.

"What the hell are you?" he demanded.

I realized I was holding my Glock in one hand and a gnarly looking file in the other. No wonder he was freaked. I would have been, too, if I was in his shoes, but it was over. He had saved the day and deserved to know.

"Candace Sanderson. DEA. I was here undercover protecting Shoshanna. You did my job for me, and for that I'm in your debt. Always."

I knelt down and took a trembling Shoshanna in my arms. "It's over," I told her. "You're okay. No one can hurt you now." I removed the pen from her hand and checked the cut on her cheek. It was bleeding a lot. She would need stitches. I pulled the sheet from her bed and pressed it against the wound.

"You're not Mandy Dandermanschmidt?"

"Nope."

"And I'm going to hazard a guess that your buddy isn't Duke LeHump, the famous cover model?"

"Correct again." I smiled at Jim and rocked Shoshanna like a baby. "His name is Luke Blakely and he's DEA too."

Jim grinned and shook his head. "This is some kind of fucked up. Is Shoshanna going to be all right?" He reached over and ran his hand gently over her head.

"She'll need some stitches, but she'll be okay."

"Jim," she sniffed. "You're a good boy and I love you."

"I love you too." He chuckled. "I'm glad I was a little early for our session. I was so stoked to work together, I couldn't wait."

"Thank sweet baby Jesus in a boob tube you didn't," she said, and laughed weakly.

She was still hanging in there. My eyes filled with tears and I knew she would be okay. Sometimes trauma could change people. Make them half of who they were before—sad, closed off, and afraid. Wait . . . was that who I was? Was that what had happened to me?

Luke, Mrs. C, and Edith had snuck quietly into the room with weapons pulled. It was alarming to me and must have been downright terrifying to Jim. Luke took one look at the situation and quickly cuffed Helen, who was still out cold.

"Talk," he said to me as he squatted down and examined Shoshanna's face.

"She got in and locked the doors between the rooms," I started.

"I thought it was Jim," Shoshanna said, starting to tear up again. "I was asleep and someone knocked at the door and I thought it was Jim, so I opened it."

"Where were you?" he asked me.

"Bathroom. I screwed up."

He nodded curtly. He wasn't pleased. Hell, neither was I. Shoshanna could have died because I'd been unhappy with how I smelled.

"Excuse me," Edith cut in. "Would anyone mind if I shot the piece of trash on the floor?"

Everyone silently contemplated her question for a moment.

"You can't just shoot her," Jim gasped.

"Sure I can," Edith grunted. "And who the hell are you?"

"Um, Jim. I'm Jim Jameson."

"Love your whiskey," she told him. "So what's the feeling about a little shot in the ass or somewhere like the hand or foot? I promise I won't hit a major artery and I'll do my damnedest not to actually kill her," she lied unconvincingly.

"No," Shoshanna said. "Don't shoot her. She needs help and she needs to be put away. Her kids will be screwed up enough; they don't need to be motherless on top of it all."

Luke and I eyed each other. Neither of us condoned shooting Helen, but neither of us thought her children would be better off with her alive.

"Where's the weapon?" Mrs. C asked. "And I'm still not clear on what happened here."

"Helen got in. Shoshanna tased her. Jim knocked her out and saved the day," I said. It was short and correct and I had no desire to rehash the whole thing yet.

"Shoshanna, you have the guts of a lesbian," Edith yelled proudly, and saluted her.

"Good fucking work, Jim. What branch are you?" Mrs. C asked, reluctantly putting her Uzi away.

"I'm . . . um, a writer."

"Well, I'll be damned," she shouted, and held out her hand for Jim to shake. "You've got some goddamned big testicles for a writer."

"Um . . . thanks?" he mumbled.

"You're welcome," she bellowed. "Now where is the piece of shit's weapon?"

"Oh wow." Jim paled and his voice sounded odd. "I think I found it."

He certainly had. It was sticking out of his thigh. Somehow, Helen must have stabbed him before she went flying across the room. Edith insisted we not remove the knife. She decided she liked Jim and wasn't in the mood for him to bleed out and die. Jim, God love him, thanked her and tried not to pass out. All of the excitement and shock had masked his pain, but he was feeling it now.

"Huge fucking balls, I tell you," Mrs. C shouted, completely impressed. "That boy has balls!"

The police came, took statements, and removed Helen. After medical attention, she would be transported back to Minneapolis for processing. She was in a world of trouble. The footage of her showdown with Shoshanna had already been sent to Steve. I worried how he would feel when he saw it. He had loved her at one point in his life . . .

The rest of us . . . all six of us, spent four hours together in the ER. Shoshanna got twelve stitches on her cheek and big-balled Jim got twenty in his thigh. The knife had missed all major arteries and muscles. He was lucky.

I kept rolling around the fact I could have been the cause of Shoshanna's death, and it didn't sit well.

"Mag," Edith said, getting up in my face. "Everyone has to shit. Shoshanna's all right. You need to learn from this and move on. Drop it. Someday when I'm drunk I will tell you stories that will break your heart and make you realize that there's a fucking plan. We're all where we're supposed to be all the motherfucking time. It's not always how we want it to be . . . it just fucking is. Remember that. It's fucking profound." With that, she walked over to her sister and sat down to wait. Luke took my hand in his and stared off into the distance. He was in lala land. His own world—and I let him stay there.

"I can't lose her," he whispered. "I just got her and I want to keep her."

"She's not going anywhere." I squeezed his hand and kissed the back of it.

"What about you?" he asked.

I paused. If he'd asked me this morning, the answer would have been different, but this morning was a lifetime ago. "I'm not sure," I answered as truthfully as I could.

He nodded his head and held on to my hand tighter. If only it were that simple.

Chapter 28

"**W**ho wants pizza?" Shoshanna yelled, almost back to herself after our field trip to the ER.

We were all in my suite: Luke, Shoshanna, Jim, Mrs. C, Edith, and me. The sisters had taken quite a shine to Jim and were fussing over him. Edith took his measurements and promised him a new sweater. I'd forgotten they knitted. It was difficult to see them as anything other than crazy, smelly, locked-and-loaded assassins.

Shoshanna held Luke's hand and bounced like a little ball. "It's over," she said. "My cheek is killing me, but the wound is in a nice spot. It will look mysterious and sexy when the stitches come out."

"I've got so many fucking scars," Mrs. C boasted. "Let me show you a doozy." She unsnapped her pants and began to lower them.

"Good God, no!" I moaned, and covered my eyes. I'd already seen her boobs, I did not want to add her ass to the catalog.

"All right, fine," she huffed, pulling her pants back up. "I'll show you all later when Miss Prissy Pants leaves."

"Speaking of . . ." Luke said. "Now that this is done, I'm going back to Minneapolis. Who's with me?"

The room went silent. Looks of horror spread across Shoshanna's and the dykes' faces. Jim was surprised and I was confused. What was the problem? Shoshanna was safe. We'd done our job. It was time to go . . .

"But the pageant," Shoshanna gasped. "You are the star of the pageant. You can't leave; poor Medusa will be bald. You're Duke LeHump—my son."

"Um, I . . ." Luke was at a loss; he glanced to me for help. I shrugged my shoulders and giggled. I was fairly sure we were stuck . . .

"Jim can't do it since he was stabbed by a fucking lunatic," Edith said with her arm protectively around her new boy toy.

"That only leaves Teddy, Rocky, Cesar, and Cheech . . . and you two," Shoshanna whined, giving Luke one of those looks that he couldn't say no to. "Please?"

"I'll leave this one to Candy," he said, ducking as I tried to swat him in the head.

"You suck," I muttered, and realized all eyes in the room were glued to me. Fuck. I had no choice. I mean, what did I have to get home to? My time with Luke was limited. I knew in my heart I couldn't give up what he needed me to, so could another day or two with him hurt? Who was I kidding? My heart was going to be in shreds when I walked away. Postponing the devastation was a better idea.

I peeked over at him. He was watching me with that wicked sexy half grin and a little part of my heart tore. He was so beautiful and so . . .

"We'll stay," I said, ripping my eyes from Luke. "But after the pageant we're out of here."

"Yay!" Shoshanna yelled, and the rest of the room joined in. Edith and Mrs. C, never ones to miss a performance opportunity, did a disturbing modern dance that ended in the splits. Jim pulled himself to his feet and gave them a standing ovation. I saw the old coots eye each other in silent psychotic twin communication. Whether Jim knew it or not . . . whether he still had a living biological family or not . . . he was about to get adopted by two insane lesbians. God bless him.

The pizza arrived and we ate and laughed. It was as if nothing had happened earlier. Shoshanna was a little quieter than usual and her vocabulary was less profane, but she seemed happy and content. I was amazed at how resilient people were. How life always went on even after bad things happened. Jim was deep in conversation with Shoshanna about his book and the lesbians listened attentively. The delight on their faces was something I'd never seen. They were with their idol and the young man who didn't yet realize he belonged to them.

"Hey you," Luke said, standing in front of me with his hand extended. "Come with me."

"But Shoshanna, I can't leave her and . . ."

"She's fine. It's over and Jim's going to stay here tonight. You, on the other hand," he said, giving me a look that made everything south of my belly button start to tingle, "are not."

Everything else disappeared except Luke. *God, how was I going to say good-bye?* I stood and took his hand. I had no idea if we said we were leaving to anyone in the room. I forgot anyone else was even in the room. I placed my hand in his and I followed him. I would have followed him anywhere. I inhaled deeply and let all the turmoil in my mind fall away. I wanted to be right where I was . . . in this moment . . . with the man I had stupidly fallen in love with.

His room was dark and it smelled like him—all sexy and soapy and man. He turned on the bedside lamp and stared at me, as if he was trying to memorize me and I did the same.

"Luke, I . . ."

"Nope, not tonight. No talking tonight unless it's yelling my name and comparing me to God." He grinned and pulled his shirt over his head.

Why did he have to look like he did? He was so damn beautiful I had to sit. He wasn't the broody, angry, closed-off guy that Steve used to know. I still saw the pain and violence of his past in his eyes occasionally, but it was less now. He was open and happy and so damn sexy . . . Was it me? Did I make him this way?

"I'd ask you what you were thinking if I wasn't afraid of your answer," he said, pulling me up from the chair and flush with his body.

"When you do that, I can't think at all," I said truthfully, lightly running my fingers over his chest.

"I don't want to fuck tonight," he said, and my eyes shot to his in disappointment. He chuckled and pulled me closer, putting his lips by my ear. "Let me rephrase that. We're definitely going to fuck, but it's going to be more. I want to make love to every inch of your body and then I want to do it again. And again."

My knees buckled and I grabbed his shoulders for balance. "God, don't say stuff like that unless you want me to pass out before we get started."

"You'll pass out," he assured me as he lifted me and carried me to his bed, "but it won't be until you've come so many times you can't take any more."

"Promises, promises," I quipped shakily.

"Candace, I don't make promises I can't keep. Remember that."

And he wasn't joking—not even a little bit. At the rate we were going, neither of us would make it to the pageant tomorrow because we couldn't walk . . . much less twerk.

"I think I'm dead," I groaned, and laughed.

"Nah, you just need a little breather before you ride me like a cowboy," he challenged. Every nerve in my body jumped to attention. How did he do that? Everything that I thought was worn out came alive at the thought of crawling on top of him and having him at my mercy.

I'd been tied up, spanked, and fucked so thoroughly I was crazy to want more, but I did . . . and it was clear from his perma-hard-on, he wanted it too.

"I'm not sure you can handle me, big boy," I cooed, and ran my hands over my breasts, pinching my nipples and sending little shocks of pleasure through my body.

"Try me." His voice was rough with desire. He put his hands behind his head and waited.

"You have to keep your hands there," I told him. "You're not allowed to touch me unless I tell you to . . . and you'll have to beg."

His sexy grin made me shiver. I got on all fours and crawled to him. I rose to my knees and arched my back. His hissed intake of breath was music to my ears. "You can't touch my breasts," I said, caressing myself. "Or this." I ran my hands down my body and stopped on my stomach. "And you really can't touch this," I said as I slid my hand between my legs and pressed my fingers into my very ready and excited body. "Can you follow those rules?" I let my hips undulate as my hand teased my body.

"Yes," he ground out as his hips began to move involuntarily. "I can do that, but you better fuck the life out of me or I'll flip you over and fuck you so hard you'll scream until you have no voice."

My body shuddered and I almost came from his words alone.

"I'll fuck you," I promised. "But first I want something else."

He groaned and closed his eyes and I took him in my hand and ran my tongue over the head of his cock. He jutted his hips up and tried to push more of his length into my mouth. I pulled back and released him. "Uh, uh, uh," I scolded, and grasped his cock firmly in my hand. "You can't move. I'm doing all the moving."

"Fuck," he hissed. "Just, please. Please."

"Please what?" I whispered, pressing my rock-hard nipples into his thigh and letting my hair fall over him.

"Suck it," he moaned. "Please, baby—suck it."

"My pleasure," I said, relaxing my throat and taking as much as I could of him into my mouth. I closed my lips and sucked as I pressed my tongue along the swollen vein on the outside of his shaft.

"Oh God," he gasped, and grabbed the headboard. "Please let me move my hips, baby. Let me fuck your mouth—oh God, please."

With a nonverbal refusal, I put my hands on his hips to still him. He swore as I moved up and down faster and deeper, applying a flicking pressure with my tongue that was sending him over the edge.

"Stop," he hissed, pulling me off of him and up his body. "I want to come inside you."

"You cheated," I gasped, so turned on I was barely functioning.

He raised his head and pressed his forehead to mine. His breathing was labored and he was holding on by a thread. "Rules are made to be broken. Straddle me. Now," he said in a low voice that left no room for argument. Not that I had any plans to disagree . . .

I spread my legs and did as I was told. I slowly lowered my body onto his and felt light-headed as we became completely fused to each other. He rose up and held my hips in an iron grip.

"Don't move yet."

My insides clenched with the most intense pleasure as we stayed motionless in the most intimate way. He slowly ground his hips, hitting spots that sent colors dancing across my vision. I closed my eyes and let my head fall back.

"Look at me," he demanded. With one hand still firmly on my hip, he tangled his other in my hair, forcing me to his will. "This time you will know what I'm feeling. Not because my body tells you—because I'm going to tell you."

"Luke, no."

"Candy, yes." Without taking his hand from my hair, he lifted me and slammed me back down on him, sending white-hot sparks through me. "I'm in love with you," he said as he repeated his sexual torture.

I couldn't speak—I could barely think.

He lifted me up and down in a rhythm that wouldn't cease until we both couldn't take it anymore. "You've made me whole." The slapping of our skin plus the frightening words he uttered made the blood roar in my ears. "I'm different now and I won't go back," he grunted as he increased the speed, letting his hand fall from my hair and placing it back on my hip so he was in total control of the situation.

"Say it," he demanded, raising his body to meet mine as he forcefully brought me down on him. "Say it."

I trembled with desire and fear. Making love was one thing, saying it was something else altogether . . .

"I . . ."

"Say it, Candy. Give me the truth at least one time before you disappear."

My body jerked and a feeling of despair mixed with the most intense sexual need I'd ever felt made me scream. I rocked my body back and met his with a desperate longing from an unlocked place inside myself. He had stolen the key and I knew he would never return it.

"I love you," I gasped. Perpetual motion. I could deal with fast and hard—soft and gentle and real might break me. I rode him wildly and he held me tight. I tasted a warm salty liquid as my tears slid over my lips. The tempo danced toward violence as he crushed his mouth to mine, repeating the words that thrilled and destroyed me.

A tight coil of heat started down low in my belly and spiraled up through my body as I started to come.

"I'm there," he hissed, and he bit down on the sensitive part where my neck met my shoulders. "Come with me."

He didn't need to ask. I clenched him like a vise as my body rocked with spasms. I cried out as he shouted his release. He rode out my orgasm, pumping into me more gently than he had been. I collapsed on top of him as the aftershocks shook me.

"It's okay," he whispered, and held me close as an avalanche of tears ran down my face. "Everything will be okay."

"Luke, I . . ."

"Don't talk. Don't say anything. Just let me have this."

I stayed silent, wrapped in his arms, and wondered who was crazier—me or him. Him for thinking we could get out of our profession and make a life together or me for thinking we couldn't.

Chapter 29

We would handle the night before like the adults we were. We would avoid it. I knew I had looked better. I'd barely slept as I lay tangled up in Luke all through the night. I tried to memorize his scent and every muscle in his body. I slipped out of bed and went back to my room to get ready before he woke. The weight of the world sat heavily on my shoulders as I pretended today was simply another day.

"Are you going to wear that?" Shoshanna asked as she shoved a monster-size cheese Danish in her mouth.

"What's wrong with this?" I asked, looking down at my jeans, kick-ass boots, and icy blue-fitted long-sleeve T-shirt that matched my eyes.

"You're still Mandy Dandermanschmidt but you look like Candy Sanderson."

"Shit," I muttered. "I have to be Mandy?"

"Yep." She grinned and offered me her half-eaten Danish. "Try this, it's fucking awesome."

"Um, thanks, but I'm good," I told her as I halfheartedly pulled a hooker outfit from my suitcase.

"You okay?" Shoshanna asked, putting her small hand gently on my back.

"Yep." I smiled and gave her a quick hug as I moved toward the bathroom to change.

"You know, Candy," Shoshanna volunteered, "I just finished writing an intense chapter with Donna and Bruce."

"Great."

"Would you like to know what happens?"

"I think I already do," I said sadly.

"Nah." She laughed. "You only got to the false ending . . . the best is yet to come."

I shrugged my shoulders and slipped into the bathroom before I started to cry. Shoshanna could never understand. She believed in fairy tales and happily-ever-afters . . . I knew there were no such things.

"Jesus Christ, this shit is uncomfortable," Edith groused as she waddled down the crowded hallway in stilettos and a green rubber halter dress. "Rubber is for fucking tires. My tits are soaked."

I bit back a laugh. I couldn't have agreed with her more. I felt ridiculous in my tight leather pants and vest that was squeezing the life out of my boobs. We were a motley crew, but frighteningly, we didn't stand out in the crowd.

Shoshanna was back in her purple rubber jumpsuit with a matching purple gauze pad covering her stitches. *Where in the hell did she get that? She looked like a drunken rubber pirate who'd missed his eye when he tried to put his patch on.* Mrs. C had donned a hot pink leather miniskirt and top that she'd clearly bejeweled before she'd arrived, and Luke and Jim rounded us out in leather pants, chains, and no shirts. Jim walked a bit gingerly, but apparently the pain meds were helping.

"So, Jim, not that I care either way," Mrs. C said. "I have a question I don't know the answer to . . . I'm thinking the answer is no, but the leather thing is throwing me off."

I braced myself for a doozy.

"Are you gay or straight or bi or asexual or into . . ."

"Um, I'm straight," Jim said, cutting her off before she said something so gross we'd all be sick. He was in for a world of pain with these two and I felt for him.

"That's great," Edith whispered loudly to her sister. "I want some fucking grandkids."

"I'm sorry, what?" Jim asked, alarmed.

"Nothing." Mrs. C punched her sister in the head and put her arm around Jim. "You're looking great, baby. Just great. You have a girlfriend?"

"Not at the moment," he admitted.

"Shoshanna," Mrs. C yelled even though she was two feet from her. "Don't you have an unmarried daughter?"

Holy hell, the laugh I'd held back earlier escaped and the look on Jim's face was priceless. Those old biddies were going to try to marry Jim off to Sue Junior.

"Sure do." Shoshanna's eyes grew wide with glee as she eyed Jim in a whole new light.

"I'm . . . uh, really not on the market right now," he stammered.

"I call bullshit," Edith grunted. "Everybody needs to get laid. Right, Shoshanna?"

"That's right," she agreed. "You don't even have to marry her," Shoshanna explained logically. "Just get her knocked up so I can have some grandkiddies."

"Wow, that's quite an . . . um, offer, but I . . . um," Jim choked out.

"Watch it," Luke cut in with an evil gleam in his eye. "That's my sister you're talking about."

"Right," Jim stuttered, and checked his nonexistent watch. "Oh my God, we're late to the signing."

"He's right," I agreed, trying to help the poor guy out. "Those Street Walkers are going to get antsy. We better move it."

Jim shot me a grateful glance. Luke grinned and slapped him on the back. "Welcome to the family," he told Jim. "We're seriously fucked up."

We entered the large convention room and the crowd went nuts when they spotted Shoshanna. On reflex, my hand went to my gun, as did Luke's, Edith's and Mrs. C's. Shoshanna and Jim gave us withering looks and we all sheepishly relaxed our stance. Ingrained habits were hard to break . . .

"What the fuck?" Edith barked in amazement as the entire room of at least four hundred fans shot their arms up in the air. "Did one of you fucktards pull a weapon?"

"No." Luke laughed. "It's Shoshanna's new move. Everybody's doing it."

"Well in that case . . ." Edith and Mrs. C raised their hands along with the crowd.

"Oh my God," I said with a giggle, and hit Luke. "Are you going to leave them like that?"

"You bet I am." He grinned and touched my cheek.

We got swallowed up in the crowd before I could react to his simple gentle touch. My cheek tingled and my heart beat wildly.

Did Donna and Bruce have these same problems? Would they find a way to get a happy ending? Had I truly lost it? Donna and Bruce were not even real people.

The signing went off without a hitch. Mrs. C and Edith flanked Shoshanna with their arms in the air for over an hour. Jim stood with Luke to one side and I stood on the other. I could feel Luke's eyes on me, but I kept mine trained to the crowd. I regretted not reading Shoshanna's chapter about Bruce and Donna. I wanted to see what happened. I wanted someone else to make a decision I was too cowardly to make. I took a deep breath and pushed the mess that was my life to the back of my mind.

Shoshanna was in heaven. Her fans cried and squealed with delight at getting to meet her in person. She signed books and posed for pictures. Mrs. C and Edith posed for quite a few pictures too. I had no clue who the crowd thought they were, but it didn't matter. The three old gals were having the time of their lives.

Luke stepped up behind Shoshanna and whispered in her ear. She turned and gave him a quick peck on the cheek before she let loose with one of her ear-shattering whistles.

"All right, Street Walkers, I have to move on to my next appointment," she shouted, and the crowd groaned in disappointment. "But, I'll be at the pageant tonight because my son, Duke LeHump, is the star!"

As if on autopilot, the masses began chanting, "Duke LeHump, Duke LeHump, Duke LeHump."

"Eight o'clock tonight," Shoshanna bellowed. "I expect to see all of you there!"

As we made our way out of the room to grab lunch before the last rehearsal for the pageant, Luke copped a quick feel of my ass. "I want to peel those clothes off of you and have you ride me like a cowboy again," he whispered.

I was flustered. I thought we'd agreed to ignore last night. Wait, I had agreed to ignore it inside my own warped brain. He had agreed to nothing. This day was going to be even more difficult than I'd originally thought.

Chapter 30

The restaurant in the hotel was packed, but Shoshanna had had the forethought to reserve the back room for our party. Teddy, Rocky, Cesar, and Cheech were already sitting at the table when we arrived.

"I thought it would be nice to have a friendly meal before the boys got their game faces on for tonight," Shoshanna explained. Well, at least lunch wouldn't be boring. I expected Mrs. C and Edith to eat Teddy alive.

"Oh my God," Teddy gushed. "Love the face patch. Is that the new thing?"

"Kind of." Shoshanna laughed and introduced everyone.

I found myself wedged in next to Luke and his grabby hands and directly across from the weird brothers. Awesome. The table was round and the room was open. Mrs. C, Edith, Luke, and I had all tried to sit with our backs to the door. None of us won that battle because Cheech and Cesar had already planted their bizarre asses in that prime location.

"Are we ready for tonight?" Shoshanna asked the boys.

"Of the course we are ready for to showdown and win," Cheech said in mangled English as if it were a done deal.

"Now, Cheech." Shoshanna laughed. "That's not a very sports-man-like attitude."

"Oh, puleese," Teddy said, throwing his shiny locks over his shoulder and hitting Jim in the face. "Cheech is an overconfident brute."

"I am confident because I have the big package," he shot back, and stood to prove his point. His brother yanked him back to his

seat and everyone kept chatting as if a grown man hadn't just tried
to expose himself at the table.

Rocky, whom I'd never heard utter a word, raised his hand to
speak. Edith acknowledged his politeness, shushing the table.

"The muscular and sexy black guy wants to say something."

"Holy fucking shit," Mrs. C shouted, and walloped her sister.
"You don't say black. You say African American."

Edith elbowed her sister in the gut. "How am I supposed to
know that? I just found out earlier today that apparently the word
dyke is insulting," she grunted. "Mr. Sexy Guy," she said to Rocky,
"I'm sorry. I would never fuck up on purpose and I didn't mean to
insult you."

"You didn't." Rocky chuckled. "But I appreciate your caring
enough to say something." His voice was beautiful—low and
melodic.

"See?" Edith flicked Mrs. C in the head. "He's not mad and by
the way," she told Rocky, "I have no issues with the word dyke or
lesbo, so you can use them."

"Good to know," he said, and bit his lip to hide his grin. "I'd like
to back up my lover Teddy on his assessment that Cheech is a
brute. I also find the irony in his actions quite amusing."

Holy cow, Rocky was beautiful and smart, although he was dating Teddy . . .

Cheech looked completely confused, unsure if Rocky was making fun of him. Cesar, on the other hand, was smiling like the cat
who ate the canary. What in the hell had they been up to?

"Should I?" Rocky asked Cesar. "Or would you like to inform
the group what you two have accomplished?"

"I'd like to take the honor," Cesar said.

"Actually," Teddy cut in, "as much as I think you two don't stand
a chance against me tonight, I think what you did was disgustingly
brilliant."

Cheech was still utterly confused, as was the rest of the table.

"Get to the fucking point. I'm so hungry, I could eat a ground-
hog," Mrs. C grumbled.

"You have," her sister said.

Jim and the other boys laughed at the joke, but I gagged on my
tongue. I knew she wasn't joking. God only knew the things they'd

eaten during their time in Vietnam. I glanced across the table at the gals. As much as they made me want to pull my hair out, they also had my utmost respect. I was sure I couldn't even imagine the horrors they'd been through, yet here they were, dressed in rubber and leather, having the time of their lives. They knitted and had friends and shot refrigerators and toasters. They had made their way in a crazy world and now they had grandchildren to look forward to . . .

"What are you looking at, Mag?" Mrs. C demanded.

"I know that look." Edith pointed to me. "Seen it a million times back in Nam. Don't you go feeling all sorry for us, Mag. We're happy and good and we made it out. You're the one who didn't. It kills me a little every day to think about that."

"Don't go getting all weepy on me, you old dyke." Mrs. C put her hand on her sister's arm. "Mag's back and even if she never believes it, I do."

There was an awkward silence at the table.

"My God." Teddy blanched. "I thought your name was Mandy. I feel just awful that I've been calling you by the wrong name. I mean, Lord have mercy, you have such a tremendous bosom."

"Okay," Luke snapped, putting an end before it had begun to any discussion about my boobs. "What in the hell is the story we can't seem to get to?"

"Oh yeah, we had an orgy with the religious freaks," Cesar announced proudly.

"What?" Shoshanna shouted.

"Yeah, we screwed like ten of them. They were wild and gave head like a . . ."

"Okay," I said loud enough to stop the blow job comparison.

"Anyway—" Cesar grinned. "I haven't been able to get laid by anyone attending the convention. It's all those freaks outside who were wanting it bad."

"That be correct," Cheech added. "My package was in the demand of the great. I filmed it all on my phone and put it on the YouTube."

"You didn't," Jim gasped, and started laughing.

"Oh yes, I did," Cheech boasted. "I give the name of the organization and I tell to the world they are horny to love my package."

There couldn't have been a finer comeuppance for the crowd of haters outside. To be busted on the Internet for doing all the things that they were accusing the people inside of was mind blowing. My grin split my face and Luke's laughter set off my own.

"Not only that," Cesar informed us. "It went viral and made the national news in your country."

Cesar and Cheech were not my favorite guys. They were disgusting man-whores. However, at this moment I liked them a whole lot. Hypocritical people were one of my biggest pet peeves and the protesters out front embodied everything I disliked about organized religion. Justice had been served by way of Cesar's and Cheech's libidos. Could it get any better?

"What was really interesting was when the women did it with each other. If they'd been attractive it would have been hot, but you can't have it all," Cesar commented casually.

"Yes," Cheech added. "I just kept of my eyes to closed and let my package lead the way."

"Okay," Rocky said. "That is enough. I'd like to keep my appetite for lunch."

"So what in the hell is this contest tonight anyway?" Edith asked, flagging the waitress over.

"It's a cover model pageant," Teddy said. "Shoshanna choreographed the big number for the show."

Edith and Mrs. C were impressed. Apparently, there was nothing Shoshanna couldn't do.

"While I do love the concept, dear," Teddy told Shoshanna, "I feel a bit creatively stifled by the parameters. My fans will expect me to twerk."

"What's a twerk?" Mrs. C asked.

"Oh dear woman," Teddy gasped, appalled. "You don't know what twerking is?"

"No."

"Then I have a treat for you."

Pushing his chair back and twisting his hair up into a loose knot, Teddy got down to business. His air humping and hip grinding was truly amazing in a nightmare-inducing way. Rocky, as eloquent as he was, clearly had a weakness when it came to Teddy and twerking. Not only were they humping air, they were humping each other. Of course, not to be outdone by the competition, Cesar and Cheech got in on the action. Cheech humped the mortified waitress, who got so pissed off she kneed him in the nuts. Cesar, laughing hysterically at his brother's misfortune, defected to the enemy and made the Teddy-Rocky duet a trio.

"Well, they look like goddamned idiots with ants in their pants," Edith commented.

"I don't think the waitress is coming back," Mrs. C said sadly. "I wanted a grilled cheese."

"Tell me what you guys want," I yelled over the grunting of the twerk-fest. "I'll take our order out to our waitress." I quickly wrote down the orders for everyone and put down four extra burgers and fries for the twerkers. If they didn't like it, tough shit. They'd pretty much ruined the appetite of everyone else at the table. They'd get what they'd get . . . and like it.

The rest of lunch was uneventful compared to the beginning. I did have to remove Luke's hand from my body approximately twelve times in the twenty minutes we ate. His strategy was to latch on when I was holding my sandwich with both hands. It was a good plan until I accidentally spilled my ice water on his crotch.

"Thanks," he whispered, and winked. "I was so hard from staring at your tits, I would have had a hell of a time standing up."

"You did not just say that," I said, trying desperately not to laugh. Why his juvenile filth-mouth was such a turn-on, I had no clue. If anyone else said something like that to me, I would deck them . . . him, I just wanted to jump.

"Hey, lovebirds—" Teddy smirked. "We have to get to rehearsal. We're already late and I don't think Medusa has enough hair left to pull out."

"Let's go," Shoshanna said. "Bill's on my tab. We have a show to rehearse!"

Medusa was a wreck and the rehearsal was a disaster. Mrs. C and Edith sat quietly and watched. They seemed to be zeroing in on someone on the stage; at first I thought it was me, and then I realized it was Cheech and Cesar . . . or possibly Teddy. Whatever. They were having fun, and if I was honest with myself, I was too. Luke insisted on practicing the kiss repeatedly. I was dizzy and horny by the time rehearsal was done.

Medusa and Teddy got into it big time over Teddy's insistence that his fans would want to see him twerk. Medusa unfortunately compared his twerking to an epileptic fit and Teddy threw a shit fit of epic proportions. Rocky broke up the brawl just as it started and Shoshanna decided we should all call it a day. We were to take the rest of the afternoon to relax and primp and be backstage by 7:30, as the show was starting at 8:00 sharp.

I waved good-bye to my crew and hauled ass up to my room before I could get convinced to spend the afternoon having sex with Luke. I'd made my decision and being around him made me think I'd made a mistake. So I did what I always did when I didn't like what was going on . . . I compartmentalized and ran.

Chapter 31

Shoshanna and the dykes insisted I wear more makeup for the show than I usually did in real life. Edith offered to do it for me. After almost hyperventilating, I politely declined, reminding her that disguise was my specialty and I could whip on false eyelashes tied up and hanging upside down. She gave in, but loaned me her glittery yellow eye shadow, promising it would make my blue eyes pop.

They had chosen my outfit with care . . . a black leather halter and a scrap of black leather skirt with my thigh-high leather boots. I didn't remember purchasing that particular outfit. I was certain the old gals had bought it for me. As touching as that was, I was going to look like the hooker from hell—all ass and boobies. Whatever. I didn't really care. I just wanted everything to be over.

"Your mom must be so proud of you," Shoshanna said as she handed me a pointy studded dog collar.

Her statement startled me almost as much as the dog collar she expected me to wear. "Why would you say that?"

"Don't get me wrong. I'm prouder than hell of Sue Junior. I still can't fucking believe I gave birth to a rocket scientist. Hell, nobody can, for that matter." She laughed. "But you . . . you have passion and guts and balls. You save lives and make this world a goddamned better place."

"She speaks three languages and can shoot almost as well as me," Mrs. C chimed in. Her sister slapped her in the head.

"She shoots better than you and me," Edith grunted. "If I had a daughter, which is an impossibility since I don't like dick, I'd want her to be you."

I tried to swallow the lump in my throat, but I couldn't. It was too big.

"So back to my original point," Shoshanna continued. "You are what little girls should aspire to, not all that movie star model crap. Smart, independent . . . original."

"She gets all that from Mag the Hag," Edith said, and Mrs. C grunted her agreement.

Who knew? Maybe I was Mag the Hag. I supposed there were worse things to have been. "What was she like?" I asked.

"She was like you. Impulsive, funny, avoided real life, and found her way by taking on other people's causes," Mrs. C said with nary a curse word thrown in.

"I don't avoid real life."

No one said anything.

"I don't," I insisted.

"Of course you don't," Shoshanna said, giving Mrs. C a stern look.

I wanted to say something to prove them wrong, but anything I said would simply bury me deeper. I was feeling the need to shoot stuff, and I knew that wasn't possible at the moment. So I tried to push the silly conversation to the back of my mind.

Fuck.

What if they were right?

"Would you guys excuse me for a minute?" Without waiting for an answer, I turned and ran to my room. I grabbed my phone and dialed. I considered hanging up, but I wasn't going to avoid anymore. It was answered after two rings. I had to clear my throat three times before words would come out. "Hi, Mom. It's me, Candy."

"Hi, baby. How are you?" I could hear the concern in her voice.

"I'm good. How are you and . . . um, Dad?"

"You know what?" she said with an uneven hitch in her voice. "We're actually doing well. We started therapy and we're working through a lot of things we should have dealt with a long time ago."

"Wow," I exclaimed, unsure what else to say. My free hand was clenched in a fist and my body trembled.

"We owe you an apology," she said softly. "We were planning on driving up next weekend to talk with both you and your brother. We . . . I did so many things wrong." I heard the sadness in her voice and it tore me apart in unexplainable ways.

"You did the best you could. We all did."

"I know, sweetie. I know."

"So, um . . . Mom, I think I might have met someone."

"Really?" She couldn't hide the delight in her voice.

"Yeah, he's kind of messed up like me, but he's good and he loves me."

"Do you love him?" she asked.

I paused. Telling Luke I loved him in the midst of sex was one thing. Admitting it to my mom was another. "I do."

"That makes me so happy, honey. Mitch, and now you. Maybe we didn't screw you up too badly."

I was quiet. She didn't screw me up. She wasn't always the most present mom, but she was suffering too. I was an adult—I had a choice. I had no one to blame but myself and I was done with that.

"Candace, I want you to know something. I don't love what you do, but I'm beginning to understand why both you and Mitch took the paths you did."

"Mom, you don't have to do this."

"Please, let me finish. I worry about you, but if you're doing what you love to do, then I will try and be happy for you. If you're doing this for your sister . . . it's time to let that go. It's time for all of us to let that go."

My tears ran unchecked down my face and I knew I would have to start my makeup over, but I didn't care. I'd been waiting for this moment for almost half of my life. I tried to speak, but my words lodged in my throat.

"I want you to think about what I said and know that I love you. I always have and I always will. I just haven't been the best at showing it for a while."

"It's okay, Mom," I whispered through my tears. "I love you too. I have to go."

I hung up and sat down on the bed and had the first real cry I'd had in years. I cried for my sister, who would never experience the things I would. I cried for my parents and myself. I cried because I'd wasted time with Luke, but that was something I could change. I dried my face and smiled weakly at my raccoon eyes in the mirror. I felt strangely light and free. I was tempted to run to Luke's room and tell him what had happened, but I didn't want him to see me like this. I'd get cleaned up and I'd go lay my heart on the line.

Rejection wasn't my worry. I was more concerned about sobbing with happiness and fucking my makeup up again. I wondered if I had waterproof mascara. God, I hoped so.

"You okay in there?" Shoshanna yelled from the other side of my door.

I opened up the door and peeked out.

"I told you. You made her cry," Edith said, and dove on top of her sister.

"Get off me, heifer," Mrs. C bellowed, putting Edith in a headlock. "It was a good cry. Look at her."

Edith paused her attack and walked over to examine me. She took in my raccoon eyes and smeared makeup. She put her hands on either side of my face and stared into my eyes. "Goddammit, you're right, you stinky lessie. She's gonna be just fine."

She pulled me into a crushing hug and proceeded to dance me all over the room. Mrs. C did a toe touch and Shoshanna clapped wildly. I was never going to be normal with friends like these, but normal wasn't what I was after. Happy. Happy and whole was what I was after. And I was almost there.

Chapter 32

The ballroom where the pageant was to be held was abuzz with excitement and chatter. My stomach was queasy as I realized I was going to be on the stage with an obscene amount of multicolored inflated condoms along with some twerk-happy cover models, but I would be with Luke. Everything would be all right. He'd left before us to find out what he was supposed to wear. Medusa had procured matching costumes for the boys. It was going to be a clusterfuck, I was sure, but Luke would be beautiful in go-go pants and a halter. Well, maybe not go-go pants . . .

"We should go backstage," Shoshanna said, pushing through the crowd. Every time she was noticed, hands flew up in the air. By the time we'd reached the stage, all five hundred or so people in the room were doing *The Shoshanna*. "Edith, Mrs. C, we have chairs reserved in the front row. Jim should already be sitting there. Go make sure no one takes our seats."

"On it," Edith said, and went to pull her gun.

"Goddammit, Edith, we're not going to shoot anyone tonight. If they're in our seats, we'll just beat the hell out of them," Mrs. C told her as they walked off.

"I'm not sure that was a good idea," I told Shoshanna.

"Me neither, but I think Jim can control them. Shit, I hope he can. Come on."

Feeling like I had forgotten something, I realized I was unarmed. There was no room to hide a gun or even a knife in the scant scraps of clothing I was sporting. I hadn't left my home in years without my Glock. It was freeing and I felt okay. Weird.

"What do you think Medusa picked out for the guys?" I asked as we rounded the corner to the backstage holding area.

"No clue, but it's probably going to frighten the shit out of us."
She laughed. "Speak of the devil . . ."

Medusa turned the corner and almost ran head first into us. Oh
my God, she was a sight. She was wearing a wig—a pink one. This
was a good thing, considering she'd ripped most of the left side of
her head bald. The pink was questionable, but so was Medusa. Her
outfit was pure gold. Pure gold lamé. She had wrapped herself in
acres of the stuff and safety-pinned the entire atrocity together. I
was now in mortal fear of what the men would be wearing.

"Oh, thank God you're here. Teddy is being a diva. Duke won't
wear his costume and Cheech and Cesar aren't here yet," she
screeched, and went for her hair. She pulled and her wig slid dangerously to the left.

"Come here and calm the fuck down," Shoshanna said, straightening Medusa's pink locks. "Just relax your crack. Cesar and Cheech
will show up. They're too egotistical not to. Teddy is always a diva
and if Duke won't wear the costume, let him wear what he wants
to. He's the star and it doesn't matter if he's different."

"Are you sure?" she whimpered. "I worked so hard on this and
those sons of bitches are going to be the death of me."

"We have a great show and you are amazing," Shoshanna consoled her. "Own your power and be proud. You're a choreographer
and a director."

"And a costumer and lighting designer and a scenic designer,"
Medusa said, regaining her confidence.

"That's right. Now you just hustle your pink head out front and
get ready. I'll handle the boys."

"Thank you, Shoshanna. You're a goddess." She inhaled deeply,
adjusted her gold disaster, and pinched her cheeks. "How do I look?"

"Beautiful. Go get 'em!"

"I will," she shouted as she ran out to the front of the house.

"Holy hell," I muttered as we went to find the guys.

"Probably." Shoshanna laughed and forged ahead.

I was very clear why Luke wouldn't wear Medusa's creation. It
was hideous and wrong on every level. The men were clad in gold
speedos with feathers hanging strategically in alarming places.
The footwear appeared to be gold gladiator sandals and they had
sparkling wreaths on their heads. I had to bite my tongue so I
wouldn't scream. Other than that, they were basically naked.

Cheech and Cesar had shown up and were grinding their hips and grunting in preparation to win the crown. Teddy was twerking violently in a corner and Rocky was juggling condoms that he'd filled with either dirt or sand. Luke stood off to the side with a look of horror on his beautiful face. Thankfully, he was dressed in his leathers and combat boots.

"Shoshanna, I have to talk to Luke," I told her.

She eyed me for a moment and then grinned. "Make it quick. The show starts in twenty minutes."

"I will. I promise." I hurried over to him and stopped short. His look was guarded and he crossed his arms over his chest. "Hi," I said, trying to coax a smile out of him.

"Just say what you want to say and get it over with. This day already sucks, so you may as well go on and make it the worst day of my life," he said coldly.

"I think I can make it better," I said tentatively.

"How can you do that?" he asked, stepping back but lowering his arms to his sides.

"I can grab your crotch and stick my tongue down your throat," I purred suggestively as I advanced on him.

He put his hands on my shoulders to stop me and his eyes narrowed. "Talk."

"Okay." I took an enormous breath and I talked . . . fast. "I love you. I want to try to do this. I can't guarantee that I can give up shooting people all at once so I might have to wean myself off. I want to be with you—all the time. I have no clue what the hell we're going to do for a living, but I won't live off of you even though you're richer than shit. I have to have my own job and my own income. I'll think about having kids with you, but you'll have to sign something that says you'll change diapers and do half of everything. I will never be a stay-at-home mom. I would suck at that, so we'll just have to bring our kids with us when we figure out what in the hell we're going to do with ourselves for the rest of our lives." I stopped and inhaled since I hadn't taken a single breath during my diatribe.

"How many kids do you want?" he asked, smiling.

"I thought two would be good. Three if it doesn't hurt too much to blow them out. Why, how many do you want?"

"I was thinking two, but I'm good with four or five, if that's what you want."

"Oh my God," I gasped. "I am not having five kids. You are on crack and . . ."

He was laughing and I wanted to punch him. I was laying everything on the line and he was amused by me. I wanted to do damage, but I wanted him more.

"You are insane. You've made my life whole," he said, pulling me to him and crushing his lips to mine. "I am so in love with you it fucking hurts. The only reason I'm still here is because I wanted every minute I could get with you before you ran."

"I'm sorry. I was an idiot. I'm sorry it took me so long to figure it out."

"What happened?" he asked as he ran his hands up and down my arms, making sure I was real.

"Well, you happened and I got smarter along the way."

"Even if you had run, I would have come after you until I wore your ass down and you agreed to be mine."

"Really?" That was one of the hottest things he'd ever said. There was pretty much nothing I could do to shake him, and nothing could make me happier. "I'm screwed up," I admitted.

"Tell me something I don't know." He chuckled and kissed me again. "I'm no prize either, but I love you. I'll be good to you and I'll do my best to make you happy till the day I die."

"You already make me happy. You make me believe in things I thought were only for other people, but I'm serious about weaning off the shooting. That might be hard for me."

"Me too," he conceded. "But if we're going to do this right, we can't have cartels gunning for us on a daily basis."

"Steve's gonna shit," I muttered, imagining his reaction.

"Nope. You're wrong. I'll bet my island that this will make him very happy. Not so sure about your brother, but I can take his ass." He laughed. I grinned and ran my fingers over his lips. He was really mine.

"Get your shit together, people, we have a show to do," Shoshanna bellowed.

"I'll be right back. Stay here," Luke said. He jogged over to Shoshanna and gave her a big hug. He whispered something in her ear. She smiled and began to tear up. She ran over to me and threw herself into my arms.

"Welcome to the world of the living, beautiful girl. It's going to be such a great life." She kissed me and I stared up at the ceiling so I wouldn't cry and ruin my makeup.

"We're on in five," she shouted. "I'm going out front to introduce the show. Kick ass and take no prisoners!" With that final sage piece of advice, she sprinted away.

My stomach was in knots and I glanced around. What in the hell had I been thinking when I'd volunteered to do this? I wasn't a performer, I was a soon to be former DEA agent who liked to shoot bad guys. Fuck. I couldn't do this.

"It'll be fine," Luke said, recognizing my panic. "We'll do this for Shoshanna and then will go to my room and screw till we're blind and tomorrow we start our new life."

"Okay." I blew out a long slow breath. I would just pretend I was someone else. God knew I'd been doing that very thing for years.

"Mag, you look stunning," Teddy gushed as he adjusted himself in his speedo. "You're breasts are mouthwatering. Do you mind if I touch one? I want to know what they feel like."

"Um . . ." I looked at Luke to see if he was going to blow a gasket, but he just grinned and shrugged. "Sure," I told Teddy.

With one finger he reached out and poked it. "Ohhhh, it's firm but squishy—somewhat like a flaccid testicle."

I didn't know if I should be flattered or insulted. I went with flattered. "Thank you."

"May I?" Rocky asked from behind his lover. "I've actually never felt one before."

"Ooookay," I said. This was bizarre and funny if I really thought about it. Rocky used two fingers and poked.

"Goodness," he exclaimed with admiration. "They are like spongy juggling balls. They bounce back beautifully."

"That's enough, boys. Those are my tits you're playing with and I say you're done." Luke stepped in and stopped the boob play.

"Oh," Teddy growled, and made hand claws. "Duke is such an alpha male. We must do lunch sometime, Mag. I'd just adore hearing how the tiger is in the sack. Call me," he said as he walked off to do his final round of twerks.

"Are you ready?" Luke asked.

"No. Are you?"

"No, but I'm so damn happy right now, I'd consider twerking."

"Oh my God." I laughed and put my hand on his forehead to check for a temperature. "No fever. You're good."

"Baby," he said in a voice that made me weak. "I've never been better. Let's get this over with."

"I've got your back."

The sound of Shoshanna's voice booming through the crowded ballroom made me giggle. Her excitement was contagious and the butterflies in my stomach started a fistfight. The rush and unsettling tingle I always got when I was going into a potentially dangerous job washed over me and I paused. WTF? It had to be nerves and the fact that I was getting out of the business. I looked at Luke and the brawl inside my stomach lessened. He was my future. I had no clue where we would end up, but I really didn't care.

The guys were pumped. Rocky and Teddy were doing a final manic twerk and Cesar and Cheech were chest bumping and speaking in rapid Spanish. It was too bad Jim wasn't back here . . . actually he was lucky. I'd have to figure out a way to make him pay for deserting us. Although getting stabbed did even up the odds.

"Boys," Teddy instructed since there was no one of authority in the area. "Remember, section one is the walk. Shoshanna will call us out individually, and we will strut our stuff."

"Cesar and I will go to together," Cheech informed Teddy rudely.

"That's not what we practiced," Teddy shrieked, on the verge of a diva meltdown. "You have to do it the way we practiced or the whole night will be ruined."

"No," Cesar cut in. "We go together. We are brothers and blood is thick."

"Oh dear God." Teddy flipped his hair and paced the small backstage area in a panic. "This is just awful."

"How about this," Cesar offered. "After the big number, you and your boyfriend here can twerk and show the crowd your skills."

"Do you think?" Teddy's eyes lit up, and he began to unconsciously braid his hair. "But it wasn't rehearsed," he whispered.

"What do you have to care?" Cheech demanded. "The hairless woman of the bitch is jealous of the twerk. And even though I will win the contest because of my package, I give to you the twerk on the stage."

"Oh sweet Jesus," Teddy squealed. "I'm so excited. Rocky, are you in?"

"Always," Rocky said, and hugged his certifiable boyfriend.

"Issss settled," Cheech proclaimed, and gave us all an extra gag-inducing grind to seal the deal.

"Wait," Luke said. "I am not twerking. Period."

"No problem," Cesar said. "We can leave the stage while they twerk and come back when they're done."

Luke shrugged and rolled his eyes. "Sure. Whatever."

"This will go down in the history books," Teddy said without an ounce of sarcasm. "My time has finally come."

The boys lined up and strutted their stuff on the runway to the hellaciously loud techno pop. I had a perfect vantage point and watched the screaming women go nuts. Most of the audience still had their hands in the air, and several of the hard-cores were flicking their lighters like it was a rock concert. Teddy, Rocky, Cesar, and Cheech were in heaven, but Luke was clearly in hell. He was being a great sport and even gave a small hip roll, which set the crowd on fire. I giggled and wished I had my phone to record the debacle, but I saw the old dykes were filming away.

"How about that?" Shoshanna shouted into the mic, making me wince. "Are those guys hot, or what?"

After the boys came backstage, the show continued with awards for different authors. Medusa and Shoshanna spoke adoringly about the ten or so authors who accepted their plaques to the chants and applause of the fans. This was followed by a tribute to Shoshanna that brought tears to my eyes. The coordinators spoke of her career and her advancement of women's causes. Shoshanna blushed repeatedly and the crowd laughed and clapped.

As she was presented with a five-thousand dollar check to give to her charity of choice, the fans began to chant . . . "Speech, speech, speech."

Medusa shoved the mic back into Shoshanna's hand and pushed her to the edge of the stage.

"Thank you. Thank you," Shoshanna said, moved by the outpouring of love. "I have been writing for a very long time. It makes me happy and whole and the knowledge that you love what I write delights me to no end. Many may snub our genre, but good and important writing is just that. I believe in the advancement of women and the right of adults to have consensual, safe sex however they please. I believe in letting stories take us away from the harshness of reality and I think that combining our imaginations and brains with our passions is beautiful. I am proud to be a writer and I am humbled by your recognition of my work. I promise you I will keep writing stories if you promise you will keep reading them."

She raised her little arms above her head and did *The Shoshanna*. The crowd went berserk and unfortunately so did Shoshanna. I gasped and Luke almost passed out as she reared back and took a running leap into the crowd. Thankfully they caught her. They passed her around the auditorium while my heart slid back down my throat and into my chest.

"That was fucked up," he muttered, shaking his head. "I can't believe she just did that."

"Your mom is nuts." I laughed and leaned into him.

"Yes. Yes she is," he agreed, and grabbed my hand. "Come on, we're up."

Fuck.

I walked out onto the stage as the crowd placed a flushed and thrilled Shoshanna back up on the runway. She gave me a big thumbs-up and jogged over to the podium. "And now for the big finish," she yelled, and gave Medusa the cue for the music.

I felt nauseous as I hit my pose. Four minutes. Only four minutes and I would be home free. I could do that. Rocky came out from the back and approached me with some dance moves that made me giggle. I hadn't seen these in rehearsal and waited in fear and anticipation for the rest of them. They did not disappoint . . .

Chapter 33

Four women tried to charge the stage. They were yanked down and thrown unceremoniously off by Mrs. C and Edith, who seemed to take great pleasure in crowd control. Standing motionless in my mannequin pose, I watched Cheech. He was almost done with his tribal grunt circle, and then it was Teddy's turn. Cesar, who'd gone after Rocky, had done at least twenty cartwheels and seven toe touches. I had to close my eyes at several points because he had split his speedo. I was fairly sure he had done this on purpose, but the ladies in the audience roared their approval. When Cheech finally finished, he pointed to his crotch and made his member twitch. I swallowed back my bile. That one even shocked some of the gals in the front . . .

Teddy's approach was dramatic and alarming. He crawled on all fours, swinging his hair as if it was on fire. He slowly rose, running his hands all over his body, giving some extra loving attention to his gold-covered manbits. I tried not to snort. Glancing to the audience, I locked eyes with Jim, who was laughing hysterically. I was tempted to flip him the bird, but realized that it just wasn't the time or place.

Teddy began to hump the air slowly around me and gained speed as the tempo of the music increased. Between his twerking and his hair, he was a blur of gross. The ladies in the house disagreed. The screaming and jumping spurred Teddy to get even wilder. I was worried he might have a heart attack or drop dead from exhaustion on the stage. Nope. He finished and cupped himself as he proudly walked off.

It was Luke's turn. He was to come out and kiss me silly. I would wake up and we'd go live happily ever after. Thank God.

He walked out onto the stage and the music stopped. I looked over in alarm at Shoshanna, who shrugged in confusion. The crowd started to whisper. Oh hell, what were we supposed to do now? Luke was the only one who was unfazed with the change of plans. He sauntered out to me and went on as if the music was still pounding. He puckered up and kissed the daylights out of me. My knees gave out and I held on to him for dear life. The crowd loved it. The whistling and cheering, along with all the blood roaring in my ears, was all I could hear. Luke's satisfied smile as he held my noodley body up was gorgeous.

"Ladies," he said to the audience. "And gentlemen," he added, acknowledging Jim. "I'd like to take a moment of your time to do something very important. Would that be all right with you?"

"Will you take your clothes off?" someone shouted.

"Um, no." He laughed. "But I will flex." This seemed to satisfy the randy group.

Shoshanna rushed out and put the mic into Luke's hand. "This is my son, Duke LeHump," she shouted, and slapped him on the behind. The screaming was deafening and I was getting nervous.

"I'd like to share my story," he told the rapt group. "I've been a cover model for a very long time. It's been dangerous and satisfying. I have seen and done things as a cover model that I am not proud of, but I wouldn't change any of it. I've taken my life into my own hands on numerous occasions and it's been hell, but it's made me both stronger and wiser. It has made me who I am in this moment and I'm good with that."

I rolled my eyes at his story with two meanings as the gals in the house oohhed and aahhed. Clearly they agreed that cover modeling was life threatening.

"Hey Duke, I thought you were going to flex!" one of his fans yelled.

"Right," he said with a laugh, and gave the gals what they wanted. As cheesy as it was, I had to admit I was turned on. His body was a freakin' work of art . . . and it was mine. "As I was saying," he continued. "I've decided to get out of the cover model business and move on to the next chapter of my life. I have met my soul mate and I'd like you all to meet her. Her name is Mandy Dandermanschmidt. She's hotter than hell and an animal in the sack."

Oh my God. The heat raced up my neck and I wanted to slug

him. What in the hell was he doing? The ladies were loving it. We were a freakin' erotic romance novel come to life.

"She wasn't easy to catch," he told the audience, and winked at them, "but I'm very good at what I do and wasn't going to take no for an answer."

I gave him the stink eye and tried to leave the stage. This was not part of the plan. Where in the hell was the music? He grabbed my hand and pulled me firmly to his side. He was enjoying himself immensely and I was going to shoot him later.

"I've decided to do something and share it with all of you today. I feel my chances are better if I have your support."

WTF?

He got down on one knee, and the crowd erupted into a frenzy. I could vaguely hear them in the background, but my heart was beating so loudly in my head, I was almost unaware of my surroundings. Luke's eyes were full of mischief and adoration. I forgot we were on a stage and that I was dressed like a hooker wearing a pointy studded dog collar around my neck. I couldn't see that he was dressed in leather and chains . . . all I could see was him. The real him—the beautiful flawed man who wanted the flawed girl.

"I am so in love with you. I don't want to live another day without you in it. If you say no to me today, I will hound you and possibly handcuff you to my bed until you say yes. You are perfect for me and I am perfect for you. Will you marry me?"

Everything got blurry. My stomach was in knots and I tasted the salt of my tears. I was so grateful I'd put on waterproof mascara. My hands shook and I searched for my voice. He was insane. I couldn't believe that he'd just asked me to marry him in front of five hundred erotic romance fans, but somehow it was right . . .

"Yes," I whispered through my tears. "I'll marry you, you idiot."

"She said yes," he shouted into the mic, and the fans roared their approval. He picked me up and swung me around. Shoshanna and Medusa were sobbing with joy on the sidelines and the old dykes and Jim were doing a dance in the front row. Camera flashes were going off like fireworks and I couldn't stop my tears.

"You are fucking crazy," I hissed as I buried my head in his neck.

"I know," he said, and grinned. "And you love it."

He was right. I did. He told the crowd he'd be buying my ring on Monday and Shoshanna would post a picture on her website. He flexed a few more times and then kissed me senseless at the urging of the crowd. I wanted to call my mom and Mitch and Rena and Steve, but that would have to wait . . . there was still a twerk fest to get through.

Cesar, Cheech, Rocky, and Teddy had all come out to congratulate us. I noticed that Rocky and Teddy had liberally sprayed their bodies with oil and Cesar and Cheech had donned leather coats with the Mexican flag emblazoned across the back. Teddy's hug left me dripping in grease, but it was nothing a long hot shower with my fiancé wouldn't solve. I touched Luke's fingers to make sure this was all happening. His smile made my insides dance with joy. How in the hell did I end up getting a happily-ever-after?

"Hey Ladies," Teddy sang into the mic he'd pilfered from Luke. "Are you ready to twerk?" he grunted, punctuating each word with a spastic hip thrust.

Of course the ladies were ready, evidenced by the air humping that was mounting in the audience. Holy hell, I was glad we had a plan to leave the stage. Medusa looked as if she was going to explode and Shoshanna held her back as she went for Teddy's neck. Teddy, oblivious to everyone except himself and Rocky, turned the music up and went to town.

"Follow me," Cesar shouted above the noise. "We need to haul ass before we get forced to twerk."

"Right behind you," Luke said as he grabbed my hand. We made a run for it just as Medusa was making her way across the stage to us.

"Go, go, go," Cheech said as we hustled past the offstage area to a hallway behind the ballroom.

"There's a door to the left," Cesar huffed, and ran faster. "We can hide there till it's over."

Cesar and Cheech slowed and looked back, checking for Medusa. Luke and I ran ahead. The room was exactly where they'd said it was. The door was unlocked and we slipped in easily. I was breathing hard and laughing at the same time. The violent slam of the door behind us jolted me out of my silly place and made my insides tingle uneasily. Luke stiffened beside me and I knew we'd been had. This could not be happening . . . but it was.

We slowly turned around. Cesar and Cheech stood in front of the door. Cheech pushed the flaps of his coat back and revealed several vicious looking knives and a Glock with a silencer. His smile was genuine and it made my stomach roil. Luke was as unarmed as I was. We were fucked.

"So," Cesar said politely. "I'd like to thank you for making this so easy. It was so helpful of you to fall in love and to show up together at the same place. It saved time. You see, Cheech can be a loose cannon and I have to keep a close eye on him. He gets antsy and that pisses me off. I'd hate to have to kill my brother after I've lost so many recently."

"Fuck to the you," Cheech hissed at Cesar. "I could kill you so fast."

"Shut up," Cesar snapped. "I was fucking talking to *Candy and Luke.* Not you, you stupid asshole."

Luke covertly squeezed my hand. The only chance we had was to get them to kill each other and that was a long shot. A very long shot. Make them talk—make them monologue. They were stupid and egotistical. They would want us to know how smart they were. Playing dumb could work to our advantage.

"What's going on?" I asked, feigning confusion. I smiled and shook my head.

"Come, come now, Candace Sanderson. I've been looking at your picture for months. You're actually more beautiful in person. It will be sad to cut up such beauty, but a man has to do what a man has to do. I'm sure you understand."

"Let her leave. I'm the one who took out most of your family," Luke said.

"Do I look like a fucking idiot to you?" Cesar screamed; the veins in his neck bulged and his eyes were wild. "That fucking bitch killed my brother and then you came down and killed half of my fucking family. You're both going to die."

Cheech put his hand on his brother's arm. "You will to calm the fuck down. I will do something nice for you."

It happened in slow motion, and I knew if I made it out of this room alive, I would replay those horrific moments over and over till I went insane. Cheech pulled his gun and shot Luke point blank in the chest. He didn't stand a chance—no one would have. The impact of the bullet entering Luke's body threw him up against the wall and he slid back down it with a sickening thud. There was blood everywhere and his eyes were closed. I heard myself scream, but it came from far away . . . like it was in a movie or a dream. In those short seconds, life ceased to have any meaning for me. I should have known I wouldn't get a happy ending. Things like that didn't materialize for people like me. I knew I'd leave this room in a body bag—I just needed to make sure they did too.

"What the fuck?" Cesar shouted, and backhanded his brother across the face. "That was not what we agreed to do, you stupid fucking ass."

"I do the thing that is nice to you and you hit me?" Cheech growled, wiping the blood from his mouth. "How about I shoot you?"

"Shut up," Cesar ground out. "He was supposed to watch us kill her first. We were supposed to make him fucking suffer," he screamed, and began moving erratically around the small space. Cheech stood there, still unable to piece together what he had done wrong.

I had a fast decision to make. It was simple. Cesar could kill me, but I was going to take Cheech out. With one bullet he had ruined my life and he would die. It was my final gift to Luke. I refused to look at his dead body. I would not remember him that way. As the brothers argued, I slowly removed the spiked collar from my neck. When conventional weapons were unavailable, one made do with unconventional ones. Cesar's pacing had a rhythm and Cheech followed his brother with his eyes. It was as if they'd forgotten about me, and that was good. I steadied my breathing and wrapped the collar around my hand with the spikes out. I'd have only one chance. I was happy he'd removed his jacket; his jugular would be easier to find. The spikes were long enough that if I hit him right and dug in and twisted he would bleed out quickly. If he dropped, I could possibly snap his neck, but Cesar would be on me before that could happen.

"Cut her," Cesar hissed. "Do something fucking right in your life for once and cut her face."

I knew I could fight him, but I wouldn't. If he sliced my cheek, he would be right where I wanted him. No pain—no gain.

Cheech approached with a sadistic grin on his face and I held my ground, even offering my cheek. "Ohhhhh, little murder whore just gonna stand there? What in the heck of the fun will that be?"

I said nothing. I simply stared and waited.

Unnerved, he pulled a blade from the collection on his body and sliced down my cheek clear to the bone. The burning pain hissed through my body and I felt the warm blood gush from my cheek. That was nothing compared to the pain in my heart. I smiled at him and winked, confusing and angering him. He reared back to come at my face again, but I was faster. I was faster and better and far more precise than he would ever be. I swung my arm with all my might and connected with his neck. I heard the pop, insuring I had hit my mark. I ground the spike in and twisted to the right. His terrified screams were music to my ears. I barely even felt the severe punch to my face before the excessive blood loss made him drop like a sack of potatoes. As he hit, I lifted my foot and pierced his neck with my stiletto boot to make sure the job was done.

I'd accomplished my goal and it was my turn to die. I was actually okay with it, but I needed to make Cesar hurt.

He flew across the room and backhanded me across the face with the butt of his gun. I saw stars and I felt queasy and dizzy. Hurt him. I had to hurt him. My collar lay embedded in his brother's neck and I had nothing.

"You fucking *puta,* I wanted to do it right," he screamed, waving his gun in my face. "I was supposed to cut you up and inject you with smack and let you bleed out, but you have fucked me up." He was so angry, he was getting sloppy. "You killed two of my brothers and now I will kill you—and trust me . . . this will hurt."

He pulled his gun. His hands shook with fury and I silently apologized to Luke for failing him. Even if I could kill Cesar, I didn't want to leave the room alive. I'd had a small taste of what real love was and I'd have to be satisfied with that. Luke's sexy grin was at the forefront of my brain and I didn't push it away. I kept it there. It made me happy.

"You smile?" Cesar screamed. "You think this is funny? I'll show you funny." He aimed his gun and shot. His trembling hands screwed with his aim and he shot me in the leg. He was either a horrid shot or he was just going to shoot me repeatedly in non-kill areas till I bled out like he wanted me to.

I dropped to the floor as the burning pain in my leg ripped through my body. Landing on top of Cheech, I simply prayed to die quickly. It was wrong to be lying atop the fuck who'd murdered the man I loved, and I tried to push myself off. Grabbing the back of his pants, I pulled my chest off him, but found myself lying face to face with him. His open eyes were the things nightmares are made of, but this wasn't going to be my nightmare . . . it was going to be Cesar's.

In death Cheech was far more useful to me than he ever had been in life. His gift to me was precious and unintended. As I hit the floor next to him, my fingers landed on his gun. A rush of sheer joy and calm washed through my quickly weakening body. I leaned over and kissed his cheek. This was not quite over yet.

Cesar had gone ballistic and was muttering and swearing in Spanish. He hopped from one foot to the other, his outbursts only interrupted by psychotic laughter. I just needed him to face me. I only needed one shot. The most important shot I would ever take— my final shot.

Time moved like I was underwater. He spewed filthy names at me as he filled several syringes with heroine. *Turn to me. Turn to me, you son of a bitch.* If he didn't follow my silent command, soon it would be too late. My head was getting foggier with each passing second and the pain that had kept me going was beginning to debilitate me. *Turn to me, motherfucker.*

And he did.

"This is gonna hurt, motherfucker," I hissed, and fired. I caught a quick glimpse of shock and rage on his face before my bullet hit him right between the eyes. He flew backward just as Luke had done and I smiled. I'd won . . . yet I'd lost.

With every last bit of strength I had left in my body, I crawled to Luke and lay next to him. I wanted to die touching him. The room began to fade to black when from far away I heard voices. They were here. I tried to say hello and that I loved them too, but nothing came out. I just needed to keep Luke warm. He was cold and I didn't want him to be cold. It was so sad to be cold.

"Goddammit," Edith yelled. "What the fuck? Mag, don't you fucking die on me again."

Was someone slapping my face? Why was she so angry?

"Call the ambulance and call Steve. We need to get rid of these bodies before anyone sees them," Mrs. C said in a voice that was as hard as nails.

"Shove them in the incinerator. Burn the trash," Edith said, and wasted no time in lifting the dead brothers. What were they doing? Was I dead and dreaming or were they getting rid of evidence? It really didn't matter. I was done.

I could hear them yelling at me and I wanted to make them happy and answer, but it was too late and I was too tired. It was a relief when the darkness came. I just wanted to be with Luke.

Epilogue

"With this ring, I thee wed," Jack said, slipping the plain gold band on Rena's finger beside her beautiful diamond engagement ring.

"Back at ya, Big Guy." Rena laughed and slipped a matching gold band onto Jack's finger.

"Now, Rena, I know I'm a nontraditionalist, but you have to say the vows correctly or the karma of the wind fairies will blow dust of discontent on your nuptials," Rena's aunt Phyllis admonished lovingly. Her long flowing green robes blew wildly around her in the balmy Minnesota spring wind. Much to the horror of Rena's mom, Phyllis had gotten ordained specifically to perform the wedding of her favorite niece and the man of her dreams. Surprisingly there was very little mention of the supernatural during the brief ceremony . . . until the end. The grounds of the country club were in bloom and the air was fragrant if still a little chilly.

"Oh, for God's sake," Rena said with a laugh, also to the horror of her mother, who sat in the front row clutching Rena's father for dear life. "Fine. With this ring, I thee wed, sexy pants," she told a grinning Jack.

"That should work," Aunt Phyllis said with a sigh. She knew if she pushed it any further, Rena might possibly start describing her new husband's body parts during the vows. "I now pronounce you man and wife. You may kiss the bride."

Jack dipped Rena back and kissed the backtalk right out of her. She came up flushed and almost a little shy. Her love for her man was so clear, it brought tears to the eyes of the small group gathered to witness the joining.

"Edith and Mrs. C, you're up," Aunt Phyllis said, making a bizarre salutation to whatever invisible entity was flying around her head.

"All right, goddammit, I need everybody's attention. You two ready?" Edith asked nervously. Mrs. C stood beside her sister, holding a Bible. They wore matching black-sequined tuxedos and lime green bowties. The choice of footwear appeared to be green house shoes.

"Yes," Kristy answered shakily. Mitch stood beside her and held her up. He was so happy it was ridiculous and Kristy, despite her jitters, was positively radiant.

"I took the obey shit out," Edith confided loudly enough for the entire crowd of thirty or so to hear. "Unless you guys are into the bondage thing and I didn't know. I mean, we can leave the obey thing in and I can even add some master and sub references."

"Holy shit," Kristy gasped, turning pink. "Just take out the obey part and leave the rest like it is." Mitch bit down hard on his lip to keep from laughing and Mrs. C, recognizing her sister's faux pas, punched Edith in the head.

"What the fuck?" Edith rubbed her head and gave her sister the finger. "I'm trying to do a fucking wedding here," she yelled at Mrs. C, who was holding the Bible up as a shield against Edith's possible retaliation.

"Ladies," Aunt Phyllis cut in. "There is to be no bloodshed. The Tree Sprites don't like blood and the Swamp Trolls will destroy the reception if even one drop of blood is smeared on these hallowed grounds of Pookieladoompada."

That made everyone pause. No one knew what on the hell she was talking about, but everyone decided that ignoring it would stop any further explanation. "No prob," Edith and Mrs. C said at the same time. Giving each other a quick hug and a shrug of apology to Mitch and Kristy, the second ceremony started. It went off without a hitch until Mrs. C corrected Edith's pronunciation of a word and Edith pulled her Glock out. Steve had to come up from the group seated out front to demand she hand it over. Shockingly, she gave it to him without a word of complaint and apologized profusely to the bride and groom.

"It's fine," Mitch said, laughing. "Just get to the part where she's mine and I'm hers. Otherwise I'll pull *my* Glock out."

Edith, with the occasional comment from Mrs. C, got through the ceremony without doing any major damage. Kristy and Mitch's kiss rivaled Jack and Rena's and the small group of guests applauded with delight.

"Shoshanna, you're up," Edith grunted, clearly happy to have finished without having killed anyone.

The guests went silent as Shoshanna made her way to the front. She carried two brass urns, and her demeanor was solemn. She approached the flower-draped platform and took her place at center. She gently placed the urns on the ground in front of her and lovingly kissed them before she stood back up.

"My son Luke loved Candy more than anything in the world," she started.

"Oh, for fuck's sake," a stunning woman in the second row groused. "You don't have a son."

"Sue Junior, I have had enough of your goddamned lip. You have a brother now, whether you like it or not. So I would suggest shutting your cakehole before I let Edith and Mrs. C teach you some fucking manners." Shoshanna laid it out to her daughter, who clearly didn't want any part of what was going on.

Apparently, Shoshanna had called Sue Junior and told her she'd had a heart attack. Sue Junior flew home that very day only to find out her mother was fine—more than fine. Suffice it to say, Sue was furious and wanted nothing to do with meeting the nice boy named Jim her mother had found for her. Shoshanna's suggestion that Sue only had to get knocked up by Jim and give Shoshanna a grandchild didn't exactly go over well. No one was quite sure how Shoshanna was able to convince her daughter to come to the wedding and no one asked.

"You are fucking insane," Sue muttered, and crossed her arms over her chest. "I can't believe I'm here."

Jim sat three rows behind her, watching with narrowed eyes. He did not like the way Sue Junior treated her mother and had told Shoshanna under no uncertain terms would he never sleep with someone as bitchy as Sue. It was a match made in heaven . . .

"As I was saying before I was so rudely interrupted by my evil spawn . . . Luke and Candy loved each other dearly, and the day of their double funeral was one of the saddest days of my life."

Several guests began to snicker and Edith and Mrs. C had shit-eating smiles on their faces. Even Sue Junior seemed to be enjoying herself.

"The best part was trying to get Luke to lie still in an open casket for six hours," Rena said, laughing.

"Or how about when we put Candy in the casket and she did the rigor mortis thing. That one gave me nightmares for a month," Kristy added, giggling.

Steve and Kevin were with their children. They now had full custody due to his ex-wife Helen's extended prison vacation. The small, beautiful nontraditional family was enjoying the banter immensely. Steve volunteered a few unnecessary facts about the ass-shooting debacle, and the crowd begged for more. The wedding day had taken a turn and landed in an impromptu roast of the dead Luke Blakely and Candy Sanderson . . .

"All right, people. Calm down. The important piece and what we are here to celebrate is the fact that they loved each other and that is a beautiful thing . . . Candy and Luke wanted to be married and since they're dead and gone, I thought we could honor them by marrying their ashes on this special day too."

The crowd laughed and clapped their approval of Shoshanna's tasteless and appalling idea. A beautiful melody came from the four-piece string quartet and the guests waited anxiously in their seats.

"Are you ready, baby?" my dad asked as he handed me my cane.

"As ready as I'll ever be," I said, rolling my eyes at the mess Mrs. C had made of my cane. She had stolen it for three hours yesterday and when she'd brought it back, it had been bejeweled within an inch of its life. I smiled and grasped it firmly in my hand.

I watched the love of my life walk to the platform with my brother, his best man, to wait for me. He had not been shot through the heart as I'd assumed. The bullet had gone through his shoulder and came out the other side. He had been knocked out by the force of hitting his head against the wall from the kick of the bullet. His recovery had been fairly quick. Mine had not.

I was thinner and still a little weak. My leg was healing slowly. All major arteries had been missed, but the bullet had lodged itself in muscle and bone. Two operations had repaired most of the damage, but the cane would be necessary for a while.

The scar on my cheek was always going to be a reminder of what could have been the worst day of my life—or more accurately, the last day of my life. The crazy love of my life thought the scar was hot and I believed him. I kind of liked it too. It had a dangerous girl feel to it. Shoshanna was delighted we had matching scars and planned to write it into a book.

I placed my arm through my dad's and we slowly made our way to the fragrant and beautiful platform that held the future I so desperately wanted. The beautiful man waiting for me watched me with such fierce love and adoration it was difficult to breathe. I knew I would die for this man. I actually had died for him . . . and he'd died for me.

My father kissed my cheek and my brother lifted me up and onto the platform to stand next to the reason I wanted to live. I felt beautiful in the cream-colored strapless gown that Rena and Kristy had insisted I buy. They had been right. I would not tell them because I would lose all rights to dressing myself ever again, but I was so happy they were my friends.

I glanced out over the array of guests. Most of them I knew well, several only vaguely or through stories. Kevin, Steve, and the kids were there along with the odd couple of Mariah Carey and her sister Boo, no relation. The Careys were friends of Kristy and the old dykes and apparently could be trusted with the super secret knowledge that the dead had risen.

Shoshanna's pals, Nancy, Poppy Harriet, Joanne, and Fred were among the few who were let in on the secret. They were Shoshanna's extended family and had taken care of us at the hospital and afterward. Also present were Kim and Hugh, the Bigfoot enthusiasts, from the raid where my brother had met Kristy, and if I'm not mistaken, *and I'm not,* Hugh was beat boxing with the alarmed quartet.

My parents, dressed to the nines and affectionate with each other for the first time in many years, were beside themselves that two of their children were getting married on the same day. My younger sister was in attendance and was doing really well. We had all benefited from therapy and moving forward with our lives. I had chosen Jim as my maid of honor since Rena and Kristy were also brides today. I had actually considered Pat, but she was not in on the secret. I felt bad that she thought I was dead, but I knew from Shoshanna that Pat had laid her feelings on the line to Junsen and the two were now a hot item.

Our deaths had been necessary. In order to eliminate the threat of more of the cartel gunning for us, we had to die. Publically. The bodies of Cheech and Cesar were never found. The brothers simply disappeared. Edith and Mrs. C refused to discuss the matter, but gave each other covert looks of satisfaction whenever the subject came up. Only a small group knew the truth of our resurrection. It was safer that way.

"You ready, Pretty Girl?" my soon-to-be husband whispered. "God, that scar is fucking hot," he added, grinning.

"I'm ready. Are you?"

"I've been ready for this since the first time I laid eyes on you," he said, and I gripped my cane tighter, afraid my already weak legs might give out.

"Okay, then . . . let's um, do this," I stammered, hoping the entire gathering wouldn't notice that I was flustered and horny. The sex thing had been a no-no for a while and then dumbass decided we would wait till after we got married to re-consummate our luuurrve. I wasn't too keen on the idea of abstinence, but he gave in halfway and said as long as we didn't actually have sex, we could do other fun stuff . . . that worked for me.

Shoshanna couldn't stop smiling. She reached out and touched both of our cheeks. Her eyes filled and I knew there had been many days of pain for the people we loved. I was touch and go for two weeks and her son had refused to eat unless he could be at my side. It took five days of a hunger strike to convince the hospital administrators that he meant business. Needless to say, we caused problems at the hospital. Hell, we caused problems almost everywhere we went.

Our plan was to go away. Far away for a few years and maybe come back eventually. The nice thing was that my fiancé happened to have homes all over the freakin' world. We would start at his island and move on when we were ready. Rena, Jack, Kristy, and Mitch were joining us for two weeks and we'd have a triple honeymoon. The guys seemed a little uncomfortable with the idea of sharing a honeymoon, but pictures of the island and the accommodations put all unease to rest.

We'd have plenty of interesting material to read when we weren't busy doing *other things*. Shoshanna had a new book out, along with her friends Poppy Harriet, Nancy, and Fred. But the best and most anticipated read was *Hanky Panky in the Pokey* by Evangeline O'Hara. Not only had she dedicated the book to Shoshanna and Rena . . . she had given the main couple their names too. Rena about crapped her pants and Shoshanna thought it was the funniest thing ever. She even called Evangeline to thank her. Evangeline was doing well. She had married Yvonne and was apparently quite the underground hit among Christian lesbians . . .

"Attention, everyone, let's get this show on the fucking road. My girl here can't stand for too long yet and I want her on her feet to say I do to my son!" Shoshanna yelled.

The crowd quieted and a feeling of calm and warmth washed over me. I truly was ready to recite our vows.

"All right, you wanna repeat after me or did you memorize the damn vows?"

"I memorized them," my hot fiancé yelled. "I want to say them now and then I want to kiss her and then I want to carry her out of here and get her ass pregnant."

"You need a goddamned anatomy lesson, boy," Mrs. C grunted, and laughed.

"Enough." Shoshanna giggled and stopped Mrs. C before she decided to teach an anatomy lesson at the wedding. "Have at it, son."

He took a deep breath and gently replaced my sparkly cane with the strength of his hand. Jim held my cane and stood behind me in case I needed the support. I was surrounded by so many people I loved, and amazingly, they loved me back. But the one who meant the most was right in front of me.

"I, Bruce, take thee, Donna, to be my lawful wedded wife, to have and to hold from this day forward, for better for worse, for richer for poorer, in sickness and in health, to love and to cherish, till death do us part." He smiled down at me and I melted. I gripped his hands tighter and he leaned in and whispered in my ear. "I'll always have your back and I will fuck you senseless daily. I promise to try and raise the toilet seat, but I won't give any guarantees on that one. I will change diapers and I will watch whatever you want on TV as long as you give me a blow job at least twice a week. Does that all work for you?"

"I heard most of that," my brother Mitch moaned in disgust.

"I thought it was lovely," Shoshanna chimed in.

I blushed to the roots of my hair, which was now red—a dark rich auburn. Bruce, my husband, had a dark brown look going that he carried off beautifully. I'd thought about going blonde, but it really wasn't my color.

"Are you going to stare at me or say your vows, *Donna*?" Bruce asked with a wicked sexy smile on his very pretty face.

"I'm going to say my vows, *Bruce*," I shot back, grinning like an idiot. It was hard to keep our new identities straight, but we were getting better. It was a no-brainer what names to pick. I'd been following the antics of Bruce and Donna the entire time of my courtship with Luke. They were based on us, and Shoshanna had retired them after Luke and Candy had died. She explained to her fans why and they embraced her decision with love and support. So the names were up for grabs and we took them . . . along with the most common surname we could think of. Smith. We were now Bruce and Donna Smith and had all the paperwork to prove it. The dykes worked fast, God love them.

Vows. Now.

"I, Donna, take thee, Bruce, to be my lawful wedded husband, to have and to hold from this day forward, for better for worse, for richer for poorer, in sickness and in health, to love and to cherish, till death do us part." I leaned in and added my own special extras . . . "I promise to double down on the blow jobs as long as you return the favor. I promise not to shoot you when you annoy me. I think we've both been shot enough to last a lifetime. I think we should take one week a month when we wear no clothing at all and I'd like to have sex in the next half hour or I will explode. Deal?" I whispered, and heard my brother groan in agony.

"Deal," Bruce said.

"I now pronounce you man and wife. Kiss your goddamned bride," Shoshanna shouted and the guests clapped joyously.

"You ready?" he asked.

"Yep. Totally."

My husband, Bruce, kissed me senseless and I forgot anyone else was even there. It was me and him, together . . . forever. My own happy ending . . . God, life was fucking great.

ABOUT THE AUTHOR

Robyn Peterman writes because the people inside her head won't leave her alone until she gives them life on paper. Her addictions include laughing really hard with friends, shoes (the expensive kind), Target, Coke with extra ice in a Styrofoam cup, bejeweled reading glasses, her kids, her superhot hubby, and collecting stray animals.

A former professional actress with Broadway, film, and TV credits, she now lives in the South with her family and too many animals to count. Writing gives her peace and makes her whole—plus having a job you can do in your PJs works really well for her. You can follow Robyn at robynpeterman.com. She loves to hear from her fans.